The Forging
The Odyssey of Nathan Embers

By Jeffrey Hancock

Dedication

I would like to dedicate this novel to my wife Barbara and my daughter. Their patience with my endless prattling on about this story and the future adventures of Nathan Embers has given me the strength to put fingers to keyboard. At last, the goblins in my head have hushed their voices.

Contents

Prologue

Dear Moiraine,

    In life, choices are given to everyone. It is in the fire of these choices we forge ourselves. The measure of anyone is in the choices they make when they are alone and in the dark. I hope the decisions I have made have forged me into a man of whom you can be proud. In the diaries which accompany this letter, I have written the events as they happened to me. They are the truth. Let no one try to tell you otherwise. I hope by the reading of these events; you will gain some insight as to why I made the choices I did and how I became the man I am.

    I love both you and your mother. Sometimes I wish that love was enough to stop me from my crusades. It almost was. In my defense, Edmund Burke said, "All that is necessary for the triumph of evil is that good men to do nothing." I want you to remember, above all else, I was a decent man who tried to do what's right, one of many decent men who did their best to hold back the rising tide.

    I go now to whatever end I cannot foretell, but I want you to promise me you will go on with life. Find a decent man. Find a better man than I. Love him and marry him. Raise strong children to inherit this world. You see those gifts of life which are worthwhile in this world must survive. It will be my ultimate victory to know that what is best will endure.

Nathan Alexander Embers
"To be willing to march into Hell for a Heavenly cause."

Chapter One

A whimper then a low growl came from Blossom which woke me out of restful sleep. I threw off the covers and sat up in bed. As I tried to rub the sleep from my eyes, I told my wife, "Char, I think Blossom's time has come. I want you to stay here. I will go be with her."

"Are you sure? ... No, I should be there too," Charlene answered. I sensed she was crying.

"There is nothing you can do for the old girl. Try to go back to sleep," I reached over and squeezed my wife's hand. I stood and slowly made my way to the living room. Blossom started to growl louder. I heard someone trying to jimmy the lock on the front door. I yelled back to Char, "Call the police. Someone is trying to break into the house." I hoped to scare off the would-be burglar. My hopes were dashed. The sound of pounding, then wood splintering replaced the jimmying. It is a solid heavy door with a deadbolt lock. It should take the assailant a few moments to break through the door. I screamed at my wife, "Char, get to Moiraine, and you both get out of here!" I ran back to the bedroom and retrieved the gun safe. Whoever is breaking in wasn't frightened by my call to Char to get the police. Maybe the sight of a model M1911A1 45 in my hands will grab his attention. I unlocked the safe and pulled out the pistol. It felt righteous in my hand. It felt like a part of me. An odd feeling came to me; it said, "*Let's get to work.*" This gun saved John's life back in the Korean War. If I am lucky, it will save my family's lives tonight. I heard the door finally give way. I inserted the clip and pulled back the slide to chamber a round. I yelled out, "I have a gun!"

"Did you finally grow a pair, Mr. Clerk Guy?"

His voice sent a chill up my spine. Mark Galos decided finally to take his revenge on me. The Klingon proverb

"Revenge is a dish best served cold" came to mind. I am going to send this man to the down below place where the only food they serve is searing hot and comes with a side of torment.

"What are you waiting for, Mr. Clerk Guy? Come and get me."

I passed up an opportunity to kill this bastard once. I had been gutless. I knew in the back of my mind he would not let it go, yet, I could not bring myself to murder him. And it would have been a murder too. A merciless killing with both malice and forethought, but I couldn't bring myself to pull the trigger. Two parts of me battled for control. My morals hogtied my animalistic desire to end the insect's life. Mercy failed me, so it is my animal half's turn. I locked my moral self in a corner of my mind and told it to keep quiet. No one would begrudge me killing him here in my home. I cleared my mind and tried to slow my heart rate down. The last thing I needed is to be jumpy and unfocused. Did Char get Mo out of the house? I must trust she got our daughter out. I took a quick glance at Char's nightstand. Her cell phone is gone. Smart girl. I know she will call for help as soon as both, she and Mo are safe.

"You know your wife and child's lives are both forfeit for what you did to me. You made me waste the better part of two years. Come on now. Don't make me wait. Come to me now, and I won't make them suffer. I will be quick and merciful in the manner of their deaths. Keep me waiting, and I will indulge my darker side. Let's see, maybe I will cut off the little one's eyelids. She'll have no choice but to watch as I take her mother. I can imagine all kinds of pleasures your wife will bring me. Sweet pleasures, I haven't experienced firsthand in a millennium. Oh yes, your daughter will get one Hell of an education before her end."

I know he is trying to goad me into rushing before I am ready. It is hard not to listen. I must remain cold about this.

Through sheer force of will, I pushed his words out of my mind. *"Stay frosty,"* I told myself. I am ready. I started toward the living room.

"Maybe I'll take them both. Perhaps I'll ..."

I didn't let him finish as my blood boiled. I couldn't think. I could only react. The anger exploded in me. Kill. Tear him apart. Eat his heart. I don't think I have ever felt such rage. It felt oddly pleasant. I am alive for the first time in my life, and I liked it.

I am outside of myself. Part of me watched from a cold distance as I moved into action. I am two people; one is a mad animal, and the other an icy intellect. With a blur of speed and grace I had never demonstrated before, I dashed into the living room. My whole existence came to this moment. I would fulfill the greatest moral a man could. I would answer the call of instinct. Kill the threat to my family. I'll offer no quarter or mercy. There can only be one of three outcomes: my death, his death, or we travel down the path together.

He is across the room holding a sledgehammer. I raised the 45 and aimed without conscious thought. My weapon and I are one. Three shots barked out. The sound is deafening in this death ground, which had once been my living room. In slow motion, I saw three holes in the center of my prey's chest. His body made little jerks as each round hit its mark. I could see shockwaves ripple through his body. Victory screamed from my being. The thrill is like an orgasm of satisfaction to my soul.

He looked down at his chest as black blood oozed from his wounds. The shock of the moment must have kept him from realizing he is already dead.

"Damn, this hurt. Tight group though. I'm impressed." His voice bubbled as he spoke, and a black ichor drooled out of his mouth. "I thought you were lying about the gun. I guess you did grow some balls after all. However, I tell you this pisses me off. I'll need a new body after this night is over. I can't finish my plans in this one. It's but a small payment against the ledger of our sacrifice," he announced all this as he started walking toward me. As he approached, a foul odor hit my nose.

I was stunned into inaction. All I did was look at my gun and say, "You have to be dead, I …,," as the hammer came around and slammed into my head. All around me is the cold blackness of oblivion.

"Mr. Nathan Embers," the bailiff called.

I dozed off and started dreaming while I am waiting to testify. Mark Galos is a two-bit thug, be it a smart one, and now he is a monster in my dreams. I'll be glad when this trial is over. I stood and walked into the courtroom.

It looked like the typical courtroom scene on TV or in the movies, with deep rich wood paneling on the walls. The judge sat upon a dais directly across the room from where I entered. To the right of the dais is the witness box with a chair and a microphone. Against one wall, the jury is seated. On the other wall, is a bookcase made of the same wood as the paneling and held matching sets of law tomes in brown leather bindings. They have no creases on the spines. It is no surprise to me. I'm sure all the laws and case studies are somewhere in a computer database. It is more efficient to do research with the aid of an impersonal overgrown abacus than to crack open a book and read the law on real paper. I suppose the books function more as set dressing. Two galleries of seats bracketed me as I walked toward the witness stand. They are mostly empty except for a few onlookers. I passed Marcy shoulder to shoulder as she walked toward the exit. She is dabbing at the tears rolling out of her eyes. What did these dicks do to her?

I sat down in the witness chair. The bailiff approached me. He raised his right hand. I stood and raised mine.

"Do you swear that the testimony you're about to give before this court today is the truth, the whole truth, and nothing but the truth?" The bailiff recited the words in a droning monotone. He had said those words countless times before and appeared bored with the duty.

"I do. So, help me God," I stated as I started to sit back down.

The judge commanded, "The witness will refrain from embellishing the oath. A simple I do will suffice."

"Sorry, your Honor," I finished sitting down. The chair is a comfy padded leather one. When I lean back, it creaks a little, and the whole thing tilted a bit to the left. It is odd thinking of me tilting to the left.

The prosecutor, a Mr. Darryl Wayne, stood up, "Mr. Embers, would you please state your full name, address, and occupation for the record."

"My name is Nathan Alexander Embers. I live at 349 Mar Vista Drive in San Diego, California. I work as a night manager at a drug store."

"Mr. Embers, could you please point out the man who robbed your store?"

"Yes," I stood from the witness stand. This action started a ruckus in the courtroom as I walked toward the defense table. I heard the judge banging his gavel. Everybody except Mark Galos rose from their tables on both sides of the aisle. I stood directly in front of the defendant and pointed at the man who had robbed the store and left me bound and humiliated. I felt a hand on my shoulder, ad it started to squeeze gently. "He is the one." The bailiff started to pull me back to my seat at the witness stand. Mark looked at me with no expression on his face. Those eyes are cold, dark, and empty.

"The witness will remain in his seat unless directed to move by the court. Do you understand, Mr. Embers?"

"Yes, your Honor, My apologies to the court."

"Please have the record show Mr. Embers pointed to the defendant, Mark Galos. Mr. Embers, why did you approach Mr. Galos?"

"I didn't want anyone in the jury to doubt who I meant."

"Mr. Embers, how can you be sure he is the same man? It has been some time since the robbery."

"He has let his natural hair color return, and he styled it differently. He has a clean-cut look about him now but make no mistake; it is the man who robbed the store. I am positive it is him. I have a photographic memory. I remember everything perfectly, and those eyes I remember even more vividly."

"I see. Mr. Embers, would you please tell the jury the exact events on the night in question."

I closed my eyes for a short time to prepare myself. In my mind, images started to coalesce. Suddenly, I am in the third person watching my mental-self walking down a long corridor with filing cabinets against one wall. A floating clock with wildly spinning hands appeared above my avatar's head. The cabinets represented my memories organized for easy access. Before I started arranging my memories like this, all my recollections were a jumbled mess in my head. When John Wheeler, an American theoretical physicist, was asked what is time? He answered, "Time is what prevents everything from happening at once." My mental filing cabinets are my amateurish attempt to imitate his meaning. They prevent me from remembering everything all at once. I can't even claim authorship to the idea. However, that is a story for another time. The cabinets begin with my first stored memories and continue almost to infinity. I have considered walking to the end of the corridor and seeing what lies beyond. Does it end with the date and time of my death or at the end of my memory? The walk scares me. Oh, not the lose control of your bowels and buy new undies kind of fright, but rather the dread we all experience when contemplating our death. I increased the pace at which my avatar walked. The hands of the floating clock are spinning so fast they could fly off at any moment.

After a few more steps, I reached the time in question. The hands on the clock stopped at 7:50 pm. The mental me pulled open a drawer from one of the cabinets reached in and pulled out a file. As if by magic, a table and chair appeared. I willed the marionette of my thoughts to sit and open the file. It is no longer an avatar to my mind's eye. It is me. I looked down at the pages of the file, and they were alive. I entered them. All this took place in my mind at the speed of thought. I opened my eyes and began.

I got out of my car and walked into work. I went through the store to the break room, opened the door, and walked in. I placed my lunch in the refrigerator. It is a simple turkey sandwich on whole-wheat bread with real mayonnaise, none of that Miracle Whip crap, and with sweet pickles in it. I also had a sliced apple with the core cut out. Last in the brown paper bag is a small bag of iced Circus Animal cookies. I walked up to the keypad on the back wall and clocked in.

Mr. Wayne spoke up suddenly, "Excuse me for interrupting, Mr. Embers. Could you please skip to the time you allege Mark Galos, the defendant, came into the picture?"

I stopped and closed my eyes for a moment then opened only my right eye and looked at him. "As you wish." I closed my eye back up. In my mind, I returned to the table. Staring down at the living file of my memory, I flipped through the pages until I reached the point in time where I first encountered Mark Galos. I reopened my eyes and began again.

"Next. Good evening, sir." I said to the gentleman who was next in line at my register. He is young, his early twenties, I think. He stands five feet ten, maybe a hair more. He has bleached blond hair; I know it is bleached because you could see the beginnings of dark roots. It is arranged messy and in need of a cut. His eyes are dark and a little dull. He has a slightly nervous way about him. I

noticed the gun he showed me as he lifted his shirt. It is a small-caliber revolver, 22 I think. I am in no way an expert on firearms, but it did not strike me as a "Saturday Night Special." The only thing in my universe right now is the gun. It is all I saw.

"No heroics or everybody dies." My eyes are still on the gun when I hear a second voice.

"Please, please, please, do what he says. Oh God, you have to do as he says." It is strange. It is like he has two voices. One voice is deeper, cool, and has an odd accent I cannot place. The second voice is shaky and scared. I can't tell where the second voice is coming from, but I can hear it as clear as my own thoughts.

Well, I don't want to argue with the robber or the disembodied voice. Another customer joined the line behind the guy with the gun. I snapped back from a universe of a gun and two voices. I grab the "Next Register" sign and put it on the conveyor belt. "I am so sor... sor... sorry," I stuttered. "I am helping this gentleman here, and it will take quite some time." I tried to sound sincere. I reached over and picked up the intercom. Mister man of two voices' face became stormy, and I saw him starting to pull up his shirt to grab the gun. Quickly, I blurted. "I am going to call another clerk so you can be on your way sooner."

My eyes were on the second customer when I heard the scared voice say, "That sounds helpful. Doesn't that sound helpful?" The voice sounded like he is talking to the robber. I turned to look back at the robber. His hand started to hesitate, then slowly moved away from his waistband.

"Sure, that sounds fine. Call another clerk," the first voice is back, and he narrowed his eyes as he stared at me. I could see he is waiting for me to say the wrong thing.

"Second checker, please. Madam, if you would move to register two, Raul will be with you shortly," I slowly put the intercom back down. *The customer is looking a little miffed at me, but she is moving to check-stand two.*

The first voice spoke, "Clever and polite I like you, Mr. Clerk Guy. Keep playing it cool and smart, and we will get along just fine. Escort me back to the pharmacy."

I moved from behind the register and started slowly to lead him back to the pharmacy. I heard the second voice once again talk, "You can't do this to people. You are going to hurt someone. I won't let you hurt anyone," the disembodied voice said. *This voice is starting to sound strained as it said*, "This ends now."

With the tag-team voices fighting it out, *I wondered if this thief is a frustrated ventriloquist with mental health issues. As I lead this thug, I steered us through the aisle with all the seasonal items.* A chorus of motion-activated Halloween decorations started screaming, booing, and generally making nuisances of themselves. *The day shift has it the worst. Every kid gets joyful glee out of testing every last noisemaker. I hate seasonal displays, but this aisle has the best pick-up from the surveillance cameras. With any luck, this guy will be recognized and caught. As we approached the pharmacy counter, I could see no one is waiting to pick up their prescription. I silently rejoiced for the stroke of luck.*

"Go around to the pharmacy's side door. I want back there," Mister Creepy Voice commanded. He put his hand on my shoulder and pushed me in the direction of the door. *His touch feels cold and wrong like an oily film is spreading out and covering me. The touch lasted only a moment, but the feeling stayed. I shivered. I'll need a hot shower to shake the cold and to clean off the film when this is all over.* We reached the door. "Open it."

"It's locked," I replied.

"You've been playing it pretty smart, Mr. Clerk Guy, so don't start acting stupid." I reached into my pocket for the keys. *"Easy. Pull those keys out slowly."* I fumbled with the keys trying to find the one that fit the door.

"Don't hurt him. He's doing as you asked," the second voice was still straining. I finally found the correct key despite my trembling hands. It took me three tries before I could fit the key into the lock. I opened the door and saw Marcy doing some restocking. The pharmacy must be slow tonight. Well, things are going to get busy in here pretty darn quick.

She looked up with a start. *"Nathan, you know you aren't supposed to be back here."* She noticed my pal with the two voices and a gun. Her eyes grew wide.

"Close the security curtain. This will take a few minutes, and I want some privacy while she works," I obeyed him lickety-split.

Marcy looks like the merry-go-round of her thoughts is about to spin out of control, *"Marcy, look at me."* I put my hands on her shoulders, *"Calm down.'* I am trying to get her to look me in the eyes, *"This gentleman promises no one will get hurt if we do as he says. We can do that, right, Marcy?"* Her breathing is getting faster. She wouldn't look at me. *"Marcy. Marcy. MARCY!"* She jumped and finally looked me in the eyes, *"You can do as he asks, can't you, Marcy?'* I am nodding my head yes the whole time I spoke and willing her to relax. She started calming down.

"You are just Mister Helpful tonight," his voice is calm, but I could see sweat beading down his face. Maybe the second voice is gaining the upper hand. *"Alright, Miss, I have written down all the different meds I want. Bring me each one, all you have in stock."* He handed her a folded piece of paper. She opened it up and read it. A puzzled look came over her face, *"Don't think about it and just get me those meds."* Marcy grabbed an empty box and went about her task. *"Hurry, Miss. I am not in a mood to be messed with,"* It took her maybe two minutes to collect everything on the list. She handed the box to the robber. He grabbed it

and his shopping list. He glanced down at the collection of bottles. "Is this all of it? It looks light to me," he growled.

Marcy broke into tears, "It's everything on the list. We don't carry much stock on those drugs. They're mostly special order."

"No, don't hurt her. I think she is telling the truth," the second voice was pleading. "I'll stop fighting you."

"Very well, with this caper going so smoothly, I can be magnanimous. However, I can't have you getting help while I finish up with him. Turn around and put your hands behind your back.' Marcy did as instructed. Mr. Magnanimous pulled a roll of duct tape and a tie-wrap out of his pockets. Tie-wrap - You know those plastic strips electricians and computer nerds use to bundle up wires. Cops use them, too, as cheap handcuffs. He handed them to me, "Wrap her wrists. Do it right. I'll be checking. If it's too loose, well, let's say it will ruin the rest of her short life."

I took the tie and wrapped Marcy uptight, maybe even a little too tight, "Don't try anything, Marcy. So far, he hasn't hurt anyone. Play it safe." Tears are streaming down her face, and her nose was running, but she was quiet.

'Excellent. Tape her mouth shut. I don't want her making a sound.'

'Can I wipe her nose first?' I asked as I turned and looked at him.

"Be quick. This is taking longer than it should."

I wiped her nose on my sleeve. Yuck. I held her cheeks in my hands and looked her straight in the eyes, "Ok. You're fine, Marcy, stay quiet. As soon as he is gone, I'll come back and free you," I tried to instill confidence in my voice in hopes Marcy would remain calm and not try something which could get us hurt or worse. I placed the tape over her mouth and helped her to the floor, "Don't do anything."

The thief checked over my tie-wrap job then proclaimed, "Good enough. Now, to the office," he glared down at Marcy, "Listen to him girl and don't try anything or your boss will pay the price first," he emphasized the last word.

We left the pharmacy quickly but not rushed. He is doing every step of this hold-up with the practiced calm of someone who has done this many times. "Why are we going to the office?" I asked myself. He hasn't shown any interest in the cash in the registers. He can't believe I can open the safe. Oh God, he needs privacy for what he's going to do next. Oh crap, oh crap, oh crap.' My knees started to wobble. Suddenly, I feel hot. Everything is starting to spin like I am going to faint. "Wait. Calm yourself down. Breathe. Yes, breathing is helpful. Don't panic. He hasn't hurt anybody, yet. Maybe he wants something else. Yes, if he planned to kill people, he would have had Marcy come with us. He has something else planned," my mind raced. "Sir, if you want to get into the safe, I don't have the combination. All the drugs are kept down in the pharmacy. Don't waste your time. You should go."

I heard the second voice join in with, "He's right. You should go."

"Don't try to tell me what to do, boy. I won't hesitate to rub you out," the creepy voice stated in the strange accent.

'Boy? What did it mean? I had at least fifteen years, maybe twenty on him and rub you out? He must have seen too many gangster movies.' I pondered.

We made it to the office without further conversation. The place is a mess. An old metal desk with a faux wood grain finish sat opposite the door. An equally ancient chair is behind the desk. On the far wall behind the desk and chair are some shelves. Books and company manuals filled them along with the hard drive and monitor of the surveillance system. Filing cabinets line one wall. Opposite the cabinets is a large two-way mirror which overlooked the sales floor. Two folding chairs faced the front of the desk. Papers and folders are strewn all over the desk with little regard for order. Mike, the General Manager, has a system to the way he keeps his desk. It had something to do with Chaos Theory, I think. Never clean Mike's desk. This is Rule Number One. I made that mistake once early in my tenure at the drug store. He made me scrub all the carts with a bucket and sponge. It is the favorite duty he would assign anyone who pisses him off. Usually, the guys who power-wash the sidewalks at night would hose the carts off, but not if you are Mike's "special friend" this week.

"Sit down and clam up," the strangely accented voice told me. He looked out the two-way mirror. He didn't appear to get agitated. The floor must have looked quiet. He walked around behind the desk, pulled out a pair of wire cutters from his coat, and cut the power cord and feeds to the hard drive. He moved the drive to the desk, disturbing some of the paperwork as he did. Oh look, he wants to be Mike's "special friend." Next, he cut the phone lines. "Okay, let's have the cell phone," he commanded.

"We aren't allowed to carry a cell phone while on the clock. Mine is in my locker in the break room."

He looked at me like he is going to burn a hole through me with heat vision. "Empty your pockets and turn them inside out. Take off your watch and ring, too. If you lied to me about the phone, little Ms. Marcy will be accompanying me on a little road trip. I assure you she won't like the ride.' I put the contents of my pockets on the desk a wallet, my keys, eighty-seven cents, a half-full container of Tic Tacs, and a small wad of lint. I took off my watch and placed it next to my wallet. As I went to pull off my wedding ring, I hesitated. I had never removed my ring during my entire marriage. Damn, if I am going to do it. A fire started to burn inside my chest. My heart started to pound. My jaw tensed. "Mr. Clerk Guy, I see something I don't like. I see wheels turning behind those eyes. Think about it. Is your *life worth the ring?" My chest fell. The rage ebbed away. I am beaten without even a fight. I took off the ring and placed it next to the contents of my pockets and my watch. "I'm impressed. You didn't let your emotions rule over you."*

"He's done all you asked. Don't hurt him. Let him and the girl go," the second voice pleaded.

He began looking through my wallet and found the picture of my wife and daughter. A sick kind of smile came over his face. "Cute girl. She favors her mother, I see. Tell me how did you get so lucky? Based on what I see, your wife is slumming it with you as a husband."

"It's what I've always thought. I believe I won the wife and daughter lottery. I'd love to talk about the family all night, but all the paperwork from the robbery is going to keep me late tonight. So, if we could finish up here?"

"Why? Are you in a hurry to die? It's the plan, you know. The next step is to put two bullets in your head." He pulled the gun and pointed it right at my face. I stared at the working end of the barrel. My eyes moved up to his. He thumbed back the hammer of the revolver. I heard it click into place.

"This is it. God, don't let my wife and daughter see me dead with two holes in my head," I prayed. They say your whole life flashes in front of your eyes before you die, but the only thing I see is the eyes of the man who is murdering me. They are cold and empty. He looks bored. I sensed more than saw something change in those eyes.

"You have made this whole endeavor go more smoothly than I had hoped. No one has been hurt, and only meds were taken. Which makes this whole enterprise low priority for the police. All evidence of me will be gone when I go. The only things left will be eyewitnesses to this caper. Hell, the girl won't even remember my hair color. So, tell you what, I'm going to save the cost of two bullets and leave you be. Of course, I will have to make sure I get enough

time to make my get-away.' He pulled another tie-wrap out. What is he wearing, a freaking utility belt? "Tape your mouth shut." I complied. "No calling out for help. Sit down behind the desk." I moved to the slightly nicer chair behind the desk. "You get to pretend you're the man in charge. Well, you get to pretend you're in charge," a slight smile, more of a smirk, came to his face over his attempt at humor. "Put your hands behind your back. No, around the chair back too, you idiot. You will be in here for a while I think, so try to stay comfy." He grabbed a couple of sheets of paper off the desk and pulled out a pen from his pocket and started writing. He held up the messages for me to see. "Do Not Disturb' is written on one. He taped the other note to my chest. "Start counting to five hundred and don't even try to free yourself until you finish. Oh, one last thing. You need to pay for the moment you attempted to grow a pair," he picked up my wedding ring and smiled. "This will cover it," he popped the ring into his pocket. He grabbed the hard drive. As he left the office, he taped the note with "Do Not Disturb' to the door. He is gone.

After I finished counting - I wasn't going to fool around with this guy - I tried to free myself, but my efforts failed. It is somewhere around ten minutes later when Raul discovered me.

I closed my eyes and took a deep breath. I opened my eyes. I am back to the here and now. "That is exactly what happened."

"Thank you, Mr. Embers. I have no more questions for the witness at this time, Your Honor."

From the judge, "Ms. Refrain, your witness."

I looked over at the defense's table. Besides Mr. Galos, there are seated four lawyers: three men and one woman. I hate lawyers. To paraphrase the movie Other People's Money, "Lawyers are like nuclear weapons: once someone uses one, it screws everything up." For what I would take as a simple robbery case, someone is dropping an awful lot of nukes.

The three men in rather ordinary, although well-fitting, navy blue suits and dull ties, sat at the defense's table. Fresh yellow legal pads sat in front of them like placemats for a grand banquet. Number two pencils rested on the right-hand side of each pad: knives ready for carving. I can guess what's on the menu. I had met each one of these hacks before. Oh, I am sorry. "Shysters," when each had his chance to depose me. I told each of them the exact same account of that night as I told the jury. I am not sure what they could possibly want to ask me, but mine is not to reason why. Mine is to recite and die…of boredom.

The fourth lawyer, a woman I had never met before, stood. I have seen some beautiful women in my day, "Hi honey. Are you listening? You are way prettier," but this goddess is…is…is perfect. Of all the gin joints in all the towns in all the world, she had to walk into mine. She stands about five-foot-six. She has brown hair with red highlights which caught the light. It fell in soft curls around her face. Her face is oval-shaped with bright eyes of hazel. I did not get a clear picture of her age, early thirties, I think. She is young for a senior partner in a major San Diego law firm, "Refrain and Associates." Her skin is flawless and youthful. She has perfectly arched brows which are neither too thin nor too thick. She does her makeup in a fashion with no heaviness, no missed chosen color; in fact, you could hardly tell it is there. Perfect. Surprisingly, she is not dressed in what you would call a business fashion. She is wearing a bright yellow dress which buttons up the front with a white collar, but no lace. The dress is belted around the waist in matching white with a buckle of polished brass. The dress is mid-thigh in length. She is slender, but not overly so. One of the three extras from the Matrix movies handed her a piece of paper he had pulled from a file. She stood there a moment looking at the paper. You could tell by her demeanor Ms. Refrain is the big boss, she's in charge. She's the boss, headwoman, top dog, big cheese, head honcho.

Sorry, I channeled the movie Airplane there for a second.

I wanted to be strong, so I played the melody to the song, a Simon and Garfunkel tune, "I Am a Rock," in my thoughts. The title from the song fits the situation. I need to be strong. Sometimes I enjoy this quirky memory of mine. I can replay any song I have heard, ever. It is kind of like having an internal "iPod," only without the earbuds that keep falling out and a limit on how many songs it can hold. At least, I hope there is no limit on my memory. Damn, that's a gloomy thought: I could run out of memory. I would be stuck in some lame version of Fifty First Dates but without the happy ending and cool boat.

The judge coughed, "Ms. Refrain."

"Sorry, Your Honor," she looked up from the paper she was reading. "Mr. Embers, this should not take long at all."

I turned off my mental radio station. I heard in my thoughts the Duff Beer guy from the Simpsons say, *This is K R A P signing off. Oh yeah!* " Note to self: hire a better voice for my mental radio station's disc jockey. *"Duff Man is sad."*

"I have a few questions for you," Ms. Refrain stated with an almost musical quality. "Your statement to police on the night in question is word-for-word exactly the same as your testimony here today. Could you explain this?" Ms. Refrain asked.

"What is there to explain? It all happened exactly as I said. It was the truth then. It is the truth now. It was the truth when they deposed me," I responded, pointing toward See, Hear, and Speak no evil.

"In my entire career as a criminal defense attorney, I have never witnessed that. In my research, I have failed to find a case where it happened before. You must have rehearsed your part very well." Before I could form a snappy comeback, she faced the judge. "Your Honor, I would like to show the jury some video of the witness's depositions to my associates?"

"Objection, your Honor, if the defense wants to present evidence, they can do so during their phase," Mr. Wayne affirmed as he rose.

"It goes to credibility, your Honor," Ms. Refrain countered.

"I will allow it."

"Thank you, your Honor," she smiled as the judge ruled in her favor. She motioned to Manny, Moe, and Jack at the defense table. One of her minions put up a projection screen across the courtroom opposite the jury but angled to let the judge and yours truly see the screen also. Another one grabbed a laptop and placed it on a table in front of the screen. He immediately opened it up and started typing away. Finally, the last one carried over a projector and put it on the table. He started connecting the laptop to the projector with some cables. As each man finished his task, they walked back to the defense's table and sat down. They did all this with the efficiency of a NASCAR pit crew.

Ms. Refrain walked over to the laptop and pressed a key. Three images came into focus on the screen. Each image is of me, in all my glory, sitting at a table. "Mr. Embers, are these images of you?" I responded in the affirmative. "Are the date and time stamps correct and correspond to the dates and times you were deposed at my office?" I told her they are correct. "Would you please watch a few minutes of your depositions?"

I wonder what would happen if I answered no thank you. She hit another key on the laptop, and the images came to life. I watched as my image recited what happened in triplicate. The show went on for only a couple of minutes before the judge instructed her to stop.

"Mr. Embers, this video of your depositions shows you using the same cadence, facial expressions, and why, you even took breaths at the same moments in your testimony. I find this remarkable and highly suspect," she smiled the way a spider smiles when her web starts to wiggle. "Mr. Embers, could you be a talented actor?" She did not wait for an answer. "I applaud your performance."

My retort was brilliant. "Oh yeah," I took a second and sighed. "It is not a performance. I have a unique memory. I call it an "Infinitely Indexed Memory Bank" like in the old sci-fi movie Earth Vs. The Flying Saucers. Some people refer to it as photographic memory; however, the correct term is Eidetic memory. I believe my memory even goes beyond that definition. The fact is I can recall with exact precision anything I have ever experienced: every conversation, every book I have ever read, every song I have heard, each movie I've watched. All of it. Everybody experiences this to a lesser extent. There are moments in all our lives when an event chisels itself into our memory. The assassination of JFK, the Challenger explosion, and the Twin Towers are all examples of when an event so ingrains itself we can remember every last detail. My whole memory is like that."

Still smiling, "Why, it would be amazing if it is true. However, I find it strange a man, such as yourself with perfect memory as you claim, would be working as a night manager at a twenty-four-hour drug store. With this kind of memory, why you could work in any number of careers which are, shall we say, more upwardly mobile. So, tell me why, Mr. Embers, you would not study to be a doctor, or stockbroker, or even a ... "

"Lawyer?" I interrupted.

"Attorney," she countered.

"Whatever," I snapped back, "I had higher aspirations than being a lawyer." As I made the statement, it must have looked like I ate something that tasted nasty. I leaned back in the chair, and it creaked. After waiting for a beat, "Lawyers don't create anything. They never build up. They only tear down. In other words, I didn't want to become someone who takes a slice of everyone else's pie. I want to make a pie of my own." I looked away for a moment. "The truth of it is I made some poor choices in life. I have missed opportunities; I was lazy in my youth. You name it. My failures are why I never became upwardly mobile, as you put it. Now, it is too late to change. I have a wife and child to support. I don't have the luxury to do things by the numbers anymore."

"I see." She crossed back to the defendant's table and picked up a binder. "I have a report here from a Dr. Lapse of UCLA," she held up the binder. "He tells of a study he performed on memory. He writes about one subject, in particular, whose memory…"

"Ok, quit the games and ask your questions," I yelled.

She looked at me again and smiled. It is a pretty smile.

"Ok. Let me help this along. Did I participate in the study you mentioned? Yes. Is the subject Dr. Lapse talked about me? Yes. Let's get on with it," I motioned with my hand in a rolling manner.

"Very well, Mr. Embers, as you wish. Let us get right to the heart of the matter. You say you have a perfect memory, but in fact, your memory has a hole in it. Does it not?"

"I would not use the word hole so much as a slight flaw," I ground my teeth as the admission came out.

"Flaw, hole, the point is it is not, in fact, perfect. You lied," she accused me making those little quote marks with her fingers as she said "perfect." I hate that. She is staring at me, unblinking straight in the eyes.

This woman must have earned an A in "Bitch 101".

"This flaw you speak of what is it? Oh, and please be precise. We would not want to have to call you back in order to clear up a lie."

"Misunderstanding."

"Whatever."

I take it back: she earned an "A plus with honors."

I broke eye contact first. I lost the stare down. "With my memory, it is not only remembering the facts but rather when I recall events, I experience the flavor of it all over again everything including the emotions, fear, joy, disappointment, etc. However, I can't remember tastes as clearly as everything else." I took a breath and steadied myself. "However; I don't see how that fact has any bearing on this case. I sure as Hell didn't stick my tongue down his throat!" Several people in the courtroom broke out in laughter. The bailiff, who had been looking so bored earlier tried to cover his laughter by pretending to cough. Even one of the Matrix boys is laughing.

"Order. Order," the judge demanded as he banged the gavel.

Now it is Ms. Refrain who broke her stare and turned toward her right-hand man as it were. A flash of anger crossed her face. She is not quite as beautiful as before.

"Even with this flaw, as you call it, I would have to say it is quite a blessing," she announced all the while never turning her attention back to me until she was finished with her statement.

"It's enjoyable at times. Oh yes. I can recall with fondness things like the first time I made it to second base with a girl, Veronica. We were both fourteen." My internal radio station started playing *"In the Summertime"* by Mungo Jerry. "She had braces, freckles, and the cutest little button nose. We kissed behind her parent's house in the avocado grove there. Her breasts are becoming evident. I was able to slip my hand under her…" The judge cleared his throat and broke my chain of thought. The sound of a needle being pulled across an LP ended the song. I pondered with a smile on my face for a brief moment. *"I wonder how you are, Veronica? Safe and happy, I hope. Thanks for the memory."*

"Forgive me. That memory gets my heart racing every time," I readjusted my position in the chair. It creaked again. "Where was I?" I glanced at the jury. Based on the slight smiles on their faces, some of the jurors seem to be enjoying a walk down their own memory lanes. "Yes, I don't only have happy recollections. I also remember all the boring daily routine stuff too. All the time I've spent brushing my teeth, every time I've pulled up my socks, grocery shopping, those are entertaining recollections there. However, those memories are but a sample. I also remember the bad times. I remember every faux pas I ever made. I remember every cruel remark I ever made to a person who had never done me wrong. I remember every petty action, childish behavior; I remember everything. I remember every time I was sick with the flu, every time I had a migraine, every time I've tossed my cookies. I even remember every time I have ever stubbed my freaking toe. I remember everything. I can also remember those moments of living Hell. I remember the day I realized my father was never coming home again. I remember my mother's slow death. It's like a time-lapse movie in my mind. I can recall each day of those five years it took her to die. I remember her wasting away to the shell of her former self. I can also remember with agonizing clarity the time I failed my daughter and almost killed both her and my wife. I relive that particular nightmare at least once a year. Thank you very much."

A wave of melancholy hit me. It washes over me like the tide stretching to reach the high-water mark. Every time I even mention that night, it tries to drown me in bitter regret at my failing as a man. Stop thinking damn it! Oh God, I wish I could travel back in time and change that one mistake. I would pay any price, even my life, to correct that one instant.

I dropped my head and took a deep breath. After a moment, I spoke. "Imagine, Ms. Refrain, every hurt lurking in the back of your mind. Imagine every disappointment you've experienced in life taunting you. A single word from a friend, colleague, loved one, acquaintance, or stranger can invoke a torrent of memories to flood over you. Picture your memories becoming like a drug. You'll spend countless hours reliving ecstasies time after time until you realize you are missing the here and now. Maybe sometimes you won't care about what you're missing. Envision all the pain, every tear, all the hours your broken heart has ever cried out in your soul. All that is yours to savor in absolute and perfect clarity. Think about it, Ms. Refrain, think about it for a moment," I had to take another beat to steady myself. "Do you know what the kicker is? Do you?" I turned and looked at the jury. I screamed, "DO YOU?" I was out of my seat and leaning out of the witness box. I realized what I was doing and sat back down. Calmer but with a great deal of intensity, "I will tell you. I remember remembering. A blessing?" I stopped for a moment and let it sink in. "No, it's a God damn curse."

Through sheer will, I invoked strength in myself. I blinked back the tears forming in my eyes and swallowed down the lump in my throat. God, help me. "May I have some water?" I asked the judge.

"Bailiff, give Mr. Embers some water." The bailiff was already bringing me a glass as the judge issued the order.

I took the glass offered. I drank deeply. I set the glass down and looked at it for a few seconds watching the water condensing on it slide down to form a ring on the lovely wood. I thought I heard the court reporter sniff. I looked up, and by their expressions, I could tell the three associates, Manny, Moe, and Jack, did not understand, that or remind me never to play Texas Hold'em with them. Ha! Remind me. Sometimes I even think funny.

"It was a moving monologue, Mr. Embers. Is this another performance?" Ms. Refrain asked with a little mocking in her tone.

I looked at the judge, "I need a short break."

"Your Honor, if I could continue, I will be through with this witness in a moment," her voice once again had a musical quality to it.

Before the judge could rule, I made the mistake of mumbling something under my breath. "I am sorry, your Honor. I didn't hear the last few words the witness stated," the court reporter announced.

"The witness will repeat his last statement, and please speak loud enough for everyone to hear."

"Your Honor, I don't think the court…," I fumbled my words.

"Mr. Embers, you will repeat your last statement."

"Yes, your Honor. I turned to face Ms. Refrain and the other attorneys at the defense's table. In a clear and loud voice, "I said, I swear all you lawyers are pricks."

"Lord knows it is true, Mr. Embers, but while you are in my courtroom, you will keep a civil tongue in your mouth. I think we can all use a little break. We are recessed for fifteen minutes," the judge banged the gavel. Most of the court stood up and filed out the door.

I worked my way down the hall to the washroom. I traveled there in no real hurry. I went to the sink and washed my face in cold water. The crispness of it brought me back to reality. I have a mind to walk out and go home. Of course, it will accomplish nothing except get me arrested and thrown in jail for contempt. They would let me rot there for a few hours until I apologized for being a bad little boy. Lose another day to this foolishness? I don't think so. I had to get a grip on myself, but getting caught gripping oneself in a public bathroom would cause its own legal problems. So, I took a deep cleansing breath in through my mouth and out my nose. Why do they call it a cleansing breath? My lungs felt just as dirty as before. After my revelation, I blanked my mind and headed back to the courtroom.

Some people are milling around the hallway in front of the courtroom door. As I approached the group, an older lady dressed in slightly out of fashion clothes caught my eye and walked toward me. This woman had been sitting in the gallery while I had given my testimony. Without breaking eye contact with me, she took my right hand in both of her hands, "Mr. Embers, I have been watching this trial since it began. I watch a great many trials. It gives an old woman something to fill her days. I love watching people. Some days it's boring. Some days you learn quite a bit, and other days, like today, you hear a witness who touches you. You touched me today. I am so sorry for you. I can't imagine what it must be like. However, you know your gift doesn't have to be a curse. I would give a great deal to spend another day, even if it was only the memory of a day, with my Albert." Before I could answer her, she gave my hand a little pat and turned away.

Compassion; who would have ever thought I would find some here? She is right. Everything is a matter of perspective. It would only be a curse if I chose to make it one.

The door into the courtroom opened, and the bailiff stuck his head out, "Court is reconvening."

Well, back into the lion's den. I entered and made my way around to the witness box. As I sat, I surveyed the room. I purposefully didn't make eye contact with the she-wolf and her cubs. Everyone is in their place. The woman who spoke to me in the hallway is no longer sitting in the gallery behind the defense. She has moved to the prosecution's side of the courtroom. In her own way, I think she is telling me she is on my side. As our eyes met, I gave her a little wink. She mouthed the words "you're too young." I laughed to myself and nodded. I finished my survey of the room. The screen and laptop are gone.

Then it popped out at me like a bad 3-D movie. All the legal pads which were pristine during the whole of my testimony had several of their pages flipped over and curled tightly under the pads. The Wicked Witch of the West must have been giving instructions to her Flying Monkeys or observations or whatnot during my absence. No worries. It's not like I'm the one who is going to be worrying about dropping the soap in the shower during my stay in the pokey. I wonder if it's why they call it the pokey.

As the judge came into the courtroom, the bailiff commanded, "All rise." Why he said it I don't know because we are already getting up?

The judge banged his gavel rather lightly as he adjusted his position behind the bench. "Ms. Refrain, you may continue."

"Thank you, your Honor. Mr. Embers, why did you make your last statement? Surely you knew better than to use profanity before this court."

The vision of Leslie Nelson popped into the view of my mind's eye and recited, *"Yes, I do and don't call me Shirley."* I hushed the bored part of my mind.

"Believe it or not, Ms. Refrain, I consider myself a man of honor. I took an oath, to tell the truth. The statement was what I mumbled, so I repeated it. Besides, I felt some relief getting it off my chest."

"I see. I have a few more questions. Then I will be all done, Mr. Embers. In your testimony, you stated you heard a second voice besides the perpetrator's. Who was speaking?"

"Like I said, I heard a voice. I did not see another person."

"Did the perpetrator have a radio with him?"

"None that I saw."

"Well, Mr. Embers, how do you explain this second voice of yours?"

"Maybe he's a ventriloquist." My remark received a couple of chuckles.

Ms. Refrain had a "we are not amused" look on her face. "What about the accent you claimed the robber had? My client has no such accent. He was born and raised here in San Diego. How would you explain this?"

"All I can tell you is what I saw, thought, and heard that night."

"I see Mr. Embers. Only a few more questions and you can go back to your life, sir. Could you please finish your retelling of the events of the night in question?" Ms. Refrain asked in a matter of fact manner.

"What else is there? He left. I was freed. End of story."

"There are your interactions with the police, Mr. Embers. Please, only a few questions more."

"Tell me, do attorneys ever get straight to the point? Or do you always have to go around the barn?"

"Interesting observation, but not a wholly original metaphor, Mr. Embers. What is the name or names of the police officers you talked with after the alleged robbery?" Ms. Refrain asked.

"I recounted the robbery to Detective Frank Hawkins. Are we done? I'm tired. This entire day has been shot, and I would like to rest a bit before I have to go to work tonight."

"No, Mr. Embers, this is another one of those pesky misunderstandings of yours. I need the names of every officer you talked with that night."

"Oh, for crying out loud. Let's see; there was Officer Meier. He told me to relax, and a detective would be with me soon to take a statement. Another gentleman I talked with was Officer Bender. He offered to bring me a cup of coffee while I was waiting for the detectives. I asked for a Diet Pepsi instead. I hate coffee. Last, there was Detective Ralph Daves.

Ms. Refrain looked startled. "You answered Detective Daves, Detective Ralph Daves?"

"Yes, Detective Ralph Daves. I had met him once before years ago." I looked at my watch. "Can I go now?"

"Your Honor, if I could have a moment to confer with my associates?" Ms. Refrain asked in her musical way.

"Very well, Ms. Refrain."

I haven't any clue as to what she is up to. I only wanted to be done with this tale told by an idiot. At this point, the idiot doesn't care.

She leaned over and whispered something to the nearest stooge. He stood up and left the courtroom. "Your Honor, something new has come to light. I ask the court, in the interest of justice, to recess for an hour so we may retrieve a vital document?"

The judge looked up at the clock "It's a bit early for lunch, but alright we are in recess until one o'clock." Bang went the gavel.

Crap. I thought they would be done with me before lunch. I didn't pack a lunch, and the mention of it made my stomach growl. I knew I wouldn't like it, but I headed to the gagateria anyways. I grabbed a tuna on wheat, some salt and vinegar chips, a banana, and a Diet Pepsi. Sometimes I'm glad I can't remember tastes well. This meal is one such occasion. They put celery in the tuna salad. Tell me please, who in their right mind, puts celery in tuna salad? If you are looking for a little crunch in a sandwich, make a peanut butter sandwich with chunky style peanut butter.

Eating this meal gave me the urge to make some real tuna salad using my Mom's recipe. It will be great for my lunches next week. Like it will even last a week. Every time I make it, I end up sneaking a few forks full each time I open the fridge. I opened the pantry and fridge at home in my mind. Yep, we have everything I need to make some kick-ass tuna salad. Assuming, of course, my wife hadn't

32

used any of the vital ingredients since the last time I took a mental note of everything in the kitchen.

I went back to court as it is about time to reconvene. We did the "all rise," and the judge did his gavel banging again. The judge said, "Ms. Refrain, you may continue with the witness, and I'll remind you Mr. Embers you are still under oath."

Both Ms. Refrain and I spoke in unison, I said, "I understand, your Honor," and Ms. Refrain said, "Thank you, your Honor." It is both creepy and amusing at the same time.

"Mr. Embers, in your earlier testimony, you stated you talked with Detective Ralph Daves on the night of the robbery. Is this correct?"

"Yes, it is."

Ms. Refrain is showing a slight smile. It is the kind of smile which scares me a little bit. "And you have this perfect memory of yours?"

"Yes, I do. What's your point?"

"May I approach the witness, your Honor?"

"Yes."

Ms. Refrain picked up a sheet of paper off the table. She walked toward me and handed it to me. "Mr. Embers, would you please read this and tell the court what it is."

I glanced over it quickly. "It's a death certificate."

"Whose death certificate is it, Mr. Embers?" She wasn't even trying to conceal her smile.

I read the name. "Ralph Daves." He was an acquaintance, a fine Cop and a decent man too. I am sorry to learn he had passed. I had met him back in 1978 when the PSA jetliner and small aircraft collided over North Park. When I heard the crash, I rushed to help if I could. Freaking vultures had beaten me there and were robbing the dead. One man was running around with bolt cutters cutting off fingers to steal the victims' rings. Ralph Daves arrived after I did. He went about arresting the creeps I pointed out. If I had been the one carrying the gun that day, I am not sure I would not have shot them where they stood. Robbing the dead is low even for a low-life.

I will have to say a few words over his resting place. He was a decent man. It's a worthy epitaph for any man.

"What is the date of death, sir?"

I read the date out loud, and as the words sounded from my lips, my heart sank. The date read two weeks before the robbery. "But it can't be; I talked to Ralph."

"Well, Mr. Embers either you remember the date wrong, or you talked to a ghost." She received a few laughs on her own. "And if you remember the date wrong, could you not have mistaken the defendant, Mark Galos, for the man who robbed the store the night in question?" She paused to let it sink into the jury's collective mind. As I was about to come back with a brilliant remark, she burst out with, "I don't believe your memory is quite as remarkable as you think it is."

"No. My memory is perfect. Mark Galos robbed the store. I talked to Detective Ralph Daves that night. This death certificate is wrong, not me." The world is crashing down on me. I almost don't believe myself. It seemed like I could hear the jurors' doubts in my mind. My head began to pound with a headache, a migraine, and it feels like one that will torment me for days.

Ms. Refrain took back the death certificate and handed it to the judge. He gave it a quick look then handed it to the bailiff. "One last question, Mr. Embers. And I promise it is the last question. Out of curiosity, what did the sign the robber taped to your chest say?" A big damn smile is on her face now. She knew what was written on the sign. She is pouring salt on the wound.

"Coward." It was Mark Galos' turn to smile. I am broken, but I tried not to let it show.

Ms. Refrain turned around, and as she walked back to her seat, she pronounced, "I have no more questions for this witness, your Honor."

The judge ordered, "The witness is excused."

I left the courtroom without another word. I am a beaten man, but I walked out tall and confident in hopes it would help convince the jury I spoke the truth. My head pounded in time with each step to my car. This mental monster is building up to be a Hell of a migraine. I'm not sure my little tricks for getting rid of it will work on this one.

I left the courthouse for my car. The headache wasn't lessening one bit. It would not be safe to drive home with the distraction of a migraine, so I had to take drastic measures. I sat in my car and took a moment to focus my thoughts. In my mind, I gave my headache a form. I saw a giant swinging a big club and pounding the ground in rhythm with the pounding in my skull. He stood maybe three times my height, dressed in leather armor reminiscent of something a Roman soldier might wear. I created a vision of myself to fight this monster. I have dressed in armor also. I am wearing a chainmail Hauberk and coif. I am armed with a Katana. It is strange I would wield a Katana wearing chainmail. Oh well, we fought each other, giant headache versus a giant pain in the ..., on the terrain in my mind.

I sliced at his legs and parried his club. With every stroke of my shining blade, I drove him toward the trap I had laid for him. Slowly, I pushed him back until at last, I backed him into the vault of synapses I had created. I flung the door closed on this giant of a headache. I spun the combination of the safe. I heard the giant pounding against the walls and door of the trap. With each beat of my heart, his pounding lessened until finally, there was silence in my mind. It should do for a little while. I had learned the trick when I was young. The only problem with getting rid of headaches this way is they always come back stronger. I eventually must let the migraine run its course. The last time I forestalled a headache like this one more than twice, I was bedridden for three days. All light and any sound which reached me are like driving nails into my eyes and ears. Only my begging kept Char from calling for an ambulance. I can't imagine what would happen if I tried to use the trick four times.

Well, with the headache under wraps, it is time to be homeward bound. The music started up in my mind. *"I'm sitting in a railway station got a ticket for my destination…"* Simon and Garfunkel, you have to love them.

Chapter Two

A perfectly agreeable day here in America's Finest City shot to Hell. I looked at my cell phone for the time; then, texted my wife to let her know I am on my way home. If I hurry, I can still make it for dinner with my family. Unless it's a special occasion, my wife, Charlene, serves dinner promptly at five-thirty PM. Well, with my schedule of working graveyards, it is more like my breakfast, not dinner. That which we call a meal by any other name still tastes yummy. I hope it's meatloaf tonight. I can use the comfort of some comfort food like meatloaf tonight. Char makes it with crumbled bacon in the mix. You can't go wrong with bacon. Pork fat rules baby. Meat and potatoes. Those are the meals I like best. I know my diet lives somewhere in the sixties, but hey, it's what I grew up eating.

As I made my way to hearth and home, wife and child, I tried to clear my mind of the events of that night and this day. So far, the void of no thoughts eluded me. I can't let it show. My family deserves better than to share my burdens. I walked up to the door, took a breath, and put on my game face. I opened my front door. It's showtime.

I entered the house to a chorus of, "Daddy's home, Daddy's home," from Moiraine. My daughter, God love her, she makes my life worth living. She makes me want to be a better man than I am. Yes, Charlene saved my life, and Moiraine makes my life worth living. Mo stands three feet tall with brown hair cut in a bob with bangs. Her eyes are the color of hazel, which changes shade depending on what she is wearing. She has these cheeks which puff out ever so slightly. Her smile fills the room, and she always smiles. Her personality matches her smile. She is a friend to all.

She wants everybody to be friends and everybody to be happy. She is also a very outgoing child. Even when we are doing something mundane like shopping for groceries, she will introduce herself to fellow shoppers, "Hello. My name is Moiraine. You can call me Mo. Do you want to be friends?" I am sure someday she will make a fine cruise director. It's very sweet. She has made numerous people smile while doing an otherwise joyless task. Her friendliness also scares me to death. She has not learned everyone can't be your friend. I hope she remains ignorant of this fact a little while longer. When she does learn the lesson, I pray it is a gentle lesson. I also pray I will be there to comfort her sorrow.

We named Moiraine after a strong female character from a series of novels by Robert Jordan. Both my wife and I were reading the Wheel of Time series when she was preggers with Moiraine. Somehow the name felt right. We never even considered a boy's name. Many parents want to know the gender of their children before they are born, but we didn't. I wanted it to be a surprise. I am a little old fashioned. No, wait. Retro, yes, make it I am retro. It sounds cool, and I tend to be lacking in cool.

Mo ran through the house to greet me at the door. "Daddy, Daddy, Daddy," poured out as she threw her arms around my legs and squeezed, "I missed you."

"I missed you, too. How was kindergarten today?" I asked, already knowing her answer.

"Good." We answered in unison. She giggled as she looked up at me. She is so loving and trusting. I am her, Daddy. I can't; I won't screw this up. The relationship with my father was a screwed-up mess. I learned early on not to trust his promises. If he told me he would pick me up on the weekend, and we would spend some quality time together, more than half of the time he didn't show. When he did show up, we never did anything fun. Most times, we would go back to his apartment and watch television. I won't even call him my father. He was more like a sperm donor with visitation rights. The only lesson he ever taught me is how not to be a dad. They say a man has two opportunities to have a father-child relationship in his life, one as the child and one as the father. I was cheated out of the first one. I'll be damned if I'll miss out or screw up on the second. I know someday she will see one of my many flaws, or I will disappoint her, or the words I say won't take away the pain, but not this day. Today I am still Daddy: teller of bedtime stories, slayer of closet monsters, and her hero.

"Luuuuceee, I'm home," I yelled in my best Cuban accent.

"You're more like Fred than Ricky," Charlene proclaimed in a deadpan voice. "Dinner is almost ready." Charlene is my beautiful wife. She has dishwater blond hair which falls in ringlets down to her shoulders. Her eyes are creamy jade green. She stands at five feet five inches tall and has a classic hourglass figure. And believe me when I say none of the sand has run out. I have always preferred women with some curves. Oh, a couple of times I have raced on a straight track with only a couple of bumps on the road, but when you take the curvy road there is always something new around the bend, and the view is spectacular. I could wax poetic about every inch of her figure, but I don't kiss and tell.

When she is working in the house, she moves with purpose and speed. She is the kind of person who has a place for everything and everything in its place. In other words, she is a bit of a pain in the butt. I tend to be messy. I will leave the dishes until tomorrow or wait to do laundry until the only clean clothes I have are the ones I just put on. Hey, the world could end and who wants to spend their last hours doing housework?

"What's on the menu?"

"Broiled halibut with orange butter."

Oh my, another gourmet meal from the kitchen of Ellie Mae Clampett. Hell, I don't even care tonight's main course is halibut. You see, the only fish I care to eat is deep-fried, covered in tartar sauce, and has the last name of "sticks."

"Go ahead and sit down. Moiraine, did you finish setting the table?" Char asked from the kitchen.

"Yes, Mom." She answered, all the while hugging my legs. She looked up at me with a proud expression, "I helped cook dinner. Mommy let me stir the butter and put the mushrooms in the salad."

I steered Mo to the dining room table. Before I sat down, I went over to Blossom's bed to give her a pet. Blossom is our dog; well, my wife's dog. She has had her for sixteen years. Blossom is your basic mutt. As best as we can tell, she is a mix of cocker spaniel and golden retriever. She is a smallish dog with a golden-brown coat which is short on her upper half and hangs long and low on her lower half. The poor thing hardly makes a sound or moves from her bed anymore. She lays there, wagging her tail as I petted her, "What kind of day did Blossom have today?" I asked over my shoulder as I gave the old girl some attention.

"She had a pain-free day, I would say. She stayed in her bed except to eat and do her business," Char responded as she put dinner on the table.

Blossom gave my hand a couple of licks. "Hey, old girl, how are you doing?" She looked up at me with her big brown eyes. I think she is trying to tell me something. Those eyes conveyed many thoughts, some of which saddens me to ponder. Thoughts like it's ok to let me go. I have had a love-filled life. "I know girl. I know," I scratched her behind the ears then left for the dining room table. I sat down and looked across the table at my wife, "It's not fair to her. She deserves better."

"I know I just can't think about it right now, okay?"

"What's not fair, Daddy?" Mo asked as I started my dinner.

"It is grown-up talk, Honey. Eat your dinner." Normally I'm of the belief if a child is old enough to ask a question, they are old enough to hear a truthful answer. However, when the answer would hurt Moiraine, I'm a bit of a coward. We all dug into the grub. This dinnertime was mostly quiet except for the yummy sounds. Mine almost sounded genuine.

When we finished with dinner, Mo cleared off the table. She always likes helping, and it has been less traumatic for us since we bought plastic plates and glasses.

Charlene and I lingered at the table while Mo made her trips back and forth to the kitchen. "How did it go?" Charlene asked with concern in her voice. She reached over the table to take my hand. We sat there holding hands and were just being together for a moment.

"It didn't go well. The big boss did the cross-examination. I am pretty sure I blew it." Pretty sure, hell if I had been on the jury, I wouldn't have believed me. "It doesn't matter. Let's do the dishes," I started to stand, but Char stayed seated, holding my hand. I sat back down and looked in her eyes. She knows it is getting to me. In her loving way, she is telling me she is here for me. I can't tell you the strength this simple compassion gives me.

Let me tell you a little secret we men have: we are weak. Oh, we can pump iron, lift that bale, tote that barge all week long and twice on Sundays, but in our hearts we are weak. Some men are driven, focused, and single-minded, but it is not the same as strong. Strength is going to a job day after day you hate to provide for your family. Strength is standing up to a greater force than yourself because it's the right thing to do. Strength is watching your child fall and not running to her aid over every little hurt. All these strengths and more I have not mentioned are given to a man when he is loved. If a man's strength can be measured by

41

how much he is loved, then I believe I am the strongest man in the world.

After another moment of being together there at our dining room table, we stood and went into the kitchen. Mo had finished clearing the table and ran off to her room for some reason or another. As I started into the dishes, Charlene was putting the leftovers away. Charlene became quiet, and I began to feel a vibe happening, "What? Aren't you going to help?" I asked over my shoulder.

"Nope, I'm enjoying the show."

"Enjoying what show, pray tell?"

"Watching your cute little butt wiggle." A silly little laugh came to my ears as her hands reached around my waist. I could feel her pressing up against my back. She leaned into me hard as she rested her head between my shoulder blades.

"Why, Miss Charlene, I do believe you are getting frisky," I voiced with a southern accent and a slight hint of naughty in my voice. An idea hit me. Smack. It didn't hit me as much as came to attention.

"Getting frisky? I've been frisky all day," she answered with an animalistic undertone.

"Do you think we can get away with a nap while Mo watches some TV?" Nap you see is the parents' universal code word for mattress Olympics, flying on the starship intercourse, or hot monkey love. Take your pick. No matter what you call it, it's all pure old plain wholesome fun.

"You know I don't like her watching TV when we're not in the room," Char asserted half-heartedly.

"Two minutes isn't going to hurt her," I teased.

"No wham and bam for this girl, Mister!"

As far as I am concerned, the dishes are done. "I'll put the Wiggles on. She'll be singing and dancing her heart out while we trip our own light fantastic." This is going to be what the doctor ordered to turn this day around. "Mo, I'm putting the Wiggles on," I yelled to the other room.

"Hooray!" came from the direction of Moiraine's room as well as the sound of her little feet scampering towards the living room.

I rejoiced in the warmth of my wife's embrace a moment longer and then went to put the DVD on.

The Wiggles are four men wearing hand-me-down Star Trek costumes dancing and singing to children's music. They don't sing well, the production value of their shows and movies are amateurish, and Moiraine loves them. She will dance and sing in front of the television for hours if we would let her. I have learned some kids love to hear the same bedtime story over and over. Not my daughter, no. Her favorite thing to repeat, ad nauseam, is the Wiggles. Sometimes I think if I hear about the "Five Little Ducks" again, I will explode.

Okay, Mo is distracted, for the time being, my wife is already waiting for me in our bedroom, the only thing left to do is to play some mood music on my trusty internal iPod. *"Maestro if you are ready, a little Barry if you will?"*

"The Duff Man is always ready. Oh yeah! K R A P is on the air with a request coming through on the Love Line."

The music started to play in my mind. *"Looks like we made it..."*

"Not Barry Manilow, you idiot, play Barry White." I thought to myself.

"Duff Man is sorry. All you asked for was Barry." Everyone has to be a comedian, even my own mental minion.

Now let us proceed to the exciting part of this evening's entertainment. I entered our bedroom, ready to start. I was ready to get started ten minutes ago. Hell, I might have finished nine minutes ago without Charlene. I closed the door behind me and locked it. No child interruptus tonight. Charlene is already undressed and only half under the sheet. The sheet was draped to cover all the strategic locations, although an ample portion of her cleavage is exposed along with most of one leg. She has a "we are going to be naughty" smile on her face. I sat down on the bed next to her and leaned in to kiss her.

There are many kinds of kisses. There is the kind of kiss you give your daughter to say goodnight. There is the awkward kiss you launch on a girl at her door at the end of your first date. There is even the kind of kiss you give your Aunt Margret because your mother makes you. This kiss started light and gentle with the warmth love bestows only after years when a couple has grown comfortable with each other. This kiss; however, did not stay light and gentle. A thirst built up in both of us. The hunger gnawed at us. We had to partake of each other, to join, to express the animal sides of our nature. Charlene started to pull at my clothes. As each moment passed, her hands became more frantic. As she tried to remove my shirt, she popped one of its buttons. I heard the button hit the floor. In a breathless whisper, Char said, "I'll sew it back on tomorrow." We scrambled to remove the rest of my clothes. If this were a classic old movie, the camera would pan to an object in the room. So, mister cameraman, please pan away. There is going to be a slight intermission.

Or two.

It was epic. On the, "did the Earth move for you?" scale, I would give it a solid nine-point-eight. If we ever reach a ten, I will be a dead man. I will be a dead man with a smile on his face, and my wife will be a widow with a story to tell the girls at Mahjong.

We laid there in each other's arms basking in the afterglow. I could lie here all night, but it is getting close to the time I must leave for work. I stood to take a quick shower. Char put on a robe and went to see what Mo is up to. I dressed in my ever so stylish uniform, combed my hair, and otherwise made ready for my night of work. I went out into the living room to see my daughter arguing

44

with her mother about getting ready for bed. I am running late. "Goodnight everyone, I will see you in the morning."

"Daddy, don't go. I don't want you to go," Moiraine pleaded as she came running to the front door.

"I have to go, Honey. It's what this daddy does. I have to go to work."

Char came in behind Mo. "I'm with you Moiraine. I don't want him to go either, but daddy does have to go to work, so give your daddy a kiss goodbye." After my kiss from Mo, Char laid one on me. It was a bit passionate for in front of the carpet shark. She hugged me hard and whispered in my ear. "I didn't pack your lunch. You will have to come home for it. I'll be waiting up in bed for you," she gave my ear a nibble.

"We took a nap before work. Now you say to come home for lunch too. You haven't been this frisky since you were carrying Mo. You know all things considered; today hasn't been too bad after all."

"Today hasn't been bad, but I will be at lunchtime," Char said as she sneaked her hand down and gave my tush a friendly squeeze. I jumped a bit in surprise. Yes, today is a good day after all. Well, hi ho hi ho, it's off to work I go. I left without any further fuss.

Work, as always, is a mind-numbing routine. I sold some sundries, turned all the products in my sections to face front, and I watched over the new-hire, Mark. He's an okay kid. Sorry, I did not mean to imply he is a baby goat. Lunch, on the other hand, lingered in my thoughts the rest of the night. And yes, she was very bad. Bad in the enjoyable way only she knows how to be.

Chapter Three

My shift is over at the store, so I headed home. It is time to get Moiraine up and ready for school. After a relatively uneventful commute, I arrived home and opened the door to my abode as quietly as I could. The house is still, except for the thumping of Blossom's tail against her bed. I crept over to her and bent down to give her a good morning pet. Whispering to the old girl, "How was your night?" I walked over to the back door and opened it up for Blossom. She slowly made her way out the door to do her business. With all the stealth as I could muster, I went into my bedroom. I stole a moment to look at my wife as she slept in our bed. In the movies and on television, women are always draped in a seductive pose in the morning. Not my wife. She is curled up in a half fetal position with the covers tightly wrapped around her body. It reminds me of a pot-sticker. Yum, Chinese food sounded yummy. My stomach growled at the thought. I want to give Charlene a little extra sleep this morning, so I turned off the alarm clock. She deserves the extra rest for her actions above and beyond the call of lust last night. I smiled to myself and left our room. I gently closed the door behind me then made my way to Moiraine's sleeping chamber.

I opened the door to my daughter's room to behold the nightmare. While Charlene loves an orderly house, our darling daughter takes after me, but she brings messy up to the level of an art form. If there is a clear spot on her floor, I could not see it. I worked my way through a minefield of Barbies in various stages of undress, half-finished colorings, and clothes carelessly discarded here and there. You see when the mood strikes her, my daughter will wear numerous outfits in a single day, and I could see she had been moody as of late. I leaned down and started the morning ritual of waking my daughter. I started tapping her forehead in beat with a song my mother would sing to me. "Wake up, wake up, you sleepy head. Get up, get up, get out of bed…" I sang until those beautiful eyes opened.

"Good morning, Daddy. What's for breakfast?" Moiraine narrowed her eyes as she looked up at me. "You can stop. I'm awake," Mo announced in a slightly irritated tone as she stretched. She never liked the way I wake her up in the mornings, but after all, traditions are traditions.

"Your request is played once again on K R A P. Oh yeah," the little DJ voice in my head proclaimed.

"Who every day must scramble for a living, feed his wife and children, say his daily prayers…"

"Please, no show tunes this early in the morning." With the thought, the music from *Fiddler on the Roof* faded away.

"Tell you what, Mo. You can help me fix breakfast if you don't wake your mom and get ready with no hassle." My daughter jumped out of bed and headed to the bathroom. The speed of her actions rivaled her speed on Christmas morning. I tell you true. I think she left a contrail. Mo loves to help in the kitchen. For a five-year-old, she's a pretty decent cook. Sure, she's not allowed to operate the stove by herself, but she makes some mean scrambled eggs, and her toast is to die for.

After making my way out of ground zero, I started pulling the eggs, cheese, and whatnot out of the fridge for breakfast. The doorbell rang. Who the Hell can it be so early in the morning? I hope they didn't rouse my wife. I opened the front door and looked out to an empty porch. A distinctive meow reached my ears from down by my feet. "Diego, how did you manage to ring the bell, and why are you calling so early?" He looked me straight in the eyes, blinked, and then ran past me into the house.

Diego belongs to my neighbor and landlady, Mrs. Blake. He is, in fact, one of many cats which belonged to Mrs. Blake. She has a whole clowder of them in her half of the duplex. Diego likes to come and visit my daughter every day or so. He tolerates my wife and me, but he enjoys my daughter. He had never come a calling so early before. Oh well, try to figure out a cat, and he'll do the other for spite. I don't mind Diego visiting Mo, even this early. I have one rule about him in this house. Don't feed him. If you do, he'll never go home, and besides, we already have a pet, Blossom, and she is a good dog.

I heard a giggle, and the word "Kitty" come from the direction of Mo's bathroom. Diego must have found his target. Well, Mo will most likely be a little late getting to work on breakfast.

So, I started things in the kitchen. If I am lucky, I will be able to surprise Char with breakfast in bed. The noise of stirrings came to my ears. Maybe next time I can surprise her. "Top of the morning, my love." Charlene shuffled through the living room toward the dining room table. Her hair is a bit messed, and there is a crease mark on her face. She looks like she had slept hard. Her movements and appearance remind me of a zombie from a George Romero film. *"Brains must eat brains!"*

"Coffee. Did you make coffee?" Char mumbled barely audible.

"No. Sorry hadn't started it yet."

"What value has a man who doesn't start the coffee when he gets home?" Char mumbled barely audible. Yep, she's my wife, and she doesn't do mornings well.

"You thought I showed you my worth last night." My statement brought a slow-growing smile to her face.

"You did earn your salt last night, but I would be happier with coffee in my hand," Char sat there, making no effort to enter the kitchen and help me. Moiraine entered the picture carrying Diego. The cat appeared to be enjoying the ride. I could hear his purring all the way over here. Mo put Diego down then kissed her mother good morning. Moiraine turned to me and proceeded to pout.

"Daddy, you promised I could help," Mo stood there looking at me with her arms crossed. It is all I could do not to laugh. She had taken a pose which mimics her mother to a tee. I'm so in trouble.

"Well, get in here," I told her. We made and ate breakfast in short order. My wife had finally risen from the grave since she has had her morning caffeine fix. She managed to motivate Mo to finish getting ready for school. All that remained on the morning to-do list is for me to make ready for my second job.

I changed out of my uniform and put on jeans and a tee-shirt. The shirt I picked out is one my daughter had given me last Christmas. It was a Disney mass-marketed Grumpy shirt. It read "Grumpy Zone." I looked at myself in the mirror. My little less than handsome face looked tired. My eyes are red, and I noticed wrinkles had started to make their presence known at the corners of my eyes. My five o'clock shadow gave my face a dirty look, and I need to run a comb through my hair. Screw it; I put a baseball cap on my head. It is time for me to don the mantle of my office. I put on the sleeveless vest and rested it on my shoulders. I tied the straps in front. I could feel the power of my vestment surround me.

I reached out my hand and took up my shield. And a powerful shield it is. Designed by the powers that be, to halt the movement of speeding missiles and offer protection to those who are placed in my charge. I put my shield in its holster across my back. Its handle protrudes up at an angle between my shoulder and neck for easy reach. I picked up my magic silver amulet and placed it around my neck. I could feel the weight of it against my chest. It felt reassuring. A shock wave would travel through the air like ripples on a pond every time I invoked its power. People would heed its call and obey my commands every time it sounded. Fully dressed, I looked again into the mirror. No longer did a mere man stare back. A guardian of the innocent stood in the mirror. I am prepared for what this morning might bring. My wife called out from the other room. "Are you ready? Moiraine's going to be late if you don't hurry."

"I'll be right there," I called back. I put my keys and cell phone in my pocket. I walked out to the front door where my wife and daughter are waiting. I took my daughter by the hand, and as we walked out the door, I attested, "I am ready to take my place and stand between the forces of darkness and those I have pledged to protect."

"Nathan, you're a crossing-guard, not a sentinel of the watch," Charlene lovingly mocked.

While I play at being the fool sometimes, I took an oath to watch over the children as they crossed the street to school. I take oaths seriously. I pride myself on being a man of his word. My word is my bond; you know old-fashioned. In the world of today where double-speak and "If you didn't get it in writing," are the norm, I do tend to be an anachronism.

I had made peace with myself over what being a crossing guard meant; at least what it meant to me. I would, without hesitation, throw myself into the path of an inattentive driver if it would save a child.

Well, maybe not if it is George. The little snot-nosed fifth-grader kicked me when I pulled him back onto the curb a couple of weeks ago. And his parents aren't any better. They called the principal the same day complaining I "touched" their son. The investigation lasted long enough to view the video footage from the red light camera. What most people don't know is the red light cameras in San Diego are video cameras. They are constantly recording the intersections where they are installed. The police view each violation and send you a still from the footage along with a hefty bill, thank you very much. The video clearly showed me grabbing little Georgie boy by the collar and yanking him back onto the curb barely before a car whipped around the corner to beat the cross traffic. It also caught my favorite fifth grader kicking me in the shin. The officer present at the viewing asked if I had wanted to press assault charges against the boy. Tempting, but I am already involved in one too many court cases. Even after watching how I had saved their son from crippling injuries or a trip to the undertaker, they didn't thank me.

There was a time, in years gone by, a man would admit it when he was wrong and shake your hand to mend fences. Not George's dad, no. Well, I didn't take the job of a crossing guard for the thanks. I took the job because it needed to be done and done right.

"Love ya," I said as I kissed my wife goodbye.

"Love you too, my little Walter Mitty," Charlene replied.

Hand in hand, my daughter and I walked to her school about half a mile away. It is about seven twenty-five AM. The morning had a bit of a chill about it. My lungs hurt a little as I took in the cold air. Listen to me, complain. I live in San Diego where the average year you could count the number of bad weather days on your hands and have fingers left over. I have turned into a wimp in my old age. I could have grown up somewhere else where they have real weather and not this perpetual sunshine.

We arrived at the corner. I pushed the idiot button on the traffic signal. It is the button every idiot pushes when he gets there. We stood there, waiting for the signal to change. I started our routine. "Are you going to have a productive day? Make sure you listen to your teacher. Eat all your lunch. Play nice." Moiraine answered in the affirmative. As we talked and waited for the light to change, other children and a few of their parents began to wait at the corner too.

The light changed. I pulled my sign from its holster and blew the whistle. It is time for my daughter and the other children to make their way to the opposite corner. After seeing traffic has indeed stopped, I stepped into the crosswalk and signaled those waiting to begin their trek. My daughter stayed at the corner. "Come on, Mo. You have to cross the street to go to school." She stood at the corner, shifting her weight back and forth from one foot to the other. She shook her head as I urged her to cross. The signal is about to change, and everyone else had finished crossing, so I went back to the corner where my daughter is standing to wait for the next batch of kids. "Honey, what's wrong?"

"Daddy, I can't go to school today," she confessed on the verge of tears.

"Are you sick?" She shook her head. "Well, what is it?" The waterworks started. I feel so helpless when she cries. We went back and forth while I crossed more students. After about fifteen minutes, we heard the final bell ringing calling the kids into class. "Come on, Mo. You have got to tell me what's wrong."

"I didn't do my homework. Are you mad at me?"

"Oh, is that what's wrong, Honey?" It's such a trivial problem in the scope of life's obstacles. But it isn't to her. To her, this represented a major stumble. "Don't worry. I will talk to your teacher. I am sure you can turn it in a little late. Tell you what: when you get home this afternoon, I will help you with it. Okay?" She shook her head yes, wiped away her tears, and steadied herself. I pressed the button for the street light and grabbed her hand while we waited. Her problem is solved for the moment. The light changed, and I helped her to cross over to the other side. We raced to arrive at her classroom in time.

I had a brief conversation with Mo's teacher. The homework it seems is a meaningless exercise to teach the children about what is expected in school. Mo's teacher fully expects more than half the students to miss the deadline. It is a lot to ask kindergarteners. Finger painting and recess is what the kids should be doing at her age, not have responsibilities. There is time enough later in their lives. Now is for the joy of being alive. I returned home. The walk back gives me a few minutes to reflect on the events of the day. This day had been a Hell of one. Not only was I run through the wringer by Refrain and Associates, not only did I have to still go to work, but now Moiraine has a crisis I need to deal with when she gets home. Sometimes you can't catch a break.

I heard my bed and pillow calling to me, "Nathan, come and curl up with us. Be embraced by our cozy goodness."

"Yes, I will be there soon," I called back to my bedroom furniture. I walked through the front door to see my wife had already cleaned up the kitchen. My wife, the White Tornado. Mr. Clean has nothing on her. I have been up for over thirty-six hours, and I am beginning to drag. I shuffled to the bedroom. Low and behold Charlene had also made the bed. Tell me why she would do that knowing full well I am going to crawl into it as soon as I returned home? It is the sign of a sick mind. She has twisted priorities I tell you.

I could hear the shower going. Char is getting ready for her day at our daughter's school. My wife is the art docent there. Docent is a fancy French word meaning "She who does not get paid," but she loves working with the kids. It's all well and right, but you know, how about a little something for the effort?

I peeled out of my clothes and put on my jammies. I slid in between the sheets and into the arms of Morpheus. Ah, "to sleep, perchance to dream." Let me tell you: sleeping in the middle of a perfectly fine day is no picnic. I have lived like a vampire for far too long, working at night and sleeping during the day, but a man does what he must do to provide for his family.

I wish I could provide a little more. Oh, we get by. I make enough to pay the bills, but living in Southern California isn't cheap. There hardly isn't any left over for extras in life. The only vacations we can afford are day trips in the area or maybe a movie a couple of times a year.

We eat out only on birthdays or other special days. A man should be able to provide more than "needs." He should be able to give his family some "wants" too.

Okay, Nathan, still your mind. You'll never fall asleep at this rate. Wait. I am asleep. This is weird. I am dreaming I am still awake trying to get to sleep. I feel a strange floaty sensation and fuzzy on the sides. I love these lucid dreams. I can indulge my imagination. What shall I be this time? Shall I be a wizard and call upon powers both subtle and gross to smite my enemies? Usually, when I would call up an image in my dreams, it would appear. Not this time. I stayed there all floaty in my bed. I looked around. Yep, this is my bedroom.

I've had lucid dreams on and off as long as I can remember. I have always wondered if it is a side effect of my perfect memory? Well, my almost perfect memory. My inability to remember tastes only started to bother me when my mother became ill and no longer could cook. I would give a great deal to taste my mother's biscuits and gravy. It is comfort food at its best. Charlene does a fine job in her efforts, but for some reason, it is not the same.

I heard my wife finishing up her shower. The sounds are muted and warped like listening underwater. She stepped out of the bathroom naked except for a towel wrapped around her head. Okay, it's one of those dreams. I'm okay with that. I don't need to be a wizard tonight or today rather. You know what I mean. I sat up in bed and tried to pull the covers open for her to join me. The covers didn't move, and my wife didn't even look in my direction. She started pulling various unmentionables out of the dresser and started to put them on. Hey; what kind of dream is this? All show and no action makes Nathan a frustrated hubby.

"Char?" I waited for a moment. Nothing. "Char," a little louder. Again nothing. "CHAR!" I screamed as loud as I could. She turned and looked at me. She dismissed whatever thought was in her head and went back to finish getting dressed. This dream sucks. I want to go somewhere else. I feel like I am moving but not moving. It is like the feeling when you're in a carwash, and you see the brushes go by in your peripheral vision. It tricks your mind into believing you are moving. It feels like that, but it lasts more than an instant.

I am at work, the site of a thousand boring memories. I don't want to dream of work. If I can't play in the realms of fantasy and I can't play with my wife, let me dream of my daughter.

Again with the carwash thingy. My daughter's classroom is before my eyes. The kids are all sitting on a rug in front of the teacher. They are listening to her read a story out of a book. Every time the teacher paused, she would show them the illustration on the page from the story. She sounded as watery and muted as my wife. This is strange. In my dreams, I usually know what figments are saying. I don't see them say it, but I understand. I can see the teacher speaking. I see the kids fidgeting on the rug. I see the walls decorated in numbers, colors, and shapes all in perfect detail. I hadn't noticed at first, but my bedroom was in perfect detail too. Work also was exact in detail. This is not right; I don't understand this.

I want to wake up. Wake up you middle-aged fart. I am being pulled out of my daughter's classroom. When I switched location before, the movement was forward. This time I am falling backward. I am looking up at a scene which is quickly getting smaller as if I am falling straight down a circular shaft. *"Lassie girl, go tell Timmy I am trapped in the well!"*

I jerked awake in my bed. My heart is racing, and sweat is covering my face. It was the weirdest dream I ever had. Believe it; I remember them all. I sat up and looked around. The room is dark and quiet. Charlene had pulled the blackout drapes before she left for my daughter's school. The clock showed I have been asleep for a couple of hours, but it feels like only moments. I sat there on the edge of the bed for a few minutes, trying to calm down. After my heart slowed to a normal rate, I stood and went into the kitchen for a drink of something. I grabbed the milk out of the fridge and drank a couple of swallows straight out of the carton. Char would have a fit if she saw it. I should wipe-off my fingerprints to be sure I'm not found out.

I put the milk back and closed the fridge door. There is a new piece of art on the door. It is a crude painting of our family outside in the sun. We can't let the school psychologist see this. She would think something is wrong. A happy child with parents still married, and all of us enjoying each other's company, it doesn't happen anymore.

I'm too cynical.

I kissed my fingertips then touched my daughter's Picasso like rendition of herself. "Love you, Mo." Moiraine has the same love of art as her mother. I've seen Mo sit and work on her art for hours on end. Such dedication in a five-year-old is rare.

The few hours of restless sleep I had is nowhere near enough. I need more solid sleep. I went back to my bed in hopes a repeat of today's earlier performance would elude me. I slid back into bed and drifted back into a blissful sleep. The alarm rang. It is time to rise and shine as it were. I jumped into the shower and took a long and a near scalding one. It is the only luxury in my life; that and Diet Pepsi. I love my Diet Pepsi. It's "My Precious."

While the water delightfully washed away the dirt and sweat, I shaved my face to a smooth, baby butt finish. Well, at least as best I could with a cheap disposable razor. I finished up as the hot water started to run out. I completed the rest of my daily routine. I went into the kitchen to grab a quick snack. I pulled out a slice of bologna and wrapped it around a sweet pickle, poured myself a tall glass of milk, and indulged. It is time to get ready for the afternoon shift as a crossing guard.

I redressed in my slick crossing guard outfit and headed for my corner. Near the end of my shift at the intersection, my wife and daughter came into view.

"Daddy," my daughter yelled as they approached.

"How was school?" I asked with a grin on my face.

In unison, we both said, "Good!" It is a game we play every day. If we don't play it, Moiraine feels slighted. I hugged and kissed them both. They waited there with me while I finished up my shift. We walk back home hand in hand with Mo in between Char and me. Oh, children, nature's form of birth control.

You know, even though I can't provide some of the desires in life, I've got it sweet. To Hell with the rest of it. I have my full measure of happiness right here with me. As long as my family is safe and well, I can't complain.

This is how my days mostly go. A little boring, maybe, but fulfilling. At least that's how they were going for about the next two weeks. I opened a letter in the mail from the District Attorney's office. It stated the case against Mark Galos had been dismissed with prejudice attached. Big lawyer words telling me I screwed up, and the villain gets to go free.

I stood there reading the letter and could not believe it. No explanation. No nothing, only a form letter thanking me for my service in this matter. I started shaking; my anger is building. This punk had robbed my store, threatened Marcy (the pharmacist), stuck a gun in my face and only on a whim decided not to put two lead slugs in my skull, called me a coward, and stole my wedding ring. With this thought, I rubbed the empty place on my ring finger. The indentation is still there on my finger as fresh as when I took it off that night. I could not see anything but his face. The anger is so intense I thought for sure I am going to turn green and rip out of my clothes.

I am not sure how long I stood there rereading the letter hoping I missed something. With time my anger transformed into determination. By God, he is going to pay. No matter the effort or how long I had to work on it, he is going to pay. I grabbed the phone and dialed the DA's office.

After six rings, the operator answered, "San Diego County District's Attorney's office, please hold." Before I could even take a breath to speak, she put me on hold. Music is playing over the phone. It is a scratchy and distorted recording of "Dust in the Wind" by Kansas. I don't know how long I have been on hold, but it felt like an eternity. I started doodling on the pad of paper we kept by the phone. It is a strange drawing; it looks like several Japanese characters of some type and a symbol above them. The symbol looks like a five-petal flower with thorns in-between the pedals. The whole symbol is encircled by a thin band. I don't remember seeing this symbol before, and I don't read Japanese. This is a new experience for me. It is oddly familiar, but I know I had never seen it before. I would remember. Too strange. As I was most puzzled about my sketch, the operator came back on the line.

"Can I help you?"

"Please connect me to Assistant DA Darryl Wayne."

"I'm sorry, sir, but Mr. Wayne has already left the office for the day. I will connect you to his voice mail."

"No. Please ..." Click. Damn, she was quick.

"You have reached the desk of ..." I hung up before the blasted recording could finish.

I looked at the clock. I had been on hold for over an hour. I needed to relax a bit. I took a breath, closed my eyes, and requested an Enya tune from my internal iPod.

"This is K R A P on the request line Enya's "Only Time*" from the album A Day Without Rain."*

I let the music wash over me like a gentle waterfall from a mountain stream. I let it wash away my anger. I let it wash away my frustration. I let it wash away my weariness. I did not let it wash away the purity of my purpose. It is a rock in my soul. The waters of calm flowed around it without eroding it.

It is Friday, so Mr. Wayne would have to wait till Monday. But bright and early, I would be up to confront our illustrious Assistant DA. The rest of the day went on without a hitch. Time to go to work. I dressed and ready for work.

"Is there something wrong?" Charlene asked as I started to head out the door. "You were a little distant and remote this evening."

I didn't want to share the contents of the letter until I had confronted Mr. Wayne. It is too fresh. I didn't want my anger to build up again, and she deserved better than to see my rage. In truth, it scared me how angry I got. "I'll tell you later when I have rolled it around in my mind a while."

"Well, don't let it get lost in there," she taunted with a hint of a smile on her face all the while tapping my forehead with her finger.

"Mo, Honey, give me a kiss goodbye." Moiraine came running and planted one on me, and a hug to boot. "Bye, all. See you in the morning." I walked to the car pausing only long enough to hear the locks on the front door turn. I got in the car and headed for work.

Chapter Four

I arrived at work with no fuss and no muss. I locked my car and started toward the doors. They slid open with a swish like doors from Star Trek; only these did not have stagehands operating them off-camera. I started walking back to the break room to put my lunch in the refrigerator and clock-in. As I walked through the store taking note of some of the things which needed to get done tonight, I noticed Larry in aisle six. He is busy rotating stock and putting fresh Coke, *"Yuck,"* on the shelves. "Hey Larry, what are you doing here? You're scheduled to work days."

"I don't know. Believe me; I'm not too thrilled to be here either. But Mike called me into work. So, here I am," Larry announced to me without glancing my way. "Oh, Mike's in his office. He told me to send you up there as soon as you clocked in."

"Head up to the big cheese's," I made my way to the office as I had a zillion times before. I knocked on the door. I heard Mike's voice tell me to come in. I entered to find Mike standing by the security window looking out at the floor. Sitting behind Mike's desk is another man, Mr. Waters. I had met him only once before when I was promoted to night manager here at work. He is a balding man with only a fringe of brown hair on the sides of his head clipped close. He wore black-horn rimmed glasses. Dressed in a standard two-piece gray suit and black tie, he conveyed a sense of self-importance in his manner and speech. He only glanced at me as I entered the room. Mike's desk is void of the usual clutter, except for a small file which lay open.

"Have a seat, Mr. Embers," Mr. Waters offered.

"You can call me Nate," I answered as I took a seat.

"We have a few things to go over before you clean out your locker, Mr. Embers."

"Excuse me, clean out my locker? Mike, what's this all about?"

As Mike said, "Corporate sent down the word you are to be laid off," he hung his head down. He didn't say it, but I could hear in Mike's voice he did not agree with the decision.

"As I said, Mr. Embers, we have a few things to go over. First, we must review your employment record. I see you have been working here for about seven years and were promoted a little over three years ago. Is this correct?"

I felt like I had been gut kicked. The interview continued like this for the next ten minutes with Mr. Waters asking questions and me answering. I am in a daze. What the hell could be the reason for this? The store's numbers are sound. It had been a twenty-four-hour store since it was built about 15 years ago. I don't think they are reducing store hours. I am stumped.

"Very well, that answers all my questions, Mr. Embers. If you could read and sign this," Mr. Waters handed me a sheet of paper.

I took the single sheet of paper and read it. Without getting into each of whereas and whereto, they are firing me and not telling me why. "I don't understand. It doesn't tell me why. I want to know why."

"We are not required by California employment regulations to have a reason to give you a pink slip, Mr. Embers. Please sign the paper acknowledging your firing, and we'll be done here," Mr. Waters recited it with no passion in his voice. I could see it is only a task to him. Pick-up the dry cleaning, fill the car with gas and fire Nathan Embers. He could check that off his to-do list. Normally I would have a snappy comeback to all this, but I am too stunned to think of one. I signed the paper and handed it back. Mr. Waters placed it in the folder with the rest of my employment record. Is this all my service to this company is? A file. Sheets of paper to be filed away and forgotten, then one day shredded. I spent the better part of over seven years here at the drug store. What am I going to say to Charlene? How am I going to provide for my family? I had never been fired before. I have been out of work sure but never fired. I don't deal well with unemployment. I become antsy. This job is supposed to be my ticket to retirement and security for my family. It isn't glamorous, but it is solid. All the time and effort is now dust.

Mr. Waters handed me another piece of paper. It is my final paycheck. "Mr. Kirkland, please escort Mr. Embers to his locker. Watch him clean it out. Make sure he doesn't take any store property with him. Then, escort him out of the building. Mr. Embers, be sure you wash your uniform and get it back to us in short order," he didn't even have the manners to look at us while he gave his instructions. He closed my file and opened another one.

Mike turned towards the door and grabbed a box. "Come on, Nate. Let's get this over with."

We walked in silence to the break room. I opened my locker and started putting my stuff in the box. The locker is mostly empty. Nothing to show for seven years of dedication. Let's see a clean shirt, some old notices about policy changes, half of an old lunch I had never finished, and assorted other crap. "Mike, what is all this about?"

"I'm not supposed to tell you, so this is strictly off the record. They think you and Marcy were working with the guy who stole all those drugs about two years ago."

"Oh, crap! You must be kidding me. Marcy, too? This is backassward. I followed all the policies to the letter. I kept my head and got that jerk out of here before he could hurt anyone. This is plain unfair."

"I told them all that. I told the suits you are a standup guy. I went to bat for you both. Corporate wouldn't hear any of it. I'm sorry, Nate. I tried."

"I know you did, Mike. I can hear it in your voice. Well, losing my job today is better than getting a couple of slugs in the head back then. No worries, Mike. I've been out of work before. I'll find something. Who's taking over the night shift? No, let me guess, Larry."

"Yep."

"Good luck with your pick. Don't get me wrong. Larry does his job, but he won't sweep the floor unless you tell him. He has never done a task because it needs to be done. No initiative him. Have you told Marcy yet?"

"Mr. Waters will break it to her later tonight. God, I hate letting people go. It's the hardest part of this damn job," Mike lamented all this while looking at his shoes and rubbing the back of his neck.

"Don't let them break you, Mike. It isn't worth it." I finished loading up the "vast" array of junk from my locker. I closed the door on both the locker and this part of my life. I threw out the old half-eaten lunch. It made a thunk as it hit bottom. With this development, I hope I don't hit bottom. I turned to Mike, "You don't have to walk me out. I know the way."

"It's no trouble, Nate, and I'm sure he's watching. I don't want to give him any ammunition." We finished walking to the front door quietly. All I can hear is the rush of air from the A/C unit and the hum of the fluorescent lights. The doors opened with a swish. I walked out. The night air is colder than it had been less than an hour ago. I looked up at the sky. Clouds are rolling in to block out the moon and stars. A storm is brewing; I could feel it in my bones.

Mike followed me to my car. He held out his hand, and I shook it. "Nate, I don't think they're going to make it easy on you. I heard Mr. Waters on the phone with some suit at corporate. They were talking about getting the word out about you. I think they plan on telling the other drug stores around what they suspect. It's a bum deal, and none of us here believe it. We passed the hat around. It isn't a fortune, but we all wanted to do something." Mike handed me an envelope. I tried not to take it. "Don't be proud. We all wanted to do this for you."

"Mike I can't take this. I've never taken any charity in my life. I'm not going to now." I tried to put the envelope back in his hand.

"Damn it, Nate. If you don't let us help, consider it a gift to your little girl's college fund," Mike took the envelope and stuffed it into my shirt's pocket. I didn't know what to say. Mike and I had never been exactly friends, but he had always been fair to me. Put me up for the assistant manager job too. He is a decent man. I respect him even if he is a bit nuts about his desk. He wished me luck, turned, and walked back to the store. There is no spring in his step. He shuffled slow and not quite in a straight line. He walked like a man convicted to spend his last precious moments in a chair which plugs into the wall. This had been hard on him, and it isn't getting any easier either. When Mr. Waters breaks the news to Marcy, Mike will have to pick up the pieces.

I yelled at Mike's back as he walked back, "Don't let them break you, Mike." He stopped for a moment and turned back toward me. We locked gazes for a moment, and Mike did a little nod of affirmation. Mike headed back to the store with a stride which no longer belonged to a broken man.

I sat in my car for a few minutes. My mind is blank. A plan is what I need. Nothing came to mind, notta, bupkiss, snake eyes. I would even settle for a "Hail-Mary" plan. What am I going to tell Char? What does a man say to his family when he loses his job?

He lies. That sounds right.

I have enough in the emergency fund to cover the bills for a couple of months, and with unemployment, I could stretch it a few more. In time, I am sure I could find another job. Yes, I'll be like a cat and land on my feet. Oh, yes, delude yourself. It will be a sound start to a new beginning.

I could hire a lawyer and make a fight of it. I have never backed away from a just fight. They had no right to fire me. They had no proof I am involved with Mark Galos. What made them think I am in cahoots with a madman? Yes, I'll hire a lawyer. Months of depositions, negotiations, offers, and counteroffers. We will come to an agreement, and when it comes time to sign on the dotted line, they will back out. We will come to another accord, and my lawyer will say we can negotiate a better deal and then we back out. Months will turn into years. It will go on and on with no resolution. If we do come to a deal, Mr. Law Degree will take forty percent, and I will get my job back. I will be working for a company looking for any excuse to fire me once again. What a joy it will be. Hire a lawyer. What am I thinking? I'm not thinking at least not with my brains.

I can't lie to Charlene. I have never lied to her before. I took a vow to love, honor, and cherish her and a lie like this would dishonor her and our marriage.

Still, I hate to be the bearer of bad news. I'll have to put some spin on it. I'll tell her I will find a day job with weekends off. That sounds believable. Maybe I will find a job in the daytime with weekends off. Yea right and maybe monkeys will fly out of my butt.

I've been delaying the inevitable long enough. I need some music to drive home by something snappy and happy. I know. I commanded my mental iPod to play *"Walking on Sunshine."* It started right up without a word from my DJ. That is strange. I listened for a moment in the dark there in my car. I keep stalling. Fear is keeping me from doing what I need to do. The fear of disappointing my wife. It's time to head home and break the bad news to Char. I put the key in the ignition and turned it. Nothing. My car didn't make a noise. Crap!

I walked around to the front. I opened the hood and looked in. Well, the engine is still there, so that's not the problem. I glanced at the tires. They had air. That's not the problem. Working on cars had never been my forte. I have always hated getting my hands dirty. I'm a lover, not a fixer. Oh, I know where the gas goes and how to start it, but that is the extent of my automotive knowledge. I may have perfect recall, but I had never read a book on car repairs. Even if I had read one, knowledge alone can't replace practical experience. This night could not get any worse.

I felt the wetness of raindrops starting to hit me. They are slow at first, but as I looked up to the heavens to ask why, it started to pour. Double crap. I slammed the hood back down and dashed back into the car before I got too wet. Evidently not fast enough because by the time I made it back into the car, I was soaked. My wiseass DJ started playing *"Raindrops Keep Falling on My Head," "Quit mocking me,"* I thought to myself.

"But I do it so well. Oh yeah!" came back from the DJ.

I was about to think it couldn't be any worse, but I stopped myself before the car's roof could be ripped away by a tornado. On the other hand, Char has always wanted a convertible. I pulled out my cell phone and called for a tow.

Click. Click. Click. The sound of keys tapping on the glass of the driver side window started before I flipped my phone closed and made me jump out of my skin. "You called for a tow, sir?" the feminine voice asked.

"Jiminy cripes, give a guy a little warning before you startle him."

"Sorry, are you the gentleman who called for a tow?" the tow driver asked through the glass. She stood there looking at me.

I opened the door and jumped out quickly, trying to avoid getting the inside of my car too wet. "Yes, I called for the tow," I stood there facing her as I spoke. She is wearing yellow slickers with reflective strips on her back, front, arms, and legs. I couldn't manage a decent look at her face in the rain. She has the hood up, and it cast shadows over her face.

"What seems to be the problem?" her voice is pleasant sweet even.

"It won't start. Other than that, your guess is better than mine."

"Well, let's take a look-see," she kind of giggled her response. She walked around to the front of the car and popped the hood. From my vantage point, I couldn't see what she is doing, and I didn't want to look over her shoulder. I hate it when someone hovers over me. So, I gave her the courtesy I would want. "Give it a try."

I got behind the wheel and turned the key. Vroom. It sounded better than when I drove it to work. Wait, I shouldn't use the "W" word anymore. I left the car idling while I talked with the tow-truck driver. "What did you do?"

"Oh, I only coaxed it a little bit. But she'll run fine for you now. You know machines are a lot like women. If you show them a little special attention once in a while, they will purr at your every touch," she closed the hood and brushed off her hands. For the briefest of moments, I could see her hands. They are rather striking. There is no grease or grime on them. I could see long slender fingers with an impeccable French manicure. I never understood why a woman would get a French manicure. It leaves your fingernails looking like fingernails with a large white stripe to mimic a free-edge and clear or blush polish on the rest of the nail. It seems pointless to me.

Since her face is still shrouded in shadows, I could only guess if I am looking her in the eyes. "New on the job?" I asked.

"No, it seems like I have been doing this forever."

"The reason I ask is your hands are beautiful. You must be extra careful while you work," she immediately hid her hands. Odd. Most women proudly continue to display a feature you compliment. She became uncomfortable and started to fidget a bit. "I'm sorry. Don't worry, it's not like I have a fetish or something," I pulled out my wallet. "So tell me. How much do I owe you? You really saved my bacon here."

"It wasn't any work. I can't charge you. We're square."

"I can't let do that. Your boss will be mad that you didn't charge me. Please. What do I owe you?" She saved me a great deal of time and effort. I couldn't let it go.

"I'm my own boss you could say. And I say no charge today. You can pay extra next time."

Next time? I hope my car doesn't break down again. Her face is still shrouded in shadow, and I felt rather than saw her smiling. I don't like to be beholden to anyone. I pay my debts. Always have. "There must be…"

Before I could finish my sentence, she took a few of those beautiful fingers and put them over my mouth. "A gift should be taken for what it is without anything more than a thank you."

An electric charge ran through my body. It is sinfully pleasant and made me feel awkward. It has been a very long time since a woman's touch, other than Charlene's, has done this to me. I took a half step back. It feels like I am cheating on my wife having this kind of sensation. I know I wasn't cheating, but it still made me feel ashamed. "Thank you," as I spoke the words, they came out slow and halting. "For the car, I mean." Wow, I sound like I am still in high school. I can be such a putz sometimes.

Most of the time.

She lowered her hand, "You're welcome," she said with a smile, "Isn't this better than the cold exchange of monies for services rendered?" She turned and started back toward her tow-truck. And as she walked, she spoke over her shoulder, "Nathan, if you feel like you need to pay me, you can always do a kindness for a stranger someday. It will earn you a little positive karma. We all need a little bit of positive karma," she got in her truck, started it up, and was on her way.

I stood there in the rain getting even more soaked as I watched her drive away. After a moment, I shook myself back to reality then sat in my car. I looked at the time on my cell phone. Well, if I head home now, Char is sure to be up still. I need to wrap my head around all that has happened today. I think I will drive around the city a bit and settle my thoughts. I turned on the car's radio to listen to some tunes. Normally when I am alone, I'll use my trusty memory for music. With so much on my mind, I didn't want to expend the concentration. I needed all the neurons I have to work this problem through.

Going nowhere, in particular, I eventually found myself on Shelter Island. I parked the car to look out over the bay. The rain had finally let up. I walked around to the front of the car. I leaned back and rested against the hood. The wind is blowing, and there is a little bit of a chill to the air, not to mention I'm still soaked to the bone. The warmth the engine is giving off kept my butt pleasantly toasty, so I weathered the chill okay. The lights of the city danced on the water as I stood there watching. I could hear the ripples on the bay lap up against the rocks which line the island. My mind is finally at rest, it is quiet, calm, and relaxed. I can think.

"You are so screwed," the voice in my head told me. *"Yea, tell me something I don't know!"* I dread telling Char the news. She worries. Mostly she worries about me. Since she saved my life, she has always worried about me. Having someone who worries about you makes you feel all warm inside.

I have been here looking out at the bay for fifteen, maybe twenty minutes with my mind blank. I am only being. I have never been one for the whole Zen thing, but I must admit it does have a certain appeal. I looked at the time again. It is safe to go home. Char is sure to be asleep by now, so I headed home.

I stopped at the corner "Oh thank Heaven for Seven-Eleven," bought a newspaper and Diet Pepsi. In the morning, I won't waste any time. Right after breakfast, I'll start looking in the Help Wanted ads. In a little display by the register, there are bouquets of flowers for sale. I grabbed the freshest looking one and bought it. The flowers will make a pleasant little surprise for my girls.

I opened the front door and entered as quietly as a ninja. I was greeted by the familiar thumping of Blossom's tail on her bed. I quickly set my purchases down and went over to give the old girl a pat. Next, I put the flowers in a vase with some water and placed it in the center of the dining room table. I turned the lights off and headed to the bedroom. Once there, I quietly changed into my jammies and slipped into bed. At first, I thought I would have a hard time getting to sleep with my body clock being backward, but surprisingly, I was able to drift off quickly.

Chapter Five

The whimper then low growl from Blossom woke me out of a restful sleep. I threw off the covers and sat up in bed. As I tried to rub the sleep from my eyes, I told my wife. "Char, I think Blossom's time has come. Stay here. I will go be with her."

Oh crap! Not this dream again. I hate it when I have recurring dreams. It's bad enough I can relive my bad memories. Now I relive my nightmares too. Not this time.

"Are you sure? No, I should be there too," Charlene answered. I sensed she is crying.

"There is nothing you can do for the old girl. Try to go back to sleep," I reached over and squeezed my wife's hand. I stood and slowly made my way to the living room. Blossom's growl started to grow louder. I heard the sound of someone trying to jimmy the lock on the front door. "Who can it be behind door number one? Give me a second, and I'll unlock it." I yelled back to Char, "Honey, we have company." Before I could open the door, the sound of pounding then wood splintering replaced the jimmying. "Oh, now you've done it. I will have to replace the door."

Char came out of the bedroom, wrapping a robe around her. "Nathan, what's going on?" She screamed, "Oh my God. Someone's trying to break in," she went running out of the room.

"Don't go running off Char, it's only a dream," I heard the door finally give way. Mark Galos pushed his way through the remnants of my front door. "Hi, Mark. I'll be with you in a second. Have a seat. Say would you like something to drink?" I turned around to head for the kitchen. When I had finished the turn, I felt a slamming into my back. I heard a snap and felt an odd tingle. I fell forward and crumbled to the ground. I have a lovely sideways view of my living room and down the hall towards my bedroom.

"What are you playing at Mr. Clerk Guy? You know I'm here to kill you."

I couldn't move. I guess my back is broken in this little dream of mine. I heard him take a few steps toward me. Suddenly his feet are in my view. I tried to look up at him, but I still couldn't move.

"Well, get up. I'm not done tormenting you yet."

"Sorry, can't help you. I can't move." He kicked me in the ribs, I think. I didn't feel anything. "Sorry, Mark. I don't feel like playing anymore," I put my will to work to end this nightmare. Nothing had changed. I didn't understand. Willing my dreams to change has always worked before.

"You go all mental on me there, Mr. Clerk Guy? Your cross-examination too much for you? Lose your grip on reality? Well, I'll get no enjoyment with you like this. Guess I will have to find someone else to entertain me." He stomped down the hall and turned the corner for the bedrooms.

Ok, this has been enough. I set my will to change the dream again. I tried so hard sweat started rolling down my face. I heard Char scream and my daughter cry. I heard the sounds of a scuffle. Mark Galos howled in pain. No. This is my dream. I am in control here, not the figments. I closed my eyes and pictured a better dream. How about a cabin in the woods with a roaring fire? I felt a kick. This time it was to my face.

"No closing your eyes. You have to watch. Keep them open, or I'll cut your eyelids off, so you'll have to watch," he had my wife by the hair. It looked like he dragged her into the room by it. He had roughed her up. There is a welt on her face and the beginning of a black eye. She was whimpering.

"Don't hurt my daughter. I'll do anything you ask. Please don't hurt her," Char took her hand and started stroking his leg. "Anything!"

"Anything? Can you die for me?" Mark Galos reached down with both hands and grabbed the sides of my wife's head. Then with a twist and a jerk, the sound of my wife's neck breaking came to my ears. "Wow. I haven't done that in lifetimes. I'm glad to know I still have the touch," he let Char's lifeless body drop. "Sorry, bitch. You're not my type." He spat on her. "That is for the bite."

"This is a dream. This is a dream." I screamed, "THIS IS JUST A DREAM!" My wife's eyes are staring at me. They are lifeless, but they still shouted accusations at me. This isn't a nightmare; it is a night terror. I feel guilty and ashamed. I failed my family. Even in this dream, agony filled my being.

"This is getting boring. There is no satisfaction in it anymore," Mark Galos took his foot and pushed my head so I could see his face. "Mr. Clerk Guy, my time is getting short. Know this. Your daughter will die also. She won't die tonight, but she will die soon. I will have a little pleasure with her at first. She will experience such sweet torment. I will extract payment from her for your debt to me. Fair compensation to me for wasted time. You could not let the robbery go. You wouldn't let it fall through the cracks. They sent me to a loony bin based on your statements. But who would not be a little crazy wasting so many lifetimes as a witness to witless fools? Yes, I won't waste what I have rightfully taken. Your daughter's life is mine now. I will let her live for a few days, perhaps a week. I will let her live with the horror of seeing you both like this before I make her pain end." He reached for the sledgehammer he used to break into the house. I saw him lift it high above his head.

"I don't understand this. I want to wake up. WAKE UP!"

"What? You think all this is a dream? Not hardly," he swung the hammer down onto my head. All around me is the cold blackness of oblivion.

"Nathan, wake up you're having a nightmare." Charlene was gently shaking me awake.

I woke with my side of the sheets and my pillowcase soaking wet. Night sweats, I hate night sweats. You have a cold, clammy feeling the second you realize what happened. "Huh? What time is it?" I asked.

"It's still early. Why are you home? Did you have a migraine again?" Charlene turned toward me in bed with her hand resting on my shoulder. The room is still mostly dark with a hint of sunlight making its presence known. It is neither dark nor light. The half-shadow of twilight gave the room an eerie noir look.

"I will tell you after breakfast. I'm going to take a shower," I started to stand, but Char kept her hand on my shoulder and wouldn't let me rise.

"Not so fast. It's not every morning I can cuddle with my man. I want to enjoy this." She laid her head on my shoulder. She took a deep breath in through her nose. She whispered, "You smell good. You smell safe," she started making lazy circles on my chest, letting the hair there curl around her finger. It tickled and felt pleasing at the same time.

I never realized how much I have missed sleeping next to my wife. I learned early on working graveyard shifts it is best to stay on the schedule, even on my days off. My health would start to suffer when I kept switching back to a daytime schedule on my weekends. Most nights, when I stayed up, I would read or play games on the computer; anything as long as it is quiet and didn't disturb my family's sleep. Sometimes I would watch them. Nothing creepy, mind you, I would wonder what they are dreaming.

Moiraine would always smile and laugh while she dreamed. My wife is a little harder to read in her sleep. I will miss watching them sleep.

Charlene lifted her head and gave my cheek a soft kiss. It warmed me. After a few moments, she lifted her head again, and this time, she gave my ear a little nibble. First, one nibble, and then another. Next, she reached up with her free hand and put it on the far side of my head and pulled my face toward her. She kissed me long, slow, and with subtle intensity. I'm beginning to get a clue, along with other things, as to her intentions.

We made love. We fulfilled each other in soft and gentle ways. It was a bonding. It was a restatement to each other and to the universe we are as one. We were quiet, not to keep from waking Mo, but more so we could better listen to the love we are sharing and reconfirming. It is all that is worthwhile in this world. Without saying a word to me, she let me know everything is alright. That everything would be alright. We reached the height of our love together. They say it is rare for couples; even long-time married couples like us, to achieve. We did our first time and most times since, not that I'm bragging.

Well, maybe a little.

I dozed afterward. It was a peaceful sleep. My nose woke me to the smell of bacon cooking. I rose and stuck my head out of the bedroom. "How long do I have before breakfast? Do I have time to take a quick shower?"

I heard my wife call back, "Go for it." I finished up the rest of my morning routine then quickly dressed in jeans and a t-shirt. As I finished tying up my shoes, my daughter came running into the bedroom.

"Daddy, it's time for breakfast. Come on," without stopping, she ran out saying, "I'm glad you're not sleeping today."

I made my way to the dining room with a slight detour to say good morning to Blossom. She responded with her usual tail thumping. "Has she been fed yet?" A chorus of yes came from the kitchen.

"Something smells tasty. What did my girls cook for me this morning?" I asked as I sat at my seat. Char brought in the last of the morning's grub and sat it on the table.

"Well, Daddy, if you looked, you would see there is yummy bacon, fried potatoes, and I made the scrambled eggies. Oh, and mom made bisquicks, too." I love what my daughter calls biscuits. In one fell swoop, she marries two different words. Twofers are such great time savers.

As Charlene sat down, she pronounced, "This morning daddy gets served first. Right Moiraine?" She emphasized. "Help yourself, Nathan."

I wasted no time in doling out my portions. They were large as my appetite is large this morning. Oh! The bacon was roasted, not fried. More of the fat renders out. It's slightly healthier for you and the bacon comes out delicious and flat as a board. It has a light maple flavor too. Char must have basted it with syrup before she put it in the oven. Next, some fried potatoes with minced garlic and a diced rainbow of bell peppers filled a large area of my plate. Then I portioned out a healthy helping of my daughter's scrambled eggs. A feast fit for a king or at least the king's fool, "What's up with this extra-special breakfast and treatment?"

"We like treating you extra special," Char stated in a matter of fact manner.

"And you brought us flowers, Daddy."

"Yes, you brought us flowers," Charlene accused with an eyebrow raised. Also, a tone of accusation came through loud and clear.

"I wanted to see how pale they look next to my beautiful girls," Moiraine giggled when I finished speaking.

Charlene acknowledged, "That was quick. But then you have always been quick, a little thick-headed, but quick." Char nodded her head slightly as if to agree with herself.

I decided to put my attention back to my breakfast. After a few bites of my potatoes, the remaining bits fell into an odd shape on my plate. I started rearranging them. They were taking on the form of, in an eight-bit graphic sort of way, the symbol I had lazily doodled while waiting on hold for the DA. It is beginning to annoy me because I cannot remember where or even if I have seen it before. It is a type of frustration I had never experienced before. I didn't like the feeling. My memory is my greatest asset, besides my rugged good looks and vast income potential. My life is filling with strange happenings, and this morning is no exception.

"Are you playing with your potatoes? It's not bad enough every time I serve you mashed potatoes you play with them and exclaim, 'this means something.' Now you are doing it with fried potatoes," Char started shaking her head.

"No, you don't understand. This has me bugged," I ranted as I showed her the potatoeized version of the mystery symbol. "I keep seeing this, and it seems familiar, but I can't place it."

"I know what it is, Daddy," Mo volunteered stretching to see my creation.

I turned and looked at my daughter in earnest. "What is it, Honey?"

"It's your breakfast, Daddy," she could hardly contain her laughter as she spoke the words. My wife had to choke back a laugh. I had to admit it was pretty damn funny.

"Love it, Mo," I gave my daughter a high five. "Where did you get your sense of humor, young lady?"

Char piped up with, "You have no one to blame but yourself. You taught her that sense of humor," she half-mocked. The conversation was sparse while we ate our meal. Charlene instructed Mo to clear off the table then to play in her room. Once Mo was out of earshot in her room,

Char settled back in her chair and crossed her arms under her breasts.

"Out with it. What's the bad news? Husband mine."

"Why does there have to be bad news?"

"Because you brought home flowers. I love you dearly Nathan, but you've never given me flowers unless there is a problem, or you feel guilty about something. You're not the only one with a memory. Husband Mine."

Crap, two husband mines. I'm in it deep. I quickly ran through every occasion I had brought home flowers and cross-referenced it with bad news. There had to be one time at least when the two didn't correspond. Charlene sat there looking at me waiting for me to admit she is right.

"Well? Did that brain of yours come up with an exception?"

I hung my head. "No, it didn't." Note to self: buy flowers for no reason in the future. I took in a deep breath and let it out, "I lost my job last night. The only reason I didn't tell you when I got home is," I took another deep breath, "I'm a coward. I couldn't face you last night with the news. I knew you would worry."

"Bullshit!"

The words "Mommy, you said a bad word," came from my daughter's room.

My wife muttered something it sounded like oh great, but I can't be sure. "Mommy and daddy are having a grown-up talk right now. Don't listen in," Char commanded in her don't question me about this voice. "It's not you're a coward. This is I'm a man, and I can't worry the womenfolk. Isn't it?" When I didn't immediately jump in with an answer, she continued, "Well, understand this mister Husband Mine." Oh my, she stretched it into a triple. "This marriage is more than a living arrangement. We are partners in this life. Well, mister man of his word, I am a woman of her WORD! I took a vow of for better or worse. It looks like it will be worse for a while. So be it. But don't sit there and try to save me. Don't protect me from life. I am not some damsel in distress hold-up in an ivory tower. I am your WIFE!" The volume of her statements steadily increased with each sentence. I sat there like a proper boy and took my lumps. We have had this one-sided discussion before, but never at this decibel level. I think my ears are bleeding.

I meekly agreed, "You're right."

"Oh, no you don't. You cannot agree with me just to make me quiet. I will have my say."

"What more is there to say than you are right? And I love you."

"I love you too, Husband Mine." The third baseman flubbed the catch, and she takes off for home folks. Safe. An in-park home run. Why we haven't seen one of those in many years. "But don't think this conversation is over."

I think her steam is letting up because she stood and headed for the kitchen to start the dishes no doubt. "I bought a paper last night on the way home, but it's not where I put it. Where did you put it? I want to start my job search."

"With a memory like yours, I would think you would look where I always put a paper if you buy one." She is obviously still working on getting her blood down. She mumbled something else under her breath too, but I knew better than to ask what. She is letting her anger control her. The sounds which came from the kitchen are disturbing the quiet. I'm glad we have plastic dishes.

I opened the paper and went straight to the "Help Wanted" section. I read it three times, but nothing looked promising. I kept hoping a new listing would magically appear, but alas I was disappointed. I started reading the rest of the paper. The comics came next. I'm in need of a chuckle or a chortle even.

Charlene finished up the kitchen as I read. When she was done, she stomped toward our bedroom, "I need some chocolate," she announced to the universe. When she returned, she had a light sweater on and car keys in her hand, "Do you want to come?" her voice is considerably softer but still resolute. Papa is not going to have any enjoyment today. And the weather forecast for tonight is chilly with a slight chance of couch time.

"Moiraine, we are leaving."

"Okay, see you soon," is the answer my daughter gave. Great, more humor from the mouth of babes.

"No. Bring a jacket or sweater. You are coming along my little jester," I yelled. I tried to take the keys from Char. She would have none of it. I guess I am going to be chauffeured today. It is something I generally don't like. Charlene drives like she's playing Mario Cart which is saying she drives fast and with little regard for other drivers. She has never been in an accident and has never received a traffic ticket, but did I say she drives fast?

We locked up the house and walked to the car. We all piled into the car or "Jezebel" as I like to call her. Mo buckled up in her booster seat. Charlene sat behind the steering wheel, and I rode shotgun.

"Atomic batteries to power. Turbines to speed," I announced.

Char started the car, "Why do you always say that when I start out driving?"

"It's a reference to the campy 1960's Batman television series."

"I know where it's from, but why do you always say it?"

"Would you rather I make a reference to the show My Mother the Car?"

She put the car in gear and peeled, I mean pulled out. We drove to the corner Seven-Eleven in relative silence. Char bought her chocolate, I bought a Diet Pepsi, and Moiraine got a small Wild Cherry Slurpee. We sat in the car indulging in our favorite vices for a few moments. The quiet was broken when Mo finished her drink with the gasping sound made by a straw trying to get every last drop.

"Moiraine, give it up. There is nothing left in the cup. Say since we are already out and about, why don't we go to the park and walk around? It has been a while since we have taken a stroll in the park." In suggesting the walk, I hope to have some enjoyable family time. We don't get enough family time, and we might as well take advantage of my unemployment to reconnect.

Charlene blew out a huge breath. "You know it sounds like a plan," Char started the car. Moiraine chimed in with a cheer of excitement. It is a short little jaunt to Balboa Park. The search for a parking space wasn't. Being a Saturday, the crowds are large, and the parking spaces are few. We lucked out and found an empty space in the lot near the Rubin H. Fleet Space Theatre.

The Balboa Park's site was created in 1835 when the 1200 acres were placed in reserve for public recreational use. The Spanish style structures there were built to hold a celebration for the 1914 completion and opening of the Panama Canal. It's a great park. I would put it up against Central Park in New York any day of the week.

Near the Rubin H. Fleet Space theatre is a fountain. Moiraine loves the fountain. She will stick her hands in the water and try to splash us. Next, she will run around it, again and again, laughing the whole time. This visit to the fountain is no different. I played along and chased her, pretending she is too fast to catch. Some other kids there joined the act and started chasing her. Mo is having a blast.

While Moiraine is playing tag with her new-found friends, Char and I are watching and talking. It was a light conversation of nothing too important. Except she reassured me everything would work out, but more importantly she took my hand and squeezed it. I feel the same jolt I always do when she touches me. We are better now.

"Mo, it's time we move along." Once she joined us, I proclaimed, "Come on, ladies. Let's take a stroll."

"Daddy, can I have a penny to make a wish?"

I reached into my pocket and pulled out a penny and gave it to her. She clutched the penny and closed her eyes. I could see Mo wished extra hard. With little ceremony, she threw her penny into the water.

"So, Mo, what did you wish for?"

"If I tell you, it won't come true."

If things become tough for us, I may have to make a midnight raid to the fountain to pay for groceries. I can picture me dressed in black trying to move from shadow to shadow in an effort not to be seen. Scooping up coins and placing them in a booty bag. The wet coins would drip a trail right to me. The papers would call me "The Drippy Bandit."

We turned away from the fountain and started our walk. We walked in a straight line toward the many museums the park offers. About halfway to the San Diego Aerospace Museum, we started to pass the Japanese tea house. A sign in front touted a demonstration of Japanese Calligraphy.

I steered us into the garden where the demonstration is being held. I want to hear what this man has to say. So, I purchased some drinks and snacks, and we sat down. We watched while the gentleman talked about the origins of the art form or Shodo as it is called. The Japanese art form derives from Chinese calligraphy. He demonstrated how a Sumi and water are used to make the ink. He demonstrated holding the brush or Fude. He talked about the traditional paper, Mulberry.

After his presentation and the crowd thinned out, I approached him, "I wonder if you know the meaning of these characters and this symbol," I motioned to ask for his brush. With an amused smile on his face, he handed me the brush. I painted the characters in easy, simple strokes. Mr. Motto raised his eyebrows in surprise and then bowed.

"I see you have held the brush before. Your strokes are most artful. You are playing with me."

"No. I have never done this before. Please, I know these characters from somewhere, and this symbol has me stumped. I can't place it, and it is driving me mad. Do you know what it means?"

"This is Japanese. It references a date in the near future, but the symbol is strange to me. No, not right. It has no meaning unto itself. This has the look of a maker's mark. I am not familiar with whose mark this may be or what kind of work it is for. You are right; it is most puzzling."

"Do you know where I can find out more about it?"

"This little mystery is intriguing to me. Please to allow me to investigate it. May I have this?" He lifted my sketch. I nodded yes, and he placed it into his portfolio.

"If you find out anything about it, please give me a call," I wrote down my name and phone number for him. I thanked him for his time and trouble. I dismissed all thoughts of the maker's mark, which have been driving me nuts. It is handled. Either I would learn what it is from or I would not.

We all enjoyed the rest of the day in the park. We ambled in the Arboretum. We listened to some street musicians. Moiraine danced to their music. She so loves music. We rode the Merry-go-round. I even caught the brass ring for the first time. We people watched, had some lunch, and just were together. I love my family. I don't know what I would do without them.

By the time we returned home, Charlene is treating me like everything is okie dokie between us. I dodged a bullet there. I hate sleeping on the couch. I can't get comfortable on the damn thing. I am a little taller than the couch is long. If I sleep with my head nestled perfect, my feet are elevated. If my feet are comfy, my neck gets a kink in it.

It's a poor metaphor for my life, but I'm no writer.

The rest of the weekend was pretty normal for us. We played some board games. I won at "Pretty Pretty Princess." I think Mo threw the game to see me wear all the plastic jewelry. We worked in the garden. This year Charlene had managed not to murder the poor plants. I love my wife, but she has a black thumb. Charlene cleaned rooms which are already clean. I tried to stay on her good side by helping. I attempted to clean as well as she does, but she would come up behind me and reclean where I had already been.

I tried my luck on the internet for a couple of decent job prospects. I logged the results in my perfect memory. All is well with the world again. Everything except I had no job.

Chapter Six

Monday morning is the start of a new week. We followed our usual routine of getting Mo off to school. I did my shift as a crossing guard. When I returned home, Charlene and I passed at the front door. We exchanged kisses and goodbyes as she went on to Moraine's school to do her art docent gig. I made ready to go out looking for work. I put on a dress shirt and tie along with a pair of slacks. I didn't believe I would get an interview right off the bat, but on the slight chance I am lucky I need to look professional. The first visit of the day; however, is going to be to my favorite Assistant District Attorney's office. I planned to exchange some choice words with him the bulk of which I would not want my daughter to hear.

Mark Galos had gotten off scot-free, and I wanted, I needed, to know why! I have a not so sneaky suspicion it is my fault. Sneaky suspicion more like it is out in broad daylight wearing fluorescent clothes and waving semaphore flags. If it is the case, it is one more item in a long list of failures in my life. I had been a boy with such promise, but now I am a man of mounting disappointments. I have to get my thinking straight. Everything is riding on my shoulders, a whole world of worries. Well, this Atlas is not going to shrug.

Mark Galos scares me. I fear he is not going to let it go. In my dreams, he has been coming after my family and me. The whole time I gave my testimony, I could feel his eyes on me. It felt like I was being sized up by a predator. His eyes held the cold reptilian quality of a Komodo Dragon getting ready to strike. If a Komodo's prey manages to escape after the bite, it is still doomed. The Dragon follows and waits for the victim to slowly die of blood poisoning, a most painful death. A Komodo Dragon's saliva is home to a virtual soup of nasty bacteria. The recipient of the love bite withers slowly and dies. I'm afraid this is what Mark Galos will do to me. Nip me in some way then back away and watch me burn up with fever. Thinking about the way he looked at me on the witness stand sends a shiver down my spine. It feels like somebody doing the hokey pokey on my grave.

"You put your left foot in, you put your left foot out ..." The song came in loud and clear as I pondered my sorry state.

"Ok, Mr. K R A P, that is quite enough!" The sound from my internal iPod died down. As I made ready for the day, I plotted out a route to hit some of the best prospective employers in the area after my visit to the DA's office. Time is a commodity I can't afford to waste. I locked up the house and got into Jezebel. "The lady told me if I give you a little special attention once in a while, you'll purr at my every touch. So, here goes." Before I turned the key, I gave the dashboard a little pat. "Who's my girl. You know I love you." I turned the key, and she started right up. I pulled out of the driveway and made a beeline for Mr. Darryl Wayne's office.

The drive is pleasant enough, despite the rude drivers on the road. The building which houses the county offices is in the old downtown section of the city. It is an uninspired square monstrosity of eleven stories called "The Hall of Justice." It looks like a seven-year-old made it out of a small and limited set of Legos.

The saying "there's no such thing as a free lunch" comes to mind every time I try to park here in the downtown of America's Finest City. In San Diego, there's no such thing as free parking. I'm sorry but public buildings should have free parking. Twelve bucks to park over an oil stain on a few square feet of concrete is plain nuts. Not even any cashews or macadamias, just plain nuts. They should do parking like in Las Vegas. You slip the valet a few Georges, and he parks your car. He brings your car out, and you slip him a few more almighty dollars. Yep, it's how I'd run it. I think I'll write to Congress and set them working right on it. Hell, it would be the most reasonable bit of joy out of Washington in over 200 years. They could tout it as a jobs bill. Maybe I should run for Congress.

I doubt I could be elected with me being honest and all.

I made my way into the building. I grabbed the elevator up to Wayne's World. The elevator is empty except for a man in an average cut blue suit standing in a corner at the back. He must have missed his floor coming down because he didn't exit the car. He looked bored to the extreme. The music playing is *"One"* by Three Dog Night, but it is the crappiest Muzak version I had ever heard.

I exited the elevator onto a quiet floor filled with hallways and doors. I had been to Darryl Wayne's office before when he wanted to go over my testimony for Mark Galos' trial. I weaved my way through the labyrinth of corridors to his lair. I pulled open the door and entered the reception area. His secretary is seated behind a desk with a computer and a phone bank. This woman is attractive. She has jet black hair cut into an asymmetrical bob and sported some large gold hoop earrings which seem to spin like gyroscopes. Her outfit, what I could see of it, is as black as her hair and cut in a deep swoop which is a little too low for an office setting. From my position standing across the desk, I received a view a single man would have appreciated. This married man enjoyed it too.

I tried not to look at the adequate deep cleavage which is exposed. The only problem is my eyes kept being pulled down from her face by some magical force beyond my comprehension. Char has always touted window shopping is harmless, "But don't buy anything." Sure, like I believe her. I could swear Char's nose got a wee bit larger after she said it.

The secretary was diligently typing away at the computer without a look in my direction. I coughed to no avail. All I heard was a guttural, "huh," out of her while she continued to type. She stopped typing, clicked the mouse a couple of times, and turned to face me.

"Who do you have an appointment with?"

"I don't have an …," but before I could finish the phone rang. The secretary put up her hand in the universal gesture for this phone call is far more important than you. She picked up the phone and began ignoring me. "Ms. I was here before the phone rang. Please Ms.," she continued with the phone call while I stewed. After a short epoch, she finished with the call. "As I was saying I …," but before I could finish the door I had come through opened. A messenger walked in. Without an "Excuse me," he nudged me aside and handed a large manila envelope and clipboard to the secretary.

"Anything going out?" he asked as he is looked at his watch and made a note on the clipboard the secretary handed back. When the secretary didn't immediately answer, he looked up and gave me a nod then was out the door he came in. With the foolishness done, I could finally tell her I needed to talk with Mr. Wayne.

As I was about to open my mouth, a buzzer went off, and a man's voice came on. This is like some bit in a bad sitcom. My blood pressure is going up, and my heart began beating faster. I'm sure the little vein on my temple started dancing to a Latin rhythm. The voice on the intercom sounded like Mr. Wayne's, "I need you to call Detective Jun and have him come in today to go over his testimony for the Abram's case."

She replied, "Yes, sir." The office is finally quiet. I waited for a beat to make sure nothing else is going to knock, or ring, or buzz.

Nothing. Victory is mine. I took a breath to begin.

The door leading to the private offices and meeting rooms opened. Daryl Wayne leaned into the room, "Can you place these in the Bruter file?" Darryl told his receptionist as he placed the paperwork on her desk. He turned to go back through the door. I jumped around the desk and stretched to grab the door to keep it from closing.

"Mr. Wayne, if I could have a moment of your time?" I tried to keep my voice level but based on how I feel. it came out a little harsher than I meant. *"Take a breath. Get yourself under control."*

His secretary chimed in with, "I was about to tell this gentleman time in this office is valuable, and he needs to make an appointment."

Mr. Wayne took a quick look at his watch, "I can give you five minutes, but no more." I followed him back to his office. The room is as I remembered it. His desk is neat with no papers out. Everything on it is arranged just so. Pictures of the family were placed in the corner of the desk. A large blotter covered the work area. A fancy pen and pencil set made of exotic wood, teak I think, is in its place right behind a nameplate reading Daryl Wayne. A Newton's cradle and other office toys are arranged on another corner of the desk. There is no clutter whatsoever. It is the sign of a sick and twisted mind. "So, what can I do you for Mr. Embers? Oh, please have a seat," he leaned back against the front edge of his desk as he gestured for me to take a seat.

I sat in the chair. I looked up at Mr. Wayne. My neck hurt from the odd angle, and I exploded, "What the Hell happened in the Mark Galos trial?" I sat there unblinking waiting for an answer, "Well?"

He opened his mouth for a second, then change his mind. He walked around his desk and took a seat. He sat there a second taking a moment to compose his words. He played with the Newton's cradle. The sound of its click-clack began to annoy me. He put on what I considered a false smile and gave his canned speech, "Well, nothing is guaranteed in a trial, Mr. Embers. We fought the good fight, but this time it wasn't in the cards." Two clichés in one sentence. I am not impressed. A hat-trick would have earned him at least a chuckle.

"Come on, Darryl, spare me the canned speech. I need to know. Was it my fault?"

"Okay, Mr. Embers, I'll give it to you straight," he stood and leaned across the desk. He braced himself on his fingertips. The gloss of the table reflected his fingers, reminding me of the old joke about a spider doing push-ups on a mirror. With a heated voice, he replied, "Yes, it was your fault, Mr. Embers, you blew the case. You were the case. You and your so-called perfect memory. We had him. A relative low-level crime his attorney should have pleaded out, but we had him. Until you claimed to have seen a dead man. You talked to Detective Ralph Davies, a fine cop. You smeared his memory. Tell me, did Mark's parents offer you a little incentive to blow the case? Tell me off the record. I won't hold it against you. You wouldn't be the first to let a scumbag slip away for a few pieces of silver. My solid record took a hit all for a minor robbery from a no-name two-bit punk." The click-clack of the desk toy is echoing in my skull.

His words hit me hard. As his barrage battered at my rage over what had happened, the headache I had subdued after the trial began pounding to be released from its confines. I should have taken care of it before today, but I had hoped, in vain, it would not reappear. But they always come back. By the time Mr. Assistant DA had finished his little tirade, the giant of a migraine had escaped. It had grown. What was once a giant, has become a titan.

Where's Zeus when I need him?

"Can I see your trashcan?" Darryl hesitated, so I repeated myself with a low toned command which sounded more like a growl. "Let me have your trashcan." He reached to the side of his desk and picked up the can and handed it to me. I poured its contents out on the floor beside me. Mr. Wayne started to make a fuss. I leaned my head into the can and threw-up my breakfast. Darryl stopped his protest in mid-sentence. I guess he is a bit shocked.

Over the years of headaches and the vomiting which follows, I have learned how to predict the time of hurling with uncanny accuracy. After the giant broke out of its confines, I knew I had only moments before the spewing began. I had no time to make it to the restroom and stick my head into a porcelain altar. I had to act quickly, or I am going to need new dress shoes.

The headache had subsided somewhat after I tossed my cookies. For a few brief moments, it would give me a break long enough to function for a time. I stood and looked around the office for a tissue. I grabbed one and wiped my mouth. I threw the soiled tissue in the waste can and received an oh so lovely look at, and a whiff of the contents of my stomach. Strange, I don't remember eating that.

"Well, has the truth of the matter caused you to be sick with yourself?" asked the idiot.

I looked him in the eye. The fury of my emotions fully evident on my face. I replied, "I'll be back," to the room as I turned around and walked into the hallway. I took the wastebasket with me. I must have looked like a zombie walking the hallway towards the men's room. No one is using the facilities as I entered. Lucky them. I washed my face and took a breath. I am minimally better. I proceeded to empty, rinse out, and dry the trashcan. I returned to Mr. Wayne's office with the trashcan in hand. My five minutes must have been up because some guy in a suit is in the office with Darryl. I started to pick up the trash I had set on his floor.

"What are you doing? Oh please, Mr. Embers, you can leave it. I'll have someone clean it up. Why don't you go home and get some rest?" Can this man flip-flop or what? He must be practicing for a run at an elected office.

I continued with my efforts ignoring both him and the other suit. After I picked up the trash, I declared, "I always clean up my messes." I handed him back his trashcan and made my exit.

I walked to the elevator and when the doors opened, the same fellow who rode up with me is still there with the same bored look. The Muzak version of *"You Oughta Know"* by Alanis Morissette played while we rode down. My head is beginning to pound again. It is all I could do to keep from heaving inside the elevator car. I put my hand out to lean against the wall. The bell chimed, and the door opened. I staggered out. I forced my way to a drinking fountain where I downed some aspirin I always carry for such occasions. I know it's rude, but I splashed some water on my face right there at the fountain.

I made it back to my car. I am in no condition to drive, so I reclined the seat as far as it would go and tried to take forty winks. Sometimes sleeping, even a short nap, can relieve my brain bombs. I requested a soothing song from K R A P. The sound of Kenny G playing *"Songbird"* came over me and I drifted off.

I slept, but it was a restless sleep. While I could still perceive the migraine, it is no longer an unbearable throb. I dreamed disjointed bits of horror and past nightmares. Mark Galos reigned supreme in most of those torments. Finally, I had some peace in my fitful slumber. The dreams stopped. I slept the sleep of the dead.

I woke with a start. What time is it? My cell phone read it is close to starting time for my afternoon shift guarding the crossing at my daughter's school. Damn, I slept most of the day away. What a waste. The migraine is there in the back of my head waiting for me to hear a loud noise, have an angry thought, or become frustrated to return to the forefront of my perception.

I had to beat feet to make it on time to my daughter's school. I made it home with no time to spare. I grabbed my stuff and took-off. Normally I would park the car at home and walk to my station, but I had no time today. I parked the car on the street near the crossing. I donned my mantle and whistle. I could hear the school bell go off as I walked up to the corner. All went well until about halfway through my shift.

The hair on the back of my neck started to stand up, and I feel like I am being watched. My head began to pound slowly as the headache reared its ugly head. As I turned around, I spoke words which chilled my blood.

"Mr. Galos, I have been expecting you."

Chapter Seven

He stood there in front of me about an arm's length away. He had the look of death about him. He appears to be sick or at least recently up from a sickbed. His hair is unkempt, and the pallor of his face is ghostly. The whites of his eyes had a yellow cast to them. He is wearing a heavy dark wool peacoat, and his hands are in his pockets. The slight smirk on his face betrayed his intention. He is here to murder me. He is going to commit this horror in front of these innocent children, and I couldn't do a thing to stop it.

"Don't do this," I calmly asked. "Not here. Not in front of the kids. I'll go with you wherever you want. I won't put up a fight. Please spare the children." My head began to throb with the migraine again. It is coming back with a vengeance.

"What, no begging?" Mark said with a blank face.

"Would it convince you to do this somewhere else?" I said, looking straight in the monster's eyes.

"No, it wouldn't," he said casually. "But I so wanted to see you beg, Nathan. You don't mind me calling you Nathan, do you? At times, it seems like we are old friends. You pissed me off as only an old friend can," his strange accent is back.

If I keep him talking long enough, maybe one of the parents will think it's fishy and call the cops. The longer I delay him; the fewer children will be around to witness my death. "Sure Mark, in fact, you can call me Nate. Amazing job with the accent by the way. Nice trick getting rid of it for the trial. Could you answer a question for me? Who had the voice I kept hearing? Did you have a partner with a radio?" I tried willing the children to leave, but there are always some who hang around for a while waiting for parents or siblings.

Pound.

"Some things are going to remain a mystery, my old friend. If you had only minded your own business, I would have left you alone to your pathetic empty life, but you had to be a hero in the courtroom. Well, you know what they say about heroes, don't you?" Mark paused and waited for my answer.

"Will Rogers said, 'Being a hero is about the shortest-lived profession there is.'"

"I had never heard it before, but so true in your case. I had plans requiring precise timing. I could have ended their suffering. They have paid too high a price for this world already. Now, they will have to ante up a little more. They will get their just due eventually, but I can do one thing for them. I can eliminate the thorn who kept me from freeing them." Mark Galos said with righteousness in his voice.

Pound. Pound.

"Who are you talking about?" I asked, trying to stall for more time. I had to keep him talking. Something is nagging at me from the back of my mind, but I can't quite put my finger on it. "Who needs freeing? Maybe I can help."

Pound. Pound. Pound.

"Isn't that rich. You helping me? You can't help me. Why you can't even help yourself, Mr. Clerk Guy. Wait, you got fired, so you aren't Mr. Clerk Guy anymore. You are a nobody, Nate," he said my name in a mocking tone. "I thought it fitting taking away what little you had. Like a deadly silent knife out of nowhere. Yes, it was me who dropped a dime on you to your employer. I had Marcy, the bitch, fired too. A pleasant twist of the knife."

A parent spoke out to the world at large "People should watch their language around children."

Like a viper, Mark Galos pulled a revolver out of his coat pocket and pointed it at the lady. "Keep your mouth shut, or you'll buy one of these in the head, BITCH!" The mother gasped in shock. Some of the children started crying. Other parents started grabbing their children. Everyone started running in all directions. "Make a move, Nate, and I'll end her and as many of these brats as I have bullets for except the last two. Those have a previous engagement with your head."

Pound. Pound. Pound. The pain is blinding. I can't think. I am still missing something, but I didn't know what. In the pandemonium all around me, I could hear a distinct voice calling out.

"Daddy." My daughter's voice sent an electric jolt to my soul. I knew what has been nagging me. In all that happened, I had forgotten my own family was on their way to the corner. Walking home together is something we do every day after school, and it had slipped my mind. If I had my wits about me, I would have tried to escape and lead Mark away on a merry chase. Now my wife and daughter are in danger too.

In my mind, the headache appeared again. It is a monster indescribably large and hideous. It is dark and billowing like a Texas tempest. Pieces of my memory churned throughout it. They are distorted and twisted. In my mind's eye, I saw myself standing before the agonizing gale. I felt no more significant than a grain of sand being tossed about by the whirlwind. I reached down into myself for strength to the very pit of my being and screamed at the storm. I hurled the force of my will and pushed the migraine back. I pushed it, again and again, further and further until it was the grain of sand and I the whirlwind.

Mark Galos' head turned in Moiraine's direction, and a smile of realization came to his face. Time slowed down. Time stopped as he swung his arm around to aim. As the end of the barrel passed my head, I reached out and grabbed his wrist. I pushed his arm up as I heard a shot ring out. A part of me prayed the bullet would miss its mark as we wrestled for the gun. Somehow, I seized the revolver around the cylinder and prevented it from spinning around to the next bullet. Despite his looking sick, this man is freakishly strong. He is throwing me around like a dog with a rat in his teeth. I held on to the gun with all I am worth, but it isn't enough. My grip is slipping, and soon, he will have it free. In the distance, I heard a siren. The sound is growing louder as it approached the corner. Someone must have gotten a call off to the police. The cavalry is on its way. He must have heard it too because he paused for a moment and looked in the direction of my approaching rescue. He redoubled his efforts and finally managed to leverage the gun away. I am on the ground with him above me. The siren is growing louder.

He said, "I'm looking forward to our next little party, Nate," he turned and ran away.

I started to stand. I forced myself to look in the direction where my daughter's voice had come from. She is alive and crying. At her feet is my wife. She is crumpled up in an awkward position. I scrambled on all fours, not taking even a moment to regain my feet. Dear God in heaven let her be alive, I prayed.

I quickly checked her, and she is still breathing, but only barely. Her pretty white blouse is quickly being stained red with her blood. I can hear Mo crying. I want to grab her up in my arms and rock her. Tell her her mother would be fine. I want to comfort my daughter. I want her to comfort me. If Charlene's life is to be saved, I can't waste any time comforting Mo or myself. I ripped my wife's blouse open. The buttons shot in all directions like empty phantoms of the bullet which mutilated her body. I found the entry wound. I am not sure, but by its position, it looks like she took the round in the heart. I yelled for help, but no one came to my aid. I pulled out my cell phone dialed 911 and put it on speaker. The siren started fading. The police car must be on a different call. Only the wildest of luck had interrupted Mark and chased him away. I hope I haven't use up all my luck. I am going to need all the luck I can muster.

Over the speaker of my cell phone came "9-1-1 operator, what is the nature of the emergency?"

"My name is Nathan Embers. I am the crossing guard at Greentree Elementary School. There has been a shooting with one victim. Send the police and an ambulance as fast as you can. The shooter's name is Mark Galos. He left the scene traveling westbound on foot. He's five feet ten inches tall with bleached blond hair. He is wearing a dark wool peacoat. The victim's injuries are severe. Please, send help as fast as you can," I could hear the operator begin to ask questions, but Char didn't have time for questions. I turned my attention back to my wife. Blood is spurting out of the wound in time with her heartbeat. I tried putting pressure on the wound, but it didn't stem the flow. I kept upping the pressure until I was sure any more would break a rib or two. And if I broke a rib, it could puncture a lung. An idea came to me. It is a wild, crazy Hail Mary Pass of an idea. I wasted no time because I have no options.

My daughter is crying and calling for her mommy to wake up. I have to help Moiraine, almost as much as my wife. "Mo, I need you to listen to me. Hold your mommy's hand and tell her you love her. I want you to say it over and over again. I want you to look at your mommy's face and don't look away," I didn't want her to see what I am going to do next.

I took the index finger of my right hand and inserted it into the entry wound in my wife's chest. I probed around with the tip of my finger going deeper and deeper until I felt what I am after. I started to feel the lub dub of her beating heart. I could also feel a warm pulse of blood. I probed deeper and found the hole the bullet made in my wife's heart. I reached deeper into her chest and plugged the hole with my fingertip.

Charlene's face is still pale, and her breathing is shallow. It feels like her heartbeat is slowing. It is hard to tell for certain through my finger. I need to do something more, but what? "Char, listen to me. You have to fight. Don't give up. You have two people here who need you to stay with them."

I heard Mo chime in with, "Yes, Mommy, I need you." That's my girl.

"Damn it; fight. Hang on with all you have. You listen to me. You have never backed down from a fight before, and you're not going to back down on this one. Fight! Tell your heart to beat stronger. Tell your lungs to take in air. Will your body to heal itself," faintly in the distance I heard a siren. Hurry up damn it. Get here already. My wife needs you. This is taking too long. How long has it been? No more than a couple of minutes for sure. All of a sudden, my focus expanded beyond my wife, my daughter, and myself. I realized we are not alone. I could hear the soft cries of children and murmurs of "Mrs. E" all around us. One of the parents present, I didn't know who, place a rolled-up jacket or sweater under my wife's head. As soon as I thought, *"Damn it, someone get these children away from here. They shouldn't see this,"* parents started pulling kids away.

"Daddy, I'm scared. What if mommy dies?"

"Don't say that. Don't ever say that," I screamed to Moiraine, "Your mother is not going to die," I looked at my wife. She is all too pale. I screamed at Char. "Do you hear. You're frightening your daughter. Now fight to stay here with her. When the doctors said you could never conceive, you fought them. When you were carrying Moiraine, the doctors said you could never safely carry a baby to term; you fought them. When they said to save your life, you had to terminate the pregnancy; you fought them. You won those battles. You proved you are strong. Use your strength now, and fight for your life. Damn it FIGHT!" I'm not sure, but did her expression change briefly? Did she have a glimmer of determination on her face? Maybe I am deluding myself.

I feel drained, and my hand was starting to cramp up. Through my fingertip, Char's heartbeat feels a little stronger and a little more regular. The color in her face is returning; Moiraine noticed her mother's improvement also. She stopped crying but kept up her talking. The paramedics and ambulance arrived. Everything started to become a blur of questions and movement.

Once the paramedics determined Char was stable enough for the ride to the hospital, we all loaded up in the ambulance. To keep my finger where it is doing the most good required a feat worthy of Chinese acrobats. I ended up on the gurney straddling my wife. It is awkward, but it works. My daughter rode upfront with the ambulance driver. The short drive took forever.

The Emergency Room is a blur of organized chaos. A flurry of doctors and nurses began giving and taking orders. I didn't listen. I kept all my attention on Charlene. I spoke to her. I relayed what the doctors are doing. I told her about all the weird dreams I've been having. I talked about how our daughter is growing up to be a fine young lady and a better than average stand-up comedian. I told her I love her. I tried to be strong. Oh, God how I tried, but a phantom of doubt grew inside and started to torment me.

The doctors did all they could for Charlene in the E.R. They had to take her up to surgery. I took another free gurney ride; only this time, it is up an elevator. They pushed us right up to the Operating Room's door.

"Okay, folks. We are going to do a little ballet here," the lead doctor said. "As soon as Mr. Embers removes his finger from his wife's chest, we move. Take her into the O.R. stat. Don't waste time prepping her. I want to crack her chest and see what we have. Does everybody know what their job is?" General murmurs of agreement came from the surgical team. "Let's get ready. Someone help Mr. Embers off the gurney. Are you ready, Mr. Embers?"

"Ready as I'll ever be," I whispered what I hoped would not be a last I love you to my wife.

"Mr. Embers, go. Remove your finger."

I hesitated for a second, then removed my finger. Instantly all sorts of alarms went off on the monitoring equipment connected to my wife. The surgical team moved like clockwork. They rushed my wife into the O.R. and left me standing there with my bloody and cramped hand. I stood there a few moments trying to understand everything that has happened in the last hour.

I went to the nearest restroom to wash my hand and work the cramp out as best I could. My hand ached. I have to find the ambulance driver who is watching after Mo. I returned downstairs to the E.R. and wasted no time searching. "Moiraine!" I yelled out and got several dirty looks from both patients and staff. I don't care. I heard her reply immediately. I made my way toward the sound. I found her sitting next to the ambulance driver hugging a teddy bear. When she saw me, she came running for all she is worth. We hugged and cried.

"Is mommy, okay? Can I see her? Is she coming home tonight? Why did the man hurt mommy?" Moiraine said without pausing to take a breath.

"Of course, your mommy is going to be fine." I had lied to my daughter for the first time. I don't think she can handle the ugly truth. I don't know. If Charlene doesn't pull through, I will pay for the lie many times over. I left her other questions unanswered for the time being. I hugged her again and stroked her hair. Am I comforting her, or is she comforting me?

The ambulance driver stood up and said, "I have to be getting back to work. I hope your wife recovers quickly."

I stretched out my hand to shake the driver's hand, "Thank you for staying with my daughter. You went above and beyond for her. I owe you one. Moiraine, Honey, you need to give the man back his teddy bear. Another little girl may need it."

"Sir, she can keep it. They are donated to the city for such occasions. It helps the young ones deal with tragedies like this one," he turned and started walking back to his ambulance.

My daughter called out, "Jerry." He turned and watched as my daughter ran up to him. While holding tight onto the teddy bear, she crooked her finger motioning for Jerry to bend down. Jerry did as he was instructed. Moiraine wrapped her arms around his neck and hugged him, then she kissed him on the cheek, "Thank you." I could see tears welling up in his eyes. The raw emotion on the man's face showed he has not gotten so jaded from witnessing this kind of tragedy while on the job. A little girl with a simple kiss, and thank you can still touch his heart.

A little pang of jealousy hit me in the pit of my stomach. Another man has been a hero to my daughter. I feel sad, but mostly, I feel ashamed for being jealous. While Mo is saying her goodbyes to Jerry, I made a call on my cell phone to Charlene's father. I told him Char is in the hospital and he needed to be here. We made arrangements to meet in the surgical waiting room upstairs. I grabbed Mo's hand. I took her to the Hospital's cafeteria for a snack and to kill some time while Char is in surgery. I tried to talk Mo into having a banana and a glass of milk, but she wanted Cheetos and Hawaiian Punch. I don't have the strength to fight her on it.

With snack and teddy bear in hand, we rode the elevator up to the surgical floor where we began our vigil in the waiting room. It is a plain room painted in Navajo White. The chairs have no padding and are upholstered in a grayish fabric. All the magazines are well out of date, a few by years. An old television is sitting on a rickety stand. The temperature is too cold, and the whole room smelled of disinfectant. We picked seats which gave us a view of the TV. Mo sat quietly and ate her Cheetos, offering a few to her teddy bear and then to me. I have to smile. After all she witnessed and all the Hell she has endured, she can still be a little girl. I prayed she doesn't have to grow-up for a time yet. I also know if circumstances turned ugly, she would quickly learn a lesson in grown-up life.

"Thank you, Mo," I took a couple Cheetos and ate them robotically. I didn't even taste the enriched corn meal, ferrous sulfate, niacin, thiamin mononitrate, riboflavin, folic acid, vegetable oil (corn, canola, soybean, and/or sunflower oil), cheese seasoning, and assorted other ingredients. Note to self; I should never read food packaging. No peace of mind can be found there.

It wasn't long before John, Charlene's father, showed up in the waiting room. John is a man from the greatest generation, which is to say he had fought at the tail end of World War II and in the Korean conflict. He had an air of an unspoken sorrow about him. He is a smallish man of only five-foot-six and walks with a little hunch which only exaggerated his short stature. His gray hair, which is cut close, is only evident on the sides of his head. He is wearing brown slacks and a white short-sleeved dress shirt. Moiraine saw him and immediately went running into his arms.

"Grandpa," is all she said before the tears started anew. John held her and consoled her as only a grandparent can. They had always had a special relationship. Along with a huge amount of spoiling, John had given her unconditional love all her life. Once the tears had faded, John turned on the TV and sat Mo back down in a chair.

I stood and walked to him. We shook hands. He still has a firm grip from years of working with his hands. John is a craftsman of the old school. He made fine furniture with hand tools and sweat.

We sat down and spoke in hushed tones, "What in the blazes happened to my girl? Tell me everything."

I started at the top with the robbery. I worked my way through the trial and ended with the shooting. I told him everything without going into such detail my perfect memory would overwhelm me. I don't think I could relive the events of today without breaking down. John took it all rather well considering his only daughter is on a knife's edge between life and death. I think if our roles were reversed, and Moiraine had been shot, I would be screaming in agony. After our conversation, we sat in silence each of us alone in his thoughts.

We had waited in purgatory for about two hours when two doctors dressed in clean scrubs, thank God there is no blood on them, came into the waiting room.

"Mr. Embers, could we talk to you outside please?" The lead surgeon asked. He is a man of mid to late fifties with grey streaks through his black hair. He was shorter perhaps five-foot-six or seven. He has an aura of command about him, which gives him the illusion of being taller. He is a man accustomed to giving orders and having them obeyed without question.

I started to stand, and out of the corner of my eye, I saw John starting to rise also. When he was about halfway out of the chair, he sat back down. I guess he thought I had the right to know first. John and I have never had what you would call a close relationship. I give him the respect due to the father of my wife. He tolerates me, the man who stole his little girl, and give me the respect I am due. Hanging around together and being best buds had never been in the cards for us.

I walked out into the hallway with the doctors. We all moved out of earshot of the waiting room. I am glad they don't want my daughter overhearing our conversation.

"Mr. Embers, I am Dr. Gastil, and this is Dr. Hazer. Your wife is out of recovery and is in the intensive care unit. If there are no further complications, I believe she will make a recovery. We were unable to save the fetus, however."

I saw Dr. Hazer grimace slightly at hearing the term fetus. I nearly exploded in a cloud of bone, blood, and bits. A flood of emotion rushed into me. Char is pregnant again. Two miracle babies? Char is no longer pregnant? We lost a child we never even knew was there. My wife is still alive. I didn't know what to feel. Should I feel joy Char is still alive? Should I feel sorrow our baby never had a chance to live? My emotions are being tossed about like a mobile home in a tornado. I tried to hold on to my sanity. I barely did. I told myself to deal with what is in front of me. I could grieve later. "I'm sure you did everything you could to save the baby," I told myself to hold on, just hold on.

"There was nothing we could do. By the time it was apparent your wife was miscarrying, it was too late," Dr. Gastil replied with no emotion in his voice.

"Are you telling me you didn't even try to save the baby?" Such anger began to build in me. I am beginning to loathe this little man. I started to shake. I clenched my fists so hard my nails cut into my palm. I felt drops of blood dripping from my hands. It is all I could do to keep myself from tearing into him.

"Mr. Embers, if I had diverted my attention from your wife in a hopeless attempt to save the fetus …"

In a low growl through clenched teeth, I said, "If you say fetus instead of baby one more time, I swear here and now I will rip your throat out with my teeth and spit the ravaged piece back in your face." I startled Dr. Gastil with my words, and for an instant, I saw fear in his eyes. My feelings of raw hatred are building. I am a pressure cooker filled with emotion with more being pumped in every moment. I am beginning to frighten myself.

Dr. Gastil recovered and said, "Mr. Embers, I don't know what platitudes you want me to say. I made the call to save the life I could."

Platitudes? How about a little grief for the unborn life which was lost? "Was the baby a boy or a girl?"

While Dr. Gastil began looking through my wife's chart to give me the answer, Dr. Hazer chimed in immediately with, "A boy, Mr. Embers." I could hear some pain in this man's voice.

I turned to look into Dr. Hazer's eyes. "I know he was in charge, but tell me truthfully, doctor. Would you have tried to save my son's life?" There was a pause, then Dr. Hazer's eyes darted to Dr. Gastil. "No, doctor. You look at me. Don't look at him for guidance. I don't care if you are a first-year resident. You tell me the truth of it. Would you have tried?"

Dr. Hazer's took a breath and said, "Yes, I would have tried. But Mr. Embers, it would have done no ..."

I lifted my hand to interrupt the man. I said, "Thank you, doctor, for your honesty. I can hear in your voice the truth of it," I turned back to Dr. Gastil, "You're fired. Dr. Hazer will be in charge of my wife's case from here on out." I took a deep breath and exhaled trying to expel my anger with my breath like the relief valve on a pressure cooker about to boil over.

"Mr. Embers, I don't think you understand. While Dr. Hazer is not a first-year resident, he is not yet, with all due respect, ready to take on a case of this magnitude. If you will allow me to recommend a ..."

I interrupted this man, I won't call him a doctor and said, "I don't give a rodent's rectum what you have to say from this point on. I have no respect for any physician who would not even try. I want a doctor who will take a one in a million shot. I want a doctor who will sweat, work, and bust a gut trying to save the life of my wife. Frankly, Gastil, I want a healer, not only a doctor. You are dismissed, sir," I refused to watch his reaction or listen any further to the man. "Dr. Hazer, please tell me about my wife's condition."

"She is in I.C.U. She has not yet regained consciousness. The bullet penetrated one wall of her heart and lodged itself in the other side. We repaired the damage to her heart, but she is still weak from the surgery. She crashed twice on the table. We brought her back the first time in less than two minutes, but the second time she was gone for seven minutes. We are not sure yet the extent of any brain damage she may have suffered. All we can do is wait and see."

"Thank you, doctor."

"I have a question, Mr. Embers. What made you think of plugging the hole in your wife's heart with your finger? It was a gutsy move."

"In truth, it was the story of the little Dutch boy. He plugged a leak in a dike with his finger until help arrived. I figured she was dead if I did nothing. I would rather live with trying and failing than wondering and regret."

"Well, I'm not so sure you did your wife any favors. The true kindness might have been to let her pass. She may never wake up, and it's an outcome I don't believe you would have wanted for her."

"She's a fighter, doc. Don't count her out yet." I wasn't sure who I am trying to convince. Is it him or myself? "May I see my wife?"

"Of course, you can, and you can stay with her as long as you want. Check-in at the nurse's station in the I.C.U. and they'll show you to her room."

"Thanks, doc." I went back to the waiting room to give Char's father an update on her condition. John is staring off into the distance, and Mo is asleep leaning up against his arm. I looked at the time on my cell phone. It is later than I thought. Time sure flies when you're in mental anguish. I gave John the news about Charlene's condition. I can see some of the worry fade from his face, but not all of it. I could not, however, tell him about the baby. I had not yet come to grips with the news myself. I think he will understand my not telling him before Char knows.

"John, could you take Moiraine home with you? I want to stay here a while longer. I'll call you if there is any change."

"It's always a pleasure to have my favorite granddaughter spend the night," John said with an amused look.

Without opening her eyes and with a yawn, Moiraine added, "I'm your only granddaughter."

I picked Mo up out of the chair. She snuggled into the crook of my shoulder. I could carry her forever this way. John stood slowly. A grimace flashed on his face. The chairs must have played a holy terror on his back. We started to make our way to John's car.

We had not gone half a dozen steps before Mo said, "I love you, Daddy and you too Grandpa." Those words made me feel as if a mule kicked me in the heart. In the space of a few minutes, I had been sunk to the bottom of despair only to be lifted to the heights of joy. Who knew four words could have such power. Nations have fallen, and dynasties have risen with less power.

We walked the rest of the way to John's car in silence. I put Mo down in the backseat. John opened up the trunk, and I pulled out a spare car seat and installed it. Having two car seats had made life a little easier when it came to Mo visiting her grandpa. Switching one car seat back and forth is a pain in the patootie. I maneuvered Mo into the seat and buckled her in. She is out. Poor thing had to deal with things a child should never have to deal with. No wonder she is so tired.

I gave John the key to the house, "Here. Get whatever Mo needs for the sleepover, and if you can do me a favor, feed Blossom for me while you are there," he took the key and put it on his keychain. "Thanks for all your help, John," we shook hands again. I started to walk back to visit Charlene.

"Nate, wait a moment. Right now is not the time to say what I have to say, but when you have finished seeing to my dau... umm, your wife, and you get some rest. I want to talk with you. It's important," I could see it in his eyes what he has to say has great meaning to him.

"Sure thing, John, as soon as I can." I turned and started the long lonely walk to my wife's room. I have had a myriad of tasks to keep my mind preoccupied but with nothing to distract my mind, my thoughts drifted. Memories came flooding in. I am afraid of one memory. It is a memory all too close to the present reality. The past is looming over me. It is breathing down my neck. It is threatening to overwhelm me, to drown me, to destroy me utterly. And though this memory would indeed destroy me someday; right now, it only wanted to drive me mad.

I managed to make it to my wife's room without being washed away with the tide. She is laying there motionless with tubes and wires attached to various body parts. She is breathing. Her heart is beating. She is alive. I hadn't been sure until just this moment. She looks a mess and beautiful at the same time.

There is only one chair in the room. I pulled it over to Char's bedside and sat down. As I am sitting there, it occurred to me they must have bought the chair as surplus from the inquisition. I can sit in it till the rapture if it means Charlene will be fine. I leaned over to give Char a brief kiss. I told her everything would be okay, and I love her. I sat and watched her for a few moments hoping to see any kind of reaction. Nothing. I guess it is too much to hope she would awake with a kiss from her prince charming. Okay, it is too much to hope she would awake with a kiss from her frog.

Since she is out of surgery and on the mend, the day's weariness is overwhelming me. I placed my hands on the railing of her bed and rested my head on them for a moment. I fell asleep before I knew it.

I dreamed. I nightmared. Over and over, it repeated the same nightmare which has been plaguing me. Each a variation on the last, but never could I beat Mark Galos. No matter how I fought, he beat me. No matter if I ran, he would find me. And in every dream, my family suffered my fate alongside me. After about a gazillion reruns, I woke with a start.

I lifted my head. "This crap is getting old."

"What's getting old?" I heard Char say behind me. I about jumped out of my skin. What's this? Charlene is still in the bed with all the gizmos attached, but it is her voice I heard. I stood and turned around. Char was there looking at me. Okay, call a shrink. Put me in a rubber room. I must be madder than a spring hare. Or I want my wife better. Something is wrong with wife number two. She is slightly blurry and a bit translucent. "Are you real?" I blinked and shook my head to clear my vision.

She smiled at me. "I think I'm real. Are you?" She reached out to touch my cheek.

I know she is touching me, but I didn't exactly feel it. I feel its warmth in my soul. It is the warmth I always feel at her touch. But my cheek feels nothing. It is like I had been shot up with Novocain. "What do you mean, am I real? Whose wonderful delusion is this anyway?" She pointed at the chair I had been sitting in. There I am sitting in it with my head resting on my hands. "What the, lose my PG rating, is going on?" I turned back to look at my see-through wife. She smiled. I swooped in and pulled her close to me. The feel of her filled me. If this is a dream, I don't want to wake up. I heard my cell phone go off, and with a start, I woke up. This time there is no dreamy see-through wife. Only the all too real nightmare of my wife in a hospital bed clinging to life.

I read the text from John. It said Moiraine is well and in bed with the teddy-bear in a chokehold. I check the time. I had been here longer than I should have. I made my goodbyes to Char and headed home. I was halfway to the elevator when I realized my keys are not in my pocket. I headed back to the room to look for them. As I walked in, I saw a nurse leaning over my wife.

The nurse is in one of those old-fashioned uniforms with the all-white dress and matching hat. Nowadays, you only see those at Halloween time when women wanted to fulfill a man's fantasy with a sexy costume. This, however, is not a costume. This is real and old school. If someone is still wearing one of those, she must be older than dirt. "How's she doing?" I said as I started looking for my keys. The nurse jumped with a start. She turned and looked at me. She is not older than dirt. I would put her at somewhere in her late twenties. She is an attractive woman with a figure to rival my wife's, not that I noticed. She also has a perky upturned nose. "Sorry. I didn't mean to scare you. So, how is she doing?" She didn't say a word. She looked around the room like she is trying to see who I am talking to. "I like the traditional uniform by the way. With everyone wearing scrubs, it makes it hard to tell a nurse from a doctor or an orderly," I found my keys. They were under the chair. When I straighten back up after retrieving my keys, the nurse was gone. She was a little rude, not answering me.

Well, with my keys in hand, I headed back home to catch forty winks. When I arrived, the house was dark, cold, and felt empty. The house is empty except for Blossom. The only sound I can hear is the thumping of her tail. It is unnatural to have the house this quiet. I stripped off my clothes and put on my jammies. I looked at our bed. We have slept every night of our marriage in this bed.

Moiraine was conceived in this bed. Char and I whispered dreams and hopes to each other in this bed, and now it is empty. Somehow it doesn't feel right to sleep in our bed without Charlene next to me. I grabbed a blanket and pillow and headed for the recliner in the living room.

I made a silent vow to myself. The next time I would sleep in our bed, it would be with Char. I sat down in the recliner and leaned the chair back, put my feet up, and spread the blanket over me. Everything is copacetic and cozy. Blossom began to whimper. "All right girl," I patted the side of the chair and Blossom slowly stood from her bed and ambled over to me. I reached down and picked her up and placed her on my lap. She yawned, thumped her tail a couple of times, and went to sleep. I followed her fine example soon after.

Chapter Eight

The alarm on my cell phone went off, and I opened my eyes to behold my empty house. I had slept without dreaming. I felt relief to have a night free of mental turmoil. Blossom's tail began to wag a mile a minute. I guess she liked cuddling. In a way, it had been comforting for me as well. I opened the back door and let Blossom attend to her business while I attended to mine. I decided to turn on my internal iPod. It started up with "Ain't No Sunshine" by Al Jarreau.

"Ain't no sunshine when she's gone and she's always gone too long anytime she goes away…". The song fits my mood.

I went to the kitchen, opened up the chill chest, and pulled out the last of the Diet Pepsi there. I popped it open and took a long deep swallow. It slightly burned the back of my throat as it went down. It felt satisfying.

I am in a state of shock and disbelief. My biggest enemy is my mind. If I dwell on the events of yesterday, I know I cannot function. I have to go on. I have to purpose myself with what has to be done. I have to start my day like any other day. It seems wrong. With soda in hand, I turned the shower on, made it as hot as I can stand, and got in.

The drops of water are hitting me like shards of liquid glass slicing into my skin. It feels agonizingly sweet. I stood there under the hot blast and took another deep swig of my soda. Caffeine and a hot shower, God bless America. It invigorated me better than a few more hours of sack time would. I skipped the razor. I have more pressing matters than to look "Oh so pretty today." I dried off, brushed my teeth, and finished dressing by putting on a pair of comfortable old blue jeans and a tee-shirt which said, "I'm a legend in my own mind." There is no point dressing extra snazzy since I have no time for job hunting today.

Scratching at the backdoor told me Blossom is done with her routine. After I opened the back door, she moseyed over to her bowl. Her kibble is waiting for her, along with a doggie treat. She is moving slower these days. It won't be long until she leaves us. I hope she has strength enough to hold on until Charlene is well recovered. It would send Char into an emotional tailspin if she weren't here when it happened.

I grabbed the phone and called for a relief crossing-guard for the day. Next, I dialed the number of someone I had no interest in talking to. After a few minutes of making arrangements on the phone, I am ready to head out the door. But, before I left for the day, I spent some time and attention on Blossom. She is going to be alone most of the day. I felt sorry, but I had important matters to see done. I turned on the television and set the channel to the "Animal Planet." I hoped it would grab Blossom's attention and keep her company.

I locked up the house and started to get in my car when a tan sedan pulled to the driveway and blocked my car from leaving. Two men got out of the car and approached me. One I recognized as Detective Frank Hawkins, who worked the original robbery case and the other gentleman I am unfamiliar with.

"Detective Hawkins, how are you doing?" I said as I stretched out my hand. The detective ignored my hand. Frank Hawkins is a nondescript man of average height and weight. The most distinctive feature about him is he had no distinctive features. He is the kind of man one would not recognize after a casual meeting. My eyes seemed to slide off his face and hardly registered what they had seen. This fact, most likely, worked well for him during stakeouts or undercover work.

Detective Hawkins left my hand hanging there with my offer unanswered. The passive-aggressive crap always cheeses me off. What is he about today? I kept my hand out for a moment more before I turned toward the other gentleman and offered my hand to him. "So, who is your partner here? I haven't had the pleasure."

"I am Detective Joe Houser." He glanced at my hand then back to my eyes. Twice I was left hanging? I wonder who pissed in their Cheerios this morning. What can I say about Joe Houser? He is built like a fireplug, a short man and nearly as wide. His stance didn't say he had a chip on his shoulder like most short men with a little power. No, he carried himself like a man confident he could handle whatever came his way. His blue eyes betrayed an intensity which could burn a hole to the back of your skull.

It always feels awkward when another man leaves you hanging. Now two men had given me the brush-off. I tried not to take it personally. I failed. "Have you picked up Mark Galos yet?"

"We have some questions about the events of yesterday, Mr. Embers," Detective Hawkins said.

"You'll have to come with us," Detective Hauser added.

"I have a few errands I have to take care of along with seeing to my wife and daughter. Can we set up a time this afternoon when I can come in and give a statement?"

"No, Mr. Embers. You need to come with us." Joe grabbed my arm in a vise of a grip. He wasn't trying to hurt me, but he would leave a bruise if he squeezed any harder.

"Am I under arrest?"

"No, Mr. Embers. You are not under arrest, but there are some matters about the shooting we need to clear up. So, if you'll come with us," Joe said in a mockingly polite manner as he started to pull on my arm.

"If I am not under arrest, then let me focus on my family, and I'll see you this afternoon. I will answer any and all questions you may have."

"Sounds like he's trying to avoid talking with us, Frank. Maybe he has something to hide? Mr. Nathan Embers, I am placing you under arrest for obstruction of justice. You're going to be rotting in a holding cell for a while. Then maybe you'll be willing to talk with us."

I am becoming angry, and I don't have time for this crap. I tried to pull my arm free, but Joe swung me around, slammed me into the car, and started putting cuffs on me. "Oh, you saw it, Frank. He tried to keep me from putting the cuffs on him. He's resisting arrest. We'll have to add it to the list." He whipped me back around and got in my face. He must have been standing on his toes like a ballerina. "Try to resist again, and I'll make sure to lose the paperwork. You'll rot for a couple of days instead of a few hours." Joe needed a Tic-Tac in the worst way. No, make it three.

"First, you'll never make those charges to stick. B, you take me in now, and I swear to you I'll lawyer up and refuse to say a word. Third, Detective Hawkins sir, I would like to point out if you look right up there," I motioned with my head, "My landlord, Mrs. Blake, is a rather paranoid, but a sweet old woman. She has video cameras with microphones all around her property here. She is an agoraphobic. I'm sorry I should use smaller words for you guys." Whoops, there goes my mouth again. I'll have to talk to it later. "She is afraid of everything and everyone. You see, she hasn't left her house since her husband died. She, no doubt, is watching and recording what is happening. She looks on me as the son she never had. No doubt, she is on the phone with your fellow officers. Telling them how a couple of crazy guys are attacking her tenant. I think it would be wise if you rethink what you are doing here. So, why don't you save us all a great deal of trouble, time, and, in your case, paperwork. Let me do what I need to do. I give you my word I will come in, and you can question me to your heart's delight." It is a real effort not to start mouthing off more at these idiots in cheap blue suits, but I don't have time for a game of 'Ring Around the Rosie.'

"What value is the word of a liar? Under oath, you swore you saw Detective Ralph Daves, a fine officer, and close friend, weeks after he died. I think you made a deal with the creep Galos. So, what was your take from the drugs he stole?"

"I can't explain what happened, but I am no liar, and I keep my word."

Detective Hawkins pulled his partner away from me, and they whispered with each other for a few moments. When they were done with their confab, Frank said, "Take the cuffs off him, Joe." Joe spun me around again and unlocked the cuffs.

I turned back and rubbed my wrists. Detective Hauser had been a wee bit too enthusiastic about putting those cuffs on me. "Thank you." It looks like I won this round, but there is no need to rub Houser's nose in it. "As I said earlier, I give you my word. I'll talk to you before the day is out. Say about four?" The detectives walked back to their car.

As they got in, Frank said, "Four o'clock. Sharp."

Joe added, "Don't make us come looking for you." The doors to the sedan slammed shut. Then they drove off.

What was that all about? They can't think I am anything but a victim of a vengeful nut job. I looked up at the video camera and made a mental note about finally fixing it for Mrs. Blake. I am surprised the bluff worked. Not being able to lie convincingly is why I never play poker. I took a deep breath and sat in my car and drove to my father-in-law's house.

Ringing the bell at John's door, I immediately heard my darling Mo gleefully scream, "Daddy, Daddy, Daddy." A shadow fell across the peephole. I heard both locks on the door being unlocked. John opened the door and motioned for me to come in. He does not look well at all. He is bent more than usual, and there are dark circles under his eyes. The creases in his face are more pronounced too. I don't think he got a wink of sleep last night. I felt guilty I had been able to get a few short hours of rest.

"Come in. Come in. Take a chair. That's what they're for."

Moiraine pushed by her grandpa and wrapped her arms around me. She hugged me long and hard. She is scared. I don't blame her. I'm scared too. "When is mommy coming home?"

"Just as soon as the doctors say she can." I pulled Mo off me and maneuvered over to John's couch. His home is always in shipshape order. With all the fine handcrafted furniture conveying a warm feeling of comfort. The coffee table has several photo albums open over it. John started flipping them closed as I sat down.

"I was showing Mo some pictures of her mommy when she was a little girl." As he straightens up the albums, I could see his eyes start to well up. "Darn allergies acting up." John is a man of the old school. You don't show emotions at least not to other men. He pretended not to be hurting, and I pretended to believe it was allergies. "Has there been any word yet from the doctors?" He asked as he walked out of the living room and into another part of the house with his arms full of the photo albums.

"Nothing yet, but you know what they say no news is good news." Clichés and platitudes are things I say when I don't know what to say.

John returned with a wooden box a little bigger than a cigar box. He set the box down on the coffee table and sat down in one of the leather wingback chairs. He sat on the edge of the chair. "Mo Honey, why don't you get some of the drawing things you keep here and draw your mommy a picture to cheer her up."

"That's a great idea, Grandpa." Moiraine stood and ran over to the large china hutch. She opened a drawer, pulled out some paper and crayons, and began to work on her masterpiece. Despite how I feel, I smiled. I noticed John is smiling too. Little girls, if anyone tells you there is no magic in this crazy world of ours, remind them of little girls.

"Nate, this isn't easy for me to say. But I wanted you to know some things before it's too late to say them. I'm sure it's no surprise to you, but when you and Char first started dating, I didn't like you." We both chuckled. "My first impression of you was of … well, let's say I didn't think you were right for Charlene. I didn't believe anyone was right for her to tell the truth. Over the years you proved my first impression of you was wrong. You're a worthy man. I couldn't have hoped for a better man to marry my little girl or to be the father of my granddaughter."

My God! We are having a moment here. I felt a swelling in my chest and a lump in my throat. "John, I don't know what …"

"No. No. Let me finish. It wasn't meant for my Marlene and me to have a son. But if we had had a son, I like to think he would have been like you. So, I want you to have this." He motioned to the box. "It is in my will you are to get this, but in light of what happened yesterday, I want you to have it now. Go on now open it."

Reaching over, I picked up the box. It is warm to the touch. The box is made of a hand-polished walnut deep and rich. I lifted the lid, and inside was a 45-caliber pistol. Déjà vu all over again. In my reoccurring dreams of Mr. Psychopath, this gun had been a major player in most of them. John didn't strike me as the kind of man to own a pistol. It has been well cared for. It has the dull sheen of recently being oiled. I picked it up … *Flash.*

My heart is racing. I am on the ground, trying not to make a sound. Next to me is some poor Joe who had bought it. In the confusion of the firefight, I lost my rifle when they overran our position. Looking around, I couldn't see where this guy had dropped his rifle, but I saw he still had a sidearm. Quietly I pulled it free of the holster. Thanks,

119

buddy, I owe you one. The sound of three or four people moving through the bush reached my ears. I tried playing possum. If it is our guys, I am alright. If it is the North Koreans, they might take me for dead. I heard the rustle of dry grasses as someone moved through them. Oh God, they're North Koreans, their whispering gave them away. A few more footsteps, then more whispering. They are taking the boots off the Joe next to me. I started to feel them tugging on my boots. They started to roll me over. As soon as my hand is clear, I'll start firing. Now! I can't see. I just fired my weapon at any movement...

What the hell? I started to feel drained and weak. My heart is trying to pound its way out of my chest. Suddenly I am shaking and cold.

"Are you all right, son? You look like you're going to sick-up." John asked. He stood and went to the kitchen. He brought me a glass of water. I drank. I am surprised I even managed to get some of it in my mouth. My hands are shaking so badly.

"Thanks. Give me a minute. I guess what's happened has finally gotten to me," I lied. I couldn't tell John what I experienced. He would think I'm nuts. It happened to me, and I think my set of encyclopedias is missing a few volumes. After a few minutes of trying to lower my heart rate, I turned my focus back to the gun.

After I pulled back the slide, I checked the chamber for a round. It is empty. With the safety off, I dry fired the gun. The action is smooth. It both feels strange and familiar at the same time. I have never picked up a pistol before, yet I knew what to do.

"I see you know your way around one of those babies. Good. If you take proper care of it, it will take care of you. You see this gun saved my life in Korea. It may save your life or the lives of people you love." John turned and looked at Moiraine for a minute, "I hope you won't need it. But if you decide to use it, son, don't let anything worry you about it. You see I took this off a fallen soldier. I'm not exactly sure why I kept the gun, but every year on the anniversary of that day I take it out to the desert and fire off a couple of rounds. Then I break it down and give it a good cleaning. It'll get the job done. Be sure not to lose it because there's no way anyone who finds it would be able to return it to you. If you get my meaning." John looked me in the eye with an intensity I had never seen before. John stood from his chair and walked over to where Moiraine is drawing. A smile came to his face as he looked at her artwork. He turned back to me and said, "A man has a right to protect his family against the evil in this world. And if what you tell me is true and I have no reason to doubt you, that man is pure evil."

I put the 45 back into its box and closed the lid. "It saved your life. You'll have to tell me the story sometime."

"No, son, I don't," John said with finality in his tone. He sat back down in his chair. "It's a hard thing taking a man's life. Whether you answered the call of your country, protecting the lives of your family, or preserving your own life, no matter the reason, you are never quite the same after. I wasn't." We sat there for a moment, looking at each other. The only sound in the air is the scratching of my daughter's crayons on the paper.

"Can I have some juice please?" Moiraine asked as she continued her coloring.

The question broke the tension. "Why of course you can," John said. He stood and went to the kitchen to fulfill my daughter's request. "While I'm up, can I get you anything, Nate?"

"No, thank you, John. I have some things to see to before I head over to the hospital. Can you keep an eye on Mo for a while more? If this is too much or you need some time for yourself, I can make other arrangements."

"Oh, God, heavens no. It's no trouble at all. She has been a great comfort to me." I stood as John put a glass of juice in front of Moiraine. She grabbed the glass and took a big drink. I made my way to the front door. "As soon as Mo finishes her artwork, we'll be heading over to the hospital ourselves. I guess we'll see you there when you are done with your errands."

"It will most likely be a couple of hours until I get there. Bye Mo, I'm leaving."

I heard her running to the front door. "Huggies, kissies, kissies, huggies." She jumped into my arms as I bent over to give her a hug and a kiss. I felt strength filling me as her love flowed. I need strength now more than ever. I said my goodbyes to Mo and John. I turned and walked out the door and waited to hear it close and locks to engage. I got in my car and started her up. Before I started to pull away, I noticed Moiraine looking out of the window watching me. As I tapped the horn, she smiled and waved.

The drive to my appointment was uneventful and quiet. I kept both my internal iPod and the car's radio silent. I needed the quiet to empty my mind of all the turmoils in my life. I finally arrived at my destination. I exited my car and made the walk to the building entrance. It has been quite some time since I had been here last, it is exactly as I remember it.

I made all the arrangements. The appointment took a couple of hours; however, it seems as though it was over in a few blessedly fleeting moments. I am finished with my errand, so I headed to the hospital. When I entered my wife's room, both John and my daughter were there holding vigil. "How's she doing?" I asked as I walked to her bedside.

"Nothing new to report, but I'm worried. Charlene should have woken up," John whispered to me to keep his worries from Mo. "Still, she is holding on. It must mean something." John grabbed hold of Moiraine's hand and said, "Come on, Bug. These old legs of mine need to be taken out for a walk once in a while." They exited the room so I could have a few minutes alone with Charlene. I brushed her hair with my fingers. Tears started rolling down my face. I cried silently for my wife. Time, since the events of yesterday, had not passed at its normal rate. What felt like a few minutes were, in fact, hours and when events dragged on for an eternity, only moments had passed. I don't know how long I was there watching her and crying, but I was interrupted by a cough. I quickly wiped my eyes and turned. Dr. Hazer is standing in the doorway.

"What's up, Doc?" I could slap my mouth for letting that one slip out. Humor in adversity is my fallback position. I hope I don't fall back any further. "Sorry, I couldn't resist myself. How is my wife doing?"

"Well, all appears fine. Considering all she has been through; her vitals are fairly strong. I am concerned she hasn't regained consciousness. I would like to run a CT scan. After the bullet hit her, the fall to the ground may have given her head a jolt. There is no external injury to her head, but I want to cover all the bases."

"Whatever you want, Doc. Show me where to sign." Dr. Hazer handed me a clipboard with a form on it. I didn't even give it a cursory read. I put my Nathan Alexander Embers by the x. "Is there anything else you need from me like blood, a kidney, my left nut? If I have extra of anything she needs, all you need do is ask for it. Even if I don't have an extra, you can get it from me."

Dr. Hazer gave an amused little smile. "Why don't we hold all those in reserve." I returned the clipboard and form with my signature on it. The doctor left without further comment.

Alone with my wife again. It is quiet except for barely perceivable sounds from the other rooms and the nurses' station. "It's all my fault. This would never have happened to you if I hadn't pushed them to prosecute mister bleach-blond psychopath. Why did I push so hard? I know because I wanted to be vindicated after my cowardice. Because I wanted to prove to myself, I made the right choice in not fighting. Could I have been more wrong? I should have fought him. Defeat and death most assuredly would have been mine, but it would have all been done and over with." I could hear Char's voice in my head as clear as if she was talking.

"Nathan, you are an idiot. Of course, you did the right thing. You gave Moiraine and me over two more years with you. You had no idea he was going to assault our family. Be at peace, Husband Mine." I even imagined her taking hold of my hand the way she would when I have a troubled mind.

As I am leaving, I take a look at Mo's artwork. It is a rendition of her mom lying in a hospital bed with a nurse by her bedside. Cute. I have to hand it to Moiraine with everything she has been through in the last twenty-four hours she has held up like a real trooper.

I pulled out my cell phone and texted Char's father, "the cops want to talk to me. I said I would meet them at 4. Take care of Mo." I sent the text on its way and left my wife's room. The trip to the police station will be another silent journey I would rather not have make.

I arrived at the station with time to spare. I told the desk sergeant I am here to give a statement to Detectives Hawkins and Houser. He picked up his phone and buzzed the detectives, "He's here." There was a pause, he said, "Okay." The sergeant told me to wait, and someone would be right with me.

About five minutes passed before another uniform came into the waiting area and asked, "Nathan Embers?" I thought he was going to lead me back to the detectives' desks, but instead, he put me in what I guessed is an interrogation room with the obligatory crappy set of chairs and an old metal table. The room was painted in a World War II-era faded olive green. There is a two-way mirror on the wall opposite of one chair. It is cleverly disguised as a mirror. The desk sergeant told to sit down. In an upper corner is a video camera with a glowing red light on it. I blew it a kiss. The room has an odor. It is a mix of old sweat and vomit. After about ten minutes of what I can only assume is meant to have me sweat it out, I stood from my chair and approached the two-way mirror. I fogged up the mirror with my breath and wrote in the condensation "Can we get on with it? Love, Nathan," then sat back down. My little act of rebellion got an immediate response.

In walked the men of the hour. "You're late," Detective Hawkins announced.

"We don't like to be kept waiting." Detective Houser chimed in.

I sighed. "Okay, guys, somewhere along the line we got on the wrong track here. I don't think I've done anything wrong, but if it gets us moving in the right direction, I apologize for my part in all this." I motioned with my hands to the room. I met their gazes in turn. We all sat there looking at each other for a couple of beats.

"Let's go over what happened at the corner," Hawkins said as he broke the silence.

I repeated the statement I gave the cops on the scene. All over again, every sensation thought, and fear slapped me around again then kicked me while I am down. My hand even began to cramp with the memory of putting a stopper in the hole in my wife's heart.

"Nice touch the part where you said you were afraid for the kids. I'm sure it will play well with the jury." Houser said. "Now that you have gotten to recite your well-rehearsed statement, I want the truth."

"It is the truth absolute and unedited."

It is Hawkins turn to talk again. "It isn't how Mark tells it."

My heart raced. "You have him? Here? The bastard tried to kill Charlene. She's not out of the woods yet. She still hasn't regained consciousness. I want him put in the darkest dankest hole of a cell you have." He is going to pay.

Hawkins interrupted me "He says everything was your idea from stealing the drugs out of the pharmacy to blowing the trial so he would get off if he were caught. Said you masterminded the whole job. The poor kid got mixed up with the wrong guy if you ask me. Tell us the real story, but this time, none of your fancy memory tricks. I want you to use different words."

They want me to impersonate a thesaurus the smartest of all dinosaurs. "I can't do it."

"Why not?" asked Houser.

"My memory doesn't work like that. I can give you the gist of what happened, but there are no details. It's like reading a dull story. Believe me, I wish I could remember the way everyone else does. It would make my life less painful."

"Let's hear it," said Houser.

So, I gave them the Dragnet version. Just the facts. "Mark Galos ambushed me at my crossing-guard job. He pulled a gun on a woman who made a comment to him. My daughter yelled out my name. The bastard turned the gun toward her. I wrestled him for the gun. It went off and struck my wife in the heart. End of story."

"Tell us again," Hawkins said.

Over and over, they had me repeat this same story. The cops kept asking for details with different words. They tried to trip me up by saying I told it differently last time. These guys are like a bad rerun of Law and Order. This went on for hours.

My phone chimed with a text message, but before I could even read it, Hawkins grabbed the phone out of my hands. "When we're done, you can answer."

I boiled and stood up in a jolt. "NO! You WILL return my property right now, and I WILL answer it. My wife is in the hospital. Maybe dying. Maybe they need me to consent to something. If you do not return to me what is mine right now, I will…" I could swear I heard a voice telling me to take it easy. It told me they are only doing their jobs. I took a breath, waited for a beat, and sat back down. "I am sorry." The anger drained out of my body down through my legs. "Would you at least read the text so I can have some peace of mind? I'll die the death of a thousand cuts to my soul if I have to worry."

Hawkins looked at the text and told me it said, "Goodnight, Daddy, love you. I think mommy likes my picture."

"Thank you." I turned my eyes down to my hands. In a humble voice, I said, "Can I go? I think we finished here."

"Frank, I am going to get some coffee. Want some?" Houser said as he stood. He took off his jacket and placed it on his chair back. He also loosened his tie. Houser walked to the door. He waited for a moment.

Hawkins replied with a non-committal grunt. He also stood and took off his jacket and loosened his tie.

"I'll take an extra hot double latte stirred clockwise with nonfat whip swirled counterclockwise and drizzled with caramel. Oh yes, and a scone."

"Take your time, Joe. Take ten, guys." Frank said to the air. He turned toward the camera and made universal gesture we all know and love. He pulled his thumb across his neck. The little red light went out on the camera. Oh crap. Frank moved quickly. He flipped the table out of the way and started reaching for me. "I am tired of your smart-ass." As he reached for me, I fell back in the chair and lifted my feet. With my feet braced in his gut, I let his momentum carry him up and over me. I rose to my feet faster than I thought I could. It was faster than Frank did. I did a mental double-take. Frank scrambled up and reached for me again. I took hold of his hand and twisted his wrist in a direction which made him pivot and lose his balance. How the hell did I do that? The door burst open, and all the cops in the world came rushing in. I let go of Frank's hand. I am immediately subdued and cuffed, I offered no resistance.

"Officers, officers, you have it all wrong. Frank here stood to stretch his legs and got a debilitating cramp. He fell to the floor. I was only helping the detective up." I looked Frank right in the eyes.

"Yeah, it's what happened alright. It hurts like hell." He started rubbing at his right calf.

I could feel the officers holding me down relax a bit. Someone entered the room. His voice boomed out with "What's going on? Frank?" I could only guess the voice came from Frank's superior.

"Nothing, Captain. Guys, you can let him go." I could feel my cuffs being unlocked. I craned my neck, but I could only get a glimpse of the Captain's back as he went out of the room.

I heard the captain yelling, "I want to see the playback of this room, and I want to see it now!" There was a pause and some mumbling then even louder, "What do you mean there is no playback? Oh, the camera was off, was it?" The Captain came back into the interrogation room. He is a big man with a barrel chest. His hands are firmly planted on what I guess are his hips. His figure is straight up and down from the waist. By his manner, there is no doubt he leads these men. He started looking at each cop in turn, and each left with no comment. The strain of many years in a stressful job showed on his face. It is cracked with deep lines like a piece of well-used leather. Once it was only the Cap, Hawkins, and me in the interrogation room, the captain broke the silence. "Mr. Embers, I am Captain Wayne Sergeant. No jokes, please. I've heard about you." He stretched out his hand and offered it to me. Oh, I like this guy. We shook hands. He had a firm, steady grip. He squeezed hard enough but not too gentle and not so hard he broke bones. The "Goldilocks" of handshakes. I returned the handshake in kind. "Mr. Embers, I think I know what happened here. Do you wish to file a complaint?"

I started thinking. Both men are looking intently at me. What had Frank Hawkins done? Did he injure me in any way other than waste my time? In fact, I had gotten the best of him in the tussle. Imagine, I kicked his ass. In a purely testosterone chest-thumping Neanderthal way, I am proud of myself. I had mouthed off at him. Do I need anything else on my plate? "Captain Sergeant, nothing happened. Detective Hawkins here only got a leg cramp as I said."

"Are you sure this is how you want to play it?"

"There is nothing to play," I said with conviction. Maybe we can put this interrogation in the past.

"Very well, Frank, make sure you don't have any more leg cramps. I mean, it no more. Let Mr. Embers go on his way unless you have something other than your gut to go on?" Captain Sergeant said in a way which conveyed he expected to be obeyed without question.

"No, Captain. I've nothing to hold him on." Frank spoke meekly like a beaten man. The captain left without further comment. As soon as the captain left the room, Frank Hawkins demeanor changed. Anger flashed across his face. "Don't think this changes anything. I know you're dirty and I don't owe you anything for my leg cramp. Stay here while I do the paperwork to release you." He stomped out and slammed the door shut.

I righted the chairs and table and sat down. I closed my eyes and tried to relax.

"Don't let him rattle you, kid. You don't know why he's acting like a prick," was said by a familiar gravelly rough voice.

I opened my eyes in startled surprise. I pushed back in the chair and stumbled to my feet. "Detective Ralph Daves, aren't you dead?"

Chapter Nine

"Yeah, kid. It surprised the hell out of me too when I found out."

Detective Ralph Daves is standing in front of me, big as life. Well, big as death. He stood about five-foot-ten inches tall. He is a man well past his prime. Grey hair covered his head cut in a short businessman style. He is easily sixty pounds overweight. Jowls hung on the sides of his face, and he has a bit of a turkey wattle under his chin. His breathing sounded labored, and it has a hint of a rattle to it. His cane, ever-present in his left hand, helped steady the man from a knee injury received in the line of duty. Ralph did not look well, but considering he is dead...

I must have snapped. All the stress has finally gotten to me. They'll lock me away with Nurse Ratchet somewhere. What's going to happen to Moiraine? Her mother is knocking on death's door. Charlene's father is too old to raise Mo. She'll become a ward of the state. Ever since that damn trial, my life has been FUBAR. I wish Mark Galos had put two slugs in my head. At least it would have been quick, and my wife and daughter would not be in jeopardy.

My face must have shown shock because Ralph spoke, "Calm down, Nate. You're not crazy. Think about it. We talked the night you were robbed."

"Why didn't you tell me you were dead?" Now there's a sentence nobody expects to say. "I would have kept my mouth shut about talking to you." Look at me talking with a ghost. No wait, maybe Mark did put a couple holes in my brain. Maybe I'm dead, and all this is my personal Hell. It feels like Hell.

"I didn't know I was dead. Things were a little foggy around me. Talking to you that night started to clear away the cobwebs. When the trial came up I was in the courtroom with you, but you didn't see or hear me."

I am scratching my head with this bit of information. Can I see ghosts or not? I had two paths I could follow as I see it. I could deny what is happening to me. I could treat it like an oxygen-starved slow death spiral of my brain before my ultimate demise. Any moment now all this would end. My life would fade to black. Based on what has been happening lately, the idea had a certain appeal.

The other path I could follow is what I perceive as reality. My wife is in the hospital. The cops think I have something to do with it, and I have some drug craving jerk who has had a psychotic break stalking my family. Which is real? What is the truth? Inquiring minds want to know.

I thought of the talk John, and I shared. The words and feeling of our conversation came back to me with the clarity my memory affords. I thought of the look in Blossom's eyes. The trust those eyes conveyed. The comfort I felt at sleeping with her in my lap. I thought of my daughter's laugh, it is so infectious and genuine. I thought of the warmth of her hand in mine as we walk to and from school. The joy I experience at each of her victories in life like her first step, her letting go of her favorite pacifier, and so many others. I've experienced the heartache that would stab at me every time she fell. The agony I feel holding myself back from picking her up and brushing her off. I remembered the pride I felt when she learned she could pick herself up and brush herself off. And finally, I thought of the love my wife and I share. I remember the ecstasy of being one flesh. The slow dragging sorrow at being apart, the wondrous joy of being reunited, the arguments she always wins, the other arguments I always lose, and the creeping fear which filled me. The fear I would lose them both when she carried Moiraine to term. Those things are the truth. They are real.

If talking to ghosts is only a fantasy which makes the nightmares of Mark Galos easier to handle, then better the illusion which exalts me.

"Okay Ralph, what's with Detective Hawkins." Oh, my God I realized I've turned into Jennifer Love Hewitt.

"Nathan, you have to understand why he is coming down so hard on you. When he was still a rookie, I had asked him why he became a cop. He told me this story." A look came over Ralph Daves as he began it is a look of mourning, a look of helplessness.

"When Frank was twelve, he was walking home from school with his kid sister. They were approached by a stranger. The kid had good instincts. He told his sister to run. Frank tried to fight him off. The son-of-a-bitch beat Frank bloody and left him for dead. His sister ran, but she wasn't fast enough. They found her body a few days later. That animal did unspeakable things to her." Ralph remained silent for a few moments. "They never found the bastard. His father blamed him for his sister's death." Ralph let it sit in the air for a moment. "He said some even more harsh things to the boy. It scarred him something fierce. I don't think Frank has ever been the same since. When something endangers children, he sees nothing but his sister. It's like he's fighting the drifter all over again. It ties him up in knots. It also fires his blood. There is no better bloodhound if a child has been hurt or is endangered. All he needs is the whiff of a clue. Then we'll follow the trail to the perp."

"And now for some twisted reason, I've become his white whale."

"Looks like it, son. Best to give Frank a wide berth at least until he learns you had nothing to do with Mark Galos."

I think I've begun to understand Hawkins a little better. I'll still kick his ass if he tries to touch me again, but I understand. "Tell me, Ralph, how do you know I had nothing to do with the psychopath?"

"Over the years as a detective, you develop a gut instinct about those things. Besides anyone who saw the way you reacted to those lowlifes robbing the dead in North Park that dark day would know you couldn't have been on the take with Mark Galos. Also, you're no liar, kid. I can see it in your eyes."

The door to the interrogation room opened with both Detectives Hawkins and Houser filing in. They walked right through Ralph's apparition. It was creepy. Ralph didn't seem to mind, and the detectives didn't notice.

Frank Hawkins slammed a file folder and pen down onto the table. He opened the file to reveal a form with some small print. "Sign it," Detective Hawkins commanded.

"What does it say?" I picked up the form and started to read.

"It's not a confession if it's what you are worried about," Frank said.

"No, it only state's you are declining to file a complaint," Detective Houser said. He sounds pretty reasonable, not at all like he did during the bad cop/bad cop routine.

Ralph Daves moved around behind me. "Yeah, kid. It's the form alright." I picked up the techno quill and signed the form. I tried to hand it back to Detective Hawkins.

"Leave it on the table." Hawkins groused, turned his back on me, and left the room. Detective Houser slightly shook his head no, accepted the form from me, and left the room behind his partner.

As I turned to Ralph, I started to say, "I'm glad ..." Ralph is gone. He disappeared in the ether as it were. "Rest in peace, Detective Ralph Daves."

I thought I heard a whisper of "Thanks, kid," in Ralph's voice but, I wasn't sure. After a moment to contemplate the day's events, I made a beeline out of there to my car. I could see someone had left a note on my car. Oh great, someone had bent my fender or scratched my car's paint. My heart sank as I grew closer. It is not exactly a message from an honest driver who had tapped my car. The note is

the distinctive yellow color of a parking violation. I had
parked longer than is allowed. I grabbed the ticket and
stuffed it into my pocket. I started to laugh. First, it was an
amused chuckle, and it built up from there. Next, I was
laughing so hard I couldn't catch my breath. "Okay, what's
next; a flat tire?" I questioned the universe. I started
laughing anew. While still trying to catch my breath, I
walked around my car to make sure my luck isn't running
that bad.

As it is getting late and I am bone tired, I headed home.
My stomach growled as I realized I haven't had anything to
eat since this morning. I hit the drive-thru of some fast-food
chain. I am not even sure which one. I am only filling the
hole in my gut, and I didn't care with what.

I returned home to Blossom and The Animal Planet
channel. I took care of Blossom's needs and set myself up
for another night in the recliner. I feel so alone.

All my life, I have had a running battle against
depression. Before I had met Charlene, I fought the battle
with Cognitive Therapy. I wouldn't try to feel happy. I tried
not to feel down. If a depressing thought or a painful
memory invaded my consciousness, I would not fight it
straight out. I ignored it. After a time, I noticed I was not
getting depressing thoughts quite as often. The whole
strategy is based on the chemistry of the brain. Somehow
the balance gets out-of-whack. The chemicals start to
propagate themselves, and you spiral down and down until
you are drowned in a cesspool of depression. But if you
can break the cycle of chemical production by stopping
yourself from feeling down, you can give yourself a chance
to one day feel better and then eventually feel happy. I
always related the process to trying to escape a riptide.
When you are caught in a riptide, and you try to swim
directly to shore you will tire yourself out, get nowhere,
and eventually be pulled out to sea and drown. The whole
trick to escaping a riptide is to swim parallel to shore. You

are carried a little further out to sea, but you can move past the danger and eventually make it back to shore. I need a shore. I am so tired of swimming.

I am weary, but I guess Morpheus is not stopping by my house tonight. I need to distract myself. I searched through the files of my memory. I want to call up a time before all these nightmares in my life. I want a memory from before Charlene came into my life. I know my happiest memories are of her and my daughter, but if I remember happy times with them, I don't think I can stand the pain. Instead of picking a memory, I decided to let my mind wander.

We pulled up to my school. "There you go, kiddo." My mother would sometimes call me that.

"I don't want to go to school today."

"What's wrong? Do you have a headache?" My mom always understands about my migraines. She gets them too. She turned and looked at me. She reached up and played a little bit with my hair. It always makes me feel so safe.

"No, Mom. That's not why" I looked down; I feel ashamed.

"Tell me what's wrong. I can't fix it if I don't know what's wrong." Her voice sounded so good. Sometimes it feels so comforting to hear her talk.

"Nobody likes me. Dave, I hate him, pushes me, and calls me names. The teachers never see him being mean to me. I want to go back to my old school."

"I'm sorry, Honey. We moved, and you can't go to your old school. Tell you what you can stay home today. I'll call the school and talk to them." My mom started the car, and we drove home. We were quiet the whole drive home. My mom unlocked the door to the apartment and let me in. "Okay, there you go. Stay out of trouble. Don't make a mess. You can watch TV. I won't bother asking you to clean your room, but it would be a great surprise if you did. You know the number of the shop. Call me if you need me. And

don't open the door for anyone. Okay, I'll see you at dinner time."

"Do you have to go to work today, Mom? I don't want to stay by myself."

"Nathan, we've talked about this before. I don't have a choice. I have to work to pay the bills around here like the rent for this apartment, the lights, and the food we eat."

"Doesn't dad give you money?" I knew I shouldn't have said it the second it came out of my mouth.

"I'll give it to you straight. When your father is here, he gives me the money, but your dad isn't here. He loves us. He just doesn't care enough to be here all the time. I'm sorry I didn't pick a better man to be your father. I have to go. I'll see you tonight," she closed and locked the door.

I watched TV for the rest of the day. I worried about going to school tomorrow. I don't think Dave is going to leave me alone. Maybe I can hide from him at lunch and recess. The phone rang once then stopped and rang again. It is my Mom's secret way to call, so I knew it is her calling. "Hi, Mom, what's up?"

"Honey, I'm going to be late getting home. You'll have to take care of dinner yourself. Don't make too big a mess in the kitchen. Get to bed on time. I'll give you a kiss when I get home. Oh, I called your teacher, and she said she will keep an eye out for trouble between you and Dave. Goodnight, Honey." The phone clicked as she hung up.

The next day of school, Dave started to pick on me again. When I tried to get away, he started to hit me and pushed me down to the ground. I got beat pretty bad until the principal broke up the fight.

The principal had us wait in the office while he called our parents and told them what happened. Dave's mother came first. I heard her hollering at Dave, "I told you not to start any more fights. Wait until your father gets home tonight."

My mother arrived a little while later. "Sorry, Honey, I had a lady under the dryer and couldn't leave. Oh my, are you okay? Your face is pretty bruised, and you have a shiner coming in."

"It hurts, but I'm fine. Can we go home?"

"No. I need to talk with the principal." She stood and banged on his door. The door opened, and she immediately launched into him, "I called yesterday and warned his teacher about that bully. Why wasn't he being watched, and how is that bully being punished?"

"Mrs. Embers, I was not aware of your call, but even if I was, we cannot keep an eye on every child every minute. As far as punishments go, I have decided to let this slide with just a warning to your son; however, if he gets in any more fights, I will suspend him."

"Suspend him? My son does not start fights. I meant the other boy."

"Mrs. Embers, it is between the school and his parents you have no voice in the matter." After their exchange, we left.

After we got home, my mother had a talk with me, "Nathan, did you hit him first?" I said no. "Okay, you don't start fights. How badly did you hurt him?" I told her I didn't hit him. "What? You didn't fight back. Well, that's not right. My son is not a coward. Nathan, you have to stand up to bullies. If you don't draw a line, they will keep pushing you and pushing you. Next time he might bully someone else, and then it would be your fault for not stopping him. You have to fight. Winning or losing is not the point. Standing tall is the point. Promise me if this Dave starts a fight again, you'll fight back as hard as you can."

"Mom, you're telling me to fight him?"

"No, I'm saying you stand up to him. Hit him just as hard as he hits you. Make him pay a price, so he thinks twice the next time he tries to bully someone."

"What if he beats me up again?"

"As long as you fight back and don't run away, you will make me proud."

"I don't know. Dave hits pretty hard."

"Pain doesn't matter. What was it the character, Dr. Spock, from Star Trek said?"

I rolled my eyes a bit, "You mean Mr. Spock? He said, 'Pain is a thing of the mind. The mind can be controlled.'"

"Exactly The pain is of no matter. Do you think his fists can hurt you worse than your migraines?" My mother looked straight at me, waiting for an answer.

"No. Nothing has ever come close."

"Nathan, you can't be afraid of doing what's right because you may get hurt. My son is not a coward." My mother put her arm around me and gave me a little squeeze. "Let me tell you a story. The Spartans of ancient Greece, one of their city-states was called Sparta. The boys of Sparta, from an early age, were taught how to fight and to stand against their enemies. The mothers of that city would say to their sons before they went to war 'Return to me with your shield or on it';" she looked at me intently. "Do you know what it means?" I shook my head. "It means fight and don't give up, with your shield, or die fighting as best you can, on your shield."

I grudgingly said, "Okay, Mom. I will fight back, but he really does hit hard."

What a crappy memory of a crappy day. Why did that day come to mind? I yawned and stretched, then settled myself down to sleep. The fact is I don't think I could stay awake if I wanted to.

Morning came as morning does. I made ready for the day and set off to pick up Mo at John's house. It is time she returned to school, and I returned to my low-wage couple of hours a day job at the crosswalk.

I rang the bell at John's house. "Good to see you, Nate. Come on in. Any news?"

"Sorry, John, I don't have time. I'm heading over to the hospital after dropping Moiraine off at school. I'll give you an update after I talk to the doctors. Is Mo ready?" I looked at the time on my phone, we would barely make it.

"Hi Daddy," came from Moiraine's head as she peaked around her grandfather's leg. "Do I have to go to school today?"

"Yes, you do. Your mother would give me the rough side of her tongue if I kept you out of school any longer. Besides, I'm sure, your friends and teacher miss you."

"Okay, Dad. Grandpa, huggies kissies." John stooped to give Moiraine an extra-long hug and kiss.

We are off to her school. The drive is quiet. I've had a great many quiet drives lately. I'd rather have Char miffed at me and telling me off than this non-noise.

We arrived at the corner where I help children cross to school. There piled about waist high are flowers, candles, balloons, a few stuffed animals, some posters with well wishes, and an array of colorings I could only take as portraits of my wife. I almost broke down right there. Every child at the coroner said a few words to Moiraine. A couple of mothers gave Mo hugs. One father put his hand on my shoulder and gave it a little squeeze. I am touched by the display of support from a gentleman I saw every day yet had never shared a conversation with.

As I crossed the first group to the opposite corner, I noticed the spot where Charlene's blood had been washed clean. One clean patch in an otherwise dirty blacktop is a metaphor of my life and Charlene's, at least until Moiraine came a calling. Walking down from the school is the Principal, Ms. Canon, and another crossing guard.

"Mr. Embers, we need to talk," came from Ms. Canon. "Would you please follow me?" She motioned for the other crossing guard to take over.

I followed her up to the school administration building and back into her office. "Have a seat, Mr. Embers." I haven't been called to the principal's office since I was in grade school. I'm glad they don't have the paddles anymore.

"What's the problem? I called in yesterday and arranged for a sub to cover my shifts."

"No. It has nothing to do with your absence yesterday. Why no one expected you to work yesterday. In fact, I am surprised you came to work today. Let me say we are so sorry about the altercation with your wife yesterday. Tell me, how is she doing?"

"It was not an altercation as you put it." Why do people insist on using polite words for gritty reality? "She was gunned down in the street by a crazed madman," I took a breath and calmed down a bit. "The last I heard she was hanging on. I will be leaving for the hospital shortly after we are through here. I will let you know if anything changes."

"Well, we all hope and pray she will be on the road to recovery soon. The kids miss her terribly."

"Yes, I was touched by the shrine that was erected at the corner for her. I know she loves the kids as much as they love her."

"There is no easy way to say this, Mr. Embers," Ms. Canon looked quite upset over what she is about to say.

"I've found straight out works best. Pull the bandage off quickly as it were." My gut didn't like the way this is going.

"The district has instructed me to give you notice. You are no longer to be the crossing guard here at Greentree Elementary or anywhere else in the district," Ms. Canon is visibly shaken. I think she's taking this harder than I am.

This doesn't surprise me. In fact, I should have seen it coming. "Can you tell me why?" She pulled out a couple of sheets of paper from the top drawer of her desk and handed them to me. They are copies of a letter and some photographs. The pictures are of three children who attend school here at Greentree Elementary. I recognized each one.

To the staff and parents of Greentree Elementary School. So long as Nathan Embers works in or around your school, no child is safe. If I see him there on the grounds or anywhere within a two-block radius of the school, a child dies the next day in front of their friends. The second time I see him there on the grounds or anywhere within a two-block radius, two children will die the next day in front of their friends. I think you can figure out the math of this word problem. If you close the school or alter the children's schedule in any way, I will strike them down in their homes. The streets will run red with the blood of the innocents if I am not obeyed. To show my noble intentions, no child will die this week, but if you don't take this warning seriously, the children will pay. Please inform Mr. Nathan Embers he is not to run or hide from me. The day of his reckoning is coming. The manner of his death is yet to be determined. Please tell him the police can't help him. If he goes to the police for help or protection, it will only get cops killed. Tell him when the time comes, he must face me like a man and not like a coward. To prove to you this letter is in fact from me and not some hoax I have placed my thumbprint at the bottom of the page. Yours Truly, Mark Galos. Have a nice day."

I crushed the letter in my hand as I finished reading it. I let the paper fall to the ground. It is an impotent act of defiance. It is all I have been since that night at the store. Impotent. The son-of-a-bitch. It's not evil enough he came after me at the crosswalk; now, he will come after kids or cops if I don't wait around for him to kill me. What am I going to do? What can I do? Too damn little is what I can do. "I assume since this is a copy the police have been called and they confirmed this letter is indeed from Mark Galos."

"Yes, they confirmed it's from him. They asked us not to inform the parents. They are afraid he will keep his promise. I have to ask you not to tell anyone. I'm also to tell you the police want you to contact them as soon as possible. They are not taking any chances about Mark Galos watching you, so they want you to call them at this number." Ms. Canon handed me a business card listing Detective Frank Hawkins.

"How am I to get Moiraine to school if I can't come within two blocks?"

"We have made arrangements to have a special services bus to pick her up and drop her off." Ms. Canon stood up and held out her hand. "I'm sure you understand I would like you to leave as soon as possible. If he is watching you, I don't want to antagonize him. I'll pull Moiraine out of class and tell her she is taking a bus from now on."

I shook Ms. Canon's hand and started to leave her office.

"Mr. Embers, I'm sorry, but I need the vest, whistle, and stop sign back." I removed the vestments of my office and placed them on her desk. All the while, the opening song to the TV show Branded played in the background of my thoughts.

"...Branded, scorned as the one who ran. What do you do when you're branded, and you know you're a man..."

How well the song echoes my feelings. I left Ms. Canon's office without further delay. In my retreat, I took a detour to the teacher's lounge. They have a vending machine there, and I needed a Diet Pepsi. I put a dollar in the machine. It came back out. Crap! It's my only single. I tried in vain again. Crap, I want one in the worst way. It's comforting to have the cold feel of the can in my hand, the crisp sound of the pop-top as it would open, and the tingle as it went down my throat. I need one right now. I need something normal right now. I tried reversing the creases. No luck. I tried rubbing it on the edge of a table. No good.

Okay, I'll give it one more try. I put the dollar into the machine. Wait, I hear it whirling and clicking then silence. My dollar came back out.

I screamed at the universe, "Okay, God. Come down here and fight me fair!" I pounded my head against the vending machine. In my field of view, as my head rested against the vending machine, there appeared a delicate French manicured hand with a dollar bill in it.

"Give this one a try."

I swapped my dollar for the one before my eyes. I put it in and presto-change-o my Diet Pepsi was spit out of the machine. "Thank you, Ms." I turned, and no one is there. Strange, wait a minute I know that hand, the tow truck driver. She must have a child enrolled here.

I popped the can and chugged the Diet Pepsi until it was gone. It burned so joyfully as it went down. "Alrighty then," I said to no one in particular. With the minor victory, I marched out of the school.

I crossed the corner I used to guard and stood looking at the improvised shrine to my Charlene. It is strange. It is like I can feel their well wishes for my wife. It is like the buzzing you hear when you walk close to high power lines, but beyond hearing it, it is more like remembering hearing it. While I was there, a young boy came running for the light. He is not going to make it. I threw out my arm, stooped a little, and grabbed him as he would have entered the crosswalk.

"I'm late, I have to cross."

"Timmy, right?" of course I am right. "Hold on. There will be another light in a minute. You could have gotten hurt." Timmy looked up at me, and the expression of recognition came to his face.

"You're the crossing guard. Where's your sign and stuff?"

"I am not the crossing guard anymore." I'm not anything anymore. Like a ship, without a rudder, I am adrift with no course.

"You helped Mrs. E, didn't you? Is she going to be okay? This picture here," he pointed to a picture of someone in a classroom overlooking children at work, "I drew it to help her feel better." Breathe Timmy breathe. "She's pretty. If she weren't married, I would marry her." I couldn't help but smile at the statement.

"My heart hopes she will recover too. Get ready the signal is about to change. And yes, you are right, she is pretty. I think I would try to marry her too if she weren't already married. Okay, it's green. I'll cross with you." *It is my last and unofficial crossing there at Greentree Elementary.* It makes me feel a little sad this part of my life is over. The sense of satisfaction I have looking over the children at this crossing is lost. With Timmy's picture in hand, I headed back to my car. Tapping the dashboard, I said, "Come on, Old Girl. We have the wife to visit." Off I went.

I walked into my wife's room. John is there talking quietly to his daughter. John looks worse; the strain is starting to affect him. I love Char with all my heart, but I can't imagine the torment John is going through. A man should not have to contemplate outliving his child. I stepped back out to give him a few moments more. As I turned to walk down to the waiting room to kill some time, Dr. Hazer came walking up.

"Mr. Embers, I'm glad you are here. This will save you from getting an impersonal phone call." My heart sank. A welling of emotions came pouring up. I suppressed everything and steadied myself. "I have the results of the CT, and it's worse than I feared. I'm afraid your wife suffered a stroke while she was in surgery. It affected some key areas of her brain. I'm sorry to tell you this, but it is only a matter of time. All we can do is make her comfortable."

"I've heard of new drugs which are supposed to help stroke victims. What about one of those. If our insurance coverage is a problem, I'll pay any price. I'll cover any charge."

"Money is not the problem, Mr. Embers. It's too late for those drugs. Those drugs must be administered within a few hours of the onset of a stroke. The parts of her brain which were cut off by the stroke have already died. It's not something we can fix. For all intents and purposes she is already dead; her body just doesn't know it yet," Dr. Hazer said all this with pain in his voice, but also with the practice of someone who has said these words to others.

"Did you tell her father yet?" I could not look at Dr. Hazer in the eye. I looked down at my right hand instead. It is the one I used to plug the hole in her heart. I could see my wife's blood. Her blood is on my hands. I had killed her as sure as if I had pulled the trigger myself. Out, damned spot! Out I say!

"No. I can explain it to him if you want."

"It should come from me. How long does Char have?"

"It's not an exact science. She could pass away in a few days or a few weeks. No more than four weeks at the outside. Tell me, is your wife a strong woman?"

"She is herculean."

"I would say you have some time before she goes. There will be changes which will tell us when she is close."

"I would like to take her home. I know she would rather be there surrounded by family than here in a cold hospital."

"Moving her might hasten her death, or she may even die as she is being transported."

"Does it matter? Home and with family is what matters."

"Very well, I will sign an order she is to be released to hospice care. I had a hunch it would be your request. Here are the representative's name and the number to Geneva's Hospice. They can help you with all the forms and arrange for transport." Dr. Hazer handed me a card and pamphlet to explain hospice care. "I hope you and your family will never need my services again," he stretched out his hand. I shook it. A fine firm handshake and warm too. I thought all doctors soaked their hands in ice water. Dr. Hazer took a few steps away, paused for a moment, turned around, and walked back to me. "During our training to become doctors, they tell us we need to be detached from our patients, objective. I failed that part of my training. Mr. Embers, Nathan. May I call you Nathan?" I nodded. "Nathan, I know I am supposed to be the spokesman for reason and science, but I want you to know I believe this is a wondrous universe we live in. There are many unexplained phenomena, things which defy logic, and there are miracles. My own hands have done things in the operating room, which are beyond my skill. All my training and experience tells me your wife is going to die, but I hope, against all reason, she will be one of those miracles." As we shook hands again, Dr. Hazer leaned in and whispered, "By the way, I liked the way you told doctor self-righteous-pompous-ass off."

I went into Charlene's room. John had finished his one-way conversation. He is sitting there, patting her hand. I gave a little cough to let him know I am there. He straightened up in the chair. He pulled a handkerchief from his pocket and blew his nose. "John, we have to talk." I don't know if it is in my tone, the words I said, or the fact Char had not shown any improvement, but John already knew what I was going to tell him. He sat there and wept. I couldn't cry with him right now I have too many things I must do. When John stopped crying, I told him of my plans to take Char home and about Hospice care.

"Damn right she should pass at home. There is something I've been working on. It's a gift for her birthday.

146

I would like to finish it before you take her home. How long do you think I have before they move her?"

"My guess is no sooner than tomorrow afternoon. What are you making?"

"It's a surprise, my boy. I have to hurry if I want to finish it." John managed to stand up. The last few days have not been easy on him. He leaned down and kissed Charlene's forehead. "I'll give you a call when I'm done and ready to bring it over."

"John, don't push yourself too hard. Charlene would not want your health to suffer over a birthday gift for a dying woman," my voice cracked as I said dying.

"You let me worry about it," John moved out of the room fired by his purpose.

I placed the picture Timmy had made for her on the nightstand next to the picture my daughter had drawn. I sat down in the torture chair next to her bed. I started telling Charlene about the plans to take her home. I started telling her about Mark Galos' threat, the fact I can talk to ghosts, and a thousand other details of the last few days. It is like a dam burst, and it was spewing out of my mouth. It is comforting to talk to her. I only wish she could talk back.

Three times a chime sounded over the speakers, and then came an announcement, "Code blue, room 862." It repeated three times. There is some bustle outside my wife's room with doctors and nurses running down the hallway.

A man stood in the doorway wearing a hospital gown. He is of average height with graying black hair which needed a comb, and he is also in need of a shave. He said, "Excuse me, buddy. Do you know what's going on?"

"I don't know what to tell you. I think someone is in trouble down the hall. I would try to stay out of the doctors' way."

The man stood there a second. He cocked his head like he heard something. "I think I hear some music calling me.

See you around. Oh, I hope she gets better." He turned around and started walking away. He gave me a complete view of his full moon. It is a sight I wish I could unsee. As he walked away, he started to fade away with no smoke, no mirrors just gone.

Well, that's something you don't see every day. I felt a shiver run down my spine. I pulled out my phone and called Geneva's Hospice. I made all the arrangements to have Charlene moved to our house and have her needs cared for until the end came. It confused me as to how easy it is to make these preparations for Char. Will her final preparations be as easy? Somehow, I knew they would not.

My phone went off. I saw who the caller is and sighed. "Hello, Detective Hawkins, how are you this day?"

"None of your so-called humor, Embers. Why didn't you call the moment you left Greentree?" Detective Hawkins' anger is oozing out of the phone.

"Sorry, Detective Hawkins, but I've been a little busy with my wife's dying and all."

"Oh…, I'm sorry. You have my sympathy. Still, you should have called. We have a madman to catch." The tone of his voice changed a bit. Well, what do you know, he's not a total dick after all. "We want to put a tail on you. We plan to catch him as he tries to kill you." Okay, he's back to being a dick.

"I have an idea. Catch Mark Galos before he tries to kill me. You know. Do the whole Law and Order thing." The theme to *"Law and Order"* played in my mind.

"What do you think we've been doing since your wife was shot? More than half the damn force is out looking for him. This Mark Galos is a ghost. The last sighting of him was your 9-1-1 call. We don't believe he has left the area either. The letter was not mailed. It was left at the school."

"What about his parents? Did you stake their house out?"

"We're not stupid, Embers. His parents say he hasn't been there. I don't think they would lie either as they want him caught too. Okay, Embers, maybe you don't understand how this goes, but I'm the cop, not you. Besides, we have some other ideas beyond putting a tail on you. If Mr. Galos contacts you in any way, let us know and for heaven's sake, stay away from the school. In fact, best not to go near any schools. If you go near a school and a kid so much as skins their knee, you'll wish Mark Galos had shot you. We'll be in touch." Frank Hawkins hung up the phone. Galos had them rattled. Threatening children like this, he has to be crazy. What the hell did I do to deserve such hate? I put my mind to work on it as I have other problems in the past. Something will spark an aha moment.

"Mr. K R A P playing Aha as requested."

"...Take me on Take me on..." I grumbled in my mind and the music stopped.

I sat there with Char for most of the rest of the afternoon, but it is time for me to return home. I have to be there when Moiraine is dropped off by the bus.

I waited for the bus by the curb in front of our house. It pulled up right next to me. It is one of those smaller buses more like a van. This van is equipped with a lift and an extra-wide door for handicapped children. The driver opened the door and activated the lift to let my daughter out. I said to the driver, "You know she can get out the regular passenger door."

The driver answered me by saying, "State regs say we have to use the lift. I don't think the committee which thought up the rules ever considered a non-handicapped child would ever use it. Our tax dollars hard at work."

I grunted my agreement. Moiraine is saying goodbye to the other kids on the bus and hugged one young girl in a wheelchair. She stood on the lift and waited.

"Wee," my daughter invoked as she rode down. It is not exactly an E-ticket ride, but she enjoyed it.

"Come on, Honey, we have to make the house ready."

"Ready for what, Daddy?"

"Your Mom is coming home for a little while. I'll tell you more when we are inside." I turned to the bus driver, "Thank you for bringing her home safe."

He walked around to the driver-side door and opened it. "It's what they pay me for." He drove off to his next stop.

The afternoon and evening were not amusing. Cleaning house has never been my strong suit. Explaining to Moiraine her mother is coming home to die is a misery I would wish on no one. I think she understood as best as a five-year-old can. Still, I think it is not real to her.

When bedtime came around, she wanted to sleep where her mother usually slept. I saw no harm in it, so I let her. I kissed her goodnight then tucked her in on her mother's side of the bed. Mo had the teddy bear from her ambulance ride with her. I tucked him in too. She took in a deep breath. "It smells like Mommy." I felt a tear roll down my face. As I made my way out of the room, I could hear Moiraine whispering words of comfort to her teddy bear.

Life is going to be tough without Charlene to help me raise Mo. John had raised Charlene for most of her life without the benefit of her mother. Maybe I can pick up some pointers. These thoughts invaded my mind as I started drifting off to sleep.

Chapter Ten

I could feel myself floating up, yet I stood in my living room. Looking all around me, everything is clear, but there is no light. Looking down at the recliner, I could see myself sleeping with Blossom on my lap. These dreams are the strangest. Walking through the house to my bedroom, I saw Moiraine is asleep with the teddy bear in a death grip of a hug. Is Charlene dreaming of Mo? The instant I thought of Char, but before the thought was complete, I stood in the hospital room where my wife lay. The false sense of movement is going to make me toss my cookies one day. Taking motion sickness pills before bedtime is a definite plan if this keeps up.

"I wish I could talk to you." Her body started to look fuzzy then it is like she lifted herself up, but her body remained in the bed. She is translucent. In fact, more so than the last time, I had one of these dreams. She stood there, smiling at me. I reached out to touch her cheek. My hand passed right through her. You would think I could touch my own wife in my own dream. I screamed my frustration.

"Nathan, not so loud people are sleeping." Her voice is rapture to my ears, but it is softer than before. I strained to hear her. "Nathan, I'm scared. I've tried to wake-up. Nothing I do seems to help. What's wrong? Why can't I wake-up?"

What am I to say to my dream? Not only is she dying in the real world, but she is also fading in the twilight world of my dreams. "The doctor says you're dying." I couldn't bear to see these visions any longer. Willing myself to leave, I began to feel the strange moving without moving sensation.

"Nathan, don't leave me alone." I could hear Charlene start to cry.

I am in my living room again. My body is still there in the recliner. My heart sank as the words my wife said faded in my ears. Suddenly a notion hit me. Smack right down to the pit of my stomach. I sat back down in my body. My eyes instantly opened. Blossom stirred, and I pick her up off my lap and put her down in her bed. Without any protest, she quickly went back to sleep.

A glimmer of hope sent me on a mission. Quickly I dressed. With a spare blanket from the closet, I bundled Mo up in it. She never even woke up. She nuzzled into my shoulder. Frantically I raced out to the car and put Moiraine in her car seat. I drove like a man possessed for I am possessed with the hope of somehow my wife still lives. We made it to the hospital in record time. Stabbing at the up button of the elevator, I said, "Come on. Come on," I pushed the button again. It is a futile gesture, but I don't care. The bell dinged, and the doors opened. The ride up to my wife's room took forever. My daughter stirred in my arms.

"Daddy, where are we?" She said as she yawned.

"Go back to sleep, Honey." The bell rang again, and the doors opened. I pushed past the doors as the space allowed. With my daughter in my arms, I ran to my wife's room. The room is dark, but enough light leaked in from the hallway I could see the shadowy shape of my wife in the bed. I turned on the light and walked up to her bedside. Tear tracks are running down the sides of her head. My wife had been crying. The room started to spin. Putting Moiraine down next to her mother in the bed, she rolled over a bit and snuggled up to her mom. Mo took in a breath.

"Mommy," Moiraine said.

Setting down in the chair by her bed, I tried to understand it all. Did I talk to Charlene in my sleep? She was crying as I left in the dream. She is crying here in her hospital bed. Dr. Hazer said she is dead and her body just

152

didn't know it yet. Is my wife dead? Is it why I could talk to her? Is she still alive, and that's why I could only talk to her in my dreams. Am I grasping at straws? There are so many strange things happening to me. I gazed around the room to see if Rod Serling is talking to the audience. So many questions, and so few answers.

Once I felt my legs were steady again, I walked to the nurse's station. "Ms., I am visiting my wife. She is the woman in room 865. I think she is waking up; I saw her crying. Please, come check," there is near panic in my voice.

"Her eyes are most likely irritated. It happens all the time, but I will check on her." The nurse came into Char's room. When she saw Mo sleeping in the bed with Charlene, she became frustrated with me. "Sir, your child should not be in your wife's bed. Please remove her so I can work." I wondered if they put this nurse on the night shift because she is such a bitch when there is no need. She began doing all those things nurses do. She checked Char's pulse, looked in her eyes, checked her blood pressure, and tried to wake her. "I am sorry, sir, but there is no change in her condition." The nurse left. What was I thinking? It was only a dream. I stood there with Moiraine in my arms and looked down at my wife. Grabbing a tissue to wipe the tears off my wife, I leaned down and kissed my wife tenderly on her lips.

Whispering into Moiraine's ear, I said, "Okay, my little crumb cruncher, let's return you to your bed."

"Goodnight, Mommy." She said with a yawn. Mo had never even opened her eyes.

The switch clicked loudly when I turned the lights back out and closed the door. Driving us home, the song *"All I Have to Do Is Dream"* by The Everly Brothers is playing gently in the background of my thoughts.

It is my turn for bed. I tried to recapture the magic of my last dream. The dream did not come. I am failing at a great many endeavors as of late.

The alarm on my cell phone went off. It is time to make ready for the day. I got Moiraine up and dressed for school. Breakfast was made and eaten. How quickly I had started to slip into a routine without Char. The thought tortured me with guilt, and I broke down and cried.

We waited for the bus at the curb. It came by shortly, and Mo was off to school. My heart sank, missing the walk to school, with no longer crossing the kids at Greentree, and yes, I even miss my old boring, run-of-the-mill life.

My phone went off with a text from John saying he is on the way over to the house with Charlene's birthday present. Well, I didn't want to wait twiddling my thumbs, so I started in on the household chores laundry, breakfast dishes, and the like. At about ten a.m. I phone went off with a text from John asking me to come out and give him a hand with Char's birthday present. What the …?

There, parked in the street, is a U-Haul truck with John standing beside it. I walked down to the street to see what John had in mind. He looks grave. His face is chalky and had a fine sheen of perspiration. His breathing is a little labored also.

"John, sit down. You look worn-out. Take a rest. They said they are bringing Charlene over later this afternoon. We have hours to unload the truck." He nodded a couple of times, and I helped him to slowly sit down right there on the curb. "Can I get you a glass of water or something?"

"No, Nathan, thank you. A breather is all I need. I've been up all night doing the finishing touches on Charlene's birthday present."

"What did you make her?"

"Oh, wait till you see it, son. I made her a bed a fine canopy bed. I made it with these." He held up his hands. "They had the magic last night my boy. I have been

154

working on the bed off and on since Charlene was about Mo's age. I never had the time to finish it. I never made the time to finish it. I was too busy with life. You know getting food on the table. Making sure Char had all the things she needed. But I finished it last night. Well, early this morning."

"John, you worked yourself half to death. Is it so important?"

"Important!" John raised his voice and started to stand. I gently pulled him back down. "I promised her the bed, and by God, I am going to see she got it! I had promised her the bed, but I kept finding things more urgent. Now it is the most urgent thing I could do for my little girl. Lord knows I tried to do right by her my whole life. It is the one promise I ever made to her I never fulfilled. I am going to keep my promise to her even if it killed me."

"John, you look like it almost did. You sit there awhile. I'll get her bedroom ready for the bed." He shook his head yes and sat there. I went into my bedroom and stripped the bed of the sheets and blankets. I dismantled the bed and took the pieces and placed them out of the way in the living room. I looked at the space where the bed was expecting to see a warren of dust bunnies. There is not one bunny. "My God woman, did you ever do anything in this house but clean?" Then I remembered a few things we had done in this house which weren't cleaning. I smiled. A cold shower is in order, I think.

I started the process of unloading the truck and moving everything into the bedroom. The bed is a huge California King. How did John load it onto the truck by himself? I remembered my own musing on women and the strength they give men. It seems it is not only the woman we share our life with who gives us strength, but also our daughters who can give us strength. I understood how he loaded the truck. As I unloaded the truck, I refused any help from John. He has me worried. I am going to need his wisdom and insight if I am going to raise Moiraine by myself, so I promoted him to a supervisory position.

The bed is made of a luxurious walnut wood deep and rich. It is solid too, and the whole thing fits together like a giant three-dimensional jigsaw puzzle. The really amazing thing is it doesn't need any bolts or screws, no hardware at all. All the seams met perfectly. There are no gaps. You could not fit a sheet of paper between the boards. He even managed to align the grain of the wood to match up. I put the bed together, and if I didn't remember how it all came together, I could not find the joints. The headboard is a marvel. It is one large piece, carved with a beautiful mural. Beginning on the left is a depiction of a young John and Marlene looking down into a crib at Charlene as an infant. Next, there is a little girl at play in a room filled with dolls. As my eyes followed the scenes, moments appeared in the wood from Charlene's life. The first day of school is next. Then a scene where she is as a young teen with two faces back to back with one side playing with dolls and on the other side looking into a mirror and putting on make-up. The next scene is Charlene as a young woman wearing a cap and gown with a diploma in hand. Next, there is a scene of Charlene in her wedding dress. You could clearly see the detail of the lace in her gown. John captured her beauty too. The last scene of the mural is of both Charlene and me looking down into a crib with Moiraine fast asleep.

Awestruck is the only way I can describe how I feel. "John, this isn't a bed. It's a work of art. Charlene would have loved it. I wish she could have seen it."

"Me, too, my boy," I could hear the regret in his voice.

"I'm not sure I like the idea of you and Marlene's likeness looking down on us while we sleep. I guess I could cover you guys up at night." It got a bit of a chuckle from John. "John, I'm going to need your help in the years to come. Moiraine is going to need your help in the years to come. I want you to know because your daughter will be passing; it doesn't mean you won't be a part of our lives. Our daily lives. I am also going to make you a promise. I will not marry or even date so long as Moiraine is under my roof."

"Son, that's a long time to be without the comfort of a good woman." I could sense a true feeling of concern from John.

"Moiraine will have a tough enough time in this world without having to deal with the drama of a step-mother. Perhaps after Mo is up and out, I'll marry again. I tell you though, Charlene will be a hard act to follow." I paused for a moment. "John, why didn't you remarry? I'm sure you had the opportunity."

John gave me a little smile, "The same as you." I've never been affectionate with John. A handshake or a pat on the back has always been the extent of our relationship. But I felt an overwhelming need to pull him into a hug. He returned the demonstration in kind. It lasted only a moment.

John helped me make the bed ready for Charlene. I pulled out Char's favorite bed linens. They are way too flowery for my taste so, Char uses them sparingly. She only pulls them out a few times a year. She always puts them on the bed on the first day of spring and a couple other times as her mood demands. As John and I worked, I couldn't help but notice what a striking woman Charlene's mother was. Her face is familiar. "John, I can see where Charlene gets her beauty. Your wife was very attractive. Char keeps a picture of you in the house, but she has never put any pictures of her mother out."

"Well, she passed away when Charlene was only a little older than Moiraine. I didn't have the heart to keep pictures of Marlene around. It broke my heart every time I saw her picture. It still does." John sniffed. "Oh, she was a beautiful woman. The carving of mine didn't do her justice. Here let me show you." John pulled out his wallet and showed me a picture of Marlene. The photo is old, creased, and tattered. It showed them both mugging for the camera. He was in his army uniform, and she was wearing a nurse's outfit. He is right, the carving didn't do her justice.

A nurse's outfit? The nurse in Char's room was the spitting image of John's wife. I looked at the carving again with new eyes. The bed is in the recurring dream of mine with the psychopath killing me. Killing us. This shit is getting too weird.

With the bed made, everything is ready for Charlene's return home. There is nothing left to do but wait. John and I chit-chatted for a time, then I made us lunch. It was nothing fancy. I made grilled cheese sandwiches, and we split a can of tomato soup. Normally it is one of my favorite lunchtime repasts. Today it tasted of ash. My wife is coming home to die.

Ding-Dong. The doorbell went off. Standing at the door is a middle-aged woman with short brown hair styled to give it height. Her face had a pinched look to it like she had been eating lemons. She wore blue scrubs with a pattern of yellow ducks covering them. "Nathan Embers? Hello, my name is Ms. Barton. I'm the hospice nurse assigned to this patient. I believe they told you to expect me." She started to come right in. When I didn't move out of her way instantly, she put her hand on my chest and started to gently push me until her path was clear. "I need to see where the patient will be placed."

"My wife, Charlene, will be staying in our bedroom. Follow me." I lead her to the bedroom, where she started her inspection.

"Yes, yes this will do handsomely. Lovely bed by the way," she said as she reached out and caressed the wood. "I assume you plan to sleep elsewhere." I nodded. "Good. I need you to bring in a chair. Please make it one with some cushions my back, you know. Here is a list of supplies I will need for the patient's care." She handed me a short but precise list of supplies. "I also will need a list of allowed visitors for the patient."

"Her name is Charlene, not patient."

"Mr. Embers, let me explain to you. Make no mistake. I am not here for your comfort. I am here for Charlene's comfort. With you, I am all business with your wife. I will be a caregiver. I have been with hospice care for fifteen years and counting. I learned a long time ago you need to stay a little distant from the family of a patient. You may request another nurse if you like, but I don't think you'll find a better one."

"I want it clearly understood she is a person and not a nameless patient."

"Of course, she's a person, Mr. Embers," her voice had changed. It is now filled with kindness and compassion. "Understand this before your wife passes, she and I will be friends. I will grieve when she passes. But, before all that, I must be business first, so nothing interferes with her care. Can you understand that?" She is looking at me straight in the eyes, waiting for my answer. There is a belief you can look into a person's soul when you gaze into their eyes. Here is a decent soul, a little gruff maybe, but a decent soul.

"Yes, I can understand. Can you pardon me for being a little touchy?"

"Nothing to pardon. Now I need a list of people allowed to visit and everyone who lives here." I gave her the information she requested. After filling out and signing a plethora of forms, Ms. Barton went to tell the ambulance drivers they could bring in Charlene.

I went shopping for everything Ms. Barton said she would need and to get out from underfoot while Char is being settled. John stayed behind to mind the fort and continue his role as supervisor.

When I returned after shopping, the ambulance was gone. I grabbed the bags out of the car and headed inside. I am greeted by the sound of Blossom's tail thumping and John's gentle snoring. He is stretched out on the couch. The poor guy was tuckered out from his labor of love.

I walked into my bedroom and set down the bags. Charlene is in her bed hooked up to a small monitor on the nightstand. Somehow, she looked more at peace. Maybe on some level, she knows she is home. Ms. Barton is sitting in the chair in the corner of the room, quietly knitting a scarf or sweater or whatnot. I asked, "How did she handle the move?"

"She handled it quite well. Your father-in-law, on the other hand, had a hard time of it."

"It has been hard on him. It has been hard on all of us." After an awkward pause in the conversation, I asked, "Is there anything I can get for you coffee, tea, or a Diet-Pepsi?" She grimaced at the Diet-Pepsi. Obviously, she is a woman with no taste.

She said, "No, thank you," and went back to her knitting.

It is about time for Moiraine to return home from school, so I walked out to the curb and waited for the bus. I wanted her to see me there, waiting for her. It was close. The bus arrived a couple minutes earlier than yesterday.

"Hi, Daddy. Is mommy home?"

I held out my hand to my little girl, and she took it. "Yes, Mo, your mommy is home."

"Is she going to get better now?"

I couldn't bring myself to answer. Together we walked into the house. She dropped her backpack at the front door and went running to her mother. I shook my head and picked up her backpack and put it in her room. I could hear her talking to her mother. She was telling her about her day and how all the other kids are asking about her. My heart ached at hearing the hope in this little girl's voice.

John woke up from all the ruckus my little crumb cruncher made. He stretched as he said, "Oh, I'm sorry falling asleep on you guys. It was very rude of me."

"No worries, John. It's just as well you woke up I have something to talk to you about. Can I ask you to do a favor for me?" John nodded. "Can you be here tomorrow when Mo gets home? There is a matter I need to attend to," I tried to keep my voice light, but some emotion squeaked out.

"What's the matter, son? Is it something I can take care of for you?"

"Thanks for the offer, John, but this matter needs my personal attention." Looking at John while I talked is too difficult, so I had to feign disinterest while I walked into the kitchen. "It's not a big deal, but I have to take care of it tomorrow." Banging pots and pans in the kitchen like I was starting to get dinner ready, but I am in no mood to cook. My mood is awful; therefore, the food would taste awful. "You know I don't feel like cooking. I'm going to take Moiraine out for some dinner. Do you want to tag along?"

"I'd love to Nate, but I'm still weary from my efforts last night. I'm going to head home, make a sandwich, and turn in early." He stood up and walked to the bedroom where Mo is still talking to her mother. I followed him in. Moiraine is up on the bed next to her mother sitting cross-legged and having a merry old conversation. Nurse Barton had an even more sour look on her face. She obviously didn't like having Mo up on the bed with Charlene. John leaned down to his daughter, held her hand, and gave her a kiss on the forehead. "I'll see you tomorrow." He looked at Mo. "I'll see you tomorrow too." He turned around and left the room.

"Come on, Mo. We're going out for dinner. Ms. Barton, would you like us to bring you back something?" She answered in the negative. I picked up Mo and headed to the car.

Moiraine's mouth is going a mile a minute talking about how great it is to have mommy home, and she should wake up soon. I hate to say it, but I tuned her out a bit. My heart can't take it.

With all the distractions of recent events, I have neglected to fill the car with gas. It is running on fumes. I stopped at the local gas station to fill the tank. While I was standing there watching the counter spin up, I noticed an elderly woman trying to put gas in her car and failing miserably at it. She tried and tried to get the nozzle in correctly, but couldn't manage it. I couldn't stand to see her helpless anymore. I finished my fill up and walked over to her.

"Excuse me, madam. Are you in need of a little assistance?"

"Oh my, heavens, yes. My husband usually takes care of the car, but he can't leave the house anymore, and this is the first time I've needed gas."

"No problem. Let me show you how to do this." I demonstrated all the steps from paying for the gas first to inserting the nozzle into the tank to putting the nozzle back. "Have you checked the oil lately?"

"No, I haven't. Is it important?"

Smiling, I said, "Yes, it is. Let me show you." First, I showed her how to open the hood. I located the dipstick and showed her how to check the oil. "You might want to take an automotive course at a community college. They have classes to teach people, like you, basic car care."

"I will look into it. Tell me, how much do I owe you for your trouble?" She reached into her purse and pulled out her wallet.

"I couldn't take anything. I really didn't do anything."

"No, I insist," she pulled out a five-dollar bill and tried to push it into my hand.

I refused to close my fingers on the bill and took a half step back. "If you feel like you should pay me, take the money and give it to the Red Cross, or Jerry's kids, or any charity you wish, but my chivalrous nature won't let me take it."

She slowly put the money back in her wallet and closed her purse. "Very well, young man. I want to thank you for being my hero today."

"I'm no hero."

"You are to me." The next car in line blared its horn. The woman turned from me to look straight at the driver, stuck out her tongue, then flipped him the bird. I choked on a laugh. She returned to her car and drove away.

Returning to my own car, I started it up and headed for the restaurant.

"I saw what you did, Daddy. You helped the old lady. It was nice, but why did you help her?"

"She needed help, and I had a debt to pay back."

"You're funny, Daddy, but I still love you," Moiraine went back to entertaining herself for the rest of the drive.

We returned straight home after dinner. Moiraine, untold, started to get ready for bed. She zipped off to do her nightly chores. Walking into my bedroom, I saw Ms. Barton talking to my wife as she attended to her evening needs. She didn't notice me standing in the doorway. After listening for a moment, I began to feel like I am eavesdropping on a private conversation. With a little cough, I walked in. Ms. Barton immediately stopped talking to my wife. She finished up what she was doing for Char. She went back to the chair and her knitting.

"Any changes?" I asked as I looked down at my wife.

"She had some trouble breathing, so I gave her something to ease it. Other than that, she has been quiet."

"Please tell me she is not in any pain."

"No. She is resting quite comfortably."

"What time does your relief come?"

"There won't be a relief nurse. I like to stay with the patients... I'm sorry. I'll stay with her until the end. It is how I like to work if you don't mind?"

"No problem. I think Charlene would like it. When you need privacy to take a shower or whatever, just lock the bedroom door. Oh, to give you a heads up, I will be gone most of the day tomorrow. Charlene's father will arrive sometime before Mo gets out of school to see to her needs." I grabbed my toothbrush, razor, and assorted bathroom needs. I also grabbed the clothes I am going to wear tomorrow, so I wouldn't disturb Ms. Barton in the morning. "Well, I'll be turning in. Goodnight."

"Goodnight, Mr. Embers."

"Considering everything, I think you can call me Nathan or Nate if you prefer."

"I thank you, Mr. Embers; however, as I said before, our relationship is a business one. I prefer to use last names. I think using first names tends to blur the line between the nurse and the family. In my business, it is hard enough without getting attached to the family as well."

"I never considered that. It must be difficult doing what you do."

She answered as she continued with her knitting and never looked up. "It has its rewards. Goodnight, Mr. Embers."

I guessed the conversation is over, so I turned around and left the room. After readying for bed, I checked on Moiraine's preparations. She was done getting ready for bed and was quietly coloring in the living room sitting next to Blossom. Blossom's tail was thumping in her usual rhythmic pattern. Sitting down on the couch and watching Mo do her art is peaceful. The time passed swiftly as we sat there together in the living room, but it is starting to get late. "Mo, it's time for bed." She put her coloring away, then went running to give her mom a kiss goodnight. After she was done saying goodnight to her mom, I guided her to her own bed.

"Okay you, we need to tuck you in." Moiraine crawled into her bed. "Tuck, tuck, tuck, tuck," I said as I pushed her covers into her sides as she laid there in her bed. I gave her a kiss and started for the door.

"Daddy, can I have my teddy bear?"

"Sure, Honey." I retrieved the bear from the dark day and put it right beside her. I started my retreat again.

"Daddy, can I have the guys too?"

"Are you okay, Honey? You haven't slept with all the guys in a long time." The guys are all of her sleeping toys. It is an assortment of Buzz Lightyear, Jack Skellington, and assorted Winnie the Pooh characters.

"I'm fine. I just miss them all. Can I sleep with them?"

"Of course, you can." I gather the guys up from their respective places all over her room. I put them all around her on the bed all the while muttering something about coming in with flamethrowers to clear out the mess.

"What did you say, Daddy? I didn't hear you."

"Nothing, Honey. Go to sleep now." Slipping out the door, I made my escape. It is still too early for me to go to bed, so I turned on the idiot box. Not wanting to disturb Ms. Barton if she is trying to sleep, I turned down the volume. As usual, there is nothing on worth watching. Maybe Char has been right; we should have cable canceled and use the savings for more important things. When I had asked her what things, she smiled and said shoes. I asked her how many shoes a woman needs. She only smiled again and didn't answer. Do I really want to know the answer to my question? Nope. I value my sanity too much. My eyes grew heavy, and I drifted off to sleep on the couch with the TV on and the remote in my hand.

Chapter Eleven

I lifted out of my body. Okay, this is getting old. Everything is as it was when I went to sleep. The weird light which is all around is augmented by the glow of the TV. What tortures does my mind have in store for me this night?

Moving through the house, I made my rounds. Moiraine is doing well in this dream of mine. Ms. Barton is snoozing in the chair in my wife's room. Charlene is resting in her bed. A strange glow is around her bed. It is subtle, but there is no denying the radiance of it. It is a soft white glow. The understated light cast no shadows in the room. It is like seeing the light in retreat, but there nonetheless. "Charlene, I want to talk with you." She didn't rise. Again, I asked Charlene to get up. Is she stirring? No, wishful thinking. My soul is weary of these half glimpses of my life. Now even in my dreams, I cannot be with the woman I love. Maybe this is the way my subconscious is trying to tell me to give up the last whisper of a hope I still hold in my heart.

Traveling out of the bedroom, I know not where my feet are taking me. I just walked. It is trash day in the neighborhood. Trashcans and recycling bins lined the street. Note to self put the trashcans out in the morning. Thanks subconscious.

About a block away from the house, I noticed two men sitting in a dark sedan. My vision must be better in dreams because I could see them clearly. I walked up to the car and looked inside. Even with my face right up to the glass, they didn't notice me. The back seat is covered with trash, a few to-go bags from various fast-food chains, and innumerable empty coffee cups from the local convenience store. Either these guys have been here quite some time, or my brain is telling me to clean out my car.

What part do these men play in my dream? Their whispering to each other is muddled, and I can't make out the words. There is another person on the street, too. He was dragging a large trash bag with him. He is moving slowly, checking the recycle bins for cans and plastic. It's a tough way to make a few dollars. If I don't find another job soon, I might be doing the same thing.

The stars are out tonight, and I watched them for a time. Wonders in the dark. I have always marveled at the heavens. In another life and at another time, I wanted to join the ranks of astronauts. It is a dream I had from the earliest time I could remember.

My mother, the ever so practical woman, said *"Nathan, darling, it's not realistic to want to be an astronaut. Why thousands and thousands of men try for those jobs. Why don't you think of something else you would like to do?"* Even if I didn't have a perfect memory, I would remember the heartbreak at hearing those words coming from the most important person in my life. My reply is clear in my memory, as well.

"Mom, you shouldn't take a man's dreams away from him." Those were wise words coming from a four-year-old. The will to stick to my dream left with those cruel words. My mother took my dream and threw it on the ground. She put on her tap shoes and did a Flamenco dance on it. Oh well, should-a, could-a, would-a.

The homeless guy had passed the car with the two men in it. Turning back to the house, as I walked, I heard four sharp barks. They had the familiar muffling all sound has in this kind of dream. Startled, I turned to see where the noises came from. Both men in the car are slumped over, and blood is splattered all over the windshield. The homeless guy was running down the street.

Waking with a start, I asked myself, "Did I hear something? Oh, it must have been the TV." I switched it off, and I went to check on Mo. She is as I had left her. My wife and Ms. Barton are okay too. With my rounds completed, I settled down in the recliner with Blossom on my lap.

The alarm went off. Mo woke up, and I told her to get ready for school. I made breakfast for everyone in the house, Ms. Barton included. With breakfast in hand, I brought it to the hospice nurse.

"Thank you, Mr. Embers, but I have my own food." She pointed to an Igloo lunch box.

"Oh, this is better than anything you could have brought. Come on, give it a try. If you don't like it, flush it down the toilet. I'll never know the difference."

"Very well," she took the plate of food from me and ate a forkful. By the change in her expression, she must be pleasantly surprised at the taste. I do one mean breakfast if I do say so myself. And I do say.

Mo, with backpack, brown paper sack lunch, and me in hand walked out to wait for the bus. Something is happening down the block. There are police cars, a police van, and an ambulance. There are so many flashing red and blue lights if a person living with epilepsy lives on this block, they better stay inside today.

From my vantage point, I couldn't see the commotion. I am blocked by a crowd of people. Then there was a break in the crowd long enough for me to get a look. I could see a dark-colored sedan with a large splatter of blood on the windshield and two gurneys with body bags on them being loaded into the ambulance. The world is spinning. My head exploded with an instant headache. What is happening to me? Oh God, I can't take anymore.

"Daddy, are you okay?" Moiraine asked with the sound of tears in her voice.

My daughter's voice stirred resolve in me. No choice, I must take more. Quickly, I subdued the headache with my little trick. *"It won't last long."* There I am on the ground.

"Yes, Mo, I am fine. Daddy slipped." She helped me back up.

"You scared me. I thought some mean man had hurt you too."

How true her words are. A mean man, an evil man, had hurt me. He hurt me more deeply than any bullet could penetrate. He sliced away a part of me more than any knife could. For what armor can protect a man from a shadow blade to the heart? Moiraine's school bus is about to arrive, so I had to put my musings on the back burner. She boarded the bus and bid her goodbye for the day.

No time to dawdle, because my dreaded task awaits. The ritual of showering, shaving, and dressing is mind-numbing today. The dark suit fit reasonably well. We never had it tailored, because of money and I don't wear it often. Once I finished dressing, I took a hard look at myself in the mirror. An aged man looked back. The memory of myself before all this tragedy entered our lives, compared little to the vision in the mirror. Dark circles had invaded the space around my eyes. The wrinkles I had noted are beginning to be more pronounced. The skin of my face is sagging on my skull. Not only have I aged, but I look hard. *"Dear God, please let me be hard enough for today."*

My cell phone went off. It is Detective Frank Hawkins. I let him talk to my voicemail. There are more pressing things to do today than to talk to him. My phone went off again. It is Frank again. He sure is a persistent little bastard. I turned my phone off. No interruptions. In case I needed to make a call, I grabbed my wife's phone and put it in my pocket.

"Ms. Barton, I am leaving for the better part of the day. Here is a number where you can reach me if there is a change in my wife's condition. My father-in-law, John, will be here later to see to my daughter."

Everything on my to-do list is done. It is time to set off for my destination. Twenty minutes later, I arrived. The limousine is already waiting for me. Standing next to the limo is a young man in his early twenty's. He is wearing the classic black uniform of a limousine driver, hat included.

The driver tipped his hat and opened the door for me, "Are we waiting for anyone else, sir?"

As I climbed into the back of the limousine, I said, "No, only me."

"Very good, sir. Do you need to make any stops before we head to the destination?"

"A drive down the coastal route and seeing the ocean would be soothing. Will we have enough time?"

The driver looked at his watch. "I'll make time, sir." He closed the door then took up his spot behind the wheel. He started the engine and rolled down the window between the front and back seats. "There is a full bar in the cabin. Please feel free to have a drink if you like. Would you like me to turn on some music?"

What a question to ask a walking iPod. "No, thank you. Not to be rude, but I would like to make this drive in quiet solitude."

"As you wish, sir." The driver rolled the window back up and gave me my privacy. We started to move.

This is my first limo ride. I had to admit it is pleasant. The atmosphere is both reserved and lush. The ride is quiet and smooth. The thought of not having to deal with traffic made my blood pressure drop a few points. Yes, if I ever win a lottery for a butt load of money, I'm getting a driver. Of course, for this to happen, I need to buy a lottery ticket first. But I'm just saying... We are out of the city traveling north on the I-5. I looked out the window to my left and could see the Pacific Ocean. Well, part of it at least. The hazy grey of the mornings here in Southern California spoiled the view a bit. The sun would burn off the haze soon enough. The ride back promised a better, clearer view.

Normally a long car ride would give rise to indulge in some memory replay. Not today. Not this drive. I need to be here in mind, spirit, and intent. Silently and alone, I watched the coast go by. Being alone now is a portent of my life to come. Charlene is dying and soon would be gone. For me to even envision marrying another woman, is wrong. Charlene would be one hard act to follow. I would have Moiraine in my life, but our time together is counting down. Similar to John saying goodbye to his little girl when Char and I wed I too will someday see Moiraine leave my home to build her own. To let a daughter go is the ultimate demonstration of a father's love.

The limo came to a stop, and the driver lowered the privacy window, "We have arrived, sir." The driver came around and opened the door for me. I got out and looked around at the park-like setting.

We are at the top of a hill which looked out over the entire cemetery. I am here to bury my son. The thought burned in my mind and across my heart.

It is a relatively small facility. I knew this location was perfect right from the moment I saw pictures of it, but the photographs did not do it justice. It feels peaceful. A gentle breeze touched my face. About twenty yards away stands a white cross at least twelve feet tall. In the opposite direction is a large oak tree which offers shade to visitors. All-around on the graves, which spread out before me, you could see flowers of every variety also dotting the landscape are small American flags. In another section of the graveyard, another funeral is taking place. Dozens of mourners saying their last goodbyes to someone they loved. I feel alone.

The sun is out in force now. Its warmth reached into my bones. How ironic this weather is to me. Hollywood would have you believe it always rains at funerals, a blatant metaphor for tears. My son gets damn picnic weather. I'm burying my son today. Such agonizing pain, how can a man be strong when his son dies for no reason? How can a man be strong when his child has fallen without meaning? How can I be strong? There is no being strong. There is only enduring.

A young woman approached me from the gravesite. She must be the director. She is about five-foot-seven with blazing red hair cut in long layers. The breeze played with loose strands of her hair and brought them across her face. She is dressed in a black pantsuit with a white dress blouse under her jacket. She had a green scarf around her neck tied in a big knot and tucked into her jacket. If my mood had not been so dourer, I would have given her a second look.

"Mr. Embers, first let me say, all of us at Alan Brothers Mortuary offer our condolences for your loss. Everything has been prepared per your directions. We can begin whenever you are ready," she politely waited for me to answer.

"I'm ready. Let's begin." I started walking to the tent they had set up to provide shade for mourners during the services. A lone folding chair is there under the tent. One chair, as I am the only mourner. The only one to mourn a life unlived.

As we neared the gravesite, the director asked, "Would you like to carry the coffin from the hearse to the gravesite?" I nodded, I was afraid to speak. The fear my voice would crack, and the dam on my emotional control would burst. I slowly walked to the hearse. In the back placed on a fine linen cloth was the tiniest coffin I had ever seen. My son was only a little over three months old in the womb. The casket can sit in the palms of my hands. They had asked if I had wanted a viewing. My heart could not bear to look upon my son's body. Imagining him as a full-term baby is all I can take.

My hands and love cradled the casket, as I walked to where he is to be laid to rest. A gravesite worker gently took the casket from me then lowered him into the ground.

I walked back to the chair waiting for me under the canopy. There is no member of any clergy to say words over his grave. The words they would say would only be a hollow solace to me. At this moment, my faith in a creator has been rocked to its very foundation. How could any loving God allow this to happen? What justification can there be for this? I know someone of great faith could find some quotes to try and ease my pain. But there is no easing of this pain.

They started lowering my son to his final resting place. It is the cue for the music to start. I selected three songs to be played the first is *"What A Wonderful World"* by Louis Armstrong: "I see trees of green, red roses too. I see them bloom, for me and for you..."

The second song to be played for my son is *"Somewhere Over The Rainbow"* as sung by Israel Kamakawiwo'ole: "Somewhere over the rainbow. Way up high..."

The last song is *"Tears Of An Angel"* by RyanDan. This song is for me. "Cover my eyes. Cover my ears. Tell me these words are a lie..."

There I sat for a moment after the last song died out. The funeral director walked up to me with a container filled with earth. "Mr. Embers, would you like to throw a little earth into the grave?" I looked up at her. "Some people do. It gives them a sense of closure." With a small handful of earth, I walked to my son's open grave. The headstone is already in place. It's a small marker which said only "Baby Embers, Son." It looked dark; the hole which is to be my son's grave. I took a deep breath and tossed the earth into the hole and onto my son's casket.

My emotions from the events of these darkest of days have been caged within me so as not to interfere with what needs to be done. Everything I had been holding in check came out. My knees screamed in pain as I fell to them, but the physical pain is an insignificant drop to the ocean of my heartache. I cried. I cried for the son I would never know.

Tears fell from my face for the child my wife would never know was growing in her womb. I anguished over the brother Moiraine would never have. Grief filled me that John would not be able to teach his grandson how to work with wood. But more than these sorrows, I cried over the truth I would keep from all of them. The truth he even existed.

Time does not exist while I am on my knees before my son's grave. In time a hand touched my shoulder. Turning to look at the hand of the one who interrupted me, I saw it is a slender feminine hand with a French manicure.

What the …? I know that hand.

Standing I looked to the owner of the hand. There is no one standing next to me. Slowly I spun around looking in turn to each one of the funeral workers there. The only woman there is the funeral director, but her hands did not have a French manicure. Her nails are painted with an understated red blush. My imagination must be getting the better of me. To the funeral director, I said, "Thank you for all you have done. It was lovely. I think I would like to go back now."

"Of course. Again, I would like to extend my condolences. The driver will take you back." She motioned me towards the limousine.

The limo is waiting for me. The driver opened the door and tipped his hat again. I said, "Thank you" and entered. He wanted to know if I wanted the scenic route again. My answer was, "It doesn't matter." While sitting in the back of the limo, I did not turn to the windows and look outside on the return trip. My vision was focused inward. Flashes of memory came to my consciousness.

Something was building in me.

The drive did not register. Over and over my memory showed me not only moments since the night Mark Galos robbed the store, but times from my whole life.

Something is growing.

I did not like what I saw in those memories. Time and time again, I had taken an easy path over the one of greater trial.

It kept growing.

For all my talk about being a man, I had never stood up and fought for what is right.

Growing.

I had run. I had talked my way out. I avoided conflict. Even when my own life was on the line, I backed down. I had been a coward. I am a coward in thought and deed.

It is burning and still growing.

Mark Galos had robbed the store. He had threatened Marcy. He had threatened me. He stole my wedding ring. He endangered the children at Greentree. He shot at my daughter. He put my wife in a deathbed. He murdered my son. The son-of-a-bitch is going to pay. The police have been worse than impotent. There is no one I can turn to.

I am ablaze.

JUSTICE WILL BE RENDERED ON THAT MONSTER, AND IT WILL BE ME WHO BRINGS IT.

"Sir, we are here." The driver had the door open and was leaning into the limo. His words had brought me back to the here and now.

"Oh, yes, thank you," I mumbled as I got out of the limousine and shook the driver's hand. Dazed and a little confused, I wondered, am I going to murder a man? My mind answered the question. Yes, I am. But how?

"It was a touching service, sir."

"Yes, it was. Thank you." Pulling out my wife's cell phone as I walked to the car, I called John to check on my wife and Moiraine. I am sure Detective Hawkins is still trying to contact me. John assured me all is well and to take whatever time I needed. "Thanks, John. I owe you one."

I had to think this through. At Balboa Park, there is a grassy area near a stand of trees. I like to sit there when I have major thinking to do. Finding my spot, I sat and let the wheels spin in my head.

How am I to kill Mark and get away with the crime? What am I saying? It won't be a crime; it will be justice. I need to be careful. If he turns up dead, the first person they will look to will be me. The best way would be at a distance. Take him out sniper style. I'll need a fine rifle. The police are surely watching me. Those poor cops outside my house were executed by the psychopath for no reason other than they were in the wrong place at the wrong time. I don't understand how I know what I know, but I know it. Say that three times fast. I must shake the police somehow. I can't risk being caught. Moiraine needs me. It is getting late. I needed to get home.

A group of joggers are running past me. One stopped in front of me and bent down to tie his shoe. Without looking at me, he said, "Don't look at me. Detective Hawkins has been trying to talk to you. You need to turn on your cell phone. Wait a few minutes until after I leave before you do it." He stretched a bit then continued his jog.

Clever. I hope Mark isn't as clever or he isn't watching me twenty-four seven. The last thing I want is another cop to die on my account. Once I was back in my car, I turned on my cell phone. Dozens of texts from my favorite detective and numerous voicemails are waiting for me to reply. I cleared all that crap off my phone. I called Detective Frank.

"About time you called me back. Don't turn your phone off again. Two good cops died last night trying to protect you. Do you have any idea where Mark Galos is?"

"My condolences about the cops. Maybe you guys should give up on protecting me. Let whatever is going to happen happen."

"It's not only about you. Mark Galos threatened all the kids at Greentree. Believe me, if I could cut you loose, I would, but you are the only lead we have. Is there anything you're not telling us?" He emphasized 'anything.' Considerably softer, he said, "You never meant it to go this far. You are in over your head. Come clean with me. I won't hold it against you. People are dying, good people, you don't want that on your head."

"Are you kidding me?" He still thinks Galos and I were in on the heist together. "I may be in over my head, but I was never in on it as you say. Once again I will tell you what happened for all the help it will bring you." Like a broken record, I repeated what happened that night and on the corner. After my tale was through I told him, "The only things I have left to say to you are my observations. He is smart and methodical. He robbed the store like he'd done it a hundred times before. He was almost bored. He has taken my testimony at his trial personally. As to why your guess is as good as mine. When he attacked my wife, he mentioned precise timing, their suffering, and too high a price for this world. I have no idea what all that meant. I don't care. What I care about is getting him caught or killed. Seeing him laid out on the street, bleeding, waiting for death to visit him as he left my wife would be my personal preference. Tell me, Detective. Can you arrange this for me?" I am screaming into the phone at this point. Based on my nefarious plan, it was a mistake to have said it.

"Calm down, Mr. Embers. We are doing our best. We'll get him one way or the other. I just hoped there was something you were holding back. Something which could shine a light on this whole affair."

"So, what's your play?"

"We are going to back off on our surveillance of you and your house. No one will be too close. It will appear you are on your own. When he comes for you, my gut tells me he will, we will be there before you can come to any real harm. If you care about your daughter, you'll want her to be somewhere else while this all is going on."

"I'm not sure. It might make Mo a madman's target. He could use her to get to me."

"It's your call, Mr. Embers, but I think you're wrong. Watch your back." Click.

Having the police back off might give me room enough to slip away unnoticed. Now it is time for me to plan a dastardly deed.

Home with my family is where I should be, so I went home. My body is home with my family, but my mind is elsewhere. I am trying to come up with a plan. Bits and pieces tumbled about in my thoughts. It all came down to four big hurdles. One, I needed to acquire a rifle anonymously. Two, I had to be able to shake whatever tail the police put on me. Three, I had to find Mark Galos when the police could not. Finally, I had to have the will to squeeze the trigger. Easy. What am I worried about? Let's see only the thousand little details which can trip me up and get me caught.

In my mind, I heard the voice of Inigo Montoya say, *"I have no gift for strategy. What I need is the man in black."* The Princess Bride, what a great movie, but I have no more time for distractions.

After I got Mo to bed, I had to get to work. I turned on the computer and began in earnest. It wasn't too long before I found the information I desired. Tomorrow is Saturday. I think Moiraine and I will take a little ride to visit an old friend.

Chapter Twelve

It is Saturday morning, and I had hoped to sleep in. My hopes were dashed, of course. I woke to a tiny finger lifting up one of my eyelids and a voice asking, "Daddy, are you awake?" Sometimes I can't wait until Mo is a teenager and will sleep half the daylight hours away. This morning is one such occasion.

"Yes, Honey, I am now." Blossom's tail began thumping away the instant my voice sounded. Slowly I stood and shook my head to clear the cobwebs out. On came the TV to Mo's favorite Saturday morning cartoons. I moseyed over to the kitchen and poured her a bowl full of her latest favorite vitamin-fortified puffed sugar. "Come and get it, Mo." I gazed into the fridge. It is pretty barren and worst of all, not a Diet-Pepsi to be had. After our jaunt today, we need to restock on provisions. A couple of slices of bologna wrapped around some string cheese will do me. Oh yes, a squirt of mustard for tang on the whole thing. I ate it while I fixed Blossom's bowl of kibble. "Moiraine, as soon as you are done with breakfast, you need to get dressed. We are going on an outing this morning. Would you like me to pick out your clothes?"

"Daddy, you don't know fashion," she answered in a flabbergasted tone.

"Me? Not know fashion? How can you say that?"

"You don't even buy your own clothes, Daddy. Mommy and I do." Unfortunately, she is right. I haven't bought myself any clothes since Charlene, and I started dating. Yeah, Moiraine is right. I don't know about fashion. It's a sad day when your child puts you in your place.

"Okay, Honey, I want to get out the door pretty quick. Go and get ready." I went to look in on my wife before we left. She looked the same. Ms. Barton is standing by Char's bedside with a tub of warm water, a couple of towels, a bar of soap, and a washcloth. Ms. Barton is whispering softly to my wife.

"Getting ready to give Charlene a bath? Do you need me to give you a hand?"

"No, thank you, Mr. Embers. I will need you to leave, however. Your wife and I will need our privacy."

"Privacy? Ms. Barton, it would not be the first time I had bathed my wife." I tried to hide a smile I am sure is growing on my face.

"Mr. Embers, please. I do my duties well, but I do them my way. I do not want you in this room while I administer to your wife. I ask you to accept my guidelines."

"Very well. I need a change of clothes, and then I will be out of your hair." Retrieving what I needed, I left. It's strange. She acts like I am more an annoyance than Char's husband. She cannot keep me away from my wife in her final days. She may find herself replaced. I took my clothes and did my morning routine to make ready for the day.

Moiraine and I are both ready to go. Texting John, I sent him a message telling him we would be out a few hours and not to worry. We left the house and climbed into the car. We are on our way.

The drive would not take long, and we would be at our destination in short order.

Mo and I exited the car. We stood in the middle of Fort Rosecrans National Cemetery. The cemetery sits near the tip of Point Loma overlooking San Diego Bay. This cemetery offers a quiet dignity to the many United States servicemen and women resting here. This is an old graveyard from the earliest days of California as a U.S. territory. The grave markers stood all around in precise rows and columns as if the soldiers interned here are at attention awaiting the call of duty one last time.

"Daddy, why are we here?"

"Moiraine, Honey, we are here to pay respects to a gentleman daddy knew for a long time."

"Is he dead?"

"Yes, he is."

"I don't like this place, Daddy."

"Mo, there is nothing here you need to worry about honey. You see all these graves are for brave men and women who served our country. This is a place of honor. It is here, so we never forget the sacrifices of these soldiers." I crouched down to be on her level eye to eye. "Do you know what a war is, Honey?"

"I hear people talking about war, but I don't know what it means."

"There is no easy way for me to explain it, but I will try. Sometimes one country will try to hurt the people of another country. They try to bully them. Soldiers, these soldiers, stood up to those bullies and said, "No, you cannot hurt my fellow countrymen. Not today. Not on my watch." Sometimes the soldiers die protecting you, me, and the other people in our country. Some of those soldiers are buried here so we can pay our respects. Say thank you to their memory. Your grandpa was a soldier many years ago. He fought in a war."

"Daddy, were you a soldier?"

"No, Moiraine, I've never served." Somehow, I feel ashamed at my admission. Not everyone joins up. Many choose other paths. Why do I feel ashamed? It is a question for another day. Today, I have other matters to see done.

"Daddy, I don't like wars."

"I don't like wars either, but sometimes they are necessary."

I looked around and got my bearings. We headed to the grave I am looking for. The marker showed the name, Ralph E. Daves. I didn't know if this is going to work. I cleared my mind and took a deep breath. In my mind, I recalled the image of Ralph as I last saw him in the police station during my interrogation.

I spoke, "Ralph Daves" and waited. Nothing. I spoke again, "Ralph Daves." This time I put a little force behind it. Still nothing. I must be nuts, thinking I could summon up a dead spirit. But I am already here, so I tried one last time. "Ralph Daves," I set my will into the attempt just like I do with my headaches. I willed him to appear.

"Sorry, kid. It took me a while to get here," Ralph materialized before me as he did at the police station.

"It took you a while? You're only about six feet away." I was peering down at his grave.

"I wasn't down there. I was back at the station."

"Why were you there?"

"I feel the most comfortable back at the station. I guess it's my haunt. So, tell me, what do you need?"

"Information, Ralph. The name, the phone number, or postal address of someone in town who can provide me with an accurate long gun. No questions asked. And I need one which can't be traced back to me."

"Oh son, what are you going to do? Don't tell me, Mark Galos."

"With extreme prejudice."

"It's not the answer, son. Let my boys do their job."

"Tell me, Ralph; you've been hanging around your old stomping grounds. How close are they to nabbing him?"

"Son, it takes time to follow up leads. You can't put a timetable on a thing like that." He sounds like he is trying to convince himself.

"He killed two cops who were watching my house. He threatened the children at my daughter's school. I can't stand by and do nothing. Someone needs to put him down. I mean it to be me. Do you have the information I need or not?"

"Nathan, you can't ask me to do this."

"The next time he strikes, it could be more cops, me, or even my daughter. As I see it, this is preemptive self-defense."

"How are you going to find him? The guys back at the station have no clue where he can be."

"I have an idea on how to find him. Don't worry. This whole discussion could be moot if my idea doesn't work."

"I wash my hands of this whole affair." Ralph stood there a moment more looking at me then looking at my daughter. "Have you considered the consequences of taking his life? When he shows up dead, my boys will know it was you."

"Will they be looking that hard? He did kill two cops."

"Some of my fellow officers will not take kindly to a vigilante doing their jobs, not kindly at all."

We bantered back and forth for the next few minutes, but in the end, Ralph gave me the phone number of someone who could help me. "Thank you, Ralph. I know this goes against your beliefs. Trust me, no one else will get hurt, and he will be off the streets." I forgot exactly who I am talking to, and I held out my hand. I think Ralph moved by instincts too because he took my hand. We shook hands for a moment then abruptly let go. I can only imagine the look on my face. The look on Ralph's face is a treasure.

"See you around, kid," he turned and walked away, fading out after three steps.

"Daddy, can we go?" I had forgotten all about Moiraine during my confab with the dead. She must have thought her dad is going nuts talking to himself.

"Did it seem strange daddy talking to himself?" I grabbed her hand, and we started walking back to the car.

"I have seen you do stranger things, Daddy." Stranger things? I thought about it for a few moments. Yep, she has.

We reached the car, and I buckled Mo into her car seat. I walked around the car. Before I opened the door, I was approached by a Marine in his dress blues. He stopped in front of me and removed his hat and tucked it under his arm.

"Sir, I need to ask you to keep the noise down. This is a place of reverence and contemplation."

"I'm not sure what you're talking about Sergeant. I haven't heard any noise, and my daughter and I have been quiet."

The Sergeant's expression didn't change. "I'm sorry, sir. But you were yelling out the name Ralph Daves. You could say it was loud enough to wake the dead."

"Well, I'll be... I had no idea anyone else could hear my call. You have my apologies. Next time I'll use a normal voice. I take it you're a ghost?"

"Yes, sir. I am."

"How did you pass away?"

"Afghanistan, by an IED, improvised explosive device."

"I am sorry and thank you for your sacrifice, Sergeant." I want to do something more for this man than a simple thank you, but what? An idea came to me. "Sergeant, your family. Would you like me to tell them anything?"

His demeanor changed. His face softened, and he stood at ease. "How can you do it, sir? My family will think it's a cruel joke. I died over two years ago."

"Let me worry about it. I'll come up with a reasonable explanation." The Sergeant gave me a message to carry to his family and where I could find them. I don't know why I made the offer in the first place. It seemed like the right thing to do. Maybe they will make it my epitaph. *"It seemed like the right thing to do."*

Moiraine and I drove home with a short stop at the grocery store. I shopped to restock our pantry and Mo made friends with the other shoppers. Besides the usual bread, milk, and other foodstuffs, I bought the fixings for some home-cooked beans. Lima beans the big ones, not those baby ones, some cans of stock, and a big ham hock. My mouth started to water thinking of those beans. I also made a separate purchase with cash.

We returned home, and Mo went into the bedroom to visit her mother while I put the groceries away. I also began presoaking the beans. I tried cooking them straight out of the bag one time. Big mistake. No matter how long I cooked those beans, they never got done. I damn near broke a tooth trying to eat those.

With the beans soaking and the groceries put away, I went to visit my wife. Moiraine is sitting on the bed next to Char brushing her hair and doing a pretty fine job of it. Ms. Barton is working on her knitting, but her eyes are on Mo. Nurse Barton did not look like she approved of what is happening. Gratefully she is keeping her mouth shut. Any opinions she had about my daughter attending to her mother would be best kept to herself. "Is there any change to my wife's condition?"

"No, Mr. Embers. She is holding her own. She has a strong will. Perhaps the best thing you and your daughter can do for her is to say goodbye. She may be holding on to life because you are still holding on to her."

"You want me to tell my wife it's okay for her to die? I have never heard a bigger load of...," I turned and saw my daughter "doodoo." Lowering my voice and talking through my teeth, I said, "It is not okay for my wife to die. She needs to fight for every blessed moment she can." I stormed out of the room.

Lunch was ready for Mo and me. It is nothing special bologna sandwiches with mayo and mustard. We had unflavored potato chips too. We ate in relative silence. Mo was humming quietly to herself. My meal tasted sour. It is fitting, since I am in a sour mood. After lunch, I picked up the table and kitchen. A knot is growing in the pit of my gut. Part of me is not happy with my choice for dealing with Mark. I wanted to clear my head, but I had been spending too much time away from Moiraine.

"Moiraine, let's go for a walk." We stepped out of the house and took a walk. The path I chose wouldn't take us anywhere near Greentree Elementary. It's Saturday, but I didn't want to risk it. Thoughts and emotions are churning in my being. If I am going to do this, kill Mark, I must quiet the doubts and fears.

Mo is having a pleasant time on our walk. She is picking up leaves and twigs, anything which catches her eye. She approached and petted all the dogs we crossed paths with, and she received doggy kisses within an inch of her life. "Daddy, when is mommy going to wake up?" There it is. I've been expecting this question in one form or another. It still hit me like an anvil in a Roadrunner and Wile E. Coyote cartoon. I took a deep breath and crouched down to her level. I looked her straight in the eyes.

"No, Honey. Mommy is not going to wake up again. I wish to God it was different, but mommy is going to die."

Tears started streaming down her face. "But, mommy is out of the hospital," Moiraine turned her eyes away from mine and started struggling to escape. "I don't want mommy to die."

"I don't want mommy to die either. If I could change it, Honey, I would." My words are a futile comfort. Moiraine started to scream in agony and tried to pull away from me. All I can do is hold her close and try to console the inconsolable. The tears started rolling down my face as well. Trying to hold them back proved I am too weak. My daughter needs my strength, and I failed her. Every tear I could not hold back burned like molten metal as it rolled down my face.

Mo raged against me. In time her screaming stopped, her tears slowed, and her struggling ended. We started the walk back home. She no longer explored. All the things she had collected were tossed aside. She is broken, and nothing I can do will fix her. This is her first real painful lesson in life. People die, even our loved ones.

We spent the rest of the day cuddled up on the couch watching her favorite movies. Moiraine fell asleep on the couch. I picked her up and carried her to her bed. As I tucked her into bed, I put the teddy bear she received from the ambulance driver next to her in the hopes it would give her some comfort in the night.

My cash purchase from the grocery store was a throwaway phone. It's a sure bet the cops are listening in on my calls to trace Mark Galos' location if he called. This is one conversation I didn't want the cops to eavesdrop on. It is time to use the number Ralph gave me. My hand shook as I punched in the number. The phone rang at least ten times but was finally answered.

"Who are you looking for?"

"Ralph Daves told me to ask for Al. Ralph said he could fix me up."

There was a pause. The voice answered, "You say Ralph gave you this number? Why didn't he call himself?"

"Ralph's dead, but he said you helped him in a little matter about ten years back. You were straight with him, so he looked the other way a time or two. He told me you two kind of had an understanding."

"Okay. I might have what you need, or I can get it. If I see a cop or even get the whiff of one on you…"

"You won't," I started to sweat. I hope I can sneak out without the police following me.

"Go to the club on Fifth and B Streets. Arrive at eleven and tell the doorman you are there to help Al with his little friend. He'll lead you back to my office. Come alone." There was a click, and the phone went dead. The clock said I had a couple of hours to kill. So, I went into the bedroom and spent the time with my wife.

A change of clothes is in order as the hour of my departure approached. I changed into dark pants and shirt. There is nothing for me to do but leave. Opening the door to the garage, I beheld where we kept everything except the car. I navigated my way to the attic's opening and climbed up and into the crawl space of my garage and my landlady's, Mrs. Blake, garage shared. Suddenly the theme song to "Mission Impossible" started playing in the back of my mind. To my ears, it sounded like I am terribly noisy. Mrs. Blake is a heavy sleeper, I hope. Climbing down into her garage, I looked around. I thought we had a bunch of junk. Mrs. Blake's garage contained the junk collected from eighty-plus years of living. Tiptoeing through the crap to the garage's side door, I opened the door which led out of the garage and slipped out. The way the duplex sits on the lot, you can't even see this door from the street. It is perfect for my needs.

Stealthily, I crept through the backyard, trying to stay in the shadows. The fence is easy enough to hop over to the neighbor's backyard. Luckily, they don't have a dog. The last thing I needed is a barking dog or a bite wound on my leg. Like a ninja, I made my way to the street through the bushes and hedges. After I cleared my way through all the shrubbery, I walked down to the nearest cross-street and called for a cab on the throwaway phone. I am in luck as my wait was only a few minutes. I told the cabbie to take me to Fifth and B streets.

The cab arrived at its destination soon enough. I crossed the street to the club. "Saxie's Jazz Joint" is the name on the marquee. I approached the doorman. He looked more like a wall, not a door. He is an African-American gentleman tall about six-foot-five. His mass is all muscle too. I did not see an ounce of fat on him. He is as large as they made Michael Clarke Duncan look in The Green Mile. His nose is broad, and his eyes are deep-set. He wears a skin-tight fade which had been done by a master in the art of barbering. He is holding a clipboard and has a blue tooth receiver in his ear. A line of prospective club goers stood against the wall with a velvet rope barring their entrance.

"You need to go to the back of the line sir, but I wouldn't count on getting in," the doorman intoned in a deep resonating voice.

"I'm here to help Al with his little friend."

"Follow me." He handed another man standing there the clipboard. He led me through the club. The band is playing a quiet set. Several couples are dancing to the smooth jazz which filled the club. The band is on a small stage set a couple of steps above the floor. The décor of the club is rich in reds with silver accents. It gave me the feeling I had been transported back to a classier time. We went through a door which took us on a tour of the kitchen, the back storeroom, and finally to a staircase.

"Turn around. No one sees the boss until I've searched him." With his massive hands, he gave me a pat-down.

"Be gentle. It's my first time." The only reaction out of him was a guttural humph.

We climbed the stairs to a door. Mr. Doorman, the wall, knocked once and held the door open for me. I had to try to squeeze by him to enter the room. As I slid by him and tried to become only two dimensional, I looked up at him; he chuckled.

I walked into the office. It is a functional office with nothing austere about it. The furnishings are a few steps above Mike's office. The desk is larger than Mike's, and it is made of real wood, no faux finish. The chair behind the desk is the classiest piece of furniture there. It is a tall, high back leather swivel chair on rollers. There are several filing cabinets. I doubt they hold any real files or records. There are two TV sets on the wall. One set showed different scenes of the club every few seconds. The other set is a top of the line flat panel job. It was playing Scarface. I smiled at the obvious tie-in with this gentleman's code phrase.

"He's clean, Boss. No weapons and no wire. I'll be right outside if you need me," the mountain of a man said then closed the door behind him.

Sitting behind the desk is a man quite a bit older than me, perhaps in his late sixties or early seventies. His skin is drawn tight over his skull in a way which gave his features a skeletal appearance. The grey hair on his head, what little there is, is clipped close. He noticed my smile as I watched a moment of Scarface. He returned the smile.

"So, Detective Daves gave you my number. How did you know the Detective?"

"North Park, 1978."

"A dark day for San Diego. I know you're on the level because Ralph told me he wouldn't keep my number in his files anywhere except his head. Ralph never lied to me in our," he hesitated as he chose his words, "dealings." He leaned back in his chair. "So, tell me, what are you in the market for?"

"I need a long gun. A sniper rifle. The best I can afford and ammo."

"Okay, before we can do business, I have to make a few things clear. First, if you're some jealous husband looking to off your wife's lover, look somewhere else. I don't get involved in that shit. I suggest you see to your marriage. Second, your target can't be a cop. The police have a nasty habit of tracking down the source of guns that kill cops. Third, strictly cash no checks, no credit cards, no IOUs. Fourth, if this gets back to me, I will sell your ass out. Do we have an understanding?"

I said in my best Jack Sparrow, "We have an accord."

"Not bad. Pirates of the Caribbean, that movie was great entertainment." He smiled and opened a desk drawer. "Have a seat." I took a seat as he threw a small binder in front of me on his desk. The title on the cover read "Say Hello to My Little Friends." I saw it had dividers. I quickly turned to the section marked rifles. Then I saw it.

Right there on the first page a beautiful color photo of an M82A1M rifle and its specifications. The gun is a 50-caliber sleek instrument of death. "This number here it's a stock number, right?"

"Cute, it's the price of the stripped-down model. All the bells and whistles are extra." He motioned for me to turn the page. Al gave a little smile. "The only person who could miss with this gun…"

"Is the sucker with the bread to buy it," I gave a smile too. I guess Al is a movie buff too. I looked at the price again.

Al said, "A little above your price range? What kind of ballpark are we talking about here?"

Based on the money I have, "Little League." I told him how much is at my disposal.

As he laughed, he stood, pulled the binder out of my hands, and said, "I thought you were a serious buyer since Ralph gave you my number, but you'll have to forgive me, I'm very busy."

"Please, forgive my being naïve about these matters. I have just started on a life of righteous vengeance and have had no dealings with businessmen such as yourself. Do you know where I might get some help? A competitor, perhaps."

"Since you're a friend of Ralph's, let me do you a favor. Nobody knows you. You don't have what they call street cred. I only agreed to see you because of Detective Daves. If you show up at any of my competitors, as you put it, you will end up robbed, beaten, or worse. Me, I am a businessman, not a thug."

"Isn't there anything my money can buy? This bastard must die. He all but killed my wife. He threatened dozens of children."

A spark of realization came across Al's face. "This man shot your wife?"

"Yes."

Al pulled open a drawer and pulled out a piece of paper. "Is this the man?" It is a wanted poster and showed a mug shot of Mark Galos. I nodded. "The cops are turning this town upside down looking for him. Bad for business you see." Al reached under his desk for a moment. Then he walked around his desk towards me. He gently placed a hand on my shoulder and guided me to turn around. We walk to the door I entered. "The money you brought let me have it. I gave him the envelope. "I want you to know I would have given you what you needed for the service of getting the cops off everyone's back, but not getting paid goes against union rules you know," he chuckled. His office door opened, and the mountain of a man entered.

"You need me, Boss?"

"Yes, I want you to take this gentleman and show him the bargain bin. Let him take whatever catches his eye."

"Sure thing, Boss. Follow me." The doorman said in a low and rumbling voice which sounded like an earthquake rolling through the ground.

He led me back to the storeroom, where he locked the doors. He moved a couple of boxes from against the wall. Then he grabbed an old wire hanger and straightened it out. He put the wire into an old nail hole in the wall. A soft click could be heard once the wire had reached its full length. A part of the back wall moved a few inches. The wall of a man pushed on the secret door until it opened fully. He led me down a small passageway. I was amazed Mr. Doorman didn't need to grease up to wiggle through. We exited the small passage into a room lined in all manner of firearms. There is everything from the mundane run of the mill shotguns and pistols to high-end special ops assault rifles with all the cool doodads. "Try not to drool on the merchandise," he intoned with a half-laugh.

"This is your bargain bin? I think I can find something here to suit my needs."

"No," he walked to the far corner of the room where he opened an old and dusty locker. It creaked as he lifted the lid. "This is the bargain bin."

I looked inside. It is filled with crap. It contained bits and pieces from some archeological dig of an ancient battlefield. "Why is Al keeping all this? I doubt it's worth any real money."

"Every year or so, the city has a buyback program to remove guns from the streets. He turns in some of these. It's easier than trying to dump them somewhere, and he makes a couple of bucks."

I started sifting through the odds and ends when I found a gunnysack. It called to me. I don't know what it means other than it is whispering my name on an unconscious level. It spiked my curiosity, so I pulled it out and looked inside. My nose is assaulted by the smell of mildew and decay. I took inventory, and it is all there, an M1917 Enfield rifle. How did I know it is all there? This is curious; I have knowledge I don't remember learning. Maybe all this is a dream after all. I set the sack aside and began searching through the bin some more. Paydirt. I found a scope to fit my prize. I quickly put it in the gunnysack. I looked around the room for the right ammo. I grabbed a box and put it in the gunnysack also. "I think this will do the job most handily. I am ready to leave." The walking wall showed me out to the street. Before I left in earnest, I turned and stuck out my hand. "Please extend my thanks to your boss for what I have here," I lifted the gunnysack and tipped my head slightly toward the bag. "I am sure this will suit my needs perfectly."

His hand engulfed mine in a strong shake. "Remember, you didn't get that here." As he voiced the statement, he glared at me and held the handshake for a moment too long. The unspoken warning and threat are clear. Based on my life lately, he didn't impress me. Oh, I believed he would kill me, but right now he would have to take a number.

The closest taxi stand is a short walk away, so I took a quick stroll and grabbed a cab back to about two blocks away from the house. The cab drove off, and I walked away in the opposite direction. After a few minutes, I took a quick look around. The street is quiet, so I snuck back into my home, by retracing my previous steps. I hid my gunnysack of firepower in my garage. I finally went to bed.

All this clandestine effort is exhausting, not to mention it caused my conscience to throw some jabs at me.

Chapter Thirteen

Our morning was uneventful. Breakfast was eaten. All the chores were completed. Moiraine is spending some quality time with her mother. I set my mind in motion regarding plans for the timely demise of Mark Galos. *"It is by will alone I set my mind in motion. It is by the juice of Sapho that thoughts acquire speed, the lips acquire stains, the stains become a warning. It is by will alone I set my mind in motion."* Well I don't have any Sapho juice, but we have pomegranate juice in the fridge; maybe that will work?

I began the work on the beans. I rinsed and drained them. I placed them in the large pot and put them on the stove. I added the stock, ham hock, and all the right herbage. I set the stove to put the beans on a slow simmer. Oh, boy, I am going to enjoy this batch. A pang of despair washed over me. How can I enjoy anything while my wife lies upon her deathbed? At the thought, I almost threw the beans out.

The doorbell rang. Oh, what fresh slice of anguish is this about? If it's the damn cat again, I'll use his guts to string a guitar. I opened the door to find a man of his mid-thirties standing at my door. He is of Asian descent. Based on the fact a limousine flying the Japanese flag on both front corners of the car is parked in front of my home, I assumed he is Japanese. He is wearing a smart navy-blue suit and tie. He is also sporting a briefcase in his left hand. Oh God, is the Japanese Government suing me? He bowed from the waist a respectful amount, but not too far. When he straightened up, I returned the bow no further than he bent.

"Please to pardon this interruption. Does a Nathan Embers live at this address?"

"Yes. I am Nathan Embers. What is this all about?"

"Very good. My name is Masafumi Asahara. I would like to ask you if this is your work." He pulled out of his briefcase a framed piece of paper and showed it to me. It is the maker's mark I had given to the calligrapher at the Japanese Tea Garden.

"Why, yes, it is. You know it had slipped my mind. Can you tell me what kind of maker's mark it is?"

"May my great-granduncle come in and sit down? He has traveled very far to talk with you. He has, I think the word is, fragile health and this trip has taxed him greatly."

"I'm not prepared for guests, but sure." The gentleman walked to the limousine and opened the passenger door and helped an elderly gentleman out. Masafumi Asahara attended to this older man and guided him to my door. The older gentleman bowed when he reached the door, and I returned the gesture. I showed them to my couch. Once everyone was settled, I offered them some ice water or Diet Pepsi. Needless to say, I don't entertain much. They thanked me but declined.

The older gentleman talked in Japanese. His nephew translated. "My name is Nobuharu Makiyama. I would like to know where you saw this mark!" Wow, they took a long trip for something a phone call could have cleared up.

"I have never seen it anywhere. It is something I doodled while on the phone. It is familiar to me. I began to see it in many places. I am sorry you came all this way for a doodle. It is a curious thing to me, nothing more."

There were a couple of exchanges in Japanese. Masafumi Asahara spoke. "My great-granduncle would ask if you would mind if he looked at your hands?" I shrugged and presented my hands. Nobuharu Makiyama took them in his hands. He examined them closely. He turned my hands over and looked at the backs. I feel like a raw diamond being examined by a jewel cutter. While all this is going on, I could sense an inaudible hum in the air. I noticed he had a tattoo on the palm of his right hand. After he finished with his examination of my hands, I looked at the palm of his right hand. The tattoo is the same as the maker's mark I doodled. This little man is smiling as I looked at his face.

"Hai! Hai! It is time. Mr. Embers please to forgive. My English no good." Nobuharu Makiyama had another exchange with his nephew.

"My uncle wishes to assure you he meant no disrespect by not using English from the beginning. He was afraid he would use the wrong words."

"Tell your uncle he showed me great respect by trying not to offend me in my home." There was more communication in Japanese. Nobuharu Makiyama bowed to me again.

I sat through another round of being left out of the conversation. Boy, this is a little tiring. "My uncle would ask you to be ready for when he calls on you to help with the crafting."

"Crafting? I don't understand."

"We all are to undertake a great adventure."

My daughter came running into the room with tears running down her face. She sat on the couch next to Nobuharu Makiyama and wiped her eyes. As the older gentleman looked down at Moiraine, a sad look came upon his face. "You cry because of your mother? I know of something which might help. Would you like me to tell you?" Moiraine nodded. "Do you have some paper?"

"Yes." Her tears stopped, and she wiped away the last remnants of them.

"Go. Bring it to me, please." She left for her room. "Mr. Embers, in finding you, we learned of your sorrow. It is a great sadness. I wish to offer you my prayers for your wife's recovery." This man bowed to me again. This time it is a bit deeper and a bit longer. My daughter returned with some of her clean art paper. The old gentleman took a sheet of paper and began folding it. "In my country, there is a story which tells if you make a thousand cranes, you will be granted a wish." The gentleman held a paper crane aloft.

He pulled on the tail end, and the wings of the crane flapped up and down. My daughter smiled. "Do you think you can make your own?" Moiraine began in earnest. What my daughter lacked in skill she more than made up for in dedication. I don't remember when I've ever seen her more intent on a project. This man is showing my daughter each fold. She is a quick study remembering most folds with only a little gentle guidance from Nobuharu Makiyama. He has a grandfatherly patience with her. In no time Mo had crafted her own crane with flapping wings and all.

"Hai! Yes, very good. Remember, it will take a thousand cranes to get your wish."

Moiraine began in earnest to make the cranes. "Moiraine honey, why don't you take it into your room." Mo picked up her paper and finished crane and went to her room. After she left the room, I said, "That was kind of you. Thank you, but my wife's doctor has said there is no hope, short of a miracle, my wife will never return to us."

"It is said while there is life, there is always hope. Do you not hope for a miracle?"

"Hope has abandoned this house," I could feel myself slipping into deep despair.

The two men talked back and forth for a short time. The younger man said, "Hai." They both stood then Masafumi Asahara spoke to me while his great granduncle slowly worked his way to the front door. "My uncle wanted me to tell you a car will come for you in three or four days. I will call you the evening before, so you know to be ready."

"Ready for what exactly?"

"My uncle makes katana, the samurai sword, in the old traditions. He has mastered all aspects of the craft from smelting the iron sand to polishing the blade. He is the only man alive today who can do the "whole enchilada" as you Americans say. My government considers him a living national treasure. They were most hesitant about letting him travel all the way here. My uncle appealed personally to Tenno Heika, His Imperial Majesty, the Emperor.

"Wow. Your uncle has Tenno Heika's ear." Wow is right. This man can ask for and receive an audience with the Japanese Emperor. That is like me asking to hang with the president.

"I am impressed you said it perfectly without accent."

"It's a gift. Thank you." I escorted Masafumi Asahara to the front door. The gentlemen turned toward me once they were on the front porch. They bowed. I bowed back. They each shook my hand. As they turned around, I asked, "What is the adventure anyways?"

Nobuharu Makiyama said back over his shoulder, "You will help us to forge a new sword. One who's like has not been known in living memory," they continued to the limousine and drove off.

Moiraine made herself scarce for the rest of the day. I am sure she is working diligently on her cranes. She must have felt some comfort in her labors because I heard her sing. Mo sings whenever she is happy. Until recently it has been an everyday event. It made the whole house seem almost normal. Then the other shoe dropped.

"Mr. Embers, we need to have a talk about your daughter," Ms. Barton said with finality in her voice. "She is disrupting my routine with my pati... Charlene. I would like her to remain out of the room when you are not there to supervise."

"Tell me, exactly what it is she is doing." Oh, I don't like where this is going.

"Well, frankly, she won't leave when I have to attend to things like bathing your wife and the like. She disturbs the quiet of the room with her talking. It is a deathbed, Mr. Embers not a therapy session for your daughter. If you don't do anything about this situation, I will have to end hospice for your wife. My job is difficult enough without having to babysit a child."

"I had no idea this was going on. Don't worry. I will take care of it. Moiraine, come here please." Moiraine came into the living room and stood next to me and looked up. "Honey, we need to talk." I listed all the offenses Ms. Barton had levied against her. "Is all this true?" Tears welled up in her eyes.

"She is mean to me. She's always saying I am in the way and go play in another room. Daddy, I wasn't playing in mommy's room. I was just – and then I – and one time-." She is crying so hard I couldn't understand any more of what she is telling me. With an explosive outburst, one statement came in loud and clear. Looking straight at Ms. Barton Moiraine blurted out, "I don't like you, and I don't like your shoes!" I nearly flew into a fit of laughter, but I caught myself. I hugged my daughter and told her to go back to what she was doing in her room.

In a reasonable tone, I said, "I will see to it my daughter doesn't upset you any longer, Ms. Barton."

"Thank you, Mr. Embers. I am glad you can see reason," she turned around and went back into the bedroom.

After a few hours, the doorbell rang, and I answered it. I took this latest visitor back into the bedroom. The look of surprise on Ms. Barton's face was almost worth this nightmare. "Mary, why are you here? I didn't call for a relief nurse." Mary is a grandmotherly figure. Her hair was gray and styled in what my mother would have called a roller set. Mary had lost her figure over time. She has no apparent curves. I hope her attitude is as grandmotherly as she appears.

"I called Geneva's Hospice and told them to send someone else, anyone else before I had you arrested for trespass. You are no longer welcome in my home. Please leave."

"I am not going to stay where I am not wanted." Ms. Barton packed up her things and started to leave, then turned back, went to my wife, and bent down to kiss her on the cheek. After seeing her display, my anger level dropped a notch. She cared far more than I thought. Maybe I could have done things differently, but I couldn't invest the time to try and find a kinder solution. She will think of me as a bad guy. I don't care. I think I may need to be a bad guy a little more often.

After an awkward pause, I asked Mary, "Is there anything you need?"

"No, Dearie. I've brought everything I need," Mary said as she put her things down by the chair next to my wife's bed. She began looking to Charlene doing all those things medical types do to patients. She checked Char's blood pressure, listened to her heart, and several other things, including checking the dressing on my wife's chest.

While Mary attended to my wife, she showed my wife caring tenderness. It was not unlike how Charlene would see to our daughter when she was sick or even me when I suffered from one of my migraines.

Moiraine came into the room, "Are you mommy's new nurse? You aren't mean like the other lady, are you?"

"Yes, Dearie. I am your mother's nurse. Ms. Barton isn't exactly mean. She has a different way of doing things." Mary looked at me and said, "She is a bit of an odd duck, though."

Moiraine piped up with "Yes, and she kept quacking at me." Mary busted out with a huge laugh. "I like her, Daddy. She can stay."

"I've worked with her at Geneva's Hospice close to ten years, and she has never told me her first name. Standoffish that one. We have some theories at the office as to why, but it's only gossip. You know, if you can't say something nice about someone, come here and sit next to me and give me all the dirt," Mary giggled a bit as she finished.

It is dinnertime, and the air has an aroma almost as delightful as I remembered my mother's beans made. I went into the kitchen to put the finishing touches to the beans. I removed the ham hock and stripped off all the meat and returned it to the pot. I gave the whole batch a stir. I took a small spoonful. It tasted superb. It tasted of home, comfort, and family. I would give anything to be able to remember exactly how my mother's home cooking tasted like. The idea of waking up on a weekend morning to the aroma of biscuits and country gravy warms my heart. The spaghetti she made was her own creation. It would set my mouth watering when I would come home and inhale that perfume. During the holidays, she would make macaroni salad. It was the only salad I would eat without complaint. Thinking about these delicacies set my stomach growling.

Enough with this trip down memory lane as I have hungry mouths to feed. I put cornbread to bake. If I can manage to save a slice for the morning, I will have cornbread and sweet milk for breakfast. The combo is another food memory from mommy dearest. It is one food memory I can recreate exactly like my mom. She used the boxed kind. You crumble the cornbread into a tall glass pour cold whole milk over it and eat it with a spoon.

"Moiraine, time to set the table," I yelled. Charlene hates it when I would yell for my daughter instead of walking the dozen or so steps to call for her in a normal voice. The cornbread is ready. I cut a healthy slice and put it on a plate. I put a heaping helping of my lima beans in a bowl and took it to Mary.

Mary's eyes grew wide as she watched me bring in her dinner. "Oh, Dearie, I was hoping you were going to offer me a bowl," she reached out and took up the plate and bowl. I stood back and watched as she tried her first spoonful. "Oh, this takes me back to the farm when I was no older than Moiraine. Thank you so much. Most families don't think to offer us nurses anything from their kitchens." She took another spoonful and said, "They're not rude. They have other matters on their minds besides manners." I turned away to fix my supper when she broke in with,

"Might I have another bowl when I am done with this one?"

"Please do. It is the greatest compliment you can give a cook to ask for seconds." I left her to her meal, and I headed towards mine. Dinner was eaten, the placemats cleared, and dishes washed. Moiraine continued with her project in the living room next to Blossom as I watched some nonsense on the television.

I told Mo, "Now, Honey, it is getting late, and it has been an interesting day. Why don't you get ready for bed?" She went to start her bedtime routine. I went into my wife's bedroom, "Mary, I will be doing some work in the garage after my daughter is asleep, so don't worry if you hear some strange noises."

"No worries, Dearie. My late husband used to putter around in the garage our whole marriage. Hearing the noise will most likely bring back some fond memories to me." I left the room to tuck Mo in and then to my labors in the garage.

I cleared a space on the workbench. Other than putting boxes of old crap on the bench, I had never used it the whole time we've lived here. I have never been a handyman. I prefer to use my head. Out of the gunnysack came all the bits and pieces for the rifle. I held up the barrel and examined it to see where I should begin.

Flash.

I am no longer in my garage. I am a passive witness behind another's eyes.

We came upon the valley. It was right open. We are to clear out them Germans.

Sergeant Early, "You men spread out." He motioned with his hands for our unit to go up the right. Right then those Germans opened up with everything they had.

I saw our boys get torned up bad. It reminded me of how our mower back home would cut down the grass. I hit the ground hard. I tried to peek at where them machine guns were. Them Germans hided those guns right good. Big shells started peppering us too.

Sergeant Early started barking out commands, "York, you and your men follow me back down to cover. Smith, Mathers, and Able you and your men make your way down, too."

We crawled on our bellies down to the ditch by the road. We all got there right away. "Sarge, what's you fixin' to do?"

"We are going to circle round and infiltrate their lines and take out those guns." We got a going keepin' out of sight of them Germans.

We were able to get behind them and overrun their headquarters. Those boys got surprised right good. We managed to capture a whole mess of men getting' ready to counterattack our boys in the valley. We were fixin' to march those guys to rear when a machine gun opened up on us. Six of us dropped dead right then and three other were wounded bad. I took count there was just eight of us in fightin' form left. I was the only one who had any stripes left on his arm, so I had to give the orders. "Alright you seven stay here with those prisoners. Make sure they don't start no mischief." I started workin' my way to get at them Germans when they got a sight of me movin'. That gun started spitting at me. I had no time to get to cover so I just dropped down. They were tearing up the ground all about me. I started yelling up to them Germans, "Give up that gun and come down I don't want to kill you." I was in a good spot to pick some of them off sharpshooting. Okay, I tried. One, two, three of them Germans got what for. I hear them boys yelling orders at each other. "Come, you guys, give up." I started picking them off. They couldn't get a shot on me, so I just kept it up. I ran out of ammunition for my rifle. I drew my 45. Just then the machine gun stopped. I peaked my head up a bit and there was six Germans jumping out of a trench and coming at me with a pig sticker at the end of their rifles. As they charged me, I got them one at a time with that 45.

"Halt, Halt. We surrender," that voice said some more words of that German talk and the remaining Germans up that hill started coming down with their hands up. I told them boys to go on down to the rest of my men. After the last of them march by me, I headed back down myself.

"Well boys, how many of them Germans do we have here?" I asked.

"Well York, you got 132 of them."

"No, it wasn't me. The Lord was guiding and protecting me all the way."

Flash.

What the hell? All these images of other people's memories are a little disconcerting. What is happening to me? It is like a whole new world is opening up. If I am not cuckoo for Cocoa Puffs, I need to learn how to control all these abilities. I only hope they can help me save what is left of my family.

I need to begin. I looked down, and the rifle is already restored. I must have restored it while I was strolling down someone else's memory lane. I've heard of multitasking, but I have never before been able to master the technique. I even have to turn down the radio while I'm searching for an address in the car.

It is late, and time to get some shuteye. But first, I cleaned up my workspace. I stored the rifle in an old sports bag. All is prepared for my nefarious deed. All this prep has me thinking. Will this endeavor make me a villain? Don't all villains begin by doing what they think is moral? They try to change the world as they think best or avenge a wrong which befell them?

I will be no villain, though. No pleasure will I take in the ending of his life. Well, maybe a little pleasure. No, it is only a job to be done. And when it is over, I will smash the rifle and throw the pieces in the bay. Though I can destroy the tool, the memory, the perfect memory, will stay with me always. It will haunt and torment me. Every day I will relive the horror to my shame. I will endure the mental agony. But every day I will look upon my daughter and say to myself, *"One more day. You can endure for her, one more day."* And when she is raised, and her life outside my protection has begun, I will travel to some nowhere, someplace where I will never be found, and stick a gun in my mouth. Oblivion. The pain will end. All my pain will end. All I ask is when the deed is done, my family is safe. These thoughts are my promise. These thoughts are my prayer.

The garage is cleaned-up, and it is time to lay down in the, growing all too familiar, recliner with Blossom on my lap and sleep. She thumped her tail a couple of times and drifted. Silencing my thoughts, I drifted off too.

I rose out of my body. These dreams come to me most nights. If they are dreams? Can I project my consciousness? Can I trust what I learn?

Enough is enough. After willing myself to see Mark Galos, I traveled and felt my version of motion sickness.

Chapter Fourteen

I came to be in a house. It had fine furnishings. This home belongs to someone who has more than two pennies to rub together. Touring through the rooms, I examined all the pictures on the walls. This is Mark Galos parents' home. There is a cabinet with trophies in it. Mark won many shooting competitions. No wonder he hit Charlene in the heart. He is well-practiced. A framed certificate read he was awarded Valedictorian in high school. My sharp whistle broke the silence. A diploma from California Institute of Technology hung on the wall too. He graduated Summa Cum Laude from there. This guy has some major assets in the old brainpan.

Why would he turn to petty crime? I don't need to know why. What I need to do is find him. He must be asleep somewhere in here. If his parents are hiding him, maybe he is in a secret room. I'm sure the police have searched this place. A well-hidden room is the only explanation for the police not finding him. I feel like I was being watched.

When I turned around, right there in front of me was Mark Galos. I didn't want to lift him from his sleep. Confronting him now will tip my hand. All I needed was to learn his location. I willed myself back home.

I woke with a start. Blossom yelped and woke too. Sweat covered my body, and my hands are shaking. With any luck, he only saw me as a dream. Of course, why would he think anything else? I had gleaned his address from a pile of mail. Sometime tomorrow I will send a bullet through his psychotic brain. Sorrow touched me. What was it John had said, *'It's a hard thing taking a man's life. Whether you answered the call of your country, protecting the lives of your family, or preserving your own life, no matter the reason, you are never quite the same after. I wasn't.'* So, I will be different. I can live with it. It won't be easy, but I can.

I looked at the time. There are a few more hours before I must rise and shine, so I went back to sleep. No dreams found me only restful sleep.

Moiraine got off to school without a hitch. Spending some time with Charlene is how I passed a few hours. "Has there been any change?" I asked Mary.

"Her breathing is slowing. It will be a while yet," she said as she looked up from her book.

"Thank you, Mary, you are such a blessing to us, to Charlene. I only wish you had come to us first. Ms. Barton was a strain. There is no ill will against her in my heart. She is the wrong piece to the puzzle of our lives." My cell phone rang, "Sure, John, I can stop by. I'll head over there in a few." Turning back to Mary, I said, "I will be leaving, and I will be gone for most of the day. I will return before Moiraine gets home from school." Mary nodded her head without looking up from her book.

At John's house, I rang the doorbell and waited for him to answer. *"What does he want to talk to me about?"* As I began to ponder the possibilities, the door swung open.

"Nate, come in and have a seat." I walked into the living room and took a seat on the couch. John sat next to me. He opened a photo album which is sitting on the coffee table. "Has Charlene ever talked to you about her mother?"

"She only said her mother died when she was young. She pretty much clams-up about that part of her life."

"She was very angry when it happened. She wasn't much older than Moiraine. Well, her mother died in an automobile accident." As John continued to talk, I could hear the emotion in his voice. "She was coming home after a late shift at the hospital. A truck driver fell asleep at the wheel and crossed the median. He hit her head-on. They said she died instantly. It was a mercy, I guess." He flipped through a couple more pages in the photo album. All too few of those photographs showed Char's mother. "Charlene was angry; she never had a chance to say goodbye. It took quite some time before she smiled again." John flipped through a few more pages then closed the book. He stood from the couch and went into the kitchen. The sounds of him puttering around in there could be heard.

While John is about his task, I looked around. The room is filled with all the beautiful furniture John had made for his home. In awe is the only way I can express my thoughts about the craftsmanship he displayed in his work. What is it like to build precious treasures with your own hands? It must be satisfying to pick out each piece of wood and to shape it, to mold it, to make it into what will be a dresser, or a china cabinet, or a bed. The sense of fulfillment gained when each piece is cut and placed together is beyond my comprehension. It seems to me when you put a great deal of energy into a creation; you invest a portion of your own life into it. Maybe that part of your life is returned to you when the construction is complete. Was God's life-force returned to him after creation?

If only I could create something even half as well with my own hands, then I could say I am a man. Once I tested my skill at making something with my hands, it did not go well. During eighth grade, I made a little wooden box in shop class. It wasn't square, the lid didn't close, and the staining was uneven. In other words, it was a piece of crap, not worth the lighter fluid needed to turn it into a small fire. When I went through my mother's possessions after she passed away, I found it along with every birthday card, Mother's Day card, and all manner of objects I had given her over the years. They were in a big cardboard box marked with a big red heart around the word "Memories." My mother must have believed I had invested some of my life into that crappy box.

Miss you, Mom.

My heart aches because she never met Charlene or held her grandbaby, Moiraine. I miss the advice she would give too. Her advice was never pertinent to the situation at the time. But years later, after I learned a thing or two, I realized the true value of those words. What advice would she give me? A bolt of lightning struck me. Crack! If I can summon ghosts, why don't I summon her? An odd queasy feeling came over me. No, calling up my mother is wrong. I don't know why, but I know it is. The odd feeling passed as I completed the thought. Well, considering all the strangeness in my life of late, it only rated a six-point-five on the strange-o-meter. So, there are only some ghosts I can call up? All the rest must have unlisted numbers, or I don't have the right long-distance calling plan.

Am I only imagining calling up specters of the past? Why do I still doubt what I did?

"K R A P has the answer." Then drumming began…
"…they're coming to take me away ha-ha. They're coming to take me away he-he to the funny farm where life is beautiful all the time…" The song faded in my memory.

Listening to Dr. Demento growing up was a mistake. Nothing good ever came of it.

I called Ralph, and he came. If I had imagined it, the phone number he gave me would not have worked. I would never have gone to "Saxie's Jazz Joint." I would not have gotten a rifle. It is real. I guess it makes me a spirit medium. Not everyone can say that. It's a skill which is very rare. I must be a medium-rare.

Groan.

The jokes are bad, but my cooking is divine.

John came into the living room and derailed my train of thought. He placed two glasses on the coffee table and opened a bottle of Jim Beam. He poured a measure into each glass. "It occurred to me we have never had a drink together."

"Oh, thanks, John, but I don't drink. My father was an alcoholic. Even at Char's and my wedding reception I had sparkling apple cider instead of Champagne for the toast. It is a promise I made to my mother. I would never drink. Keeping my word means a great deal to me."

"Good for you. Nasty stuff that demon rum, or," John picked up the bottle and looked at it, "Bourbon, or whatever your poison happens to be." John grabbed my glass and poured its contents into his glass. "I only drink it for medicinal purposes, you see." John gave me a wink. He lifted his glass to me and downed the double shot. He placed his glass back down on the coffee table. He looked me in the eye with a force which surprised me. "When are you going to let her go, Nate?"

Those words hit me square between the eyes.

John let the question sink in for a moment, then said, "She is my daughter, and I love her same as you love Moiraine. After her mother died, she was my whole life. Now all I have in my life is my darling granddaughter. Nathan, you have to say goodbye to Charlene. You have to let Moiraine say goodbye. I don't have the years left to wait for our little girl to heal from the scars of words left unsaid. Letting her say goodbye will start the mourning." Tears are flowing down his face. They traveled down the many deep creases there. "Lord knows I prayed Charlene would recover. I prayed harder than I have ever prayed in my life." John bent his head down for a moment and rubbed at his eyes. This man is still mourning the loss of his wife, Marlene, and now the loss of his daughter. All those years, he didn't say goodbye to his wife tore at his soul. Will this be how it is for me if I don't say goodbye to my love? "Nathan, God answers all prayers." He looked away, then turned back to look in my eyes again, and said, "Sometimes his answer is no." He paused again, then said, "No parent should ever outlive their child." The dam burst. His crying turned loud. I realized he is already mourning the death of his little girl too. What words do you use when no words will do?

I moved over to him. We hugged. We held each other wrapped in our grief. Suddenly he stood, grabbed the glasses and bottle, and carried it all back into the kitchen. There was a long awkward silence broken only by the sounds of John's tinkering. Eventually, John came back into the living room. As he passed me, he placed his hand on my shoulder and squeezed it. He sat back down. Looked me in the eyes again with the same intensity, and said, "She's a stubborn woman, Nate. Oh, she is like her mother that way. Maybe even a little more so. She will hang on to you and Mo until you tell her it's okay to go."

"I can't, John. I can't say goodbye to her. It would be tearing out the better part of myself if I said those words." If only I could tell John I had already said goodbye to one member of my family, my son, he might understand better. No, this is my burden to bear. Hearing he had lost a grandchild would break him even more. Inhaling a deep breath and blowing it out slowly, I tried to relieve the pressure building, then said, "I can't." I turned my head and looked anywhere but at John. He wasn't saying anything I hadn't thought myself. But it stung all the same.

"I'm not one to mince words, Nathan." He took a breath. "What a load of horseshit, and you know it. You are being cruel and selfish. She is not there. She hasn't been there since she got off the operating table. All that is left of her is a shell. Her spirit still clings to the shell. My God man let her go." John stormed out of the room.

Getting up too, I walked to the window. There is nothing I can see through the glass. My vision is turned inward. I don't like what is revealed to me. The sign the monster affixed to my chest blazed across my vision proclaiming "Coward."

I am afraid. I'm afraid to lose my wife. I'm afraid I failed my family. I am afraid to raise Mo by myself. Fear, my whole life is about fear. The only thing I am not afraid of is Mark Galos. Oh, and he is a thing too. He is a fiend; a fell monster most foul, and evil. He was a man once, but he tore up his human card the day he endangered those children at the corner. When the time comes, I know I will face the monster. And it's as clear to me as anything ever has been. When I face the monster, I will die. I have seen it a thousandfold times a thousandfold in my dreams. It sounds silly, but I know it to be true. To my core, I know it to be true. Only one other time in my life was I this sure of my future. I am resigned to my fate.

John came back into the living room. He had the bottle of Jim Beam again only this time he had only one glass. He poured a tall drink and took a long swallow. "Nathan, I don't want to fight you on this. This is a private family matter. But I will fight you if I have to. If it means getting a lawyer, I will. I'll fight dirty too. You think on that." What does he mean "fight dirty?" He poured another shot into the glass and downed it fast. "Nathan, I think you should leave before I say something I can't take back." The temperature in this house dropped a few degrees. "I don't have the stomach for any more talk."

After I walked to his front door, I stood there for a moment. My hand is on the doorknob then something stopped me. Something inside stopped me from leaving. This man is hurting. He is hurting over Charlene. He's in pain still over his wife. How can I ease his pain? I turned around and walked back to John. Here goes nothing.

John stood. The weights of his sorrows are evident in his posture. He is all hunched over. "I thought I told you to leave my house," John's bitterness slapped me in the face.

"John, may I see the picture of Marlene you carry in your wallet?"

"Why do you want to see it?" He said all this as he was pulling his wallet out of his back pocket. He took the picture out and handed it to me.

"What is her middle name?" After John told me, I studied the picture. *"Deep breath, clear my mind, and recall the feeling I had when I called Ralph Daves."* I was about to call her when John piped up.

"Nathan, please, I need to be alone," his tone is considerably gentler.

With a picture of her clearly in my mind, I called her name. "Marlene Louise Gustafson, your husband needs you." As before, I put my will behind the call. Scanning the room, it is only us living folk. After the span of three heartbeats, standing before me is the shade of Marlene Gustafson, mother of Charlene, and wife of John. "John, I wish you could see what I do. Your wife is gorgeous." Marlene smiled and blushed slightly.

"Boy, what are you playing at? Are you making light of me? Do you think I am some brain-addled codger?"

"John, don't ask me why or how, but I can call up spirits, and I can talk with the dead."

"I think you need to go. All this turmoil in our lives is making you nuts." John started pushing me toward the door.

Marlene's ghost spoke up. "John is not one who believes in what he can't touch. Tell him I said we lost a child before Charlene was born. I miscarried. It hurt him gravely. We never told Charlene. There was no need for her to know." I have more in common with this man than I thought.

As John is pushing me toward the door, I said, "John, she told me you lost a child, a miscarriage." John stopped pushing me.

"How... How do you know?"

"She told me."

"I don't believe you. I can't believe you."

Marlene spoke to me. "I told you he can be a little slow. This should convince him. Tell him we didn't start our honeymoon after our wedding. I told him we would be too

214

tired afterward, so the night before our wedding I snuck out of my parent's house and we …"

"I bet that's a story he never told Charlene."

"What about Charlene?"

"You started your honeymoon early. It was Marlene's idea too." John stopped dead in his tracks.

"I never told a soul. Is she really here? It can't be!" Spinning John around slowly, I put my hands on his shoulders. "She is standing right there." John began to straighten up. He is standing taller than I had ever seen before. "I see her. Oh God, Sweetheart, is it you?"

"You can see her, John?"

"She is right there." John pointed to her. "How? Why?"

"Yes, John, it's me. The how is him. The why: only God knows. Maybe God thinks you need me."

John sat down, "Where did she go?" A panic entered his voice. He started to stand back up. I gently pushed him back down into the couch. "Now she's back. Nathan, what is happening? My heart can't take this."

"This is all new to me." I looked back at what had happened. When I had communicated with ghosts before, no one could see them. What is different?

My hands were on John's shoulders. Once we broke contact, he could no longer see her. "I think I have to touch you."

Marlene said, "John, sweetheart, you need to let Nathan see to "his" family as he sees fit. You can't interfere. It's not right. Just as my father had to let go of me and let me live my life so too, you need to let go of Charlene to live hers."

"It's so hard. I don't want her to suffer."

I was starting to feel a head rush and gnawing hunger. "John, I think you need to finish up here."

"Sweetheart, you're a decent man. You're a better than average father too. I remember when Charlene was born. My mother wanted to keep you away. She said, 'A newborn doesn't need your filthy hands on them. Go do your work. I'll tell you when you can see this girl.' I never saw you both so hurt and so determined before. You gave her such a talking to. I don't think anyone had ever put her in her place quite like that. You used words I didn't know you knew. You did it all without raising your voice too."

"Charlene was asleep. I didn't want to wake her. I damn near told your mom never to darken our doorstep again too. It would have served her right. Try to tell me how to handle my family. Why…" The sign of realization slowly came to his face. "You're right, Marlene. You always could get me to see things your way all the while making me feel it was my idea all along. I miss you."

"I've always been here." She said with a broad grin.

"John. You better say your goodb…"

A screaming headache was mine as I woke, but it is not a migraine. Two EMTs are hovering above me with all manner of medical devices attached to me.

"Sir, can you hear me? What day of the week is it?" Silly question.

"John, what time is it? Someone has to be at the house when Moiraine gets home."

"Hush now, boy. It's not for a few hours yet. You fainted. I called these guys straight away. Got here right fast they did. It must be a slow day. I'll tell you, for a minute there I thought I was going to be the one to raise Moiraine. Those teenage years are enough to make a man lose his hair. And I ain't got the hair to spare anymore." John smiled, trying to lighten the mood.

"Sir, when was the last time you ate?" he asked this while looking in my eyes with one of those damn annoying lights. He had me follow his finger back and forth. I'll have a finger for him if he doesn't back off. "Sir, please, when was the last time you ate?"

"I had a breakfast of cornbread and sweet milk this morning. Why?"

"Mike, hand me the glucometer." The EMT pricked my finger and squeezed it. I've been called a prick, but I have never been stuck with one before. "Are you diabetic?"

"No."

"Your blood sugar dropped dangerously low. We should take you to the hospital and have you checked out." He spoke into a radio, "We need the gurney in here."

"No, no, and Hell no. I have a family to care for. Just give me a shot of something, and I'm good."

"Are you refusing transport to the hospital?"

"Yes." Mike, the EMT, started packing up and the other EMT, whose name I never got, pulled out a clipboard and began filling out some bureaucratic bologna.

"All this form says is you are refusing medical advice and will not hold me, the fire department, or the city responsible in the event of further injury and or death." I signed the form and started to stand. My head started to swim.

"John, do you have any OJ, apple juice, or any sugary drinks?"

He stood and went into the kitchen. I heard the refrigerator open. "I have a Coke-a-cola."

The thought sickens me, but any port in a storm. "Sure, thanks." I'll do penance later. The EMTs were all packed up and heading out the door. "Thank you, guys. Sorry, you came all this way for nothing. Is it customary to tip?"

"Cute, no, it isn't. Well, we are out of here. Never be afraid to give us a call if you need us. But seriously you do need to see a doctor."

"I'll do it." *"No, I won't."* Picture this; the doctor will say something like tell me what were you doing before you fainted? Well Doc, I was calling up the dead for my father-in-law...

"Here you go, Nate." John handed me a Coke, and I downed it. Oh, I don't like Coke with its spicy after-taste.

After a couple of minutes, I was starting to feel like my old self, which is too bad. I wanted to feel like my young self.

The EMTs finished packing up all their gizmos and whatnots and left. I brushed myself off as I stood. "John, I hear what you are saying. I will tell her goodbye soon. It doesn't feel right. Don't ask me to explain it. It just doesn't. I've tried calling to her as I did with your wife. Her spirit didn't come. If she is gone, I think she would have appeared."

"Nate, son, I'm a simple man and all these going ons with ghosts is beyond my understanding. I know what I saw. My wife, my Marlene, was here. It was no trick of smoke and mirrors. You called her name, and she came. So, if you say Charlene isn't gone yet, I'm right there with you."

After I took in a big breath and blew it out slowly, I said, "John, I make this promise to you. When it is time, we will all say goodbye to her together." I held out my hand to John. He shook it. The man is right. Whether or not I can call up Char, we all need to say goodbye, grieve, and move on. What I need is to come up with a plan. Right now, though, I should go home and be ready for Moiraine's return. Then I plan to make my plan, and the most important part of any plan is to have information.

The rest of the day went as the days lately have gone. Mo came home; we spent time with Charlene. Moiraine went to bed.

Now that Mo was down for the night, I need to make a couple of calls on the throwaway phone. I went into the garage in case Mary has sharp hearing. I dialed Mike's home number. Having a perfect memory can come in handy sometimes.

Mike answered a little groggily. "Sorry, Mike. I didn't mean to wake you. Things have been hectic here, and this was the first chance I had to call you."

"It's alright, Nathan. How is Charlene doing? The shooting was all over the news."

"She will be passing in the next few days, Mike."

"Oh God, Nathan. I didn't know. Is there anything I can do for you?"

"Can you see your way to giving me Marcy's phone number?" There was an awkward silence on the other end of the line. I realized how it sounded. My wife is dying, and I want another woman's number. "Marcy needs to know about Char. They have become friends since the last Christmas party." Lies, lies, and more lies. "She might want to say goodbye."

"Give me a second, Nate." The sounds of fumbling and paper rustling came over the phone. "Here it is." Mike gave me the number. "If there is anything I can do for you, Nate, just say the word. You have friends here. We want to help. You are not alone," Mike said without a touch of hesitation or reservation. There is a tugging at my heartstrings. Except for Charlene, Moiraine, and John, I have always thought of myself as being alone. When this is all over and if I don't go to jail for murder, I'll have to reexamine my belief.

The time is getting a little late to call Marcy, so I'll have to drop her a line tomorrow.

Chapter Fifteen

It is a new day and the time for action. After I saw Moiraine ready and off to school, I looked in to see if Mary had any needs. As it is a decent hour, I gave Marcy a call.

"Hello," she sounded tired. Crap I hope I didn't wake her.

"Marcy, this is Nathan from work. Can we talk?" She grunted, yes. "I know this is coming out of left field, but I remember you had a quizzical look on your face when Mark Galos robbed the pharmacy. Why?"

"I'm fine, Nathan. How are you? No, I haven't found a new job yet. Say how did you get my number?" Her sarcastic tone is coming through loud and clear.

"I'm sorry, Marcy. You are right. It is rude of me to launch into my question. I hope you can forgive me," I didn't hear a reply, so I carried on. "I can't believe you haven't gotten snatched up by another pharmacy. I know there is always a shortage of experienced pharmacists."

"Well, it seems the word has been spread around town and now everyone thinks I was in on the robbery. This is all unofficial of course. I have even gotten a call from the State Board. They interviewed me over the phone. They may pull my license. My life is falling apart. And now you call and remind me of that awful night."

"Those bastards. You need to fight them, Marcy. I'll stand up with you."

"Thank you, Nathan. It means a great deal to hear someone say those words. It seems like everyone family, colleagues, and the state are kicking me." I heard her gently sobbing then blow her nose.

"Marcy, if I can do anything, I will, but I need my question answered. Mark Galos shot my wife, Charlene. He intends to kill my whole family. I am desperately searching for an edge any advantage at all to stop him. Please," I waited for her to respond.

"Aren't the police protecting you?"

"What they are doing, I would not call protecting. The police are using me as bait to draw Mark out. The detective in charge believes I was in on the robbery too. My best guess is he wants Mark to kill me to save him the trouble of making a case against me."

The sobbing stopped "Well, I don't know what good it will do you, but he didn't want any of the drugs you would expect. The list didn't have any painkillers or opioids. Nothing on the list had any street value. All those drugs do is treat schizophrenia."

"Thanks, Marcy. I don't know if this information will be of any help, but I thank you for it. You hang in there. If I hear of an opening anywhere, I will give you a call and put a word in for you."

"Thank you, Nathan. I don't know anymore, maybe this is a sign I picked the wrong path for my life. Goodbye."

"Marcy, Marcy, wait. Don't hang up."

"What else?" She sounded resigned to despair.

"Years ago, I struggled with depression. It wasn't pretty, and it took me a long time to climb out of the emotional hole. Don't slip into hopelessness, Marcy. It won't help. You have to fight it. Fight it by not giving into depressing thoughts. I know it sounds hollow but trust me. This trouble is not your making. Something will present itself to you. You have to wait until you know what it is. It could be a new job, finding the right someone to make you feel complete, or maybe a chance to start over. No matter what form it comes in, and it will come, it will be a blessing. It was for me, and it will be for you."

"I sure hope so, Nathan. I sure hope so. I will try to take your suggestion. You know I think this is the most words you have ever spoken to me at one time," she gave a bit of a half-laugh, "Goodbye."

"Goodbye, Marcy." She hung up. The conversation was enlightening. I did a quick search of my memory, and she is correct. It was the longest dialogue we had ever had. Despite seeing each other most days, we had never connected in any way other than work-related. Connecting with people other than family, was never important to me. I have no friends. My whole life has, after Char and I wed, been about family. People should connect. I should connect. How much more could I grow if I had friends?

I must focus on trying to kill that bastard who is going to kill me and those I love. Let me inventory what I have. A gun, check. A location, check. Desire, check. I must find a way to shake the police tailing me. How? It is broad daylight, but I can't wait. Think.

I cleared my mind and willed my brain to find a solution. Twenty minutes passed with me staring off into space and thinking of nothing. Daylight is burning, and I am no closer to my goal. So, I turned on the TV to distract myself.

"...the full report on News at Five," the newscaster read. The TV cut to a commercial, "Next week a new Magic's Biggest Secrets Revealed. Watch as our masked magician tells all the secrets behind your favorite illusions." Using the remote and click. Maybe I can hire the masked magician to make Mark Galos disappear "Bippity boppity boo." No, wait ... it ... is ... coming to me. Not magic, but one of the principles of magic. Misdirection. Oh, this can work.

In the bedroom, I retrieved my workout clothes and another change of clothes. Next, I grabbed a baseball cap and a pair of sunglasses. I changed into the workout outfit and stuffed the rest into the sports bag containing my implement of justice, a Lee-Enfield 303. In my imagination, I see a slug hitting him in his melon. The thought of seeing the moment his head blossoming into red goo is most satisfying.

Sometimes I scare myself.

I went into the bedroom and said, "Mary, I'm headed to the gym to try to burn off some of this nervous energy. All this waiting has been getting to me," and it is no lie.

"No worries, Dearie. If there is a change, I will call you," she stood, stretched out her back a bit, and went to check on Char. She has caring hands. It is a blessing we switched out Ms. Barton.

With sports bag in hand, I headed out the door. I made a show of stretching a bit before I climbed behind the wheel. I drove to the gym, grabbed the bag, and walked straight to the locker room. I waited and watched. No one followed me in. So far, so good. I transformed into another person care of my nifty disguise. Exiting the gym, I walked to the curb and hailed a cab.

It was a bit of a drive. The time passed in boredom by pretending to be involved with my phone. No chit chat with the driver, I didn't want to leave any lasting impression. We arrived a few blocks from Mark's lair. I hoofed the rest of the way and found a neighbor's house, which had a beautiful view of his home.

Luck is with me as the house is empty. I walked around until I found an unlocked window. After I climbed in, I went upstairs. In the home office, I found a window facing Mark's house. It had a clear view of most of the property. I set the trap. A song by Kansas began playing in my head. *"Carry on my wayward son. There'll be peace when you are done..."* The only thing left is to wait.

Time dragged on; I've been lingering here too long. The owners may return before the deed is done. Getting caught stalking with a scope and rifle would look nefarious. Doubts and second thoughts entered my mind.

John's words came to me again, *"It's a hard thing taking a man's life. Whether you answered the call of your country, protecting the lives of your family, or preserving your own life, no matter the reason, you are never quite the same after. I wasn't."*

What am I thinking I can't do this? Kill Mark Galos in cold blood. It's not me. A man must be true to himself, and I am no murderer. I need to get out of here.

"No, you don't. Mark Galos will show any minute. Patience." The thought which entered my head is in a different voice than my own. This is weird. My brain has spoken to me many times, but in another man's voice? This freaks me out. Have I snapped? Has the stress caused me to lose my grip on reality? *"Do not have doubts. This is what we must do."*

Okay, this is close to madness. I heard a car drive up and a car door slam shut. Out, I must leave and try something else later. I saw Mark in a window of his home. My body started to aim. There are footsteps outside heading towards the house. I am trying to pack up and beat feet, but something is stopping me. My body isn't answering my call and on its own started to lineup Mark in the sights. My finger started to squeeze the trigger. No, Stop. I can't do this. I eased off the trigger and pulled the sights off Mark.

"We'll never get a better chance. Do it." My body is moving on its own. It lined Mark up again. I heard keys jingling in the door. *"Ignore it. Kill him."* My finger started again.

No, I won't kill him not like this. I tried to move, but I could not. It is exceedingly difficult to move away from the shot. My finger relaxed, then started to tighten again. I will not be a murderer. I screamed the words in my head and put all my will behind the effort "I WILL NOT BE A MURDERER! GET OUT OF MY MIND!" There was a release. It seemed like opening a bottle of Pepsi and having the Carbon Dioxide escape. My body started to obey my commands once more.

While breaking everything down and packing it away, I could hear the owner walking up the stairs. Escaping is the order of the moment. The window is no use. It is too high up for me to jump down. Spraining an ankle or even breaking a leg would be the outcome if I jumped. As quietly as I could, I crept back to the bedroom door. I could hear the home-owner approach the door. I squeezed up against the wall hoping if they opened the door, they wouldn't see me, and I could sneak out of the room before they turned and saw me. The doorknob began to turn. My heart raced. This is it.

A cell phone rang. Damn, did I forget to silence my phone? "Hello, yes, this is Ms. Miller. Okay, I'll be right there." The doorknob turned back the other way. I heard footfalls heading back downstairs. The sound of the front door opening and closing came to my ears. I took in a deep breath of relief. Too close. What would I have done if discovered?

I wouldn't have harmed, her of this I am sure. Maybe I would say I had a singing telegram for her. If it looked like she bought it, I would break out into a show tune. *"Getting to know you. Getting to know all about you. Getting to like you..."* Rodgers and Hammerstein. Am I sick and twisted or what?

The time on my cell phone is later than I thought. I had to make it back and pronto too. Exit stage right. I retreated out of the house and found a cab pretty quick. "Hey Buddy, I will make it worth your while if you take me to the gym on Washington and don't spare the horses." We tore out of there. He did not disappoint. I handed him the most generous tip I had ever given.

"Thanks, but no thanks, bud. In ten years of driving a cab, I have never had someone say, don't spare the horses. I have always wanted someone to say it," he chuckled and drove away.

In the gym's locker room, I changed back into my workout clothes. I can't go back outside without looking like I had the workout of my life. What to do? Ah! The memory of when I tried to do a half marathon should do the trick. Without any real training, the race was a disaster. By the end of the first mile, I was soaking wet in sweat and sucking wind. Oh, the stupidity of youth. As the memory came back, I began to sweat and hyperventilate. I stopped the heavy breathing, but my clothes are starting to sport a large cross of sweat on my chest, and my pits are equally sopping. A sports drink will complete the illusion, so I hit up the vending machine on the way out the door. I started guzzling it down as soon as I stepped outside. I sat in my car for a moment. I still had some time to kill, so I went to the park.

Back to my favorite stand of trees and patch of grass in Balboa Park. In the middle of the trees alone, I lost myself in thought. The sign is right there back on my chest again. Yep, I'm a coward. What am I to do? I failed my wife, my child, and myself. When it came down to it, I couldn't pull the trigger. Mark will eventually fulfill his promise. He will destroy me. He all but killed Charlene, and he will kill Moiraine. In an added bit of torment, he will do the deed in front of me. He will kill me too or worse. He will leave me alive to wallow in misery, knowing I let my family die.

As I sat there with my head hung low, a pair of stylish sandaled feet came into view. The feet in those sandals turned, and the lady attached to them sat next to me on the grass. "I'm sorry, Ms., but if you don't mind, please let me sit here by myself. There is a pretty piece of grass over there." Without looking the lady in the eyes, I pointed to a patch of grass about ten feet away.

"Well, you're not being very social. Perhaps I wanted to sit next to you. Maybe I was going to flirt awhile with a handsome man who looks like he could use a friend," the owner of the sandals announced.

Her voice had a familiar sound to it, but I am in no mood to devote the necessary mental resources to search my memory. "So sweet," I said then held up my left hand "but as you can see I am bound to the ring. One ring to bind me in the land of matrimony where the shadow lies. Well, you would see the ring if it had not been stolen from me." I put my hand down. It feels like the ring is still there as if it is a phantom limb. The torture laughed at me as I tried to dismiss the sensation.

A hand touched my chin and gently pushed it up. A jolt of excitement went through me like Charlene's touch does. The hand looked familiar also. It is graceful and sported a French manicure. French manicure? I looked up startled to gaze into the eyes of a striking young woman. Her eyes are gray and had a softness to them. They also conveyed wisdom beyond the age of the owner.

"Why so glum? Turn your frown upside-down."

Her voice echoed through my mind. My heart both dropped and jumped. "You're the tow-truck driver. You also swapped a dollar with me so I could get a Diet-Pepsi. I sorely needed it then too. Next, you showed compassion at a funeral no one knew about. You left so quickly. I didn't have a chance to thank you."

"You can thank me now."

"Thank you. I don't understand why you have done all these things for me?"

"Everyone needs a little help once in a while, and helping people is my job. That or giving people a little payback when they deserve it," she giggled a bit.

"How did you know I needed help? I understand you are a tow-truck driver. Be it the prettiest tow-truck driver I've ever seen. Your child must go to Greentree Elementary. Those are a couple of cases of being in the right place at the right time. But how could you even know about the funeral? My own family didn't know about the funeral."

"First things first, for a man with old-fashioned ideals let me introduce myself. You can call me Karma." Now that I can get a real look at her, I can see she is tall for a woman this side of five-foot-eleven. Based on her figure, she could work the runway at any fashion show. She is young too. She is in her early twenties, I would say. Her golden blond hair is loose about her shoulders and flowing gently in the breeze. She is wearing bold black eyeliner. Her eyes jumped out at me when I gazed into them. Her lips are painted cherry red and popped as well.

"Karma, it sounds like the name of a character from a bad urban fantasy novel. Let me guess you have sisters named Faith, Hope, and Charity." She tilted her head and gave me an expression of displeasure. "I am sorry. I was a little snarky."

"Yes, it was a bit snarky, but I accept your apology. And no, I don't have any sisters. I do have what you would call a cousin named Epiphany. I don't like her. She keeps taking credit for everyone else's ideas."

"Now that's comedy," I said with a smile on my face. "Why are you following me? Do I owe you money?"

"I'm not sure you are ready to know. Let's say you are a little investment of mine and leave it at that."

"Investment? Never mind my life has been so kooky lately what is one more kook?"

"I am no kook as you put it. I have been following you, though. You have done me proud," the Cheshire cat grin on her face said I know something you don't. "You have a unique energy about you. Your energy is unfocused, but there none the less. It is what attracted my attention. From time to time, I have looked in on my investment. I lent a hand if you needed it. I only watched when you didn't. You have not disappointed me. I think you will do swimmingly." Her Cheshire grin of hers came back, and she looked as though she was holding back a laugh, "You must learn the ways of the Force if you're to come with me to Alderaan."

"No. No. And no! You have it all wrong. You are supposed to be an old man, and I should be a young, naive farm-boy with wanderlust and a destiny to save the world. I am only a middle-aged, washed-up, ex-crossing guard with delusions of being a man."

She crossed her arms under her breasts, "Are you done with the self-pity?"

She is right. Self-pity is getting me nowhere. "Yes. Yes, I am." With my decision, I feel a new confidence. The turnaround was quick, but I have always been quicker than I look.

"With all of the stresses in your life, your self-imposed barriers are finally beginning to break down. Whether you realize it yet or not, you have potential, but before we can start, you need to deal with Mark Galos. Know this. He is more than he appears. And remember you have made me proud and if they knew what you have done, Charlene, John, and Moiraine would be proud of you too."

"What did I do to make you or more importantly, my family proud?"

"You chose not to pull the trigger. You had more than enough reason to murder the son-of-a-bitch, yet you did not. It is easy to kill a man who deserves it. It is difficult to show him mercy, especially if no one will ever know what you did. Well, I know what you did. So, I want to give this back to you as a reward." She reached into the clutch bag she was carrying and pulled out a simple gold band and offered it to me.

"How did you know I chose not to murder mister psychopath?"

"You have so many questions, and I don't have the time. I'll tell you this would all go easier if you would only go with the flow." I took the ring. It is warm to the touch. I looked at the inscription on the interior surface; it read "Together Forever." It is my ring.

"How did you get this?"

"Mark tossed it away after the robbery. I picked it up, and I have been waiting for the right time to return it to you."

It slipped right on and nestled into the indentation on my finger as though it was never missing. "I can't thank you enough for my ring back. It means a great deal to me. Silly, I know, to be emotionally tied to an object."

"Is it? Your daughter, Moiraine, such a sweet and gentle child, has been carrying the teddy bear with her since that terrible day. Did you know she has been taking it to school every day in her back-pack?"

"No, I didn't know." Guilt struck me at the realization I had not been as observant with her as I should have been.

"I wouldn't concern yourself with it. It is harmless and she, in her own way, is trying to make your burdens lighter. She knows you are hurting because of your wife's plight. Remember your daughter's love can be a source of strength just as your wife's love is."

I looked in the distance, "I don't know where to go to from here."

She placed her hand on my shoulder, and I looked back to her, "I can't tell you, but I have faith in you."

"Thank you. It has been too long since a lady has said those words to me. It is comforting. Too little comfort has been mine lately." I smiled at her, even though it felt hollow. "You say things as she would."

"Well, she is a woman of a gentle nature, and gentle-natured women think alike, but more importantly, she is right for you. I can see both she and your daughter have had an exponential effect on your growth as a man." She smiled back at me and said, "I approve of them. I think this is enough for the time being, Nathan." She stood with her proclamation.

"What is it you want from me?" I stood also.

"Why, Nathan, I want you to become a hero," she started walking away.

"Heroes often die."

"Not the smart ones," she said over her shoulder. She had made her way to a crowd of people and started to disappear from my sight.

This has been one strange encounter. How strange? Compared to seeing ghosts? Not so much. It is way past time to do some right thinking. She said there is more to Mark than there appears to be. I must break down this problem. Do one step at a time. It works for both problem solving and square dancing. How can I protect my family? How do I deal with Mark himself? How do I live with myself if I fail the first task but accomplish the second? If I win the day on all fronts, I can go back to my life? If I fail both tasks, all I'll have is oblivion.

Simple. Why have I been stressing?

In my dreams, I have been less than impotent protecting my family, and he finds us if we run. Change the game. Think outside the box. I must turn things around.

Lightbulb.

It might work. I must marry the plan with intent and action. I started for my car at a pace close to a power-walk. Karma is right. I needed to stop see-sawing and act. My first step is to confront Mark Galo's parents. Queue ominous music. The theme to *Alfred Hitchcock Presents* started playing in my head *The Funeral March of a Marionette*," I wonder if Mr. K R A P is trying to tell me something?

The drive to Mark Galos parent's house was agonizingly slow and filled my soul with dread. What am I going to find? Would my knock be answered with a shotgun blast to the face or tender mercy?

There is plenty of parking on the street, so I found a spot close by. It is a long walk up to the front door made longer by my anxiety. Mark's family home is a fine house, more like a mansion. It has two stories with tall white columns around the whole house. It had a red roof and red shutters. The porch extended all the way around the house like an old Southern mansion. It is a bit out of place here in America's Finest City. Most of the older homes touted a Spanish Ranchero style.

Arriving at the door, I rang the bell. A woman's voice called out "Who is it? You are standing in a shadow, and I can't see you." I took a step back so she could see me.

With my best humble look, "My name is Nathan Embers, madam. I testified at your son's trial."

She gasped, "Get out of here. I don't want you here. Leave before I call the police. Please leave. If Mark is following you… Get out of here. Oh God, please leave." There is panic in her voice.

"I will leave in a second. Let me have my say."

"No, leave my property now."

"I know Mark is in hiding here. Don't ask me how. Tell him I'm sorry. Tell him I hold no grudge. He won his freedom fair and square. Ask him to please leave my family out of it. Kill me if he must, but to have mercy on my family." I heard a bolt being thrown back and a lock turn. Mrs. Galos showed half her face through the chain, which kept her door from fully opening.

"Mr. Embers, I don't know what happened to my son, but I know what he is now. He is a monster. I know he shot your wife. He will be back to finish the job. I have no doubt. He almost killed me. I have no son. He is dead to me. Please leave before he thinks I am helping you and changes his mind about killing me," She shut the door, threw the bolt, and locked it. She shouted through the door, "Please, go."

"I am going," I turned and right in front of my eyes stood Mark Galos. My heart jumped. I immediately started to tremble as the fight or flight response kicked in. After a split-second, I noticed he looked different somehow. He didn't look sick anymore. There is no craze look to his eyes. His expression is sorrowful.

"Mr. Embers, why are you here?"

"Your voice. It is the second voice I heard during the robbery. I don't understand. It is like you are two different people."

"You can hear me! Finally, I can be heard. And no, the thing living in my body is not me. We are two different beings. I'm a man. He's the beast."

"You have two personalities, like Dr. Jekyll and Mr. Hyde?"

"No, Mr. Embers. He was a voice I started hearing in my head. A voice not my own. Over the years he started to push me out. Tell me, Mr. Embers, do you think I'm dead? I think I am."

I reached out and touched him. It felt similar to when I shook hands with Ralph Daves. "Yes, Mark, you are dead and are a ghost."

"How can you talk to me? Never mind. The how is not important. You are in danger, Mr. Embers. He wants to kill you something fierce."

"Yeah, I am beginning to think that. Your mother is going to freak if I don't leave. I will go someplace safe for us to talk. When I call you, please come." I drove away.

There is a place I know where I won't be out of place talking to the dead. Heading to the cemetery, about a mile from the Galos' mansion, suddenly there was a blinking red light in my rearview mirror. Crap. With a closer look in the rearview mirror, I recognized the driver and passenger to be my favorite pair of detectives Frank Hawkins and Joe Hauser. How special. I pulled over and patiently waited for the forthcoming harassment.

They approached my car one on each side. They had their suit jackets open, and the side where they holstered their guns was pulled back. Oh yes, I am one dangerous hombre. To be fair, it is standard practice. It still makes you nervous to think you can be riddled with bullets for the wrong move. Playing nice seems to be the order of the day. My hands are in plain sight on the steering wheel with my fingers spread. "What can I do for you fine officers today?"

"Cut the crap, wiseass," came from Frank. He opened my door and yanked me out and threw me against the hood of my car. He proceeded to cuff me and give a more complete frisking than the last time I went to the airport. When he was done with his version of rough foreplay, he pulled me to the curb. "Sit down." As I struggled to sit down gracefully with my hands cuffed behind me, Frank had a sneer on his face. Joe, on the other hand, looked a little bored.

"Okay, spill it. Why did you go to the Galos' home?" Frank asked it like he knew my answer before I gave it.

"Truth. I had hoped they were in contact with Mark. I asked his mother to convey my apologies and to beg for mercy. I know his attack on my wife is only the first. He plans to kill my whole family."

"Is she going to send him this message?" asked Frank.

"No. She is scared to death of her own son. She begged me to leave before he would see and take his vengeance out on her."

"Mr. Embers, you must admit it does smell a little fishy you talking with Mark's parents," Joe said with an easy-going tone in his voice.

"It may smell fishy to you, but it's only reasonable I try to get the word, anyway I can, to Mark. The hours are counting down until my wife dies, and I will try anything, including begging, to keep the same fate from my daughter."

"My condolences," Joe bent his head down a moment. "Do you think he will come after your daughter too?" Joe is not taking all this personal. He's only a man doing his job.

"Without a doubt. If you had been the one who looked down the barrel into his eyes, you wouldn't doubt either." Sorrow hit me, and I hung my head down. "Can you let me go? I am trying to find a way out, and you are hindering me."

Frank snapped, "You're trying to find a way out. Tell us where Mark is hiding. We will take care of him."

"Are you playing the same old tune again, Frank? Screwing up my testimony is all I did. The result: a crazy man was freed. What more do you want from me?" When nothing but silence came to my ear, I said, "Frank, I know why you are taking this so personally. The kids. Ralph told me once why you go ballistic when children are threatened."

Frank barked "You know nothing. You don't get to talk to me about Ralph. Mention him again to me, and I'll take you someplace without cameras."

"Your sister...," Frank grabbed my arm and pulled me up and not in a friendly way. He pushed me back to their car. I stumbled a couple of times. He opened the back door and shoved me in. He didn't even hold my head so to keeping from bumping my wee little noggin. He slammed the door shut. He yelled at Joe to get in.

Joe walked around the car and started talking animatedly with Frank. Their voices are too muffled for me to hear what they are saying, but I think Joe didn't agree with Frank's plan. Frank got right in Joe's face. Joe walked away and pulled out his cell phone. Frank paced back and forth a couple of times. Joe hung up his phone, turned back to Frank, and started talking with him again. Frank is not happy.

Joe walked over to the back door and opened it. "Come on, let's go." He reached in and helped me out of the car. He is far gentler than Frank. He unlocked the cuffs. "Mr. Embers, you are free to go. The San Diego Police Department would like to extend an apology to you." Joe leaned into me and said, "He has it bad. I don't think he has slept since the shooting near the school. He can't find the bastard. So, he's taking it out on you. He's a decent cop."

"I hear what you're saying." Frank was still pacing in front of the car. "The last thing I want is there to be bad blood between him and I. When this is over one way or another, and it will be over, tell him I hold no grudges. The oath to protect those kids still binds me. Even though I no longer work the corner, the promise is still in my heart. I also know you're a working man doing his job, and I hold no grudges against you. You were doing your job with the bad cop bad cop routine." Frank stopped pacing and looked me in the eye. Hard. He spat, then a little smile grew on his face. Oh, this is not even close to being over. Somehow, I could feel his thoughts. Even if the virtuous win the day and all is well in Mudville, he has marked me down in his book. Hopefully, he never gets a chance to strike a line through it.

During the walk back to my car, I half expected Frank to put a round or two in my back. With the threat averted, I started old Jezebel up and left for the cemetery. It is about the only place one can go and look like you're talking to someone who is not there, and no one will think twice on it. The rest of the drive happened without a hitch. I picked a grave at random and made the call. I thought of Mark Galos, said his name, and put a piece of my will behind it. True to form after the span of three heartbeats, the real Mark Galos stood before me.

"Hey, Mark, you look like death warmed over." He looked at me like a teacher does when a student gives an obviously wrong answer for the laughs. "Sorry, my life has been so screwed up lately I have to joke, or I would put a bullet through my brain."

"At least your body wasn't stolen by a psychopath bent on freeing his friends."

"Point taken. Freeing his friends?" I asked.

"Yes. I don't know what it means. Every once in a while, I saw glimpses of him doing some high-level math. I'm no newbie, but it was some stuff I couldn't comprehend, upper-end particle physics I think. As I said, I only got fleeting views of it."

"Say your family is pretty well off. Did he say why he wanted to start a life of crime? It seems to me like he could have shaken the old family money tree for money to buy drugs."

"He wasn't looking for a high. He used the drugs to help him quiet my voice and finally push me all the way out."

"Well, that explains that. Sorry, continue."

"Why did this happen to me? Why me? I had plans, and I was getting there too." His face showed the expression anyone gets when an injustice is perpetrated on them. It's a question to the universe.

"I don't know what to tell you. I felt the same way when he pointed the gun to my head. If it's any consolation to you, I have no qualms about trying to kill him when I face him at home. I must stop calling it, him. I must call the creature in the shell of Mark Galos. for that is what it is, a monster. What did he talk to you about when he was a voice in your head?"

"He kept trying to convince me to take higher and higher levels of math and science. He gave me suggestions as to which other courses to take. We worked on the homework together. He pushed. I went willingly at first. Then he started to try and wrestle control from me. He is a persistent little bastard. The first time he took control, I was asleep. He got up and did some internet searches. My parents thought I was sleepwalking." A quizzical look came to Mark's face, "You are taking all this pretty well. I would think most people would be in disbelief."

"I can talk to ghosts, son. All this is no more than a raised eyebrow worth of weirdness to me. This thing, for lack of better words, the shell of Mark Galos must be smited, hard, fast, and repeatedly if necessary. Whatever it is, it must die." I told my brain to start working on a plan. *"The wheels in my head go round and round, round and round, round and round. The wheels in my head..."* Mr. K R A P is doing a mashup today how clever. The music faded. I looked at the time on my cell. It is later than I thought. I needed to be home when Mo's bus arrives. With

237

a quick call to John, I asked him to head over to my house to take care of Mo if the traffic holds me up.

"Mark, is there anything I can do for you before I run?"

"I don't know. Am I destined to being a ghost until the end of time?"

"Can't you move on to whatever is next?"

"How do I do it?"

"I have no idea, son. Wait." I remembered the guy in the hospital he said he could hear something. "Mark, can you hear anything strange or unusual?"

"I can hear something like singing, but it's not with voices. It is hard to explain. It is faint." Mark turned his head and looked back behind him.

"Go to the sound, Mark. I don't know what's there. I don't hear it. Maybe it is where you need to go." Mark didn't say another word; he turned his whole body to where I guess the direction the music came from and walked. After three steps, he was gone.

I tried an experiment. I pictured Mark in my thoughts and began to call him back. My stomach started to turn, and I started to feel ill. All indications point to I can only call those ghosts which still walk the Earth. I raised one eyebrow and said, "Fascinating."

Returning to my car, I drove for home. Moiraine's bus arrived moments after I arrived home. John and I waited at the curb for Mo to exit the bus. We all walked together up to the house.

"Moiraine, put your school things away then go see your mom." I asked John, "Are you ready? I think it is time we all say goodbye."

"You're doing the right thing, Son." John patted my shoulder as he passed me and headed to his daughter's bedside. It is a long walk of only a few steps to my wife's deathbed.

She had a peaceful look as she is laying there. I touched her cheek. Gone is the electric sensation I always feel when I touch her or when she touches me.

Chapter Sixteen

I looked down at my wife. I am being selfish. She is
entitled to better than I had ever given her. Will my life be
worth living after I say goodbye? I turned and looked
down at my daughter. I placed my hand on her head.
Moiraine looked up at me with such love and trust. Yes, my
life will be worth living. My thoughts drifted to how
Charlene and I met.

She had saved my life.

*I am done with my weekly shopping at the supermarket.
I placed my items on the conveyor belt and waited my turn.
The woman checker is young but conveyed a more mature
aura. She is also rather striking in both face and figure. I
have been shopping here for some time, but I have never
been in her line before. She is dressed in a baggie uniform.
It is far too big. She must be trying to disguise her most
fetching figure. On her face is a pair of big horn-rimmed
glasses. Her name badge reads "Marge." I don't believe it.
At her station is a coffee cup from the coffee house in this
shopping center. It is one of those three bucks a cup places.
I never frequent those establishments. I hate all coffee, even
the super sweetened and extra caffeinated ones. My
particular favorite liquid vice is Diet Pepsi. I have four six-
packs in my mix of items. Her coffee cup had a different
name than her badge. As I read it, I thought it sounded
more like how she looked, beautiful and classy. I paid for
the groceries. As she counted my change back to me, our
hands touched briefly. The pit of my stomach fell, and my
heart skipped a beat. I'd heard of love at first sight but
never love at first touch. Is it love, or am I only randy? I
didn't know what to do. I took my change and said, "Thank
you." I walked to my car and loaded it up with my week's
worth of future sewage.*

Normally I would never approach a woman without an introduction. I tend to be a little old fashioned and have passed up other ladies who have caught my eye. This is different. I feel a tugging in my heart. It is unsettling. I had to talk to her. No other option even crossed my mind.

I entered in her line again with a little something I didn't need. When it was my turn without looking at me, she said, "Next, please."

I handed her the pack of gum I had grabbed. She looked over to me and smiled. My heart skipped a beat again. "Back so soon? Did you forget something?"

"Um yes." I haven't felt this awkward since middle school. We finished the transaction, and I was about to walk away. A fire erupted inside me. "Marge, I would like to buy you a cup of coffee if I may. What time is your shift over?"

"It is against the rules to go out with customers," she said sternly, but she is blushing also.

"As of right now, I no longer shop here." After a moment of silence, I said, "Just coffee." I waited what must have been an eternity, but was only the span of a few loud heartbeats.

She looked around quickly then softly told me the time her shift ended. Good, I have enough time to clean up a bit. I promised her I would be back promptly when her shift ended. I hurried back to my car and rushed home to shower, shave, and shove off.

I patiently waited at a spot halfway between the two entrances into the supermarket. I could quickly glance at either door, so I wouldn't miss her. It is about five minutes after her shift ended and she emerged. Her hair is out of the ponytail she had during work. Gone are the ugly glasses. She had applied some make-up. It is a light application to enhance rather than to cover-up. After about three steps out the door, she removed her smock. She is wearing a pull-over top which fit far better than the smock.

241

*Her figure is even more alluring than what I had imagined
was under her tent of a uniform. The neckline dipped a bit
but didn't reveal any cleavage. She is walking with
confidence and purpose. I approached her and held out my
hand to shake. I know on social occasions, such as this, you
don't offer to shake hands with a lady unless she presents
hers first. But what I want to do is touch her hand again to
be sure. She clasped my hand and a rush of endorphins
coursed through my brain like a flash flood. I am rolling on
an emotional white-water trip. Hope I don't drown. After a
long moment, she asked, "Can I have my hand back?"*

*Damn. I had forgotten to let go of her hand. I felt like an
idiot; I would know. I'm familiar with the feeling. I
released her hand and mumbled an apology. "Shall we?" I
motioned to start walking to the coffee house. We strolled
and chit-chatted about nothing important. I tried to sound
calm and relaxed. I fear I came across like the idiot who
forgot to let go of her hand. As we reached the coffee
house, I opened the door for her. "Why don't you grab us a
table and I'll place the order." I made and paid for the
order then sat down. Before we became too comfortable,
the name "Charlene" was called out by the barista. I stood
to retrieve the coffee. I returned and announced, "One iced
vanilla latte with an extra shot for Charlene." Out of my
coat pocket, I pulled out an ice-cold Diet Pepsi. My only
beef with establishments like this is they never carry
anything but coffee and tea.*

*"How did you know what I drink and how did you know
my real name? Are you some kind of stalker?" I couldn't
tell if she is serious or a little impressed.*

*"I noticed, at your workstation, the coffee cup had a
different name on it than your name tag. I reasoned you use
another name at work to avoid creeps from learning who
you are. I like that. It shows you're smart and cautious. I
bet being as pretty as you are," again she blushed a little,*

"a great many men approach you. I feel honored you agreed to spend this time with me."

She raised an eyebrow at me. "And how did you know what I drink?"

"When I went over to the counter, I jotted down on one of their cups what was written on yours." Her eyebrow is still raised, and the silence is deafening. I continued, "I hoped I wouldn't have to explain this until after we have been going out for a while. Assuming you agree to go out with me again." I started, "I have a unique memory. I can relive anything I have read, witnessed, or heard. Taste is different. I can't remember those as well. It's sad. I would give a great deal to taste some of my mother's cooking again. She passed away about a year ago."

"Oh, I'm sorry about your loss." A sad look briefly crossed her face. Then she was back to the issue at hand, "I find what you said about your memory a little hard to believe." Charlene crossed her arms under her breasts and leaned back from the table.

She's closing herself off from me. It is not an encouraging sign. I leaned back too. I rattled off every in-store special which line the shelves of the market where she works; all 103 of them. She uncrossed her arms, and her face changed.

"That is amazing. You really can remember everything?"

"Every boring or gut-wrenching detail since about the age of five."

"Wow, music too?" I nodded in the affirmative. "So, you can replay songs in your head like one of those new things. What are they called? Mp3 players?"

I gently slapped my forehead. I have been a little dense. "You know I have never thought of it that way. Thanks, I'll never have to listen to songs I don't like on the radio again."

She looked at the watch on her wrist and said, "I have to get to class. Thank you for the coffee." She reached out and briefly, touched my hand. A casual gesture nothing at all, but it still made my heart skip a beat. I stood with her, and as we exited the coffee bean brewery, I opened the door for her. I walked her to her car and again opened her door for her. She turned toward me before she got in. She looked at me for a few seconds.

This is my opening. "I would like to see you again."

"I don't know. I don't have the time. I work full-time and go to school full-time."

"Three dates is all I ask. I have found by the end of the third date you know if there is reason enough to continue." I was silent for a moment. She did not speak up. "And this coffee counts as the first date."

She didn't say anything for a second and then said, "Okay, I will go out with you twice more as you've asked. Don't read too much into this. I don't have time for someone in my life with school and work." She gave me her phone number, and we arranged to go out in four days on Saturday night.

Before she sat in her car, "Here let me get that." She reached out and plucked a piece of lint off my shoulder. She got in the car without further fuss.

I watched her drive away as my heart soared. I didn't understand. It is only a date. Yet, the anticipation is already building. I have plans to make. I went home to contemplate. On the short drive to my apartment, I had decided on dinner and a movie, a classic second date. Which restaurant? Which movie? I walked through my door and before anything else I booted up my computer. I need to perform some searches.

The days flew by at a snail's pace. Early Saturday morning, I had my car washed, fueled it up, and went for a haircut. Well, I had them all cut. I spent the rest of the day puttering around my apartment. I watched as the time approached when I had to leave for our date. All is well. The only thing left to do is to pick her up. I arrived at her house about five minutes before our date. I waited there in my car until it was exactly the time to pick her up. I knocked on her door, and it was promptly answered. She stood in the doorway. She is dressed in a white blouse and black skirt. The blouse's neckline revealed the hint of cleavage without showing too much. The skirt's hemline is about mid-thigh, and she wore nylons. I tried not to get caught looking, but my eyes did flick for a second. Luckily with my memory, I can dwell on the mental image without appearing to gawk. It's a definite benefit. I pondered her image in my mind for a moment. I must say if I were to try to judge which one of her assets is the most appealing, it would be a toss-up. I don't think you could take either one alone without the whole being diminished.

She turned her head back into the house. "I'm leaving, Dad."

I heard a male voice from inside the house. "Do you have money on you?" Charlene replied she did have money. "Don't stay out too late. You know how I worry."

Charlene rolled her eyes a bit. "Yes, Dad." We walked out to my car. My mother taught me manners growing up, so I opened the car door for her. She entered the car in a classy fashion by sitting down and pivoting her legs into the car. I received a libido amping long look at those legs. My first judgment was right. Those are some nice gams. I take it back. By all appearances, she is a classy woman. A classy woman isn't a skirt, dame, babe, or chick and they don't have gams.

We had about a twenty-minute drive to the Gas Lamp Quarter. I had made reservations at a cozy little dinner house called The Amber Glow. It is a higher-end middle-class establishment with cloth napkins. Usually, cloth napkins are a sure sign the eatery is too pricey for my wallet, but I was surprised as everything is reasonable, but *not cheap by a long shot. It is reasonable enough, so I'll be eating Top Ramen soup instead of lettuce sandwiches without the bread. This will be my last real dinner until my next paycheck, so I started chewing slowly.*

We talked about little things like where we grew up, our families, and work. I was afraid a conversation about work would come up. I grimaced inside. "I don't have what you would call a career. I hate to admit it, but I'm a rent-a-cop or a security guard, if you will, at a retirement community. It pays the bills. I'm still up in the air on what to pursue." I don't have any sense of how she feels about my admission. She has a great poker face. Yes, she has a beautiful poker face. "What are you studying in college?"

"Well, I am majoring in Fine Art, and I minor in Education." Her face brightened as she revealed this. "My ultimate goal is to become a teacher in a grade school. I love little children. They see everything with new eyes." She talked about her plans all the way through the salad and halfway through the main course. "Listen to me talking this whole time." I could listen to her talk all night. "Have you thought about going to college?"

"I did start to go to college, but I was stupid."

"You don't strike me as being stupid, in fact, just the opposite."

"Thank you. It's a long story. The cliff notes edition would be I was accused of cheating by an intolerant professor with a small mind. Needless to say, with my memory, I scored perfect on the first three exams. He claimed I must be cheating because in over twenty years of teaching, no student had ever scored so many perfects in his class. I think the kicker was on one exam a question was incorrectly worded, so I turned in my exam with the correction included. It was his word against mine. Tenured professor against a freshman student. The outcome was he had me expelled with a note placed on my transcript. When I tried to enroll in another college, I was turned down and

told as long as the note remained on my transcript, I would never be admitted to any college."

"That doesn't seem fair. Education should be open to anyone."

"It wasn't. I appealed the decision. I was told the administration would remove the letter from my file if I admitted to the cheating and made a formal apology to the professor. I know it sounds hokey, but I am trying to live by a code. I don't lie unless the truth would hurt someone for no good reason. You know, like do I look fat in this outfit?" Charlene smiled. "If I had cheated, I would have copped to it. My pride blocked my way. So, here I am in a nowhere job, hoping an opportunity will present itself. If it doesn't, I will make an opportunity."

Dessert arrived. We shared a slice of Black Forest cake. She only took one bite and wouldn't take anymore. I had to finish the rest. I looked at my watch, and it is getting time for the next round of shows at the theatre. "I thought we could take in a movie. Is there anything playing you want to see? I am open to anything; I love movies of all kinds. I hate to admit it, but I even enjoy what most men would refer to as chick flicks."

"I am having a pleasant time sitting here and talking. Do we have to go to a movie?" She smiled as she said it. My heart soared again. I like this woman. She ordered coffee, and I asked for some hot tea, Earl Grey, of course. And we talked. We talked as though we had known each other all our lives. It is comforting. Finally, the manager of the restaurant said they are closing, and we had to leave. I looked at my watch and was surprised at how long this simple dinner had lasted. It is still too short for my taste.

I paid the check and left an extra-large tip.

"Are you sure you want to leave so large a tip? Our bill couldn't have been costly enough for such a big tip. Don't feel like you need to impress me."

"Impressing you has nothing to do with it. We sat in the booth all night long. Our server could have turned over the table at least twice more if we had left right after dinner. Waiters and waitresses live on their tips. It would be unfair to take a table all night and not compensate them for it."

"You're a decent man, Nathan."

"You can call me Nate."

"I always call people by their full names. I don't know why, but it's a quirk I have." She smiled again at me as we stood from the booth. "But you can call me Char."

The name Char brought a mental image of a man getting burned by her touch. Lord knows it put a fire into me.

We returned to her house and talked a few more minutes sitting there in my car. Charlene said, "This has been a very enjoyable evening." She looked at her watch. "Well, more like early morning. I have to rest. I have work and studying tomorrow." She started to get out of the car. I started to open the door on my side when she said. "It's ok, Nathan. I can make it the rest of the way myself."

I quickly considered what her statement meant. Is she trying to avoid an awkward moment at her door? Is she trying to let me know I don't have to play the gentleman? Is she trying to escape? "I will enjoy walking you to your door. You can thank my mother. It is the way I was raised. And you don't have to worry. I will not take liberties." I had already decided on that course. This woman is special, and I want these dates to be special. I am sure most men would have already made a play. I wanted her to see I am different. She waited in the seat while I walked to open the door. I put my hand out to help her out if she needed it. She put her hand in mine and used it to help leverage herself out. I rejoiced for a short infinity at how her hand feels in mine. Once she was out of the car, I released her hand, and we walked in silence to her door.

At her front door, she turned towards me and said, "I have had a very pleasant evening."

Now to give her an out if she is only being polite. God, I hope I am reading everything right. "I know you agreed to go on another date, but I don't want you to feel obligated to keep your word. If you don't wish to see me again, I will trouble you no longer. Just know, I thank you for tonight and the chance to know you."

"Are you trying to squirm your way out of seeing me again, Nathan Alexander Embers?" The porch light is out, so I can't see her face clearly enough to tell if she is playfully mocking or miffed at me. The light came on. Her expression changed immediately. She rolled her eyes.

"Wow, a long delay for a motion-sensitive light."

"It is my dad in his own, not so subtle way, telling me to come inside. If I don't come in now, he will open the door next," she opened the door. Turning quickly back and looking in my eyes, she said, "Goodnight Nathan, I am looking forward to our next date. Call me." She entered her house and closed the door.

I don't think my feet touched the ground once on the walk back to my car. All the way back home a song from "Oklahoma" played in my head "... I've got a wonderful feeling. Everything's going my way ..."

I called her two days later. Her father answered the phone. "I'm sorry, but she's not here. I'll tell her you called," he promptly hung up on me before I could say another word. But before the line went dead, I heard a grumpy "Humph!" Me thinks he is not happy. I'll have to remedy that.

Charlene and I finally connected and arranged our third date. I knew what I wanted to do. I had made a couple of calls and talked to the people I needed to talk with. All is set.

I arrived early and waited in my car until the appointed time trying to drum up the courage. I rehearsed what I am

249

going to do and say a hundred score or more. Well, ready or not here I go. I knocked on the door and as before it is answered right away by Char. "May I come in?"

"Oh, I don't think it's a prudent idea yet," Charlene said all the while taking quick looks into her house.

"I'm sure it is not a prudent idea. However, I believe it's the right thing to do," I said with a little firmness in my voice.

"If the boy wants to come in, by all means, let him in." His voice didn't sound any less grumpy than before on the phone.

Char let me by and under her breath said. "Oh, great."

Her father is at the dining room table doing some task I couldn't quite make out. As I approached, it became evident he is cleaning an impressive old double-barrel shotgun. He is telling me something. My stomach started doing summersaults as though someone had let loose a kaleidoscope of butterflies in it. I stretched out my hand. "Hello, sir. My name is Nathan Embers." He looked at my hand and then looked up at me. He left me hanging there. Well, I am in his home if he wants to play it that way, he has the right. "Impressive shotgun. It's a Greener, right?"

He kept looking at me as he cocked an eyebrow in the same fashion Char had when we had coffee that first day. "Yes, it is. It's been in my family for a long time. So, tell me what is it you want?"

"I wanted to assure you there is no need for concern. I have nothing but honorable intentions for your daughter." I stuck my hand out a second time and was unanswered again. "Please take this as gospel, for I am a man of my word. I will treat Charlene with nothing, but respect, and I will protect her while she is with me."

I heard an "Oh, brother," come from Char's direction. I ignored it as if she had never said it.

He chimed up with a "This one has a right pretty tongue in his mouth. I've seen your likes before. Your kind say the

250

right words and act the noble gentleman. Your kind don't fool me none. You are after only one thing."

"Father! Don't say that," Charlene pleaded.

"He's right. I am after one thing." Charlene's father stood up from the table and snapped shut the barrels on the shotgun. "I want to win your daughter's heart!" I let it sink in a moment. "I know we haven't spent much time together, and normally I wouldn't admit this so soon." I paused and swallowed hard. I turned to look at her. "Every moment with her, I feel closer to her. I can only hope in time I can prove to Charlene I am a man worthy of her." I turned back to her father. "I hope one day I can earn your respect."

"Well, she's past the age she needs my permission. She can do as she likes."

"Yes, she can; however, it doesn't change that I am here showing you the respect you deserve as her father."

"You don't rattle easy do you, boy?" He put the shotgun down and held out his hand. I shook it as I was taught firm and proper. His grip has strength and it is on the edge of being painful.

"Are you two done or are you gentlemen going to start thumping your chests now?" Charlene scolded as she put her hands on her hips and looked at both of us in turn.

I looked at Char's father and spoke first. "Yes, I think we are done."

"Boy, I have to give it to you. You have spunk." There was a bit of a pause. "I don't like spunk, but if my daughter sees fit to be in your company. Well, I'll trust my daughter." There was a longer pause, and then he said, staring me straight in the eyes with a steady, steely glare. "You, I'll watch."

"Daddy!"

Her father started with, "Do you have money on you?" Charlene replied she did. "Don't stay out too late. You know how I worry." She gave him a peck on the cheek, and we were off.

As we walked to the car, Charlene said, "Well, that could have gone better."

"Yes, it could have, but at least he never loaded the shotgun." We drove in silence for a few minutes before I turned onto the I-15. I said, "I have some surprises in store for you tonight." I quickly turned my head toward her and smiled.

"What kind of surprises?"

"You'll see. We are going to do one of my favorite activities. The other one is, I want to share something with you, which is important to me." We started chatting about the mundane things in our lives; school, work, and overprotective parents. The time flew by. Even though I drive like an old woman and could have cut about fifteen minutes off our drive time, the ride was over too quickly. We finally arrived at our destination: The Moonlight Amphitheater. We are going to sit on a grassy knoll under the stars, have a picnic dinner, and watch some fine theater. We walked to our spot, spread out the blanket, and we ate my home-made tuna salad sandwiches.

"Wow, this tuna is great," Charlene said, holding her hand over her mouth and talking with her mouth full. When she finished her sandwich, she said, "I never liked tuna salad, but yours is amazing. You have to give me the recipe."

"If I did, you wouldn't need me anymore. Besides, I promised my mother I wouldn't tell anyone how to make it except my children and only if they made the same promise."

"So, you want children?" She said, looking at the stage because the show is about to begin. But I could see her looking at me out of the corner of her eyes.

"Yes, I want one of each." The show is beginning, "The Wizard of Oz." We sat there watching until the end of the show. "How did you like it?"

"I enjoyed the show, and they did a great job for an amateur production." We headed back to the car. I checked the time. By my quick calculations, the timing of the second surprise would be perfect. While we drove, we talked more. All the while, I feared this would be our final date. True to her word, we have been out three times, but I still don't know if there will be a fourth and more. Oh, how I hope there would be more.

We pulled into the parking lot for Belmont Park. Walking to the front gate is like swimming upstream. The crowd is leaving the park. It is about closing time. "Nathan, this is a sweet idea, but the park closes in five minutes." I urged her to keep walking. She stopped about ten feet in front of the turnstiles. I didn't let her reluctance sway me. I am on a mission. I approached the gate attendant and exchanged a few words out of her earshot. I motioned for her to follow. "Nathan, the park is closed."

"Trust me," is all I said. The attendant let us through, and we walked with purpose to the surprise. We entered the line for the Ferris wheel. We snaked our way to the front of the line. I shook hands with the man waiting there. He pressed a button on the control panel, and the wheel began to spin for a few seconds until a special car was in the loading ramp. In the car are a thermos, an igloo cooler, and a folded blanket. I quickly walked up the ramp to the car. I turned aside to let Charlene enter first, but she hadn't followed me.

"Nathan, I can't get inside it. I have a dreadful fear of heights."

I held out my hand towards her and said, "I will look after you. I will not let you fall." The expression on her face changed from fear to serenity. I must have said the right words. Without any further hesitation, she walked up to me, took my hand, and let me guide her into the waiting car. I placed the blanket over our laps. The operator put the restraining bar in place and sent us on our way. We rode to the top when the Ferris wheel came to a stop. As our car rocked for a couple of moments, Charlene gasped a bit and held on to the restraining bar. The car settled down, and Char relaxed. We had a beautiful view of the Pacific Ocean. It is a beautiful night, and the stars are out in force twinkling at us as if they are waving hello. It is perfect. I could not have asked for a better setting to share with Char.

"Oh Nathan, the view. It's beautiful. Thank you."

"It's not over. Wait for it." About five seconds later, all the lights on all the rides shutoff. We sat in the dark a moment. All is quiet. You could barely make out the sound of the waves. It is more a white noise which masked all the other sounds. The moment is right. I said, "Charlene, while all this is beautiful, it's not exactly what I wanted to share. I want to share a story. A memory. I have never told this to anyone before." My voice cracked.

"Nathan, I hear the pain in your voice. Please, I don't want you to be in pain. It can wait for another time."

"While there is a little pain with this memory, it is not why I have never told anyone before." We sat in the dark, smelling the ocean and feeling the breeze for a moment more. "When I was a young boy, I don't remember exactly how old I was, but it was before I started remembering everything. I told my mother I wanted to travel the stars and be an astronaut. I was serious. This was not the fancy of a young child. I felt it in my soul. She dismissed it without giving it a second thought. She told me it would be too difficult to become an astronaut. Too many people tried, and only a handful ever became one. I know she was only trying to spare me the pain of a hopeless pursuit. But her words cut me to the core. To think my mother would squelch my dream. It broke my heart. I was a broken boy.

254

As I walked away to my room to console my pain, I turned back to her and said, "You should never take a man's dreams from him," I turned back around and continued my walk."

"Oh Nathan, it is one of the saddest stories I think I have ever heard." The emotion in her voice told me she is sincere.

"When my mother saw how her words affected me, she told me we were going somewhere special. We took a picnic basket with dinner in it. We went to Balboa Park to a special place with a small stand of young trees. We laid out a blanket on the grass and looked up at the stars. She handed me some hot chocolate." I poured Char some hot chocolate out of the thermos and handed her the cup. "My mother pointed up at a star." I reached out and pointed to the same star. "That one right there. She told me in the days of the old wooden ships men would steer their ships by a star. If they followed the right star, they would always know their path is true. She told me it is my star. If I followed my star, I would always know my way is true."

I opened the cooler and pulled out a Diet Pepsi, opened it with the usual pop and slight hiss, and took a long swig. We sat there for a few minutes in the dark and silence. I reached over to take her hand. My heart raced with anticipation. Our fingers touched, and she held my hand without hesitation. She began to rub my hand with her thumb. I returned the gesture. I am in heaven. The height of the Ferris wheel is minuscule compared to the height my heart reached.

After another few minutes, the ride started to move again and spun until we reached the ramp once more. We walked back to my car, holding hands. "Nathan, how did you arrange this? Entering the park after hours and getting to ride the Ferris wheel. Having them to turn off all the lights on queue was amazing. It must have cost a fortune."

"No, its only costs were the hot chocolate and the Diet Pepsi. I know a guy. He owed me a favor. He just paid me back."

"Still, it was wonderful." It is getting late, so we headed to the freeway and back to her house. The freeway is quiet.

A car raced passed us as we cruised down the road. When the car was about a quarter-mile ahead of us, I saw one of his tires shoot off to the side. Sparks flew as the car cut across all the lanes. It didn't slow at all as it careened off the freeway and down an embankment. I pulled my car over. I handed Charlene my cell phone and told her to call 911 and to stay in the car. She started to get out anyway, *"No, stay in the car. Wait here for the Fire Department and direct them to the accident."* I said it rather forcefully. There is no mistaking my tone. She needed to do as I say.

"But I can help."

"You are helping." I softened my voice quite a bit, *"Besides, I don't want you to see this. Please, Char."* She listened to me and didn't follow. I took off for the accident.

Ten days later, I am in my recliner in my apartment. *"Star Trek, The Next Generation,"* is in my VCR and playing back on my television. The same episode has repeatedly been playing for days. I put it on once I returned home. I have been doing nothing but watching it since that night.

A knock came to my door. I ignored it. I had ignored everything since that night. I hadn't eaten, washed, or even brushed my teeth. All I am doing was drinking my Diet Pepsis, but they ran out a long time ago. The knock came to my door again.

"Nathan, it's Charlene, are you home? I have been worried." I heard a key being put in the door. My door opened slowly. I saw Charlene's beautiful face when she stepped in. *"Why haven't you called or picked up your car?"*

"How did you find my apartment?"

"It wasn't hard. Your address is on your registration."
She turned on my lights and got a real look at me. "Oh, my
God, Nathan! You look terrible. Are you sick?"

"You look as beautiful as always, but yes, I guess you
can say I'm a little sick." I turned back to continue
watching "Star Trek."

"I have brought your car back."

"You're a fine woman, Char. You can put the keys on
the table. Thank you. You shouldn't have bothered, though.
I won't be using it anymore."

She walked over to the table and placed the keys there.
She turned around and looked at me. "Nathan, what is
wrong? Look at me."

I turned and looked up at her. "I don't want to live
anymore, but I am too cowardly to do the deed straight out.
So, I have sat here. I am waiting to die."

"No wonder you look so haggard. What is this nonsense
about wanting to die?" She walked over to the curtains and
pulled them open. The sunlight is so blinding I had to close
my eyes before my retinas burned away. She opened a
window. "Let's get some fresh air in here. This place, and
you have an odor." She walked over to me and brushed a
few strands of hair away from my forehead. "Have you
eaten lately?"

"Nothing other than a few Diet Pepsis."

"What do you have here to eat?" She said this while
walking back to the kitchen. I heard several cabinets open
and finally, the refrigerator. "No... No... No... Well, this is
still growing." I heard the lid on my trash can open and
something thump. "Well, this is going to have to do until
you go shopping." I heard the noises of Char busily
preparing something.

"Charlene, it's kind of you, but you don't have to
trouble yourself."

"I don't want to hear any nonsense. My boyfriend is not going to starve himself to death." I heard more movement in the kitchen and some muttering under her breath.

I must have misheard, but I thought she said, boyfriend. My heart feels lighter at the prospect. It sank again because I knew it couldn't have been what she said. After a few more minutes she came walking over to me carrying a plate and a glass of water. All she said was, "Eat."

"Yes, ma'am." *I ate like a starving man, which I guess I am. Eggs and toast are the only things on the plate. While I ate, I realized I needed fresher eggs.* When I was done, Char went back to the kitchen and brought out my frying pan. *It had more eggs in it. I ate them without question.*

As she walked back to the kitchen with the frying pan, she spoke to no one in particular, but *I am sure it is aimed at me.* "Not a green vegetable in the house. The only thing which came out of the ground in here is a potato, and it is still growing." She started muttering some more, but I couldn't hear exactly what she said. She came back out and stood above me. "Get moving. Brush those teeth and shave your stubble off. Wait. Now that I look at you, a beard kept close and trim, would look handsome on you, but for right now clean-shaven is the order of the day, mister." *I did as commanded. I am a robot, neither motivated nor thinking. I only did as I was told.*

When I was finished, *I made my way back to my recliner and sat there. Charlene is doing some task in the kitchen. The dishes, I think. I wasn't paying attention to it. I am in my world of the memory of the night of our final date and the crash. What I saw changed me terribly. I tried not to dwell, but it is no use. I am in an endless loop of despair.*

Charlene finished what she was doing and came in and stood above me again. "I thought you would shower too, but I smell you didn't. You need to get in there and scrub, Boyfriend Mine."

"Charlene, what you are trying to do here is very kind. Have a seat." She sat down on the couch. "You don't understand. I don't see the point to all of this. All you are doing is delaying the inevitable. I want to die. The pain is too great."

Charlene had a softness in her eyes, but her voice is firm. "What a bunch of self-serving crap. If you, in fact, wanted to kill yourself, we wouldn't be talking. You would be dead. Some part of you wants to live even if you can't see it."

"No. You don't understand. That night on our way home, the man driving the car was injured. He was dying. His leg was mostly severed. I tried to put a tourniquet on it. I slowed the bleeding some, but I couldn't stop it. He was wedged in the car, and I couldn't pull him out. I was going to run back to my car to get the jack. I thought I could use it as a lever and free him enough to apply the tourniquet better. He reached out and grabbed my hand. He begged me not to go. He said he didn't want to die alone. He begged me to stay. He begged me. He asked me to be his friend. The firefighters were taking so long, and he was scared. He told me he was afraid to die alone. He told me he had spent his whole life alone. In the fleeting moments, while his life was pouring out of his leg, we talked. I mostly listened. He told me he always believed there would be time for friends and family later. His realization of what is most important was too late. It came to him there in the car with his life flowing away. I saw it in his eyes. He knew he was fading. I told him the rescue team would be there soon. I told him to hang on."

I took the glass of water Char had brought me with my eggs and downed it. I handed the glass back to Charlene. "Can I have some more, please?" Charlene took the glass, filled it with water, and returned it to me. I downed it too. I paused a moment. "He died, holding my hand in the ambulance. I can still see the blood, his blood, on my hands. *My God, I can't wash it off. I wash and wash my hands, but I still see it."*

Char looked at my hands, *"Nathan; there is no blood on these hands. You did the right thing. You were strong. I don't believe I would have been able to stay with him."*

I smiled at Char. *Her kindness is a mercy to me.* "There is more. All the while, as he was talking, it was like I could see what he said. Only it was my future. A mirror of my life was before my eyes. Every step in my life was leading me down a path, a dark and lonely path. It was a path to heartache and despair. At the end of the path, I was alone. When my sad life finally ended, I was unremembered and unmourned. I was a shallow man laid to rest in a shallow grave. Oh God, the pain is like a jagged knife being plunged in me." *Somewhere during my tale, I began crying. The tears burned my cheeks as they ran down my face. The acid of my torment was scaring my face deeply. At this point I found my head at Char's breast being rocked back and forth. Char is making comforting sounds which had no meaning unto themselves. All I know is a small amount of my pain had eased. Somewhere along the way, I stopped crying.*

"Nathan, I had no idea what you were going through, but it's over. It is in the past."

"My cursed memory won't let me forget. It plays over and over in crystal clarity." *As the events of that night started playing over again in my mind, my tears were renewed.*

"Nathan, look at me." My eyes met hers. *I feel a real connection with this woman, or perhaps I am reaching for a rope which isn't there.* "Nathan, I am here. You are not alone. I am here with you. We will get through this together. You are a caring and decent man, better than most, and any woman worthy of the title would welcome you in her life. All you have ever shown me is a kind and

gentle soul. I do not see you dying alone. I see a future for you filled with a wife and children who love you."

"Oh, Char, thank you for your mercy. I am sorry you had to see me this way. I thank you. Even if it is only for a moment, the illusion warms me in a way I don't believe I have ever felt."

"It's not an illusion. It is real. Come, the shower will help you feel better." She took my hand and guided me into my bathroom. She turned on the shower and made the water near scalding hot. You take a shower. I will leave you to it. Scrub mister! Every nook and cranny. Wash your hair too. I don't want to smell anything foul on you." She left the bathroom so I could begin. I undressed and stepped into the steam bath of a shower. After about ten minutes, I was about done when I heard Charlene's voice. "How are you doing?"

"Finishing up." I saw the shower door slide open. "I can dry myself. Thank you." Charlene slowly stepped into the shower without her clothes. She took a pose which accentuated her generous figure. If any man questions whether there is a God, all they need do is behold the beauty of the female form in all its glorious variations to know there is a creator. The vision of her brought a line from The Rolling Stone's song, "Start Me Up," to my mind. "Char, you are a teenage boy's wet dream." She blushed and averted her eyes from mine. She turned her head and looked into my eyes. "I can't believe I am saying this. I don't want this if it is going to be a one-time event as wondrous as it would be. One night with you would be like giving a man dying of thirst a single drop of water and denying him the full glass. I have done many things I am not proud to admit. I don't want you, us, to be one of them."

"What are you afraid of, Nathan? I don't bite." She paused then with a naughty grin said, "Unless you want me to." The naughty part of the smile faded, and she looked *even deeper into my eyes. "I want a full glass too, Nathan. I am not offering this out of pity. Nothing is compelling me. At least nothing more than the desire I have to be with you. Since the age of sixteen, I have only known boys. You are the first true man who has come into my life. I feel safe with you. You are hurting. Let me make you feel safe." The naughty grin found her face again as she said, "Besides you still owe me a goodnight kiss." She moved closer to me. She reached up to my face and held it with both her hands. I tilted my face down to hers, and we kissed. At first, it is only our lips then we melted into each other. We finished our first kiss. She pulled back, and we looked into each other's eyes.*

"Char, I have dreamed of that since the day you accidentally touched my hand. I fell in love with you at that moment. My feelings only grew as we began to know each other. It may not be smart to say this yet, but I love you."

She paused a second then said, "You are quite thick, aren't you? You are not the only one whose life changed." She smiled and said, "You had me at coffee, but you're not done having me yet. Not by a long shot."

I looked down at myself and said, "I haven't been taking care of myself since that night. So, you will forgive me if I'm a no-go for launch, so to speak."

"Failure is not an option." Oh, I like this girl. She kissed me again. It is the most intense kiss I have ever had, and I can remember them all. A Foreigner song started playing in my mind "I Want to Know What Love is; I Want You to Show Me..." Charlene must be able to see into the future because true to her prediction I didn't fail. In fact, I didn't fail twice.

I am back in the here and now. I bent down and kissed my wife. "Goodbye, my love. You will be missed." I leaned down and whispered into her ear because I don't want anyone to hear what I am saying. It is for her and her alone.

John is next, he took his daughter's hand and patted it a few times. "Goodbye, my little darling. It seems like only yesterday I said hello to you when you came into this world. Do not worry for us. We are a strong family, Nate, Moiraine, and I. We will look to each other." He kissed her forehead, turned, and walked out of the room to be alone with his grief.

I turned to Moiraine and told her, "Honey, you need to say goodbye to your mother."

"Daddy, I don't want to say goodbye to mommy," she turned around and went running out of the room. I heard her bedroom door slam shut, and the sounds of crying came to my ears.

I followed after my daughter. I knocked on her door. "Come in." She is holding the new Teddy Bear in a death grip and rocking back and forth on her bed.

"Moiraine, your mommy is not coming back, Honey. We have to say goodbye and let her go on without us." I was crying too. The tears are running down my face. They are little rivulets of sorrow. I hugged my daughter and rocked with her.

"But Daddy, the nice old man told me if I make a thousand cranes, I will get a wish. I want mommy to have my wish so she can wake up. Daddy, how many is a thousand? I already have a lot of cranes." She stood and ran to her closet. She opened the door and what must have been about a hundred cranes are piled up in there. "I ran out of paper. Can you get me some more paper if that is not a thousand?"

How can I tell her no? In her own way, she is trying to help. "Of course, I can get you more paper. We can go to the store right now. Clean yourself up, and we'll go." I left her room and went back to my wife. "Mary, my daughter is not quite ready to say goodbye to her mother yet. We will try again tomorrow."

"Mr. Embers, Nathan, I'm not sure she is going to last so long. She is close to the end." Moiraine came in the room with an armload of cranes. She put them on the bed next to her mom.

"Is that okay, Mary?" Mo asked as she turned and looked at the grandmotherly figure.

"Yes, Dearie, of course, it is" Mary reached into a pocket on her scrubs, pulled out a tissue, and dabbed her eyes. As Moiraine and I left for the store, Mary touched my arm and whispered to me, "Remember, it will be soon. Her breathing is slowing and erratic." I nodded my understanding. If Char leaves us before Mo has a chance to say goodbye, so be it. I will deal with the fallout. Without further delay, Mo and I headed to the store. It was a quiet drive.

When we returned from shopping, Moiraine grabbed the bundle of paper and started her task at the dinner table. I was amazed at how she worked. Her hands moved with both speed and grace. I planned to let her complete the batch of paper then tell her it is a thousand. It is a small lie, but this task is so important to her. I had to let her do it. I am probably wrong in my decision to let her try to save her mother this way, but is this any different than prayer? Both provide comfort. Moiraine will learn sometimes the answer to our best wishes or our most sincere prayers is "No." A harsh truth to say the least, but the truth is the truth.

She fell asleep at the table, making cranes. I carried her to bed. As I tucked her in, I said, "Have sweet dreams of your mother. Sweet dreams to both of us."

I entered my wife's bedroom to say goodnight to her. I turned to Mary, "Tell me she's not in any pain. The truth mind you. But I need to know she is not in pain."

Mary looked up from her book and said, "Oh heavens no, Dearie. She is resting peacefully. If she starts to be in pain, I have something I could give her to ease it."

I looked down at my wife, "Charlene, I know this is a lot to ask, but if you could stay with us a little while longer, your daughter needs to say goodbye to you in her own way. She needs to say the goodbye you never said to your mother." I leaned down and lightly kissed my wife on the mouth. I went to sleep in the living room with Blossom on my lap as she had been since the terrible day.

Chapter Seventeen

When my alarm went off, I woke and put Blossom down off my lap. Forcing myself to move, I stood from the recliner. Today is not going to be an easy fun-filled day. When Moiraine returns home from school this afternoon, she will have to say goodbye to her mother. Even if she refuses, I plan on telling Charlene it is time for her to move on. I am not looking forward to dealing with the atomic level of emotional fallout Moiraine will suffer if she decides not to say goodbye to her mother.

I made sure Moiraine is ready for the day. After she left for school, I spent most of the day with Charlene. We talked. Well, I talked, and she listened. Gently, I held her hand and stroked her cheek. It is difficult to watch her struggling so hard to stay here with us. When she would take a breath, I could hear a death rattle in the sound of it. Twice I thought she had passed because the time between her breaths was so long. I turned to Mary and asked, "Waiting for the inevitable is killing me. How can you do this job? The emotional toll…"

"Mr. Embers," she paused and smiled "Nathan, you start to grow a bit of armor around your heart, but the truth is it's difficult at best and heart-wrenching at worse. It does have its rewards, though. I know it sounds like a canned answer. But I have been with some people at the end when their own families would not. To be of service and comfort in a person's final hours is a sorrowful joy. I remember this one patient. He had been in a coma for a few months. I was with him most of the time. Not once had any family member come to visit him. I try not to judge people too harshly. I still have trouble with that family. The day he died he also woke up. It sometimes happens with coma patients."

"Are you serious?"

"Oh yes, they wake-up, some without symptoms of their ailment, to say good-bye. The human spirit can do wonders. The sad thing is it deceives some families into believing their loved one is back." She looked puzzled for a moment, "Where was I? Oh yes, the dear man thanked me for being there at his side. He said he only woke up to thank me." The expression on her face showed both sorrow and happiness as she told her tale. "We visited for a few hours then he said he was tired and went to sleep. Twenty minutes later, he passed." She dabbed at her eyes with some tissue. "Yes, it has its rewards."

"I don't think my heart could take having Charlene come back to us only say goodbye. It would break me."

"You don't strike me as someone who would break. You appear to be a strong man, stronger than perhaps you know," she went back to reading some romance novel, mind candy, or a bodice ripper, in other words, porn for women.

It is about the time Moiraine gets home from school. As I opened the front door to meet her bus, I saw John standing at the curb waiting. He knows we are going to attempt another try at saying goodbye to Charlene. Maybe he can give Mo the strength I could not. In short order, the bus pulled up, and Moiraine disembarked. John grasped her hand, and they walked up to the house together.

"How was school Mo?" I asked, hoping to play our little game.

"It was okay, I guess. I'm hungry. Can I have a snack?" Without waiting for an answer, she went to her room. She came back out with a stack of paper, sat down at the table, and started making cranes. John went to check on his daughter as I fixed her a little something for Mo to eat. I placed a plate with a cut-up apple sprinkled with cinnamon down next to her along with a glass of milk too. "Thank you, Daddy," it should hold her until dinner.

Sitting next to her, I started making cranes too. We worked silently until the paper ran out. "You did it, Mo. This makes one thousand. Why don't you put them on your mommy's bed with the other ones? She scooped up the cranes and high-tailed it to the bedroom. After I cleaned up the snack plate and glass, I followed her into the bedroom. Moiraine is talking to her mother. John and Mary are whispering back and forth to each other. Not wanting to eavesdrop, I focused on Moiraine and Charlene. After a few moments, I went to Mo, "Honey, we need to tell your mom it is okay for her to go."

"But Daddy, the cranes haven't worked yet."

"Moiraine, we need to say goodbye."

"I won't do it!" She crossed her arms and stood exactly like her mother does when she takes a stand no one can budge her from.

Mo's teenage years are not going to be stress-free.

John came over and whispered something into Mo's ear, and they walked away from the bed and faced Charlene. John's hands were resting on her shoulders.

In a loud and clear voice, I said, "Charlene, my wife, it is time for you..." the doorbell rang then a loud, persistent knocking began immediately. "What now?" I tried to ignore the knocking and started again, "Charlene, my wife, it..." the pounding grew louder and refused to be ignored. I stomped to the front door ready to give the assailants what for. Throwing open the door, I found half a dozen children and Ms. Canon.

"Mr. Embers, thank goodness you're home. We were about to give up and leave all this on your doorstep," she motioned to the dozen or so large trash bags in everyone's hands.

I took a breath and calmed myself, "What is all this?"

"We have a little surprise for your wife."

"Ms. Canon, we were ..." I was interrupted by Trevor, a young man from Moiraine's class, yelling.

"Moiraine! We are here with them." By the noise, I could tell my daughter is running for the door.

"Oh, thank you thank you. Bring them this way." A stream of children of all ages paraded past me without so much as a how do you do. Ms. Canon is last in line and stopped short of coming in. She looked at me for a moment, and I motioned her to come in too.

Shaking my head, I said, "Why not?" We all headed to my wife's bedside. It is a little crowded in the bedroom. Looking to Ms. Canon, "I don't understand."

"It is quite simple, Mr. Embers. Your daughter organized a literal rebellion at school. She organized all the kids, and I mean every last one to start making cranes. She showed them how and said it would help her mother. They were making them at recess, at lunch, at any time they could steal away; they were even making them during their lessons. I was concerned at first, but the district's psychologist thought it could help the young ones to deal with this tragedy and give them closure. So, the whole school took a day away from learning and experienced a day of action and healing. I think it helped."

"Or it could crush them with false hope."

"Daddy, Grandpa, they brought them! They brought them. Look," Moiraine opened up one of the trash bags and started pouring out its contents all over her mother. There are cranes, hundreds of cranes, and when the bag was empty, she grabbed another and started to pour it out too. All the kids joined the act. After each child finished pouring out their bag-o-cranes, they told Charlene they loved her. "Mary, you pour out some cranes too. Grandpa, please come on and give mom some." Moiraine said with a little desperation in her voice but hope too. Both Mary and John obliged Mo. Even Ms. Canon put some cranes onto Char. "Come on, Daddy, put some cranes on mommy." She stood by Char's side and eagerly watched as I placed the last of the cranes on her mom. Moiraine's heart sank as her mother didn't stir. Slowly the realization her mother is not going to wake up became hard and cold in Moiraine's mind. After another moment, Mo went running out of the room crying and yelling "Mommy, Mommy, I want my Mommy…" over and over again. Everyone watched Mo as she left. Some of the kids are tearing up too. John took off after her.

"Nathan, could you please see what is bothering Moiraine? I can't seem to get out of bed. Bring her here to me." Charlene said in a horse and raw voice. I spun so fast I thought the centrifugal force would rip my clothes off. The kids let out with a huge cheer.

Kneeling at Char's side, I lightly brushed the hair from her face. Whispering softly to my wife, "Moiraine will be fine now that you have woken up." Trying not to bring the thought to mind, but I feared it is only to say goodbye.

"What happened? Why does my chest hurt? Where am I?" Char asked with increasing panic. Immediately Mary came over and started checking my wife. "Who are you? Ms. Canon, children, why are you here? Nathan, please answer me."

"You were shot by Mark Galos." She immediately placed her hand to her chest. A look of horror came to her face. "We got you to the hospital. Char, we brought you home because they said you were dying," I grabbed my wife's hand. "Do you remember any of it?" She flinched with her mental search.

"I remember hearing the shot. I remember you yelling at me. You… put… your… finger in the wound?"

"I tried to plug the hole in your heart."

"Oh, my God Nathan, how did you have the courage to do it? I would have been an emotional mess."

"You gave me the strength. Besides if you died, I would have to do the laundry. And no hurry, but it's beginning to pile up." Char gave me the look she always gives me when she does not approve of a joke, but behind her mask of disapproval, I saw her smile.

Charlene reached up with one hand and cupped my cheek "Well, you always could touch my heart," she smiled and pursed her lips to ask for a kiss. It was a tender kiss. When we finished, John and Moiraine wedged themselves between us.

John dropped to his knees, "Thank you, God. Thank you." He began crying loud sobs.

"Grandpa, why are you crying? Mommy is not sleeping anymore. Don't be sad."

"Oh, grandpa is not crying because he is sad. These are happy tears. grandpa is happy, so very, very happy."

"I'm happy too," Moiraine said, as she grabbed a handful of cranes and threw them up in the air. Soon all the kids present gathered around and grabbed up the cranes and started throwing them up in the air and cheering. John started laughing and joined in the party, Mary also.

Mary chimed in with "This is what the doctor ordered," she laughed. "I would have paid real money to see the look on Ms. Barton's face if this had happened while she was here."

What the Hell, I started cheering too. Grabbing a handful of cranes too, I threw them in the air, and they rained down on Charlene. Moiraine started saying, "I love you, Mom," and soon all the children began chanting themselves, "We love you, Mrs. E." After all the pandemonium died down, I saw Mary use her cell phone. I assume she is informing Hospice they no longer had a patient. "Okay, children. Mrs. Embers needs her rest, and your parents are waiting back at the school. Let's get a marching. And we're walking, we're walking." The envoys from Greentree Elementary followed their principal's orders and headed out the door.

"Goodbye, children. I will see you back at school soon." Char's voice is a bit hoarse, but it is music fit for God to my ears. "Nathan, I am terribly hungry, would you fix me something?" Those words are more music to my ears too. She's hungry. I took it as a good sign.

I asked Mary, "What is safe to feed her?"

"Use the BRAT diet until we hear from her doctor. It consists of bananas, rice, applesauce, and toast. Not too much, her digestive tract has not been working for some time. It is best to start slow. I called for her doctor to come out. He needs to give her the once over." She began to whisper, "Don't forget what I said; this might be only temporary." I nodded my head, yes, but somehow in my heart, I knew Char is back.

I brought everything on the BRAT list and the largest glass we have full of ice water. Char ate a scant few mouthfuls before pushing the plate away. She did drink a large amount of water. After she ate, she was able to sit up and gave the room a quick look. "Dad, is this the bed you have been working on?" John told her it was. She turned in bed and beheld the mural and cried. "It is so beautiful. Thank you. We might need to cover your and mom's faces at night. Having you watching Nathan and me while we are," she coughed a bit and blushed, "sleeping would be a little unsettling." John nodded. At our feet, we could hear the thumping of Blossom's tail against the nightstand and one distinctive bark. "Nathan, let her up here, will you?" Doing as I was asked, I placed Blossom up on the bed. She gave Char many licks of love. She curled up next to her owner. I started to pick her back up when Char told me to leave her be. Wow, Charlene never lets Blossom up on the bed, let alone let her sleep there. Having a bullet rip through your body must change your priorities a bit.

It is about dinner time when John said, "I don't know about the rest of you, but I'm hungry. I am going to run out and pick up some Chinese food."

"Pot-stickers, Grandpa. Get some pot-stickers."

"Okay, I'll get pot-stickers. Does anyone else have any other requests?" John took my order for cashew chicken. He turned to Mary. She motioned no, but John would have none of it, "This is a celebration. What do you want?" She acquiesced and told him broccoli and beef. He turned to Charlene and said, "Sorry, you are on a diet. Only what the doctor says until you are one hundred percent." John left on his errand.

Before John returned, the doorbell rang. Charlene's doctor, Dr. Hazer, was at the door. He didn't say a word to me. He started to push his way past me. "Is she this way?" He pointed down the hall, and I nodded. He went straight away down the hall and to Charlene's side. He wasted no time. He introduced himself to Charlene, then began his examination. I leaned in, "Doctor, a moment, please." He stepped back, and I whispered, "Don't tell her about the baby. It will come better from me." He nodded his head then continued with his examination. Char gave me the eye but said nothing. Mo and I stepped out of the room to give Char and the doctor some privacy.

"Okay, you can come back in now, Dearies," Mary said as she stuck her head out.

"Well, except for weakness from being in bed so long, she appears to be in perfect health," Dr. Hazer said. Turning to Char, "You are one lucky lady. By all accounts, you should have died. I can't explain why you didn't. In a couple of days, I want you to come in for some testing. Maybe we can figure out what went right." He started packing up his bag.

"Doctor, when can I return to my normal routine? I have been in bed long enough."

"I should readmit you to the hospital, but I feel you will heal better at home. Your incision is healing up well for the most part. Tomorrow you can start pushing yourself, but not too hard. Don't lift anything more than five pounds. No housework and I understand you work at a school as well.

Please wait until I give you a complete okay before you return to work. Let your own body tell you what you can and can't do." He finished up packing and started walking for the door. I followed him out of the room.

At the front door, he stopped, turned, and looked at me, "Mr. Embers, I didn't tell her about the baby, but she needs to know. If she asks me directly, I can't lie or hide the truth."

"I know. When she is strong enough, I will tell her." A promise I won't have to keep, because I don't think she will ever be strong enough for the news. She was shot in the heart. I don't think she can take it being broken.

I stretched out my hand and shook the doctor's hand. "You saved her life. Thank you. If ever you need anything, I'm your man."

"I didn't save her life. I only removed the bullet. You saved her life. And God gave her back to you." Dr. Hazer left.

Back in my wife's bedroom, I found Char and Moiraine having a conversation. Moiraine is telling her all about the events since the shooting. Charlene is listening intently while stroking Blossom with one hand. "It's Mary, right? Mary, could you take Mo out to the living room? I want to talk to my husband in private." Mary shooed Moiraine out of the room and closed the door.

I started to undress, "This should only take a couple of minutes."

"Nathan, when I said talk I meant talk."

"I know. I am trying to lighten the mood."

"Sometimes moods should not be lightened," she said while giving her famous out with it look.

I paused, "What?" I paused again, and she looked at me. "Okay. Okay. I am worried about you. You push so hard sometimes. I wanted the doctor to emphasize you need rest." Another lie this is starting to become a habit. She accepted my answer, but I can tell by her expression she didn't buy it. We talked some more I filled her in on everything Mo didn't. I told her Mark Galos still had plans to kill me. The threat he made to Greentree if I didn't stay away. My dreams of visiting her.

"Nathan, I dreamed we talked a couple of times."

"What do you expect? Of course, you dreamed of Moiraine and me."

"They were strange dreams. It was like I was looking at myself, and once you left me alone in the hospital."

"They were dreams; don't let them upset you." Wow, she remembers my dream visits? This stuff keeps getting curiouser and curiouser.

John returned in short order with his arms full of Chinese food. I brought in some paper plates, and we all feasted right there in the bedroom. Char didn't even say a word about it. It was a magical time.

As I started clearing away the used plates and empty takeout containers, my phone rang. I went into the other room to take the call. After a brief conversation, "See you then." I hung up my phone and went back to the party.

Mary is packing up her stuff. John is quietly talking with Charlene, and Moiraine is enjoying having her mother brush her hair. Seeing my wife engaging in everyday things gave me a warm, happy feeling. It has been a long time since I've felt happy.

I announced, "Well, I have a temporary job. I start tomorrow morning."

"Good work, my boy. Any chance it can turn into something more permanent?" John asked as he stood from Char's bedside.

"No, it's for a couple of weeks at most. But it's a start." I looked at the time on my cell phone. "Moiraine, you need to get ready for bed; you have school tomorrow."

"No. I want to stay home tomorrow and be with mommy."

Char broke in "Now, Moiraine, listen to your father. Tomorrow is Friday. We will have the whole weekend to be together. Also, help your dad pick up these cranes and put them out of the way for now."

"Alright," Mo said crestfallen. She started picking up cranes and putting them back into the bags. She made the task seem like the cranes weighed as much as White Star material. She is not happy.

"I'm all packed up, Dearies. It is time for me to make my exit," Mary said as she started for the door.

Charlene sat up a bit in bed, reached out with her hands, and said, "Mary, I want to thank you." Mary put her things down and took Char's hands in hers. "You took such loving care of my family and me. Thank you."

"It has been a true pleasure. It's not often I see a happy ending when I go to work. Thank you." Mary leaned in and gave Char a light hug and kiss on the cheek. Charlene reciprocated. Mary turned around to pick up her things, but John had beaten her to them.

"Let me walk you out to your car. It's the least I can do for my second favorite nurse."

Mary asked, "Second favorite nurse?"

Char replied, "My mother was a nurse." Mary nodded and smiled.

"I think I will head home after escorting Mary to her car. The emotions of this day have tuckered me out. No need to see us out, we know the way. Okay, Mary, let's go." John started out of the bedroom carrying his burdens, and Mary followed him out.

Moiraine is taking her own sweet time picking up those cranes, so I started to help with her task. "So, Char, what do you want to do with all these? Throw them in the recycle bin?"

"Please put them in the bags for now. I have an idea of what to do with them." Char watched as we completed our chore smiling at us the whole time. "Go ahead and put those bags out of the way for now then get Mo ready for bed."

I watched her brush her teeth, get a glass of water, and waited patiently in the hall as she emptied her bladder.

She ran to her mom to give her a kiss goodnight, "Goodnight, Mommy." She reached over and gave her mom a huge kiss then went straight to bed. As I am following her to her room, she grabbed something in there and dashed by me. Back into my bedroom, she handed her mother the teddy bear she had been carrying everywhere. "Watch over my mommy. Make sure she keeps getting better. Goodnight again, Mommy."

"Goodnight, Moiraine," she replied with a tear rolling down her face and a big smile. "Our daughter…"

"is amazing. She has been through the wringer, but she never gave up hope." Pausing and bowing my head. "I did. I am ashamed to say." After my confession, I followed Moiraine to her bedroom and tucked her in. No longer is she surrounded by the guys. They had been placed in their corner as they were before this whole episode of our lives began. I think, in time, Mo will be fine. I returned to Char's side.

"Nathan, give me your hand." We held hands. The little electric jolt is there again. "You said some foolishness a moment ago. You have nothing to be ashamed of. YOU gave me back my life. It is the greatest gift anyone can bestow. Can you name me anyone else who could have done what you did? As ever you were my hero." I leaned in and gave my wife the most passionate kiss I could without her heart bursting out of her chest. After our bit of bonding, Char said, "Nathan, tell me everything that has happened with as much detail as you can without reliving the events."

She wanted the whole story, so I laid out every detail. She heard about everything except about our son. The news might jeopardize her recovery. Carrying the weight of that fact will be my burden for the rest of my life. She doesn't need to know. The song "Carry That Weight" by The Beatles began playing in my mind. Mr. K.R.A.P. is particularly cruel today. *"Boy, you gotta carry that weight Carry that weight a long time..."*

"Charlene, it is getting late, and you need your rest, so I will leave you to it." As I tried to disengage my hand, she would not let it go.

"What I need is my husband to come to my bed and share it," she said it with a slight catch in her throat.

"Only sleep, right?"

"Only sleep, Husband Mine."

"Glad to hear it. While I would love to more than sleep, I think the safe play is to wait for the okay from the doctor." Can I keep my lustful self in check? I returned Blossom to her bed and made my rounds through the house, checking to see all the doors and windows are shut and locked. Last on the list is to pick up the blanket and pillow off the recliner and put them away. Nothing left to do but getting into my jammies. It felt like heaven sliding under the covers and enjoying the warmth of my bed. I reached over to Char and gave her a goodnight kiss.

"Goodnight, Charlene."

"Goodnight, Nathan."

This is going to be sublime getting a restful sleep in my bed once again. It had been about five minutes when Charlene said abruptly, "Nathan, will you bring a towel or something to cover up my parent's faces." I nearly peed my pants. I laughed so hard. I got up and got a towel then neatly covered up John and Marlene's carved portraits on the headboard.

Returning to bed, I turned out the light and said again, "Goodnight, Charlene." I waited for a beat then said, "Goodnight, John. Goodnight, Marlene." I tried so hard not to snicker, but I am weak.

"Shut up," Char said trying to sound miffed, but she started snickering too

Chapter Eighteen

Why I agreed to help in this adventure as Mr. Nobuharu
Makiyama asked? My life has been crazy lately, but I feel
in my heart, I should go with it, or as my mother would say,
"Ride the horse in the direction it's going."

It is a glorious morning here in the twilight of the day's
beginning. Standing here on my front porch, I am watching
and waiting for my ride. Char is on the mend. My family is
whole again. I have a temporary job to bring in some cash.
I looked around and took it all in. The birds weren't up yet.
All is quiet except at the edge of my hearing I could barely
make out the whispers of traffic on the streets. The jingle of
a dog's collar is in the air as one of my neighbors is
walking their dog. For what is the briefest of moments, I
am at peace.

A limo pulled up in front of the house, and the driver
opened the back door for me. When they said they would
send a car, I didn't think it would be a limo. I walked down
to the open door and bowed in return as the driver gave me
a respectful bow. Sliding into the back seat, I quietly
watched the world go by as we departed for parts unknown.
At least unknown to me, but I think the driver knows the
way.

While I am watching the world go by, of course, I
started to brood on my failure. I must live with the
knowledge, more likely die knowing, I can't protect my
family. What can I possibly do? Wheels began churning in
what I had left of my mind. My brooding went on until we
arrived in the light industrial section of town. The driver
opened my door, then guided me to an old beat-up
warehouse. Once in, I can see a vast empty space. A few
furnishings are trying to fill the space, but they are
unsuccessful. The objects take up maybe twenty percent of
the warehouse. There is a large pile of black sand. An even
larger pile contained charcoal, real charcoal, not those

barbeque briquettes for backyard cookouts. There are also three structures inside this warehouse. One is a large furnace open at the top with a hood above to carry the smoke up and out of the warehouse. The glow of a fire could be seen. In a different area is an open hearth. It is cold, but it looked prepared so it could be lit quickly. There also is a small shrine of some sort.

Mr. Masafumi Asahara turned toward the door and walked to us as we entered. After a short bow, he said, "Mr. Embers, good. You are right on time. My uncle is waiting for us to begin. Please come this way," he motioned me toward the shrine. We walked there with a purpose in our strides. The feeling of peace I had experienced earlier is returning to me, the closer we approached the shrine.

Mr. Nobuharu Makiyama is praying at the shrine. Quietly I stood next to him waiting. After a moment, he turned toward me and asked, "Mr. Embers, Nathan?" I nodded my approval of his using my first name. "Are you most rested? It will be a long time until we sleep again."

"Oh, wait a minute. How long are we talking about? My wife woke up from her coma, and I have a family to see after."

"Your wife has recovered? What a blessing. I prayed it would be so."

"Thank you," I said as I bowed to him.

"Nathan-san, it will be three days, perhaps four, until our task is done." He bowed at me, "Hai."

"Okay, I am not prepared for this. I need to make a phone call and let my family know." Pulling out my phone, I began to dial. John was supportive of how long I am going to be gone. He was puzzled, but he also said, without question, he would take care of everything in my absence. He's a dependable man. If he said he would do something, you could bet the farm, he would get it done. We have grown a great deal closer with all that has happened in the last few weeks. Is this how it feels to have a father? It is reassuring to have a steady man like John in my life. Someone I know won't lie, cheat, or steal. It's grounding to know there is a man who is not afraid to tell me if I'm wrong or being an ass. Yes, I think this is what it feels like to have a dad.

"Everything is all set. My body, mind, and spirit are all yours for the next seventy-two to ninety-six hours. It's a long stretch. Are there some cots or sleeping bags?" With the question, everyone began to laugh. "What is so amusing?"

"Nathan-san, we will not be sleeping. If we fall asleep, we must begin again, or the work will be corrupted and ruined." He turned back to the shrine, "We must pray before we start. In the Samurai culture, they believed their sword, their katana, is their soul. Tell me, Nathan-san, what spiritual qualities would you want a katana to have?"

"If I were forging my own sword," I paused and thought a moment, "protection, I would want it to bestow protection to the weak and innocent – protection to all those who would be victims of the monsters of this world. Yes, I would want a katana of protection tempered with mercy."

"Hai. Interesting choice, Nathan-san," Mr. Nobuharu Makiyama said. "Come do as I do." The Grandmaster turned to the shrine and took a small dipper with his right hand from a trough filled with water. He retrieved some water with the dipper and poured it over his left hand. Next, he took up the dipper in his left hand and poured some water over his right hand. He transferred the dipper back to his right hand and cupped his left hand and poured more water into it. He took some of the water in his left hand and put it in his mouth. He spat out the water on the floor next to the trough. He placed the dipper in both hands, tilted it up, so the remaining water poured over the handle, and returned the dipper to its place on the trough. After his demonstration, I followed suit copying all his movements exactly. "Very good Nathan-san," the old gentleman said with a broad grin on his face. "As before, copy my actions. We pray. I pray I create good tamahagane, good steel. When you pray, you must pray for the sword to have those qualities you wish."

The Grandmaster, I guess you could say my master now, turned back toward the shrine and rang a bell once. He motioned for me to do likewise. He then clapped twice and held his hands together and bowed. All the other men there did the same, so I clapped twice holding my hands together after the second clap. I closed my eyes and cleared my mind. I prayed not in words but in emotion. Rage began to fill my being. Rage at what one monster had done to my life. The thought of vengeance consumed me. After a moment while the emotions boiled, I felt – I cannot put it exactly into words, but it felt like someone is smiling at me. A calm came to me. It is an overwhelming feeling of serenity. It surprised the Hell out of me. My emotional prayer finished on that note. I opened my eyes to find all the other men had already completed the ritual while my master and I still stood there. The old man finished only moments after I did.

My master turned toward me and gave a huge grin. "Hai, yes, it is time we begin. Yes, this is a fine beginning." He walked to the forge. He patted the side of the forge "Yes, the Tatara is ready. This is called the Tatara. It is where we…" he turned to his nephew and said something in Japanese. His nephew answered in English. "Smelt the iron sand, satetsu, into good tamahagane." The nephew, along with the other men, began adding the charcoal to the Tatara. Slowly the temperature radiating from the smelter began to increase. I picked out a shovel and started distributing the charcoal into the Tatara also.

My sense of time is off somehow, and I am not sure how long this took. Every few minutes, the master would inspect the smelter. After a time, he announced it is time to start adding the satetsu or iron sand into the Tatara. We layered sand and charcoal for what must have been hours. My back is beginning to ache. During a break, we all sat down and watched the Tatara. "The Tatara is like our wife," Mr. Nobuharu Makiyama said. "We must care for her. We listen, and she tells us what she needs. Listen to her, Nathan-san. Right now, she is saying she is happy. We can eat and rest for a time, but ever we must listen. She could get hungry for more food, satetsu. She may tell us she is cold, so we must put more charcoal on the fire. We will do this for the next three days." Mr. Nobuharu Makiyama said something in Japanese to one of his other apprentices.

About ten minutes, later the apprentice brought over a tray with bowls of rice on it along with cups of water. I was polite and took my share of plain rice and tepid water yum, yum, yum. The expression on my face must have betrayed my true feelings for the meal because Mr. Nobuharu Makiyama is grimly looking at me. "This is the traditional meal while we work." He spoke in Japanese to another apprentice. The apprentice brought over another tray, but whatever is on it is covered. The apprentice presented the tray to me. Removing the towel, I uncovered what is on the tray. My eyes beheld ambrosia, the food of the gods, an In-N-Out Double-Double Cheeseburger animal style, fries, and a large diet drink. In-N-Out is my all-time favorite burger place. Mr. Nobuharu Makiyama said, half laughing, "It is tradition to have rice and water, but not a requirement." He did a little bow toward me, then grabbed a fry and ate it, smiling the whole time

"Master, I don't know what to say."

"Thank you is proper at times like these." I thanked him and indulged. When our meal was over, Mr. Nobuharu Makiyama said, "Nathan-san, if you please, work the bellows for a time. I must see to my wife and future child." I gave him a quizzical look, and he replied, "The Tatara and tamahagane." I nodded and mentally slapped my forehead for not remembering.

In the same rhythm as the gentleman I replaced, I pumped the bellows. Watching my master examine the Tatara, I noted he is not happy. He retrieved some charcoal and began distributing it into the Tatara. He raised his hand a bit and started moving it as a conductor does while the whole time listening and watching his "wife." I altered the rhythm of my pumping in time with his hand. His hand would go up, and I would fill the bellows. His hand came down, and I pumped the handle down. We did this dance of the bellows for maybe ten minutes. He turned to me and over the sound of the smelting said, "Have you worked a bellows before Nathan-san? You follow my direction perfectly. It is good, hai."

For three days, this has been our routine. We would pour layers of sand and layers of charcoal into the Tatara, rest, eat, and watch. All of us apprentices would take turns working the bellows. Sometimes the master would give gentle instruction to each of his apprentices. By my reckoning though, he spent the most time teaching his nephew. He spent as much time with me, an outsider to this world. I hope his other apprentices don't take umbrage with me usurping their pecking order and becoming the master's number two. Thinking that, the voice of Patrick Stewart came to me, *"Make it so, Number Two."* To think the chain of events leading to this work all started with a doodle.

I am beginning to feel bone-weary. I want to sleep something fierce. The master, Mr. Nobuharu Makiyama, looked tired, but not as tired as I feel. For the last six hours or so, he has been taking small samples of the tamahagane through vent holes at the bottom of the Tatara. He is intent on how the samples looked. Every time he took a sample, Mr. Masafumi Asahara is there also. The master is instructing his nephew in the finer points of smelting tamahagane. In the end, the master tried to stand but stumbled slightly. His nephew caught him. It appears to me all this might have been too taxing for Mr. Nobuharu Makiyama. The master waved off attention from his nephew, stood up straight, and smiled at all of us. "It is ready. Hai, it is good. Come, we must hurry. Break open the Tatara. All of the apprentices went to retrieve some tools which looked like metal rakes.

Mr. Masafumi Asahara handed me a rake and said, "Come, we must help in the birth of the tamahagane." All the other apprentices had already started the process of breaking up the Tatara. I joined in the work. The heat given off by the Tatara is unbearable. We all took turns breaking it apart. When the heat grew too hot for an apprentice, he would step out, and another would take his place. Since the Tatara is mostly broken up, the heat is beginning to abate. In the middle of what is left of the smelter, laid a large chunk of metal hot and still glowing. After about an hour of watching the metal cool, we all worked together to wrap chains around the tamahagane. Like the men of old, we muscled it out of the remains of the Tatara.

As we pulled in unison, the song, "Sixteen Tons" by Tennessee Ernie Ford came to mind. So, I began singing in time with our work rhythm. "You haul sixteen tons, and what do you get? Another day..." I got some strange looks from the other apprentices. Who cares? Here I am working hard the last three days, and finally, I am not obsessing on my failures or the threat to the family. It is cathartic.

The tamahagane is clear of the debris. We all took a breather. The master proclaimed, "It is good. I am pleased." There are bows and smiles all around. One of the apprentices opened a bottle of sake and began pouring a celebratory drink for everyone. I took a cup, but only feigned drinking. Someday I may have a taste of spirits, but for now, keeping the promises I can keep is important to me.

My master came up to me and said, "We are done for a time. We must wait while the tamahagane cools. You can go home and rest. Soon we will break up the tamahagane, and we will choose the best pieces for the katana." He motioned to his nephew to come over. They spoke for a moment in Japanese. Mr. Masafumi Asahara made a call on his cell phone and spoke to someone on the other end in Japanese. If everyone keeps talking in Japanese around me, I will start learning it by osmosis.

Mr. Masafumi Asahara said, "I have called for a car and driver for you. He will return you home. Get some rest and be ready. It will only take a few days for the tamahagane to cool."

"Thank you; I will wait outside for the driver." Standing in front of the warehouse, I took deep long breaths of the fresh air. The fresh air felt invigorating. My body and soul felt better than it has in a long time. Feeling better didn't mean I wasn't weary to the core, but it is a satisfying weariness. Rarely have I done hard physical labor. I have gone out of my way in the past to avoid it. There is something pure in hard physical work, though. I may have to rethink my stance of "no sweaty work."

The limo pulled up to the warehouse. The driver opened the door for me and gave a short bow. Grime and dirt covered me from my work. There should be a towel or something on the seat to keep it from getting contaminated. A couple of extra strength air-fresheners are in order also because I reek.

The drive home was quick. Before I knew it, the driver was gently tapping me on the shoulder and saying, "Sir, you are home now." My eyes shut the instant I sat in the limo until the moment I arrived home.

"Umm, thank you." Dragging myself out of the limo and through the front door took all my concentration.

My daughter screamed, "Daddy's home. Daddy's home." She came running and nearly tackled me to the ground when she hit me with a big hug. I gave her a huge hug back and a kiss as well.

"I'm not enjoying this, but daddy needs to take a shower in the worst way."

"Yeah, you're stinky!" She started laughing hard. It is heavenly to hear her laugh again.

The shower is compelling me, but I held it at bay while I stopped to say hello to my wife. She is reading and resting in bed. She put down the book and said, "Nathan, I heard Moiraine proclaim your return. How did it go?"

"It went well. It is satisfying to be part of a team with a single-minded goal. More importantly, how are you doing?"

"Healing, I guess. I have no energy, and it bothers me that I don't feel like I can get out of this bed. I feel useless."

"Not being able to give the house a once over has got to be killing you," I said, smiling the whole time.

She stuck her tongue out at me, then said, "You know it. Now take a shower. No offense, but you stink," she said in a half huff.

Peeling out of my working clothes, I examined them one by one. Nothing can save them. Burning them is the merciful thing to do now. I wonder if there is a ritual for that? The hot shower is melting away my exhaustion. Now I am only tired, not weary. The steam of the shower kept obstructing my view in the mirror as I shaved, but I am not deterred. With a fresh razor in one hand, my favorite shave cream in the other, and a can-do attitude, I managed to remove the stubble without committing a demonic blood rite. As I stepped out of the shower, I looked at myself in our big mirror. I am oh so pretty again.

As I was drying off, Char said in a disappointed tone, "Oh, you shaved. I was hoping you were finally going to try and grow a beard. I've always thought you would look handsome in a beard, especially now because you have a little grey in it."

"I can think of a few comebacks to her remark, but I am too tired, and my bed beckons." I dressed in my jammies and hit the sheets. I fell asleep as my head hit the pillow.

Chapter Nineteen

Someone was rummaging around in the bedroom and woke me. Without moving or even opening my eyes, I said, "Sleep. Need more sleep."

"Sorry, Nathan. I didn't mean to wake you."

"What time is it?" Rising from my warm and comfortable bed, I threw off the covers and swung my legs over the edge. All I did for a time was sit there rubbing my eyes.

"It is getting close to dinner time. Go back to sleep if you are tired."

"How was your doctor's appointment? What did he say?"

"He told me I am healing remarkably well," Char said it as if it is bad news. "He said I would make a full recovery. In four to six months, I should be one hundred percent."

"Praise be." Jumping out of bed, I threw my arms around my wife. I leaned in to give her a big kiss.

"Nathan, you're hurting me," she started pushing me away. I let her go. *"She is still healing. You idiot."* I thought to myself. Char gave me a weak and unsatisfying kiss on the cheek.

There was a knock on our bedroom door, and John said, "Pizza is about ready. Come and get it."

We made our way to the dining room where the table is set with paper plates and a roll of paper towels. John and Moiraine had worked together to make homemade pizza. It is hot, delicious, and I ate more than my fair share. Charlene had a couple of bites, but she is still on a restricted diet. Bland food is the order of the day until her digestive tract gets back to full speed.

After dinner; we played a game of "Pretty Pretty Princess." John looked silly with the crown and all the jewelry on. Following game night, we retired to the living room and watched a movie while Charlene read. Moiraine is cuddling with her mother. John is in the recliner, and I am relegated to the far end of the couch. Life is back to normal.

The house phone rang. No one else stirred, so I went to answer it. "Hello."

"Hello, Nate." The voice on the other end drew out my name in a mocking way.

Turning my back on the family and lowering my voice, I asked, "Why are you calling me here? Haven't you tortured my family enough?" A little laugh came through the earpiece. It is the laugh of the shell of what was once Mark Galos.

"Not even by half. Congratulations on your wife's recovery. It will make my revenge even sweeter knowing the anguish you'll feel over losing her again."

"You listen to me you son-of-a-bitch. Leave my family out of this. This is between you and me."

His voice is remarkably even as he said, "This is between me and the rest of you pathetic meat sacks. You will all eventually pay for this carefree life you have led. We will take our just due. We will snuff out the flames of your pathetic insignificant lives like candles on a birthday cake."

"A man should know the name of his murderer. Tell me yours. I know it's not Mark."

There is a bit of surprise in his voice, "I have had many names over the countless years. You will have to remain ignorant of my real name. What would you call me?"

"A parasite for you lived within Mark Galos. You drained him of all he was. You killed his spirit and inhabited the husk of what was left."

This parasite answered in a matter of fact manner, "True. So, you know some small part of the whole. I doubt you can even conceive of the whole. If he had only stopped fighting me, he could have lived as I have lived. He would have been a witness to the return."

"What return? Answer straight out none of this cryptic crap."

"I will leave you with this. Our sacrifice was before your time. Your time would never have been without us. The debt is due, and we will extract payment. Before I go, and you begin to ponder my words, did you have a fruitful visit with the mother of this shell?" Click.

"Who was on the phone, Nathan?"

"Some jerk," I sat back down on my end of the couch. My eyes are on the television screen, but my mind is elsewhere.

"We interrupt this broadcast with this breaking news," the TV spewed. My attention immediately snapped back. "We go live to a news conference called by the San Diego Police Department." Detective Captain Sergeant walked up to a podium. "I want to thank all the media here. As you know, two police officers were recently murdered. We have learned two more officers were also slain. All four officers were working on the same case. Mrs. Galos, the suspect's mother, was also found murdered. All of these killings are tied together. We are asking for the public's help in apprehending this man," a mugshot of Mark Galos came on the screen. "We ask anyone who sees him to be cautious and not approach him. If you see him, call 9-1-1 immediately and let us know. Again, do not approach this man as he is considered very dangerous. Remember he has killed four officers and one civilian and would not hesitate in killing more if he is crossed." The screen returned to Captain Sergeant. "The Police Department wishes to thank the media for all their help in this matter. Funerals for the fallen officers are…"

Click, I turned the TV off. The sound of Moiraine crying filled the air. She had her head buried into her mother's shoulder. A look of horror is on Charlene's face as she was comforting our daughter. John's face betrayed a dour mood. My resolve is renewed to see this creature, this

291

parasite, in the shell of Mark Galos to pay for his crimes. I stated, "Maybe we should call an end to this evening and go to bed."

John stood and without comment gave his daughter and granddaughter each a kiss on their foreheads then walked to the front door. Opening the door for him, I offered my hand, and we shook. "Nathan, I am going home to pick up a few things along with my Greener. I'll be back in a jiffy."

"John, I thank you for the offer, but he is not coming here for some time. He is going to let us stew for a while more." Whispering, I said, "His killing of Mrs. Galos, his mother, is a message to me." A brief look of mild surprise flashed on John's face. "Mrs. Galos and I talked. I begged her to ask for mercy from her son. I learned you cannot ask for mercy from a monster. All you can do is kill it. He and I are tied together. Don't ask me how I know, but I will know when he will come for us. Now is the time I must prepare for my own private little war. What I am going to do? I don't know yet, but I may need you. I will call upon you when I am ready."

John looked down for a moment then reached up and patted the door frame and said to the house "Guard well my family," he turned his head and looked deep into my eyes, "each and every member of my family," he walked out to his car. I watched as he drove away.

I closed and locked, the front door. It is secure. I made my rounds checking to see all the doors and windows are shut tight and locked. Charlene had already put Moiraine to bed. Quietly I opened my daughter's door and leaned my head into her room to double-check on her.

She sat up in bed and said, "Daddy, the man on the TV. He is the one who hurt mommy, isn't he?"

"Yes."

"Is he coming back?"

"Yes, but not tonight."

"Can I sleep with the guys?"

"Of course, you can." Her cuddling toys are in their corner, so I gathered them up and placed them in her bed. "Goodnight, Honey."

As I started to step out of the room and close the door, Moiraine asked, "Can you leave the door open and light on?" Nodding, I did as she asked. I walked back to the living room and sat down in the recliner there in the dark. After a moment, Blossom was thumping her tail against the chair. I lifted her onto my lap and mindlessly petted her as I sat there.

After a time, the light came on, and Charlene was staring at me. "Are you coming to bed?" She is dressed in what are her most unflattering nightclothes. I sat there looking at her. "Come to bed. There is nothing you can do tonight."

"Helpless, I am so helpless. He kicked my ass at the corner and shot you. I don't think I can stop him when he comes for us here." My head hung low with my confession. The electric touch of my wife on my chin brought me to the now. She lifted my head, so I am looking in her eyes.

"This burden is more than anyone can handle. The whole city is after him now. The police will catch him. Just wait and see. Someone will call in a tip and bam. They will lock him up fast, and he will never be free again." She took my hands and pulled me up to my feet. She put her arms around me. My arms wrapped around her. "Gently," is all she said.

My arms held her as tenderly as I could. It is as gently as when I held Moiraine for the first time. I love my family. When this all started, I thought the greatest duty a man could fulfill is to die for his family. I was wrong. The greatest duty a man can fulfill for his family is to… kill.

Charlene released the embrace and said "Let's go to bed. I am exhausted, and you look dead on your feet." Still holding one of my hands, she led me to our bed and rest.

Looking up at the ceiling in the dark, I pondered what I must do. I drifted off.

Moiraine's screamed, "Mommy, Mommy!" I dashed to her as fast as I could with Char only half a moment behind me. I saw my daughter thrashing in bed. My daughter is still asleep and screaming, "Mommy, wake up! Please wake up. Daddy, why are you putting your hand inside, mommy? Wake up, Mommy!"

I grabbed up my daughter and started rocking her in my arms. "Moiraine, it's only a dream." She is soaking wet. Strands of her hair are matted against her face. Her pajamas felt like she had taken a shower in them. Her eyes are wide open, and the pupils dilated. "Wake up, Honey. See, your mommy is fine. Look."

A look of surprise found her face, and she reached out. "Mommy. Mommy." Charlene grabbed up her daughter to comfort her. Char rocked Moiraine and quieting her down with tender cooing.

It took maybe half an hour to settle Mo back down to normal. Char cleaned her up and in fresh jammies while I changed the sheets on her bed. During this time Moiraine kept a death grip on the teddy bear. The damn news flash brought on a night terror to her sleep. It is all too much for her little mind to handle.

The next three nights were a repeat of this scene. Moiraine would go to sleep, and all would seem okay, but she would have a night terror. Her mood grew darker every day. My lovely child was replaced by a fearful girl who had no power to call her own. What can I do? I won't stand by idly and watch her sanity slip away.

On the fourth night before Char and I went to sleep, I said, "We need to talk about Moiraine's dreams. Watching her night after night going through this is breaking my heart."

Char turned to me and said, "I will take her to the doctor's tomorrow. Maybe there is something they can do."

"It's a fine idea, but I want to do something for her tonight. I want your blessing before I try it."

"What do you want to do?"

Mustering my courage, I said, "You said when you were in the coma you dreamed of me visiting you and us talking."

"Yes."

"The truth of the matter is I did visit you in your dreams." I sat up in bed and looked away from my wife.

"Nathan, of course, you visited me in your dreams. You were under stress it gave you some comfort to dream of me just as I got comfort from dreaming of you."

"No, you don't understand. The first time I visited you was when you were just out of surgery. Somehow, I floated up from my body and heard your voice. We looked at our bodies. Yours was in a bed with all kinds of gizmos attached. Mine was resting my head on my hands. We visited another time, and you cried as I left." Looking at her, I saw her face contorting with more emotions than I cared to count. Finally, she chose only one. Disbelief won the day. "I know it sounds nuts, but it's true."

"Nathan, this is crazy talk. People don't go traveling for real in their dreams."

"You said, 'Nathan, not so loud people are sleeping.' Next, you said, 'Nathan, I'm scared. I've tried to wake-up. Nothing I do seems to help. What's wrong? Why can't I wake-up?' I explained to you the doctor said you were dying. At the time, I believed I was only dreaming too. It pained me to see a phantom of you, so I left. You began crying and said, 'Nathan, don't leave me alone.' My heart was hurting so bad, and I wanted my visits to be real. I rushed to the hospital with Moiraine in my arms, and you were crying. I saw tears running down your face." Charlene put a hand of comfort on my shoulder. "Char, those visits were real. I traveled in the realm of dreams."

She said, "I thought those were only dreams too, but everything you said I remember. I was so hurt and mad when you left me. I tried to wake up. I tried so hard, Nathan. It felt like something was pulling me the other way. I even saw my mother. I thought I was going to die." She started to cry. "I think I almost did." Gently I held my wife as she cried on my shoulder.

Whispering in her ear, I said, "But you didn't die. You came back to us. You came back to us."

Charlene pulled away and grabbed a tissue from the box she keeps on her nightstand. She wiped away the tears. With a look of determination, "What is your plan?"

"To visit Mo in her dreams. I will try to distract her with some silliness and hope she gets a restful sleep. I think it may break the cycle of terror in her dreams. Have I told you I love you? Here I tell you something I have a hard time believing and you take it all in stride." Tenderly, I kissed my wife.

When we were done with the kiss, Char said, "Sounds like a plan. What do you want me to do?"

"What I want you to do the doctor hasn't cleared you for yet," I said as I gave her a lustful smile.

"Get your mind out of the gutter."

"We've never done it in a gutter, but if you want to, I'm game."

"Nathan, let's keep our attention on our intention please."

I replied, "Yes, dear," but I kept the lustful smile on my face. "Seriously, be prepared to comfort Mo if this doesn't work. Alright, let's do it." The lights were turned off, and I laid down.

Sleep wasn't coming. Breathing in deep and let it out slowly usually helps. Nope. Commanding my body to relax, addressing each part in turn, was of no use. My thoughts are all over the place. *"Calm."* I thought. It is as if I had no weight. My dream-body floated up from my real-body. Charlene is watching me closely. She looked worried. I wish I could tell her I am here. It dawned on me the first time I did this with her in the room, she heard me. With my will, I communicated, "I am here. I will pull Mo out of her sleep now. Give me a thumbs up if you hear me."

Char said, "I'll give you a different finger if you don't stop playing around. Now see to our daughter."

I can talk to the wakeful while in this dream world. *"Cool."*

At Moiraine's bedside, "Mo, we need to talk." My little baby lifted up and was before me all translucent and floaty. Pointing to her body, "Look Moiraine." She gave a little giggle.

"Daddy, why am I out here if I am asleep in my bed?"

"It's like a dream, Honey."

"Awesome!" she giggled again. "What now?"

Children are so accepting of new things. If I did this to her grandpa, he would argue half the night away about how you can't do this. "Moiraine, let's play a trick on your mom." Moiraine nodded her head yes and started tiptoeing into the master bedroom. Tiptoeing also, I followed. "Okay, I want you to say something to your mother."

Moiraine said, "Boo." Her mother didn't respond. I motioned for her to try again, but this time, I tried to will it to work. "Boo." Charlene jumped, and at first, her face flashed a little anger, then she smiled.

"You did it, Mo!"

"This is fun, Daddy," came from my daughter. "Can we go scare someone else? Oh, let's go scare Grandpa."

"Your grandpa has seen enough ghosts lately. I don't think he wants to hear them too."

Mo gave her shoulders a shrug. "Okay." Then a grin grew on Mo's face. "TAG! You're it." Moiraine touched me and ran out of the room. In a flash, I was chasing her. I am faster, but she is a nimble little goblin. We ran around the house. This is something Charlene never lets us do. We are so naughty. I tried to tag Mo back, but she ducked under the dining room table. I would go right, and she would go left. We did that back and forth three times with her laughing the whole time.

An idea struck me like a bolt of lightning. Crack! *"This is only a dream."* I reached through the table, passing right through it, and tagged her.

"No fair! No fair!" She crawled out from under the table. "This is fun! Mommy never lets me run around inside. Will we get in trouble?"

"Not if we don't tell her." Moiraine giggled. Then a pained look took her.

"Daddy, I don't feel well. It feels like…" She is being pulled away from me like someone has a rope tied around her waist and is pulling fast. She reached out to me. She grabbed a hold of my hand, but I couldn't stop her. We both were dragged straight like a shot through the wall and into her room. She fell into her body, and I was pulled in with her.

We are back at the corner by Greentree Elementary. Maybe I am experiencing her dream somehow. Everything looked so large. All the adults are as giants. This must be what it is to see it all from her perspective. She is walking toward my dream-doppelganger all smiles. Mark Galos started to approach. He looked no different than any other parent there to pick up their child. My alter ego is talking to Mark, but as the conversation went on, Mark became larger and more menacing. My dream-self became smaller and looked to be cowering. Moiraine called out, and Mark pulled the revolver and started turning toward my wife and child. His face is twisted and distorted. He looks like the monster I know him to be. His eyes are bulging and red. His hair writhed like Medusa's hair does when she's pissed. His mouth extended ear to ear, and his teeth are glissading white needles dripping with saliva. Mini-me jumped on his gun as he swung his arm around. A shot fired as it had in the real world. Charlene crumpled to the ground. The wailing of Moiraine's voice is deafening. There is blood, a brilliant red, everywhere. It is spreading in all directions until it covered the entire landscape in crimson sorrow.

The monstrous Mark ran away laughing as he did. My dream-self had grown to a more normal size and had made its way to Charlene. The figment of me yelled at Moiraine to look away. It is harsh and uncaring. This is killing me seeing Moiraine's view of the events. She is a child and doesn't understand I did what I did to try and save her mother. My visage began to grow hideous. My hand, my right hand, became distorted into some cruel hook as it plunged into Charlene's chest. Oh God, I could hardly bear to see it. My daughter is seeing me as another monster who hurt her mother.

"Focus, I must focus." Getting caught up in Moiraine's dream is not helping her. Taking up a place next to her, I said in a calm voice, "Moiraine, this is but a dream. You have the power to end it." She is howling in her agony. With a little more force behind it, I said, "Moiraine, this is your father. Look at me.". It was no good; she is too embroiled in her terror. Here goes. Maybe I can alter this vision as if it is my dream. It is worth a shot. The scene flickered to the moment in our lives when we were throwing the cranes up in the air at my wife's bedside. It was only a moment, but it broke her torture.

Mo looked around, then directly at me and said, "Daddy?" The scene flickered back to the corner and somehow grew in terror. Again, I tried to impose my vision on her dream. This time we are on the carousel at Balboa Park. We are all riding around and laughing. In this dream, I had Moiraine reach out and catch the brass ring. She laughed and was so proud. The nightmare returned, and this time, it is an even darker beast. "Daddy, why are you hurting mommy?"

"Mo, listen to me this is a dream. You are in control. Take control. Change the dream. Use your mind. You KNOW I would never hurt your mommy."

For a moment, my words caught her attention. "Daddy?"

With a sliver of my will into the words, I said, "Think, Mo. See your favorite memory in your mind." Maybe my willpower will have some influence over her actions. For an instant, we are walking down to school. The next moment all of us are walking hand in hand from school back home. Next, she is helping her mother cook dinner. Each memory flashed faster and faster. My consciousness couldn't keep up. It is coming at me like a movie montage. It dawned on me all her memories are happy ones. Up until this tragedy, she had no bad memories, only happy ones. In her life, she has been angry, disappointed, and frustrated, but never unhappy. She needs to remember the truth, and she needs to face the terror. Through the storm of memories, I yelled, "Moiraine! take us back to when mommy got hurt."

"No! I don't want to. I'm scared."

"It is only a dream. Remember, mommy is all better now. This bad man can't hurt you or mommy here in YOUR dream."

She started crying, "I don't want to."

"Do it, or I will punish you!" Saying those words tore at my heart.

She cried out, "Mommy." The scene changed to the corner again. Everything is playing out as before. When she saw the monstrous version of Mark Galos with all those teeth, she cried out again, "Mommy."

"Mo, he is not a monster. He is a man. See him as he truly is. Remember, he looked sick. Mark's image began to flicker back and forth from monster to man. "Good, Moiraine. Keep him as a man here in your dream." He became only the man. Mr. Galos began to swing the gun around. I willed my dream-self to call out "Moiraine, help me fight this man who wants to hurt your mommy." She shook her head no at first, then anger and determination took over. She charged into the furball between Mark and me. She threw punches. She made kicks. She even jumped on his back and bit his ear. He howled right good as she did it. At the end of our epic struggle, Mark went running, but it is Mo and me who did the laughing. I gave Mo a high five. Our work here is done. We had the tools. We had the talent. It's Miller time.

"Daddy, did you see? I kicked him in his funny part." Mo laughed hard and long. "What do you want to do now?"

"You should go back to sleep now. It is time for me to return to my own body and my dreams." After I finished the statement, I was standing by my bed. I stepped back into my body and woke up. As Charlene walked into the bedroom, I sat up and asked, "Where did you go?"

"Moiraine was crying out for me, so I went to her bedside." Charlene looked troubled. "There were a couple of times where I wanted to wake her up. I felt helpless. She is sleeping peacefully for now." She turned out the light and climbed into bed. "What you tried worked. Do you think you helped her?" Char broke down. Through her crying, she said, "This is all so strange. What's happening to our family?"

Gently I held my wife and whispered, "First, yes, I think I did help her. Showing her it is her dream, and she could control it. It gave her power. Second, I don't know. Before the monster came into our lives, I thought I had a bead on life. Now it is all craziness. There is a lot of craziness I have not told you. You need to hear what I say and not judge me."

Charlene gently pushed away from me and wiped her eyes. "Nathan, I have never judged you."

"You have judged me twelve ways to Sunday."

"I have not," she said a little indignantly.

301

"Shall I name the dates and times?" Gazing at her in the dark I gave her an expression of come on now.

"Okay. Well, I never have… Then when… sometimes I hate your memory. It's so damn inconvenient."

"It may sometimes, but it has its perks. Can I tell you everything?" I started talking. I told her everything except the loss of our son. She took it all rather well. She didn't believe me about talking with ghosts. In a lot of ways, she is like her father. She won't believe it until she sees it, and even then, she will want to peek behind the curtain. "Wait here. I will be right back."

As I am walking to the kitchen to pour myself a glass of orange juice, I could hear her say, "Where do you think I would go?" Her feistiness is returning. It is heart-warming to hear, and a welcomed sign. Returning to our bedroom with the glass of OJ in hand, I turned on the light.

I sat in bed and took Char's hand. She rubbed her thumb across the back of my hand like on our third date. It warmed my insides. After I downed the juice, I placed the image of Char's mother in my mind and said, "Marlene Louise Gustafson, please come. Your daughter would like to say hi."

"Nathan, you are being…" but before she could finish her sentence, Marlene materialized in our room and smiled. Charlene's grip on my hand turned into a vise. I am going to need to put some ice on it when we are done. "Mommy, is it you?" Charlene said like a little girl. "Nathan, how are you doing this? This better not be a trick. If it's a trick, I will never give you the special something you like me to do on your birthday again."

Marlene spoke, "Charlie, it is no trick. My love for you and your father has kept me here. Nathan only called me forth."

"I've missed you. I was so mad at you for dying." Char broke her grip on my hand and held it to her heart. "Pain

Nathan, it hurts. Where did she go?" Char cried out again even louder.

"It's a shock. Believe me, I know. Should I call for an ambulance?"

"No. No, it's getting better. It is an emotional pain, not physical. It still hurts like the dickens though." She calmed down a bit. "Where did she go? Nathan, bring her back."

"She is still here. You can't see her unless you're touching me. Take my hand again." Char latched on to my hand again. "Ouch. See she is right there."

"Mom, there is so much I want to say. There is so much I want to ask."

"My little Charlie, you can always talk to me. My answering is up to him," Marlene said with a smile.

Charlene started spewing "I've tried to take care of daddy as best I could. I've gone to college. Did you know I earned my Bachelor's Degree? Moiraine, I have tried to raise her as I thought you would want me to. Mom, I've…"

Marlene walked over to her Charlie and wrapped her arms around her and began to rock Char as you would to comfort a small child. "It's okay. I have always been with you and your dad. I am very proud of the woman you have become."

"I was doing okay until your mother started to hold you. The orange juice isn't going to hold me much longer. Char, I need you to let go of me. I am beginning to feel… The room is spinning." Charlene let go of my hand. Immediately I felt better, but I am crazy-hungry. "Food! Ravenous. I need to eat. I'm going to make a sandwich or fix a bowl of cereal." When I tried to stand up, my head swam. "Maybe I'll wait here for a moment."

"Nathan, was that my mother?"

"Yep."

"How can you… never mind it's not important. Can I see her again?"

303

"Char, it took a lot out of me. I need some rest, but mostly, I need something to eat. I feel like there is a hole in my stomach, and I could eat my pillow." I tried out my legs again, and they are better. "I'm going to make myself a snack now."

"Sit back down, Husband Mine. I'll fix you something."

"It would be angelic of you, but I know you are still on the mend. It isn't…"

"Sit back down, or I'll sit you down, Husband Mine." She stood and went to the kitchen. The gentle sounds of her moving around in there filled the air. After a time, she came back into our room carrying a tray. She put it across my lap.

There is a beautifully grilled cheese sandwich on a small plate. The first bite tasted so amazing. It has a few slices of ham in the center. It is warm and cheesy. The bread had the perfect amount of crunch. I tried to eat it slowly and savor every morsel. Like a man dying of thirst, I drank deeply from the tall glass of milk she also brought. It is all delicious. This meal is the first Char had prepared since the awful day. "Charlene, a simple cold sandwich would have been fine."

"The grilled cheese and milk is not all," she said as she pulled out a bag of Hershey's Kisses from her nightstand. She doled out a handful to me and took one for herself. "You did not see that."

"See what?" I consumed my share of the chocolate trove as Char ate hers. "This is a welcoming finish to a great snack." Giving my beautiful wife a light kiss, I said, "Goodnight."

Char answered, "Goodnight, my love." She rolled over, and we both attempted to go to sleep.

Not ten minutes later, my cell phone went off. I answered it, "Yes? You have to be kidding. Tomorrow? Alright, I will see you then."

"Who was it, Husband Mine?"

"Work. They want me to come in the morning. It seems they are ready for the next step. Go back to sleep." I set my alarm for bright and early in the morning. *"There goes sleeping in tomorrow."*

Chapter Twenty

Groggily I stood, turned off the alarm before it sounded and woke Charlene. Stumbling out of bed, I made my way at a zombie's pace. Usually, I put on some strong coffee for Charlene; however, Doctor's orders no caffeine for a time yet. She'll have to be satisfied with decaf. The doc is playing it safe. It's a smart play by my reckoning. Out of the chill chest, I took my morning Diet Pepsi. I downed it quickly. The jump-starting of my heart and mind is needed this morning. My energy reserves are drained. Did I get any rest last night?

There is not enough time for me to fix anything fancy for breakfast today, so I prepared some old-fashioned oatmeal. I wish I had the time to make Irish oatmeal. Those are some stomach warming eats. Making it with cut-up dried apples and a healthy amount of cinnamon, it's like eating apple pie for breakfast. The first time I served Irish oatmeal to Mo instead of putting milk in the bowl, I put in a scoop of vanilla ice cream. Charlene hit the roof until I explained it is the same as putting milk and sugar in the bowl. She did not like conceding the point. Some of my fondest memories of Char are when I get her to admit I am right on some point or another. It's like hitting the Lotto, but a great deal rarer.

My girls assembled at the table, so I served up breakfast. Blossom's tail thumping told me she wanted something special too, so I took her an extra doggie treat. Sitting down at the table and looking at my family, I smiled inwardly. It is a perfect quiet moment together.

The clock on the wall said it is time for me to be picked up for the next step in the great adventure. I kissed my girls goodbye and put my bowl in the sink. It was perfect timing as I exited the house as the limo pulled up to the curb. Briskly I walked to the awaiting car and driver. I raced the driver to see if I could beat him to the door. Alas, I was too slow. "One of these days I'll beat you to it."

The driver gave a hint of a smile as he said, "Hai." We made the trek to the warehouse without talking. Before the driver could get to my door, I opened it. He smiled a bigger grin, shook his head, and said, "Hai," under his breath.

This is a wonderful morning. My worry the parasite, as I call it, will return and kill us has been lifted off my shoulders. Oh, he will be back, but seeing my wife somewhat whole again and helping my daughter with her night terrors gave me some needed confidence.

As I passed through the door into the warehouse, I noticed changes. Gone are the broken pieces of the Tatara and what was left of the satetsu, the black iron sand. The tamahagane is still there only it is cold. The hearth is still unlit. My master approached and bowed. Bowing in return, I heard my master speak, "Come we pray," is all he said. Then turned and began walking to the shrine and I followed. As before, we prayed. Again, I felt a sense of serenity surrounding me. It is a peaceful calm like a deep breath and exhale, which ejects out the madness of the day, week, year, or even life.

When we were finished with the ritual, my master turned and walked toward the tamahagane. He reached out and touched the huge ingot. It is mostly dark with bits of a shiny silver metal throughout. He took back his hand, then bowed to the tamahagane. He gave what sounded like an order to someone in Japanese. A helper brought me a large sledgehammer. Asahara, my master's nephew, had a sledgehammer as well. The master said only one word more, "Begin."

Asahara started swinging his hammer against the tamahagane. Bits and pieces began flying off. I followed suit and started swinging away. It feels oddly satisfying hammering the crap out of the metal. We soon developed a rhythm to our onslaught. My coworker and I are swinging in counterpoint to one another. As my stroke fell, he lifted his hammer and vice versa; it is a dance between Asahara, the tamahagane, and me. We circled the ingot slowly breaking it up. After a time, we took a break for water. Asahara took off his work shirt. Feeling heated as well, I removed my shirt. My complexion is pasty, but compared to Asahara, mine looked like I had been working the fields picking crops all my life. During our respite, the master was looking over the broken pieces of tamahagane. Some of the pieces he threw back down; others he handed to an assistant. This follower had a bag over each shoulder. He put the darker pieces in one bag and the brighter pieces in the other.

After about a fifteen-minute break, we returned to our labors with renewed strength and vigor. Time seemed to pass at a different rate as our dance had a hypnotic effect on me. Soon it was lunchtime. My mouth is watering at the thought of a Double-Double. Sadly, I was disappointed. One of the helpers brought in a couple of armloads from Rubios Home of the Fish Taco. He was loaded down with fish tacos, chips, and beans. Fish tacos are not my favorite, but they'll do in a pinch

Lunch was eaten, during which conversations between all the men present started up. A feeling of isolation is mine. Not so from the fact, I don't speak Japanese, but there has not been enough time to form bonds with these men. While listening to the rhythm of their conversations, I feigned napping in my chair. It wasn't only the rhythm I was listening to, but the emotions as well. These men shared something I did not have. They shared friendship. Other than Charlene, and we are friends, I haven't had a friend in a long time. All I have in life are responsibilities. They are enough to overwhelm a man and drag him down. They are weights tied around my neck. I have no friends to throw me a life raft. As I look back to all those I hurt in my youth, it is fit punishment that, except for family, I would be alone. The gloom is beginning to overwhelm me. I shook it off before letting it seep in any deeper.

The lunch break was over, and we returned to our task. After a time, there was only a small fraction of unbroken tamahagane left. Masafumi Asahara bowed to me and backed away from the metal. He motioned for me to continue. Again and again, I swung my hammer. Each swing is a little faster than the last. A surge of energy flowed into me. It welled up in me from my feet, through my legs, into my gut, and leaped into my heart. With the next beat, my heart sent the energy to spread into my whole body. Crying out in a challenge to the whole, I threw all my strength into one mighty swing. The tamahagane rang as pieces flew off in all directions. A gasp came from all who worked there. The hammer is too heavy for my exhausted arms, so I set down the hammer with the handle standing up. Leaning on the handle, my lungs heaved with labored breaths.

I looked at what remained of the untouched tamahagane. What was left from the heart of stone is a shiny remnant perhaps the size of a shoebox. It is dazzling. A ray of sunlight struck the shiny metal. The light was shattered into too many pieces to count with all playing on the walls of the warehouse like a disco ball from a wedding reception. The master, my master, looked to me, smiled, and bowed. The sound of him whispering something in Japanese could be heard. Somehow, I know it translates into English as "It is born. Now, it must be shaped."

Thirst gnawed at my body, so I asked for some water. One of the helpers brought me a tall glass of water. Deeply I drank and managed to get some in my mouth. Weary, I am so weary. It is a virtuous fatigue the kind I get after honest hard work. My muscles will be complaining at me tomorrow, but I'll endure the agony with a smile.

Nobuharu Makiyama walked up to me and put his hand on my shoulder. Looking at this man, I could see heavy bags under his eyes, and I felt exhaustion about him. His eyes gave a little twinkle as he said, "Nathan-san, you did very well today. Hai, yes, very well." We stood there and exchanged many words, not spoken. He nodded once at me, "Your wife, how is she doing?"

"Our family has been blessed. The doctor says she will make a full recovery in time."

"My heart sings with joy at the news. Now, tonight, go home. Take hot shower. Relax and sleep well. Tomorrow is when we really begin."

"Oh, yes, I will sleep well. It will be like the sleep of the dead, and I'll be twice as hard to raise." I said my goodbyes, then headed out the door to the patiently-waiting driver and limo. The driver is standing by the already opened door. I sat down, and we headed home. The gentle rocking of the car and hum of the engine as we traveled the streets of San Diego relaxed me enough I took a catnap during the trip home. I woke as we pulled up to the curb in front of my home. I saw John's car is on the street. It looks like we have a most welcome guest for dinner.

Walking through the front door, my ears were assaulted with the welcomed sound of, "Daddy's home" along with the happy patter of Moiraine's feet heading my way. Mo gave me an extra hard squeeze of a hug at my return. "Daddy, grandpa is staying for dinner. He said he would take me out for some ice cream

John stood from the recliner and expounded, "With all that has gone on, I thought you and Charlene could use a little alone time."

Char piped up with, "Dad, I am nowhere near healed enough for...", she paused, "alone time."

"Get your mind out of the bedroom girl. All I'm doing is giving the man who married my daughter and fathered my granddaughter time to remember what it is he's fightin' for. That monster out there has killed four cops and his mother for heaven's sake. Sometimes a man needs to restore his strength. As I see it, Nathan is going to need all the strength he can muster."

"Dad, you sound like a recruiting poster. Besides with all the heat he's getting from the police, I'm sure he is long gone."

"No, he's not. This one takes things right personal. Charlene, I've done some digging on my own just to get a better idea of what Nate here is in for. This Mark fella was locked in a hospital where they take away your belt and shoelaces. I called in a few favors from nurses your mother knew. They told me he was one cold and calculating bastard. Acted at being mental and all. Them nurses saw through it, but the head doctor knew better. Knew better my ass." Both Moiraine and Char voiced their displeasure at John's choice of words. "It was the right word, so I used it. Where was I? Oh yes. That trickster pulled the wool over the doctor's eyes and got out. The next night the nurse who sounded the alarm loudest got herself killed. The police said it was a home break-in gone wrong. The rest of them nurses knew better. Give me a nurse any day for knowing what's what in a hospital."

"Mommy, I don't understand? I am scared, and grandpa is yelling." Moiraine went running to her mother and threw her arms around her.

Charlene hugged her daughter back and made some hushing sounds then said, "Moiraine, you have nothing to be afraid of, and grandpa forgot mommy's hearing is perfect."

"Can I still get some ice cream with grandpa?"

"Yes, you can still get some ice cream. You can have any flavor you want."

"Any ice cream I want?"

"Yes, any ice cream you want." Wow! She didn't sound at all like my wife.

"Can I have a triple scoop sundae with three different flavors and hot fudge and whip cream?"

"Yes, you can," Char said, sounding a little frustrated with Mo pushing it.

"Cherries and nuts?"

"I said anything, Moiraine." Now, Char sounded near the end of her patience.

Moiraine immediately said, "Okay, Mom." Mo went running to her grandpa and grabbed his hand. "Come on, Grandpa, let's go," as she started to drag John.

"Moiraine you know better. You can get ice cream after dinner," Char said with finality in her voice. This sounds more like my wife.

Mo started to half-laugh as she said, "A girl can hope." I'm with Mo on this one. Why wait until after dinner? You may be too full to eat it then.

A chime went off in the kitchen. Charlene said, "Dinner is about ready. Everyone gathered around the table."

We all took our places while Char brought in the meal. Stunned is the only way I can describe what I feel. There is not one healthy bite on the table. There is a salad, but it is swimming in ranch dressing. I think there is more dressing than salad. The main course is meatloaf, where she puts crumbled bits of bacon in it. My arteries began clogging up, just looking at it. The side dishes are as evil as well. Real mashed potatoes with butter resided in a large bowl. Real brown gravy made from scratch is delightfully congealing in its boat. My eyes must be lying because, there sat a bowl of broccoli with cheese sauce, but not any cheese sauce. I exclaimed, "Cheese Whiz. You made me broccoli with Cheese Whiz."

"I'm sorry, but I don't call anything that comes out of a jar cheese. It is broccoli with Whiz."

Moiraine giggled "Mommy, it sounds like you put tinkle in it." John snorted but regained his composure quickly.

"Well, whatever it is, it looks scrumptious," came out of my mouth as I filled my plate with large portions of every item." It is a delight enjoying this rare treat when I stopped and looked at Charlene and said, "Okay. What gives? A grilled ham and cheese snack last night and some of my all-time favorites tonight. Are you feeling guilty or something?" With true panic, "Did you get some horrible news from the doctor you didn't tell me about?" My brain began running through some awful scenarios, all ending with Char dead or gone.

Charlene looked into my eyes from across the table. She reached out and took my hand. She rubbed the back of my hand as she does. In a soft voice which conveys a deeper meaning than only her words said, "Heavens, no, Nathan. After waking up from the coma, I have been doing some thinking. Sometimes I don't think I show you enough how much I do love you. This is only a token. A demonstration of while I keep the house and raise our daughter, you are loved, wanted, and needed. You are not only a bank account. You have value to us, more than your earning capacity. Some women forget to let their husbands know this truth. I will never be one of those women. So, I've decided one night a week we will have something you love even if it's unhealthy."

Swallowing the feelings which are welling up my throat, I asked myself what did I ever do to deserve this? If only I could grab up my wife and well, I didn't want to clean up the floor after I swept all the plates off the table not to mention, I had no desire to explain to Moiraine what we were doing. Pausing for a moment, I said, "I don't know what to say."

With a puckish grin, Charlene said, "That's a first."

"Daddy, you are supposed to say, 'I love you.' Silly Daddy, I'm only five years old, and I knew what to say."

I turned to look at my daughter and say, "Moiraine, you are right." Then back to my wife and said, "I do and have always loved you ever since the first moment we touched."

John's timing is perfect as he waited a beat then said, "Would you like me to take Mo to the movies for a long alone time like we talked about?"

Without breaking her gaze into my eyes, Char said, "Now, whose mind is on the bedroom?"

"Daddy, I don't understand. Why are we talking about bedrooms when there is ice cream waiting?"

"I'm glad you don't understand, Honey."

"Daddy, you're funny," we all went back to eating our extra special meal.

After the meal, true to his word, John took Moiraine by the hand, and they went out for ice cream. Char and I washed and put away the dishes. Char took off her apron and said, "Let's go for a walk." Agreeing with my wife, we were off to Balboa Park.

We parked in the lot near my favorite place. We strolled hand in hand to that little clearing the one with all those lovely trees. We stood there in the center of the grass and looked up at the stars. It is a real shame the city lights wash out most of the stars. With my memory, I can playback the stars fading over the years. It makes me sad. Maybe I should start a movement to clear the sky of lights one night a year. For one hour all the lights would be turned off. It would allow people to look up and see the glory of the cosmos once again. Astronomers would back the idea in a huge way. They would love seeing the night sky through their optical telescopes unspoiled by light pollution. Char leaned into me. It felt so heartwarming to have her close to me. "Do you remember the first time we looked at the stars together?"

"Don't be silly, of course, I do. You finally took my hand. I've always wondered why didn't you try to kiss me up there on the Ferris wheel? I never could figure it out."

"Fear stayed my lips."

"Why were you scared? You must have sensed I wanted you to," Char said as she turned from the stars and looked at me.

"In my teenage years, I was...," I paused and thought better about revealing that stupid painful part of my past. "... The gist of it is I didn't want to screw up what chance I had of being a part of your life."

She put her arms around me, and I put mine around her. She said, "Gently, it still hurts." After a wonderful minute together, "Odd, I was afraid of the same thing as we started dating. I hope someday you can tell me whatever it is that made you pause and change your train of thought. You don't have to hide anything from me. I'm your wife, and you can tell me anything. Besides I have already seen you at your worst." I know she means it, but she has no idea. What I did in those years can never be forgiven.

We stood there under the stars for a while more. We talked. We talked of hopes and dreams, fantasies and reality, and our child and her future. It is getting late, so we headed back to the car and home. As we headed back, Char said the idea of some ice cream was appealing. I steered us to a little shop we discovered by accident years ago. I looked forward to the most amazing handmade ice cream. We walked up as the owner is turning his sign to the closed position. We tapped on the door and pleaded our desire. He shook his head no and pointed to his wrist. There is no watch there, but his meaning is clear.

Signing okay, I was resolved to an evening free of ice cream. I started to pull Char to come along. She turned back to the door and knocked again. The owner came back and started to say no more firmly when Charlene interrupted him and said, "I love your ice cream, and I dearly need it." The gentleman shook his head yes and unlocked the door. We filed in like kids at an ice cream parlor. Wow, something changed his mind. Maybe Char flashed him.

Usually, we would split a scoop of whatever flavor, chocolate, strikes her fancy. This time we each had a cone of our own. She must be splurging. She got, let me see, chocolate and mine was vanilla bean. I paid for our cones and thanked the owner for reopening the store.

Since we are finished with our indulgences, home is waiting. It is later than we thought. The house is dark as we entered. All we could hear is Blossom's thumping and John's gentle snoring. He is laid out in the recliner. It feels like we are trying to sneak back into her father's house after being out too late. Char placed her hand on her father and quietly woke him. John stood and headed for the front door. On the way, he told us Moiraine is in her bed, and all is well. We thanked him for the time he gave us together, and he was out the door.

We quietly got ready for bed. The light is out, and we are all snug as the proverbial bug in his rug. My brain is at the point of crossing the line from wakefulness to slumber when I heard a cry from Moiraine's room.

"Damn!" Mo is having another night terror. Charlene was about to wake Mo when I stopped her. "Let's see what happens."

"Nathan, no. She is scared to death." Char tried to pull away from me, but I held her in place.

Moiraine's screams are tormenting to my heart. Char slapped at my hand to free herself. Emphatically I said, "She can do this. She is stronger than you think. Let her try!"

Mo began yelling in her sleep, "Mommy, wake up Mommy. Mommy, stay with us. I love you." My heart fell she is already past the point where Char was shot. Char began to put some muscle in her attempts to free herself.

"Stay here. Let me try something." Char had streams of tears running out her face. Her free hand was clutching her chest. First, she shook her head no. "She has to face her fears." Char grudgingly agreed, so I let her go. If I were a betting man, I would have laid odds she was going to put a move on me to get by. To her credit, she is staying put for the time being. In Mo's room, I knelt down by her bed. I whispered in her ear, "Moiraine, you are asleep. Remember, this is a dream. Your dream. You can fight him. Go back in your dream to before the mean man hurt your mom." Her expression changed. She quieted down. I turned to Char. "That helped."

Mo is mumbling incoherently, then burst out in a laugh "... funny part." We watched her for about twenty more minutes before heading back to our bed.

We laid there lost in our thoughts. There is little hope this will be the last time Mo screams in the night, but sometimes you have to hold on to hope. Sleep finally came to me but offered little rest.

Chapter Twenty-One

In the morning, Moiraine looked tired, and she was not quite herself. Gone is her playfulness. She is as dark as when her mother lay dying. Making jokes and jests didn't change her mood. She would have none of it. I hoped by the time I returned from my labors this day she would be better.

The limo would soon be here, so I went outside to wait for it. It turned the corner and pulled up. The driver raced to open the door before I reached the car. With so little joy this morning, I am in no mood to race. I didn't even try.

Pushing through the door to the warehouse, I saw all looked as it had when I left yesterday. Except for the hearth. A gentle fire was going and placed close to the hearth was a block of metal. My master approached me. He is dressed differently than before. Gone were the typical work clothes he wore last time we met. He, along with everyone else, is wearing a white smock with matching pants. On his head is a cap which tied in the back. It covered all his hair. One of the other men there brought me a set of the clothes. Everyone is looking at me and waiting. I squeaked, "Oh," took the clothes, and changed into them in the bathroom. Dressed as everyone else, I stood before the frail man and said, "We pray."

With a slight smile, he said, "Hai. You seem to be getting it." We walked to the shrine and began. My mind is troubled, and I didn't get the same feeling of calm and peace. When we finished, Mr. Nobuharu called out in Japanese to someone, and he brought a broom. He bowed slightly to his assistant and took the broom. The assistant bowed back deeper to the master. It is all very formal. It must be a tradition. My mind started to play some music, but I squelched it quickly. Mr. Nobuharu handed me the broom and said, "Sweep." Everyone else had acquired brooms too.

We formed a line at one end of the warehouse. We all started our work. Not to be silenced, my mind started playing Roger Miller's song "King of the Road." "*... Ah, but, two hours of pushin' broom buys...*" I let this song play out; it is an amusing distraction to the mindless labor.

There is no rush. We painstakingly moved across the floor, finally getting all the dust and debris into a pile. The pile was swept into the waiting dustpan held by Asahara. It took several trips to the waste can before we were done. Another assistant had a moist cloth ready to pick up the bits the broom and dustpan failed to capture. The way he diligently went about the task, I wondered if he had taken cleaning lessons from my wife.

The master motioned to his assistants, and like a ballet, they moved with order and grace. Around the hearth, which lay flush with the floor, one apprentice retrieved two boxes and placed them close by. He sat behind the boxes on his knees with his head slightly bowed. A second helper began gently pumping a bellows to stoke the fire. It is an unusual bellow instead of an up and down motion it had an in and out action. The helper sat on his knees, so he has a full range of motion. Still another helper, also on his knees, is feeding the fire and brushing bits and pieces of fuel and hot coals back into the fire with a straw hand broom. It isn't a proper hand broom; it is more a round mass of straw tied together in a bunch. The fourth and final assistant carried a bundle of heavy cloth. He sat down like all the rest of the assistants did on his knees. He sat before the block of metal with the bundle of cloth in front of him.

The master, Mr. Nobuharu, with a little extra effort, sat down on the floor near the metal block. Mr. Nobuharu motioned to the assistant sitting with the bundle. This helper untied the cord wrapped around the bundle. He unrolled the cloth. He flipped the flaps over as if he was tearing apart a fabric burrito. There is Japanese writing stitched to the interior of the bundle. The filling for this textile delight is tools. There is a pair of tongs flanked on both sides by two one-handed hammers. These hammers did not look like any hammers I've seen before. The handles are off-center perhaps by two thirds back.

Mr. Nobuharu nodded to the helper who brought the tools. The assistant bowed, and the frail old man picked up each tool in turn and examined each one. His examination was not hurried. He gave each tool his full attention. He placed the tools down on the block. I understand. The metal block would be the anvil. Using a western anvil would be cumbersome on the floor where the work is to be done. This Japanese anvil is both practical and elegantly perfect for its function. "Nathan-san, come sit here and learn."

I tried to sit down on the floor next to my master, but my legs did not move the way I told them to. Slowly I lowered myself down there, but my knees are screaming at me. Unlike my wife, I have never been bendy. I am hovering more than sitting. Everyone is watching me as I contorted. In frustration, I pounded my legs with my fists and said, "Bend, damn you." Laughter erupted from all present. "What do you call this sitting on your knees?"

Mr. Nobuharu answered, "It is called Seiza."

Asahara followed up with, "It is for formal or traditional occasions."

"No offense, but I call it painful."

"Nathan-san, you may sit as you wish if this is too uncomfortable." The frail master said.

"No. I wish to do this the correct way even if it involves a small amount of agony."

"Yes, Nathan-san, it can be a hard thing when you are not used to it." Mr. Nobuharu said in a gentle way similar to the way how he talked to Moiraine about making the cranes.

I tried to relax. My knees are nagging at me, so I put the pain in a small recess in my mind. It always dulls the pain. For me, dealing with pain, especially migraines, for so long the agony and I seem like old friends playing a game of chess. Sometimes the pain would win the contest, and sometimes I would win. This battle is one where I would prevail.

"Very well." Mr. Nobuharu turned to the two boxes. The man sitting there opened them up. One box contained broken pieces of the dark tamahagane. The other box held the large piece of shiny tamahagane along with other smaller pieces of bright tamahagane. The master picked up a piece of the brighter metal. The way he held the metal conveyed both respect, and I would say, love. He said to me, "This steel is strong; it forms the edge of the katana. It is strong like a mighty tree stiff and unbending. The tree is so strong it will not bend to wind, only break to it." He returned the shiny piece and picked up a dark bit of metal from the other box. He held the metal with no less reverence than the other. "This steel will form the spine of the blade. It is like the grass. Before the wind, the grass bends and sways, but never breaks. The grass has no strength and bows even before the slightest of breeze. We will take these two halves and marry them into one strong sword, but wise enough to yield." Mr. Nobuharu paused, and I began to think.

All this is fascinating. Think, you take raw materials sand, wood, fire, and turn them with sweat and craftsmanship into something more than the sum of its parts. It is a true act of creation, like when John made furniture. My hands have been a part of this creation. I hope my help doesn't dick everything up.

Mr. Nobuharu continued as he held the dark piece of tamahagane and picked up a shiny piece. "I have worked this craft for over eighty years. Not in all that time from my start as an apprentice at my grandfather's side until now, I have seen no better tamahagane. This metal, this tamahagane, is a gift. This promises to be a blessed undertaking." At this point, Mr. Nobuharu began to pray. I could see a sublime glow about this man. It must have been a trick of the light though.

Mr. Nobuharu took the tongs from atop the anvil, picked up a piece of dark tamahagane, and placed it in the fire of the forge. At this, the apprentice managing the bellows began to increase his pace. The fire intensified. Every few minutes, the master pulled the metal from the forge and examined it. Once he was satisfied as to the color of it, he placed it on the anvil. Asahara handed me one of the hammers. It felt strange and off-balance. Asahara demonstrated how to use the odd hammer as he began pounding the tamahagane. As when we broke up the large ingot, we slid into a rhythm. Slag flung from the work in a display of tiny fireworks with every stroke. After a few strikes of the hammers, the master would turn the metal. Sometimes instead of turning the metal, he would return it to the fire for a time. Once the piece was flat, he set it aside and picked up another piece of tamahagane, and we would begin again.

All day this went on with only breaks for lunch and water. Every piece of metal had been seen to except the one large piece of shiny tamahagane. Mr. Nobuharu talked with Asahara for a moment, then Asahara stood. He retrieved a portable writing desk and gave it to his uncle. The master took out a large sheet of rice paper, dipped a writing brush into an inkwell, and began writing.

I asked Asahara, "What is he writing?"

His answer was simple and to the point, "A prayer."

"Ah," I bowed my head and silenced my voice and my thoughts. The sounds of the fire in the forge are clear. The noise of the bellows is a steady beat. The movements of all there came to my ears. There is the sound of the assistant placing new wood in the forge. There is the sound of a bird's song from outside. I heard the gentle shifting everyone made as they sat there, waiting for the next step. Even the sound of the brush on the paper filled my ears. I had again attained the peace about me of only being. I felt as if a great burden had been shifted off my shoulders. It is not gone; it no longer weighs me down.

Mr. Nobuharu stopped writing his prayer and put away the ink and brush. He handed the writing-table back to Asahara, who returned it to its place. The frail master wrapped the large piece of tamahagane with the prayer he wrote. He left the package on the anvil and said, "The day is over, and I am fatigued. Let us rest, then return in the morning."

Everyone stood and started to mill around in gentle conversations except me. I couldn't stand. My legs are asleep, and no longer obey my commands. "A little help please." I held out my arms and Asahara, and another assistant lifted me to my feet and held me up while the feeling came back to my legs. I said, "Domo arigato," to my rescuers.

Asahara grinned, "Oh. Very good! When did you learn that Japanese?"

"Watching the television mini-series Shogun and I also listen to Styx." Music began playing in my head. Damn it. I need to watch what I think. *"You're wondering who I am Machine or mannequin."* Well, I guess it's better than Turning Japanese by The Vapors. *"I think I'm turning Japanese I think I'm..."* Give it a rest brain.

As soon as the feeling came back to my legs, I walked to the limo and headed home. My home is as I had left it. My girls gave me kisses hello. We ate dinner, had some quiet time together, and went to bed. As I was drifting off, Moiraine started screaming in her sleep.

Holding Char back while Mo is dealing with her nightmare, is no easy task. We waited in torment, but she wasn't resolving her fears. Finally, I let Charlene go, and she woke and comforted Mo. She turned her face to me and threw a look of anger at me. It was brief, but there. With the VCR of my memory, I played the moment back in my thoughts. The freeze-frame of her expression shocked me. In all our disagreements over the years, she had never hurled that face at me. I know how her heart felt when the bullet pierced it. My heart now feels the same pain.

"Go ahead and go back to sleep, Nathan. I've got this. You're working tomorrow. You need your rest," she said with her back to me while rocking Mo. With a broken spirit, I did as I was told.

Even though I slept for the rest of the night, I woke up tired. When Char finally returned to bed, I had no clue, so I let her sleep. Quietly, I exited our bedroom and closed our door. I fixed myself a bowl of something. It had no flavor, and I ate it standing in the kitchen looking at nothing. Do I talk to Charlene about the look she gave me last night? Do I let it be? Did I make the wrong call when it came to my daughter? Welcome to the state of uncertainty. My phone chimed with a text. The driver let me know he is here. No one was up as I departed.

It was an uneventful drive, and we arrived in due course. Walking into the warehouse, I saw everyone is waiting for me. "Sorry, I am late."

The master smiled and said, "You are not late Nathan-san. We are all in the right place at the right time." After I bowed to him, I grabbed my uniform and quickly dressed.

Coming out from the bathroom dressed to work, I said to no one in particular, "What I wouldn't give for a Diet-Pepsi right now." Without warning, one of the assistants came up to me holding a can of my favorite caffeine fix. "You've been holding out on me." He looked confused as I took the aluminum-can filled with liquid ambrosia and downed it quickly. The charge of satisfaction as I held it high to get every last drop filled me. The trash can beckons, so I went running to it saying, "Dribble dribble fake shoot swish." I tossed the empty can into the trash. "Nothing but net. The fans go wild." Mimicking the sounds of a crowd, I turn back to my fellows only to see them stunned at my hijinks. After a beat, laughter broke out.

Strutting to the master, I lifted my hand, pointing to the shrine, "Shall we?"

"Hai, yes, Nathan-san." We all prayed in the shrine for a time. When we were done, we took up our brooms and swept. The routine of it all is calming.

"Master, with so little dirt on the floor, why do we sweep every morning?" I asked.

"It is to prepare this place for the work at hand," Asahara answered for his uncle.

Mr. Nobuharu broke in and said, "and my master made me sweep when I was an apprentice." The old man giggled at his jest. After the sweeping, we all gathered in our places. It still hurts trying to sit on my knees. *"Knee pads, I should have brought knee pads."* I mentally put a palm to my forehead.

Everyone took their places, and we began. Mr. Nobuharu picked up the prayer wrapped tamahagane and placed it in the forge. The paper slowly browned on the fire. In a flash of blue-white flames, the prayer was consumed. All which remains is the tamahagane. We sat and waited while the metal heated. No one spoke during the heating. The only thing which can be heard is the bellows going in and out. With each pump of the bellows, the forge spoke in the language of fire renewed. When the tamahagane was ready, the old master pulled it from the forge,

Mr. Nobuharu placed the ingot on the anvil and nodded to Asahara. He stood and took up a large two-handed sledge. It is also offset like the smaller ones. I stood and took up a large sledge as well. We began.

Mr. Nobuharu used what I can only describe as a baton to direct us where and how fast he wanted the hammers to fall. Somehow, I knew without knowing where to place the strokes. The baton conveyed how fast to swing and how hard to hit the ingot. As each blow fell, slag leaped from the metal as with the other tamahagane. After a short time, the master would signal to stop, and he would reheat the ingot. This pattern repeated more times than I cared to count.

The metal began to take shape. It stretched out and flattened. Its mass diminished with each stroke of the hammer. We stopped, and the master placed a chisel on the flattened ingot. Asahara struck the tool three times with his sledge. The master moved the ingot and motioned me to strike the end. The tamahagane bent to a ninety-degree angle. The master flipped the metal, and Asahara struck it. The metal was folding back on itself. We pounded the metal for a time then it was placed back in the fire.

Mr. Nobuharu removed the metal from the forge once more. We set to beat the crap out of it again. This time once the metal was ready to be folded again, the master said, "Nathan-san, please show me your right palm." I showed him my hand, and faster than I thought this man could move, he drew a small knife from inside his white uniform and slashed me across my palm. Instinctively I tried to pull my hand away, but the grip he had on me was unbreakable. Blood dripped down from my hand onto the hot metal. The hiss of my boiling blood filled the air.

"What the Hell? Why did you do that?" I yelled.

"So sorry, Nathan-san, but it is necessary." Mr. Nobuharu bowed and released my hand.

Asahara immediately wrapped my hand in a bandage. He did a proper job of it too. I wondered if he had any medical training? After he was done, he once again picked up the sledge. Then, I guess the not so frail, old man had the chisel in place. Asahara struck the chisel as before. Once the metal was bent over to the ninety, I raised my sledge and folded the metal over. The first few swings of the hammer caused my hand to ache. Slowly as the day went on, my hand felt less and less pain.

Everything began to speed up in my perception. Heat the metal. Pound the metal. Fold the metal. Reheat the metal. Lather, rinse and repeat. Each time my hammer fell during our work, I poured a part of myself into the metal. I poured my frustration, my anger, my resolve, and finally, I poured my will. We folded the metal twelve to fourteen times. Weird how I can't remember the exact number of times we folded the metal. We finished the folding. We started in on the dark pieces of tamahagane. We fused the flat dark metal together by heat and hammer. We started folding that metal as well.

We ended our task for the day when we were done with folding the dark tamahagane. I feel drained. My uniform is soaked with my sweat and blood. We all looked drained. Mr. Nobuhara looked as weary as the rest of us combined. Worry filled me. Bowing to the master, I said, "I know this is a great adventure, but it should not take your life. I wish you would rest until you have recovered. The work can wait."

"Nathan-san, I am touched by your concern for me. I promise you this adventure will not, as you say, take my life. But tomorrow we work. With luck this next day will see an end to your part, and you can return to your life." We bowed, and I went home.

After I arrived home, I checked the thermostat because the way Char is treating me, it feels a few degrees cooler than usual. We had dinner. It was nothing special. Charlene didn't say more than a dozen words to me the whole night. It is bedtime for the family. I started to take Mo to bed, but Char stopped me. She had a glass of water in one hand and a pill in the other. "Come on, Moiraine. Take your medicine." She gave Mo the pill and water and made sure Mo took them. Disbelief struck me, and I gave Char a quizzical look. She paid no mind to me and marched Mo off to bed.

After I made ready for bed, I slipped under the coverers. Charlene didn't come to bed. Ten minutes passed when I got up out of bed and walked into the living room. Charlene is reading. "We need to talk. I was waiting for you to come to bed, but I guess we can talk out here." Sitting down on the other end of the couch, I asked, "What's up with the med you gave Mo? She didn't say anything about being sick."

Char kept reading her book and said, "I took her to her doctor today. He gave me a prescription to help her sleep." She turned a page and kept reading.

"I thought we were going to give my dream visit a chance."

"Nathan, we did give it a chance, and it didn't work." She never even turned her head to look at me as she spoke.

"It worked one night."

Charlene put her book down but without looking at me, and said, "She needs restful sleep every night. The doctor says these pills will do the trick until we can get her into therapy."

"We don't need to give her drugs to alter her mind. I can visit her dreams again and reinforce in her the knowledge she has the power to control her dreams."

She is still not looking at me as she talked. "So many bizarre things are happening. I want our boring old lives back. I want my life back."

"Then take your life back. Leave the bizarre stuff to me. You can handle the boring."

She turned and looked at me after I spoke. She had the same angry look on her face, and this time, she let loose her voice. "I used to feel safe with you, but now … I don't know. I don't like feeling afraid. I want things to be as they were. How do we go back, Nathan? Tell me! How do we go back?"

"We can't go back. We can only go forward." Charlene stood from the couch and walked out of the room. She came back with a pillow and blanket. She put them on the couch. "You're kicking me out of our bed?"

"No. I never liked the idea of one partner kicking the other out of bed. These are for me. I need to sleep alone tonight. If Moiraine has another nightmare tonight, I'll handle it. Don't bother." Stunned and speechless, how can this be? For a moment, I sat there trying to process it all. After about a minute, Char said, "I would like to go to sleep now. Please leave," so I went to bed in a cloud of disbelief.

Moiraine screamed, and I sat up in bed instantly. Looking through the open bedroom door, I saw Charlene as she entered our daughter's room. It tore at my heart to respect Char's wishes and stay out. My heart has been assaulted a great deal lately. Friedrich Nietzsche wrote, "That which does not kill us makes us stronger." My heart must be the strongest in the world.

When I rose from my restless sleep, Charlene and Moiraine had already left the house. There is a note saying nothing more than, "We will be back in time for dinner." She didn't even sign it. What to do about the widening gap between Charlene and myself? One of my usual romantic gestures won't win me any play. If I try one, I'm sure Char would show me some gestures of her own.

As I am getting ready for the day, I checked my wounded hand. Opening the bandage, I am amazed at how fast it healed. I have always been a quick healer but never this quick. There is nothing more than a raised welt where a gash had once been. Cool, I'll be able to save the $50 co-pay on stitches.

Back at the forge, everyone is in their place. This day we are shaping the metals to form the katana. The master placed both types of tamahagane into the forge. We sat in silence as the fire did its work. The shiny tamahagane was ready. The frail master pulled the hot metal from the fire and placed it on the anvil. Asahara and I began working the metal. We started flattening it out. Once the metal was broad enough, Mr. Nobuhara placed it in the forge. As the metal is reheating, he instructed an assistant. The man brought a tool and gave it to his master. It is a long and round piece of hardened metal. We waited. The fire burned, the bellows pumped, and energy grew around us.

The master removed the flattened tamahagane out of the forge. He placed it on top of the round tool. He nodded and Asahara, and I began shaping the metal around the circular tool. We formed it into a "U" shape. Once we completed the shaping, the master reheated the metal. He pulled both parts out of the forge and carefully inserted the darker tamahagane into the open end of the bright tamahagane. Asahara tapped it into place, so there is no gap between the two pieces. Again, the metal is heated.

Mr. Nobuhara removed the metal once more. He placed it on the anvil and with his baton directed us to hammer again. Slowly the sword took shape straight and true. It is done. Mr. Nobuhara returned the newly formed sword to the fire. He barked out some instructions to his apprentices, and they jumped to work. They brought over an empty trough and began filling it with water. Once the trough was full, the master took over the bellows and pulled out the glowing katana. He was unsatisfied with it and returned it to the fire.

"I have questions. I thought katanas had a curved blade?" I asked Asahara.

"The curve comes when the metal is pleased with the working. The blade will smile when it is done," Asahara answered.

Mr. Nobuhara is working intently. He paid no mind to the goings-on around him. In short bursts, he pumped the bellows as he removed the glowing blade. The color of the hot blade is unlike any shade it had been before. Quickly in one smooth motion, the master plunged the katana into the trough of water. Steam erupted from the water as the katana was quenched. The sizzling sound from the water ceased.

Mr. Nobuhara then pulled the katana from the water. The blade is happy; you could see the curve of its smile. The master examined his work. The expression of awe at what his craft had wrought filled his face.

He spoke to Asahara. My partner retrieved a long and slender box. He opened the box and inside is silk cloth. The master wrapped the katana in the cloth and placed it in the box and closed the lid. The master is smiling broadly and bowing to all of his apprentices. I didn't understand the Japanese he spoke, but the sentiment is obvious. Though he is pleased, I could clearly see the weariness in his face. "Nathan-san, your work here is done, while mine only half so. Soon the katana will be whole and complete."

"I would love to see it once it is complete. If I may ask?"

Mr. Nobuhara chuckled a bit as he said, "Yes, Nathan-san. You will see it once I am finished."

We cleaned up the warehouse before we all left for the day. The house was empty when I returned. Only the sound of Blossom's thumping tail filled the air. Fear struck me. I raced to our bedroom and checked the closet. Charlene's clothes are still there. Whew, what a relief. I heard keys in the door and the most welcome sound of my family filing in.

"Nathan, are you home? Moiraine, go play in your room until dinner."

"Yes, I am. I just arrived in fact," I called back.

"Can you help with the groceries please?" Charlene sounded normal.

In the kitchen, I started putting away everything. Char did some major shopping. We have enough fixings for two weeks or more.

As we worked to put everything away, Charlene grumbled, "Never go grocery shopping when you're hungry." Among everything she bought today the one thing I took notice of is the huge and opened block of dark chocolate. She had already had a piece of it. I am surprised. She never grazes while she shops. She thinks it's rude.

I am for a loss. Life is not hunky or dory as I had hoped it would be. Did I save my wife's life only to lose my family?

"Nathan, make yourself scarce while I make dinner," Char said with no emotion.

"Is there anything I can do?"

"If there were, I would have told you. Now, please leave."

I left only to return for dinner. Moiraine is quiet. She is not herself at all. There is no joy about her. She didn't laugh or joke. She didn't even want to dance to the Wiggles when I offered to put them on. I felt a stranger in my own home; if this is my home anymore. A cesspool of despair began growing inside me.

Chapter Twenty-Two

This has been my home life for the last two weeks.
Some nights Moiraine could fight her personal demons.
Other nights the terror in her mind would win, and she
would wake up screaming. My darling little girl is dead
inside. The drugs did seem to help but at such a cost. She
never smiles or laughs. Though it killed me inside, I did as
Charlene asked. I left my daughter alone. Gone are the
visits to her dreams, nor did I comfort her at night.
Something has to give. My role in their lives was
downgraded. No longer am I a husband and a father. All I
am is their roommate.

During those two weeks, I poured myself into the only
thing I had left, which gave me any value, work. A
permanent position anywhere eluded me. The drug store
had warned off all the other pharmacy and sundry stores in
town. One interviewer told me I had been "blacked-balled."
I took any kind of work where I could. Whether as a day
laborer on a construction site or picking avocadoes for too
little money a pound, I did it. Avocadoes, the green slimy
things, I loathe them.

Mrs. Blake helped us by letting me do some minor jobs
to reduce the rent. Hustling to getting applications out to
any business which had a whisper of a job opening was my
focus. There was nothing out there for me.

One morning the doorbell rang. Charlene answered the
door. "Nathan, this gentleman says he wants to talk to
you."

As I went to the front door, Charlene left to the bedroom
to read, I guess. She takes little interest in me anymore. Mr.
Masafumi Asahara was standing there patiently waiting for
me. One of the apprentices is with him. "Please come in," I
said as I gestured for them to enter. They both bowed to me
and walked into the living room. "Please take a seat. How
is your uncle, the grandmaster?"

The gentlemen did not sit. Asahara said, "Thank you, but we cannot stay more than a moment. My uncle has passed."

We had only known each other briefly, but my heart grew heavy at the hearing of his passing. Perhaps I will call to his spirit once they have left to say goodbye to the man. "My condolences to you and your family."

"Thank you. My uncle died as he finished this," Asahara reached back to the apprentice behind him and opened the long wooden box his uncle had placed the unfinished katana in. He retrieved the finished sword. He lifted the katana with both hands as if he were offering it to me. He brought it up to about eye level with the back of the blade facing me. He bowed his head but did not raise it until after I took the blade. I grabbed the sword with my right hand in-between his two and bowed in return

"I appreciate you bringing the sword, so I can admire the work we did together. I wish your uncle had not worked so hard. I didn't want to see the work take his life."

"You do not understand, Nathan-san. The work didn't take his life. He gave his life to the work. He knew he would not live past its completion."

Pondering for a moment, I grew quiet. I drew the katana from its sheath. It is magnificent. It gleamed in the light. It gave me a sense of pride to know not only did I have a hand in its forging, but a part of me, the blood spilled into it, would be forever a part of it. After returning the sword to its resting place in the scabbard, I tried to hand it back to Asahara as he presented it to me with both hands and the spine of the blade facing him. "Thank you. I will remember that sight for the rest of my life."

Asahara lifted his right palm facing me, shaking his head no," his palm shows the same tattoo his uncle had. It wasn't there before. "You do not understand again. The katana is yours. It is yours to wield. It is yours to name."

Stunned for a moment, then I said, "I can't accept this work of art." I once again held it up to Asahara. He refused.

"My uncle had been waiting his whole life to make this sword. Three generations passed without the making calling out to my family. Only two other blades in the memory of my family have been so made. One sits in the private museum of the Emperor. The other was lost in battle to the darkness." He paused for a moment and closed his eyes. He must have been praying. "Nathan-san, as my uncle gave up his life to the sword, so too will the sword give its life to its wielder. You are its hand. Use it wisely and with honor." Asahara bowed very deeply this time as did his apprentice and they left my home.

After I closed the door behind them, I looked at the sword in my hand. It felt lighter than I thought it would, and holding it is comforting somehow.

"Nathan, what did those gentlemen want?" Charlene asked as she came out into the living room with her book.

"They are the men I worked with a couple of weeks ago. They gave me this," Presenting the sword to Charlene. I slowly drew the blade from its resting place. As before, it gleamed in the light.

"Is that what you were working on? It's pretty, but not practical," Char said dismissively.

"When is art ever practical?"

"Fine cooking is art and practical too."

Grudgingly I said, "Point taken." Looking around the room, I asked, "Where do you think we should display it?"

"Valiant try, Nathan, but we are not putting that thing up in my living room."

The living room is mine too, but with tensions being what they are right now, I decided to let it slide for now. I placed it in a corner until the time is right to revisit this discussion.

Moiraine walked into the room and looked at us. She didn't say a word. She looked dead behind her eyes. The drug is taking her away from us. "Moiraine, Honey I have some sad news." Char dropped her book down and looked at me.

"What is it, Daddy?"

"You remember the kindly man who showed you how to make the cranes. He died, Moiraine."

In a deadpan, she said, "Okay. Can I draw?"

What is happening to her? The news should have gotten some emotional reaction out of her. The drugs are harder on her than I first thought. "Sure, Honey." Mo went into her room and brought out her coloring supplies, sat at the table, and began drawing.

"Nathan, I wish you hadn't told her. She has had enough to deal with as it is."

"What dealing with? She's not dealing with anything. Those pills you are making her take are killing the happy little girl inside. You need to stop giving them to her."

"No," Char announced as she snapped closed her book and started to stand from the couch.

Also standing, I blocked her exit from the room. "This discussion is not over. I will be heard. I have a right to decide our course of action too."

"I'm her mother. She came out of my body. Your role was over after a split second. I carried her for nine months. I almost died bring her into this world. I have greater authority. Now, let me by," she reached out and started to push me out of the way.

Without either of us realizing it, Moiraine had crept upon us and is standing there looking at us. In a flat tone, Moiraine said, "Don't fight. It makes me sad."

Charlene put her book down and squatted down to be with Mo. "Oh, Moiraine. Mommy and daddy aren't fighting. We are only talking loudly. We will talk softer."

Mo turned and faced me, "I drew a picture." She handed it to me. My heart screamed in agony as I looked upon her woe. It is a self-portrait. She had drawn herself in a cage.

336

Her mouth was opened wide as if wailing. Out of her eyes were streams of tears. In the background of her portrait, a big bellowing mass stood. It has red eyes and a mouth with a shape which somehow conveyed laughter. In its maw are large yellow teeth dripping with blood. After a moment to mourn for my daughter's sanity, I gave the picture to Charlene.

"Do you like my drawing, Daddy?" Moiraine asked with no emotion.

Her question hung in the air unanswered as I watched my wife go through the same torment as I had felt. Tears began running down her face. "Oh God, Nathan, her pain, I can't take it." Char put a hand to her chest.

"Drugs aren't going to help her. Tonight, I AM going into her dreams again, no matter what you say. I want your blessing, but if I have to, I will do it even if you curse me." Squatting down, I wrapped my arms around Moiraine and held her. She put her arms around me. It was robotic as if she was programmed to do it. Char wrapped her arms around Moiraine as well. We all hugged each other for a time.

That monster is beginning to cheese me off. I am going to end it. If the cost is my life, so be it. Hell, in my visions, I die anyway, so if I take him out along with me, I'm good.

It is time for dinner. No one feels like cooking tonight, so we went out to a local restaurant. It is more like a diner. There is no fancy food with strange names, only hardy eats. Moiraine didn't voice any choice for dinner, so we ordered her favorite Cinnamon Roll French Toast. Charlene had a Chef Salad with the dressing on the side. She dips the fork in the dressing, then a forkful of salad. She always eats her salads that way. She claims it saves calories. I had a Patty Melt and fries.

When we returned home, Char helped Mo make ready for bed. Charlene began to give Moiraine the medication. "No. We are not doing it tonight," I announced.

"Nathan, the doctor said this is what she needs to sleep until her therapy sessions."

"Doctors don't know everything. They told me you died, and your body didn't know it yet," I said it harsh and cruelly. Taking a breath and blowing it out. "I'm sorry." With my wife's hand in mine and with a catch in my throat, I spoke, "I trusted the doctors and brought you home to die. I gave up. Your father gave up. I even said my goodbyes to you."

Charlene reached up and put her hand upon my cheek, "I know. I heard it, Nathan." A tear ran down her face.

I brought Char's hand to my lips, and tenderly kissed it. Pleading, I said, "This little girl, our Moiraine, didn't give up on you. Don't give up on her."

Char turned to look at Moiraine, who is standing there waiting and said, "Moiraine, no medicine tonight. Let's get you to bed." Char took Moiraine into her bedroom. In silence, I watched from the doorway as Charlene tucked our daughter into bed. Moiraine closed her eyes and started to drift off. Charlene closed Mo's bedroom door. She clasped my hand and led me to our bed.

As I was clearing my mind and getting ready to rescue my daughter's sanity, a bolt hit me, and I sat up in bed. Throwing off the covers, I moved quickly to Mo's side. Charlene was close behind me. Char said in a panic, "What's wrong?"

"She doesn't have the guys in bed with her." I gathered up all her bedtime friends and placed them all around her as she slept. The teddy bear she received that terrible day, I placed it closest to her head. "Right now, we need all the help we can get if we are to save her." We started to leave my daughter's room when I turned and spoke in a whisper, "Protect her well this night, guys."

Char and I returned to our bed. We cuddled for a time. It is heart-warming. Maybe things will return to a more normal state in our marriage once our daughter is better. I prepared myself once again by quieting my mind, closing my eyes. I lifted myself out of my body

Wasting no time reveling in the wonder of my dream world, I rushed to my daughter. "Moiraine, I need you to enter this dream world." Mo lifted out of her body as before, but there is no glee in her mood. She is as robotic and unemotional as in the waking world.

"What do you want, Daddy?"

"You need to take me into your dreams as we did before. Do you remember?"

"I don't know how, Daddy."

"Okay. Let me try." Holding her hand, I willed us into her dreams. There is the sensation of us moving for a moment, then we are in her dreams. It is colorless. Everything in here is different shades of grey. Her dream had us in her room, but it is clean and sterile. It scared me seeing her room this neat. It is wrong, somehow. "Moiraine, is there anything you want me to see here in your dreams?"

Moiraine turned to look and pointed in a direction behind me. Turning around, I saw the scene of the shooting. Her mom is on the ground with blood everywhere. The creature and I are in a battle for his gun. Moiraine is not by her mother's side as it happened. She is off to the side about ten yards away. She is in a cage with her hands on the bars. She is crying and shaking the bars trying to break free. There is no sound, except the struggle between me and the creature. It is like someone had hit the mute button on Mo. The scene looped back to the beginning. Moiraine's mother is standing there with her when a shot rang out. It is deafening loud, and the sound is drawn out like it is in slow-motion somehow. As Moiraine started to cry, a cage appeared around her. Slowly the cage started to move further and further away. The distance is increasing between her and Charlene. When the scene ended, it looped back to the beginning again.

"Oh, no. Not again." In the dream, I rushed to the cage. With my hands on the bars, I tried to break them. My whole being needed to free my daughter. I strained and strained, but the bars would not budge. My thoughts willed a crowbar to appear in my hands, and with it, I tried to force the bars apart. They held fast. A whole clone army of myself assembled when I willed it. We put our collective hands every place they would fit on the cage. It is no better than before. My beautiful katana came to mind, and a dream version is on my back. I drew the sword. It gleamed in a light brighter than my daughter's smile. I put my will to it and tried to slice open the cage. The blade bounced off. Again, and again I swung at the cage which holds Moiraine. My efforts are futile. Not a scratch is on this prison of my daughter's own creation. Maybe I need images Mo understands. She needs images which have strength in her mind. The guys began to appear one by one. First was Winnie the Pooh, then Eeyore. Next to appear was Piglet, Tigger, and Buzz Lightyear. The instant they came into being, they animated and rushed to the bars and began their efforts. Even this cadre had no effect on the bars. Wait, someone is missing. The teddy bear. I dreamed the bear into the struggle. He arrived twice the size of the other guys. He joined the fray. She is still trapped. Nothing is working.

I left Mo's dream and returned to my body. Instantly I was ravenous as I sat up in bed. My nightclothes are soaked. My body is shaking, but not from the cold. All I could think about is food. My body didn't obey my commands. I tried to make it to the kitchen, but I couldn't even get out of bed. I gasped out, "Char, I need food. Bring me anything." She did not hesitate. She didn't even bother to make me anything. She brought a jar of peanut butter, a spoon, and a carton of milk. With a passion, I dug into the peanut butter. Straight out of the carton, I chugged the milk down. In-between bites and swallows, I said, "Sorry, about all this mannerless eating."

Char said, "I don't care. You scared me the way you sounded and looked. Do you need any more? Did it work? Is she better? What do you think?"

My eating is done. The gnawing hunger is gone, and the shaking subsided. "No, I'm fine thanks," I took a breath. "It didn't do a damn bit of good. She is trapped in her nightmare, and in this dream, she seems to be getting further away from herself. Our little girl is disappearing. Give me a minute, and then I will go back in there and try again." Taking my wife's hand for reassurance, I squeezed it and laid back down, closed my eyes, and said, "Have strength. We'll get through this."

In the blink of an eye, I am in the dream world. Standing beside me is Charlene. "How did you get here? I didn't lift you up."

"How do you know I didn't lift myself up?" She smirked a bit then she showed me we are holding hands. "Put me back so I can watch over you and Moiraine."

"Why don't we enter Mo's dream together?"

"I don't know, Nathan. What if something goes wrong?"

"We can't let fear rule us. Besides, you may see something in Mo's dream, which I don't. Your insight might be enough to tip the balance in her favor. Together we can do this for our girl. You're her mother. Now, man up, and let's do this."

"Man up, Nathan. Really?" She said with a cockeyed look.

"Okay. Woman up." I wasted no more time because our daughter's mind is at stake. I willed us straight into her dream. We both stood at the crosswalk of our grief. The loop had reset. Char is on the ground in a puddle of blood, and I am fighting an increasingly terrifying Mark Galos. Watching in a catatonic state is a Moiraine. The cage holding my true daughter is almost out of sight. It is no more than a speck on the horizon of her mind.

"Nathan, is this how it looked?" Char cried out.

"Pretty close. There wasn't that much blood on the ground, and I did a little better against the monster," I said. "We have no time to ponder. We must get to Mo. Follow me," I commanded. We ran toward the speck. It grew as we drew closer. The guys are still working at the cage. Taking up the bars in my hands, I tried to bend them. Charlene followed suit. All of us together are not budging it. It isn't working, so we paused a moment.

Char spoke to the caged and the crying Moiraine, "Hush, hush, hush. Mommy is here. Everything will be alright." Charlene tried to reach through the bars. She could not touch our daughter. Char looked at me with anguish on her face, "Nathan, I can't touch her," and her face turned from anguish to determination. Charlene once again took hold of the bars and strained against them. I took hold of them again, as well. The guys had never stopped. We all strained together.

The bars are bending, but not enough to free our daughter. The scene reset, and the cage holding our baby traveled away from us and further from the nightmare. "We almost had it. I have an idea. We need another set of hands. Stay with her. I will be right back." I willed myself to the core of Moiraine's nightmare. With my face in front of Mo's face to force her to look into my eyes, I said, "Daddy needs your help, Honey. Come with me."

Her eyes are lifeless. Forcefully, I said, "Moiraine, you need to come with me." Her eyes betrayed no change. "Mommy and I need your help." Her eyes began to focus on me.

"Okay. What do you need, Daddy?" Grasping my daughter's hand, I felt an almost unperceivable return of my grip. I willed us back to the caged version of Moiraine.

I began to help the crowd of toys, and my wife try to free our daughter. We bent the bars a bit, but it wasn't enough.

Pleading with my daughter, "Mo, help us!"

Charlene chimed in with, "Moiraine, Mommy, and Daddy need your help!" We continued to urge Mo to help us. Slowly she walked to the cage and put her hands on the bars.

"Now, everybody together!" I strained. Char strained. Moiraine started to strain at the bars as well. "Break!" I threw all my will into it.

The cage shattered into a thousand shards which flew in all directions. The air filled with my daughter's lament. The Mo which tipped the balance faded away. Char picked up our baby girl and comforted her. I threw my arms around them both and added my comforting to Char's. All the guys cheered and slowly faded away as they are no longer needed.

"Mommy, Daddy, I am so scared. That man is so mean. I thought he was going hurt me, too," Mo said haltingly in between her sobs.

"We won't let anyone hurt you," Charlene announced.

"No, we won't. We will protect you," I squeezed them both a little harder. "I think we are better now." We traveled out of the dream. My hunger wasn't even in the same neighborhood as before. I am shaking uncontrollably. I am sweating buckets and looking through a tunnel. "Char help. I think …" I knew what I wanted to say, but it is coming out all mumbled. The next thing I knew, I could hear Charlene encouraging me to drink. There is a cup at my lips and liquid in my mouth. Orange juice, I think. Swallowing seemed to be an impossible task. I had to use all my concentration to accomplish it. Slowly the fuzziness sharpened, and I was back.

Moiraine climbed into bed with us. "Daddy, I made you a crane to feel better," she said as she handed it to me.

My daughter is showing emotion again. My heart is soaring. "Thank you, Honey. I will treasure it always."

Mo giggled and said, "It's only folded paper, Daddy. You are so silly." I pulled my daughter in for a big hug.

"Nathan, do you need more OJ?" I shook my head. "I don't understand this. It's like you have diabetes, and your glucose levels are way too low."

"Me neither. Maybe when I travel in someone's dreams, it requires a lot of energy, and when I take someone with me, the amount goes up geometrically. It might be a prudent measure to put on a few pounds for safety."

Char answered in a resounding, "No. I have no desire to have a chubby hubby."

"Mommy, Daddy, can I sleep in your bed tonight?"

Char answered, "Okay, just this once." Moiraine climbed under the covers between Char and me.

After I turned out the light, I rolled over to go to sleep. "Goodnight ladies." I heard a chorus of goodnights.

Moiraine broke the silence with, "Daddy, please don't make your sleeping sounds."

"I don't snore, Mo."

Charlene answered with, "Nathan, you snore."

"I get no respect." Immediately Aretha Franklin began singing Respect. *"Turn it down Mr. K R A P I'm trying to sleep."*

Chapter Twenty-Three

As I woke up with a start, I glanced at the clock. We had slept-in. A feeling grew in the pit of my stomach. It is like the sensation when I know I will be vomiting soon, but without the urgency. Throwing off the covers, I sat up in bed. My movements disturbed Mo and Charlene. It is just as well. My mind buzzed with plans in the making.

Charlene lazily stretched and asked, "Is something wrong?"

Quickly I jumped out of bed and started getting ready to take a shower and do my morning routine. "Moiraine, Honey, go ahead and start getting ready for school."

"Okay, Daddy," Mo climbed out of bed and started for the bathroom.

"Char, I have some errands I need to do today, important errands. Can you do a few as well? First, I need you to see Moiraine off to school without me today?" I tried to put an urgency in my voice without sounding too alarmed. Charlene nodded. "Excellent. I knew I could count on you."

"Nathan, what's wrong?"

"Please do as I ask without questions, no guesses, and no women's intuition. Can you do this for me?"

"Nathan, what is..."

"Damn it, woman! If you never do another thing I ask again, do this for me." I rarely yell at my wife, but I needed to hammer down any dissent.

"O...k...ay." Then as quick as if a light switch had been turned on, she said, "Whatever you need from me, I will do. It is the least I can do for the man who is my husband," her tone is soft and compliant. I heard a touch of love in her voice too. She said I am her husband and meant it along with all that goes with the title. My heart panged, but I had no time to enjoy the sensation.

"After Moiraine is off to school, I want you to pack for us. I want you to pack like we are going on a long road-trip vacation."

"Now, you're talking. Oh, I have always loved the idea of us taking a long vacation, Nathan. It will be a magnificent road trip too." Charlene jumped out of bed then grimaced and put a hand to her chest. "We can take our time and reconnect far away from all the craziness our lives have been lately." She put on her robe, opened the closet, and started scanning her choices for the road. "Nathan, can you get our luggage out of the garage for me?"

Grunting an okay, I retrieved the suitcases. I put them on the bed and opened them up.

"Nathan, I am wondering do we have the money for a trip? Where are we going? I am still recovering maybe we should hold off?"

Throughout our relationship and life together, not only are we husband and wife, we have always been partners, too. If there are problems to solve, we bring them to the table, the kitchen table in fact. We'll sit across from each other with my left hand in her right. We take the problems, chew them up, and spit them out together. We did it so when we planned our wedding. It was the way of it when we decided to try for children against doctors' advice. It is how we chose to give Moiraine a conventional home life with me in the role of breadwinner and Char being a stay-at-home mom. And to her credit, Charlene would let me believe we came to all those decisions together.

With all the tenderness I could muster I said, "Charlene, I love you deeply and without reservation. I don't say this lightly, and I hate getting all alpha-male on you," in a deep guttural tone and intensity I commanded, "My wife will keep her word and do as I asked!"

Charlene lowered her eyes and bent her head down slightly and said, "As you wish." An almost imperceptible smile came to her lips. Movie quotes, you have to love them. Of course, she is only letting me think I won this round of our life, but if she packs us up as I asked, I'm fine with it.

I finished getting dressed and ready. The time on the clock showed I had plenty of time before the first thing on my mental to-do list. So, I sat down at our dining room table to wait for Charlene to put out the breakfast. Moiraine is trying to help her mother, and therefore, breakfast was a few minutes late. It is no concern of mine. I sat back and watched my girls working together. Blazing this moment into my already perfect memory is my goal, a perfect moment to hold dear. I wanted to see us normal one last time.

We ate breakfast. It was as perfect as I hoped. "Mo, go ahead and finish up getting ready."

"Okay, Daddy." She rushed off to her room to pick out the fashion of the day. My wife, my beautiful wife, started to pick up the dishes.

"You can do those later. I want to sit across this table, hold my wife's hand, and look into her eyes." To my surprise, Char didn't argue or become all obsessive-compulsive on me about how easier it is to keep a house clean than it is to clean a dirty house. "There is something I have never told you in all these years. I want to share it with you now." A look of concern came to her face. "It's nothing bad. It is a little something I have kept to myself. Do you remember our first kiss?" Based on how she began to blush, I reckoned she did. "I don't."

A look of confusion hit her. "Nathan, I don't understand. You can remember everything I thought."

I let the comment hang there for a minute. "I can. I have explained my mental filing cabinet to you before. Well, I also have a mental safe where I have hidden memories from myself. Sounds kind of weird, huh? It takes a great deal of mental discipline. It only works with happy

347

memories. My life would have been filled with a lot less sorrow if I could lock up terrible memories." My daughter came back into the living room to ask her mother to put her hair in ponytails. Charlene started devoting attention to Moiraine's hair. Continuing, I said, "Remembering all of the ordinary everyday kisses is a simple task, but I locked away in my safe our first kiss. Every time we're about to," I looked at Moiraine and chose my next words carefully, "have some adult time, it's like our first kiss to me all over again. When we finish, I lock those kisses away too."

Charlene did something I have never seen her do. She stopped fussing with our daughter's hair. If Char starts a task, she does it until it's done and on to the next. "Nathan, is that the truth?"

"I have never lied to you."

"That has got to be… No, it is the most romantic thing you have ever said to me. I thought you could never beat how you proposed. Boy, how I was wrong."

Wow, she must be unsettled, because she never admits to being wrong.

Charlene's eyes are welling up, and she swallowed hard. "Moiraine, wear your hair straight today." My daughter said okay without an argument and went back into her room to finish dressing. Charlene stood from the table and walked around to stand next to me. She pulled me up to my feet. She leaned into me and laid a kiss on me like rarely before. *"Oh, this is one for the safe."* It is as if I could feel her love firsthand.

Grudgingly, I pulled away from my wife and said, "If my errands didn't call, I would stay like this for hours, but you know what a B-word traffic can be." I was mindful of my words since Mo is walking back into the room and is in earshot. "Mo, Honey, give your daddy a great big hug and kiss. This one needs to last. Your last hug and kiss only lasted a few hours." I lifted her, looked into her eyes, and pulled her in close to me for a hug. When she was well hugged, I gave her a huge kiss. "Okay, that should last me." I put her back down. I made my way to the front door and was off. I tried to be strong and not look back.

If only I were that strong.

My family is standing at the dining room table. Mo is standing right in front of Charlene. Char's hands are on Mo's shoulders as if to hold her back. I smiled at them, turned around, opened the door, and walked out. I have enough time to do what needs to be done if I don't waste any time in the doing. I thought to myself, *"I hope John's an early riser."*

It was a quiet drive, and because I hit all green lights, I made great time to John's house. As I exited the car, I could hear some racket coming from the garage. My fist pounded on the garage door. With all the noise coming from John's power equipment, I didn't think he would have heard me if I went to the front door. The garage door rolled up. There was John covered in sawdust with a look of annoyance until recognition came to his face.

"Nate, what are you doing here this early?"

"Well, John, your neighbors called and complained about all the noise." John gave me a quizzical look. "Sorry, my sense of humor gets the better of me sometimes. We need to talk."

"Okay, son. Let me clean up a bit." John brushed himself off, and we went into his home. "Can I get you anything? Coffee? Tea? Sorry, I don't have any of those diet drinks you like. It's a little early, but I could pour us a touch if you like. Oh, right, you don't drink."

"No, John, I'm fine thanks." We sat down, "Before I start in with what I need to talk with you about, let me say you are looking mighty healthy and spry. There seems to be a little bit of a spring in your step. Also, I thought after finishing Charlene's bed, you were going to give up working with the wood."

"It is what I had planned too, but," he hesitated then continued, "Nathan," he looked around a bit as if to make sure we weren't being overheard, "ever since I got to talk with my Marlene it's like I'm alive again for the first time in years. Thank you for that."

"John, you don't have to…"

"No, no, I do. The truth of it is I have been waiting to die. Looking forward to it I was. You see, Charlene is not the only one who didn't say goodbye. I had Char to raise and see after. I didn't; I couldn't grieve. When she left me to be with you, I was bitter. Oh, I know it's the way of things, but it was like my only reason to keep living was gone."

"John, please…

"A little piece of me died each day. You know Marlene, and I have been having many talks. In my dreams mind you. I haven't gone all Alzheimer on you. Her and I will be together again someday where there ain't no pain," John paused a moment, and his face shone. It never dawned on me before, but these ghosts I can talk with confirm there is at least some kind of afterlife. "I just want to live a while longer maybe see a great-grand baby or two from Moiraine. Not too soon mind you, and only after she is properly wed. I don't hold with the way things seem to be going with young folks these days. When she starts bringing suitors home, I want to loan you that shotgun of mine. It keeps away the riffraff." He gave me a wink.

"It made me think about staying away." We laughed together. "Well, I'm glad to see you in better spirits, or should I say with better spirits," we both chuckled a bit again. "Talking like this is great, and I could do it for hours, but I have so many things to see done before tonight. Here is what I came to talk to you about." I gave John the low, and the down on what is happening and what I needed him to do. Surprisingly he neither challenged me nor called those men in white coats.

John handed me the paperwork I needed and said, "I'll be ready, Nate. It's not exactly what I would do, but it's your call." We shook hands, and I left for my next errand.

Quickly I traveled to the next destination on my list. Standing in front of my bank, I was waiting for it to open. An older security guard was waiting at the door until opening. There was a muffled chime from inside the bank. Mister glorified doorman turned the key and opened the door. At the first available teller, I requested access to my safety deposit box.

After a few minor delays, I managed to get at my stuff. There are only a few items inside mostly paperwork. My birth certificate, both Char's and Moiraine's birth certificates, and a few precious knick-knacks. The object I wished to retrieve is my mother's wedding ring. The day Moiraine was born, I put it in here to give to her for her wedding day. I had originally wanted Char to use it, but she decided to use her mother's ring instead. It is only worth maybe a couple hundred bucks. It will help a little bit. After I locked the box back up, I headed to a teller to clear out our vast savings. It is maybe three or four months' worth of bills. Knowing how tight Char can be with a dollar, maybe five. I traveled to my next stop.

I picked up what I needed at the local hardware store then traveled back home. After getting out the ladder, I set it up next to the broken security camera. I knocked on Mrs. Blake's front door. From behind the door, I heard her ask, "Who is it?"

"It's me, Mrs. Blake, Nathan. I am going to fix the broken camera today. Is there anything else you need me to put a screwdriver or hammer to?" A myriad number of locks and bolts could be heard as they are thrown open. The door cracked open a bit, and I could see her eye looking at me.

"Oh, Nathan, it is you." She opened the door wider. Diego made a mad dash out of the door. The mewing of her vast array of other cats is loud enough to drown out Mrs. Blake's voice. Mrs. Blake is what you would call a classic "little old cat lady." She stood about five foot nothing. Her gray hair is styled in an old-fashioned roller-set. She probably puts toilet tissue in her hair at night like my mother did in my early years. My mother supported us by working as a cosmetologist or hair-dresser, if you will, and was expected to wear her hair in the style. "Heaven must have sent you, Nathan, that broken camera has put a worry in me. Thank you, Nathan. I don't trust anyone else to fix things around the house. You're a good boy."

Inwardly I smiled. "Mrs. Blake, you need to go somewhere tonight. Is there anyone you can stay with?"

"Heavens, no. You're the closest person I have to family anymore. They're all gone now. All I have are my cats since Barney died." She paused and looked sad for a moment. "Why do I need to leave?"

Flash.

It is like reality blinked. So strange.

"An evil man is coming to kill me tonight."

Mrs. Blake's eyes widened, and her head started to twitch left and right. She looked like a squirrel on the side of the road trying to decide if it should cross the street or run the other way as a car approaches. "Leave my home; I can't leave. What do I do?" Her breathing started to quicken, and little beads of sweat started growing on her face. "Oh Nathan," Reaching over to her, I put my hand on her shoulder. She started to crumple to the floor. I supported her on her way down and made sure her landing was gentle. Counting her pulse is useless as her heart is racing. I pulled out my phone and called for an ambulance. Mrs. Blake died there on her front porch waiting for help to arrive.

Flash.

Reality blinked again. Before I said a word, I paused while I thought about what happened. Mrs. Blake is standing there in front of me. She is not dead, but she died, holding my hand only moments before. Is my imagination running wild? Perhaps a part of me is pointing out she didn't need to know the truth. Knowing could only hurt her. Quickly, I thought of a lie. *"So many lies of late. Am I still the kind of man I had tried to change into?"*

"An old friend of mine is visiting me late tonight, and things might be loud. If you stay in your back bedroom, the noise should be less. It would be a great personal favor to me if you would disregard anything you hear. You have my promise the noise won't last long." It never did in my visions.

"Thank you for telling me, Nathan. My old heart can't take any surprises anymore."

"If I've never told you before, let me say you have been a great landlord. In all the years we have lived here, you have not raised the rent. Being able to stay in one home has given great stability to Moiraine. Thank you." As I started to turn to start work, Mrs. Blake stopped me.

"The pleasure has been mine. Your family has been a joy to rent to. The rent has never been late. You help me with little things around the house. Your daughter is a joy. On her visits here, all my cats just love her to death." She paused for a moment, "With all the terrible things happening you hear about on the news these days, it is comforting knowing there are still decent people like your family in the world." She turned and went back into the house. The sound of all her locks going back to their locked positions could be heard through the door. As she walked away from the door, I heard, "Ah, do my babies want a treat?" Well, my task awaits, and I should be about it.

When I finished with the security camera, I put the ladder away and cleaned up a bit. In the house, I fixed myself a snack. Charlene wasn't home. She must have gone to visit the kids at Greentree. In the garage, I retrieved the object of both my greatest failure and greatest triumph.

Opening the sports bag, I checked on the rifle and made sure it is safe for travel. It is as I left it. With sports bag in hand, I locked up the house, climbed into the car, and headed to Saxie's Jazz Joint.

Again, I hit nothing but green lights all the way. I guess it's my lucky day. Let's hope my luck holds true. I banged on Saxie's Jazz Joint's front door. Being it is daylight hours, it took some time to be answered. Mr. Doorman opened the door.

"What do you want? The boss is busy."

"I'm fine thanks. How are you?" He answered with a deep rumble of a humph. "You know I don't think I got your name." I held out my hand, "Nathan Embers, pleased to meet you." I was left hanging a long moment. What has happened to manners these days? "You said your boss is busy, but he will want to see this." I lifted the sports bag.

With an even harsher gravel to his voice than before, "What is it?"

"Something to trade. A pearl of great price, if you will."

"Open it." He saw what is in the bag. Then faster than I thought this man could move, he grabbed me and flung me into the club. He managed some decent hangtime too. On the floor with a foot on my neck and a gun pointed at my head is where I found myself.

Slowly I lifted my hands into the universal sign for surrender. "Easy there, I am not due to die until tonight." The big man tilted his head to one side, but his aim never wavered. "Sorry, I am being foolish. Please, take me to your boss. He will not be upset. Cross my heart and hope to… Well, you know the rest. If he is, you can kill me. I will even dig the hole you'll put me in without any sniveling."

This hoss moved his foot off my neck. He grabbed me by my shirt and hauled me up. It hurt. He pulled a few chest hairs in the process. He took the sports bag from me and led me to the boss's office.

"Turn around. No one sees the boss without getting searched." He patted me down again.

"You know if this keeps up, I'll expect candy and flowers," I said as his hands ran over my body. Nothing. Is this thing on?

"Go ahead and keep the sass up. I know just where I'll have you dig the hole." He knocked on the door once then motioned for me to enter with him close behind.

Sitting at his desk, Al is looking over some paperwork. He glanced at me then opened his desk drawer and placed the paperwork there. "Mr. Embers, what brings you here today?"

"You're a businessman. Perhaps we could do some business? A little horse-trading, or a bit of bartering."

"No offense, Mr. Embers, but based on our last dealings I don't think it will be possible, and I am quite busy. Good day, Mr. Embers." He made a dismissive motion with his right hand and reopened his desk drawer."

"You're the boss, Boss, but you might want to see this." The hoss lifted the sports bag.

Al closed the drawer again, stood, and walked around to look in the bag. He opened it up and saw the gun he had sold me. He lifted the rifle up and with practiced hands opened the breach. He looked down the barrel and generally gave the gun the once over. "Mr. Embers, you must have some training in gun-smithing."

"None. The day I bought it from you was the first time I had ever held a rifle."

Looking up at his bodyguard, he said, "Good call on this one. I think you can leave me alone with Mr. Embers for a time."

"Okay, Boss. I'll be right outside if you need me."

"Mr. Embers, you have surprised me. You have restored this weapon beautifully. And you did it without losing any of the patina. I don't know of anyone who could do better.

If all your work is this good, I could use a man such as yourself in my organization."

"To be honest, it wasn't me. You could say the rifle told me what to do."

Al gave a slight chuckle then said, "Well, however you managed it, this rifle is worth perhaps twice what you paid for it. Do you wish to sell it back to me?"

"As I said earlier, I am looking for a trade." Out of the sports bag, I retrieved a folder. "In here, you will find individual pictures of my family along with some vital information birthdates, physical descriptions, etc. I need some rock-solid new identities for my family new birth certificates, passports, social security cards, the whole enchilada."

"I don't deal in such things. And even if I did, this gun is not worth what you are asking. It's not even close."

Pointing to the computer on his desk, "I assume you have internet access."

"Of course."

"You'll want to look up the serial number of the weapon."

"What you are up to Mr. Embers?"

"Trust me."

"Okay, I'll play along." With an amused look on his face, Al sent the rifle down on his desk and began typing away on his computer. After a minute, he did a double-take and reread the serial number on the weapon. He looked at his computer screen again. With a look of shock, he pulled open a drawer in his desk and retrieved two white gloves. He put them on with only a slight trembling of his hands. Al picked up the rifle and began to look at it with new eyes. After a minute of gazing at the weapon in his hands, he stopped and pushed a button on his intercom, "Tell Jake to get in here. I have a job for him."

In due course, a man came into the office, "What do you need Boss?"

"Take this," Al handed the folder over to Jake, "to Murray. Tell him I am calling in a solid he owes me. Tell him to do a Claude Rains on these people, and I want it back today before the club opens. Hurry!" Al sat back down behind his desk. He picked up the weapon again and started examining it more intently. He started, "This was in my junk box all along, and I never knew it."

"Yep. I was lucky it called to me," I waited for a beat. "Don't ask."

"I'll say you were lucky. It's almost the time of year when the city holds its buyback program. To think Sergeant York's rifle was almost melted down and lost forever." Al started examining the rifle again. He touched it as a lover strokes the object of their desire. "Mr. Embers, it will be at least a few hours before your new identities are done. You can wait out in the club or would you rather come back later, but I have more pressing matters to deal with than entertaining you."

Checking the time on my cell phone, I saw had a few hours to kill before I am killed. An idea struck me. Talking to someone special and walking in the green one last time sounded like a plan.

It is quiet on the drive to where my mother is buried. After I parked, I took the slow walk to her gravesite. Many times since the sad and relief filled day, I have come to visit. "I tried calling you and received an upset stomach for my troubles. Maybe there are some people I can't call on? This is all so new to me. Maybe I can't summon you, but it doesn't mean I can't talk to you, Mom. I miss you. You taught me so much. How do I thank you?" We talked, well she listened, the better part of an hour. We talked about everything and nothing. I want to go to one last place before the dominoes start to fall, so I left. "Goodbye, Mom, see you soon."

I am now at Balboa Park at the spot where my mother had pointed to my star. I have spent many hours here over the years. It is near a circle of trees ash, oak, maple, and others. I can playback their growth in my mind like a time-lapse movie. This place always gave me a sense of peace. It is quiet on a level which isn't based on sound. After I cleared my mind, I felt right with what I would do. In the thousandfold thousand nightmares, I had of what can happen tonight never had I tried what I plan to do now. The exact outcome is hidden from me. In every scenario I played in my mind, I die. There is no reason to believe it will end any better for me, but my family will be safe. This is what is important. Yes, my family will be safe, and I will achieve the greatest of endings; I will die so my family lives.

For the few hours, I sat in the green before leaving for Saxie's Jazz Joint and acquiring those things my family will need for their future. My final drive home was still. No music is playing on the radio or in my head. Green lights all the way, and there weren't even any rude drivers on my route. It is as if the city itself is giving me a gentle farewell.

Walking into the house, I know I am about to face an even harder battle than with the creature. John is there already, excellent. All our luggage is near the door. It is time to tell Charlene my plan and to say goodbye forever.

"Nathan, what is this all about? My dad won't tell me a thing." Char is standing there with her hands on her hips, indicating she would brook no deviation from the truth absolute, complete, and without delay.

Here goes. "The man you know as Mark Galos is coming to kill us tonight," silence hung in the air for a moment. "Don't ask me how I know. I just do," again I let it hang in the air for a long second. "You, Mo, and your dad are going on the run. You need to gather all the money you have squirreled away in the house. Grab all your jewelry of any real value as well. Moiraine, Honey, could you get your piggy bank and bring all the guys too. You will need them in the future, I think." Moiraine, without question, did as I asked and ran to her room to perform her tasks. Charlene, on the other hand, fumed.

"I don't understand, Husband Mine. You sound as if you will not be coming with us."

"It is not the path I must walk. My job, my duty, and my sacrifice will be to delay the monster as long as I can. Who knows I might even win." For a man of honor, I sure have been telling a whole mess of lies lately.

"He... is... coming to kill us tonight," surprise came to my wife's face as she dropped her arms to her sides. "It is strange. I hear the truth in your words. Nathan, I'm frightened."

Rushing in, I hugged my wife, not too hard, for her incisions are still fresh. I pulled back and kissed her with more intensity than perhaps ever before. It matters not John is right there and if he did, so what.

"Nathan, we can call the police. We can tell them he's on his way."

Still holding my wife, "In the best scenario only six cops are killed and another dozen or so crippled and we still died. The worst-case more fine cops are killed than I care to say, and we still die." Char broke the embrace, wiped away a tear, and went about the task I had set her to do. "John, your help means a great deal. Stay true to the plan. It is the only way I foresee, which has a chance of working."

"Nate, son, you don't have to stay here alone. We can take him together. We don't have to play fair like the police do. We can set up a right good ambush for the bastard. Besides, I owe him some payback as much as you."

Reaching out with my hand, I grasped his shoulder, "John, we tried many times." Confusion came to his face. "They all ended with all our deaths."

"Nate, you are talking crazy, but somehow I see the truth of it."

"I've come to believe when people hear the truth they know it," After taking a breath and blowing it out hard, I said, "The truth rings true."

Both Char and Mo returned to the living room with their respective stashes of money. Moiraine had all her guys in her arms and Charlene had a photo album in hers. I asked Char how much money she spirited away. Wow, she can pinch a penny or three. I handed Charlene a black leather pouch like the ones businesses use to make bank deposits. "In here is all the money I could squeeze out of our holdings. It's not much." Placing the ring in Charlene's hand, I said, "If you have to, sell my mom's ring. I hoped Moiraine could have it when she is old enough, but the money it could bring may be of more importance. John knows the full plan. But, here it is in a nutshell. You all load up in the car and haul ass. Pick a direction and drive. Don't look back. Don't wait and see, and don't tell me where you are heading. Don't even think about where. What I don't know, no matter how he tortures me, I can't tell him. This man is smart and cunning. He has evaded the police for weeks and taunted them while he did it. If you leave any trail at all, he'll hunt you all down. This is why you are leaving your names behind. In the pouch are new identities for all of you. You need to abandon everything which might lead to you. Throw away your old IDs, credit cards, and even your cell phones. In the pouch, you'll find a pay as you go cell phone along with everything else. Don't, and I mean this, don't call the house. Don't call me. Give it a week you can call the police. If I am dead, they should know it by then. If I am dead, throw the phone away and never look back again. He will find you if you don't."

Moiraine threw down the guys and ran crying into my arms. "Daddy, don't die. The mean man won't find you if you come with us. Please, Daddy, please come with us."

If I thought my heart was breaking before, it is now shattered in my chest. I must be strong. Their lives depend on it. I know I am right. "Moiraine, I need you to understand."

"I don't understand. Mommy almost died. You say you are going to die. No! I won't understand, and you can't make me," she is in a full-on rage now.

"Then don't understand, but accept what I tell you. Can you do it for me?" I am crying tears, which burned my soul.

Moiraine stopped crying and wiped at her tears and mine, "Okay Daddy, but I don't understand." She pulled away and started to gather up the guys. Once they were safely in her arms, she looked up at me and said, "Don't die Daddy and kick the mean man's ass."

Charlene said immediately, "Moiraine, no potty mouth young lady." Then with an accepting tone said, "But you are correct, however. Kick his ass, Nathan. I will not contemplate my husband doing otherwise. I will not."

Smiling at what Char said and trying not to laugh at what Mo said. I guess she understood more than I had given her credit for. Putting on my best game face, I said, "Okay, I won't die, and I'll kick the mean man's ass." It is one last lie before they leave.

John had been loading up the car while all this took place. Looking at the time on my cell phone, they should have been on the road by now. With the last of the luggage in my hands, I started herding my girls out of the house. They all piled in the car and buckled up. I kissed my girls one last time and said to John, "Guard them well, John." Then whispering, "I'll say hi to Marlene for you when I make it to the other side." As I said those words, I understood there is another side.

"I feel like I am abandoning you, Son," John said through the car window. He unbuckled his seatbelt and started to open the car door.

Pushing the door closed again, I said, "Nonsense, John. You fought in a war. You know in a war a general may order some troops to withdraw while he orders others to hold the enemy off. In this war, I am the general, and I need you to keep my family, our family, safe. You have done enough in this fight. Your example gives me strength, and you gave me a cool gun with bullets and everything." John shook his head at me as he rebuckled his seatbelt and started the car up.

Patting the car's hood, I said to Jezebel, "Godspeed."

Watching them drive away is one of the hardest things I have ever done. I have given up almost everything. There is but one thing left for me to give. My life, I shall place it on the altar of hope. The hope they will be safe. The hope they live long and happy lives. The hope when John passes, many years from now, it is peaceful and without pain. The hope Moiraine will find her dream and live it. The hope Charlene will find a better man than I. One who will love her and treat her right. Finally, the hope they remember only our happy times together.

"Well, Mr. K R A P, how about some mood music while I prepare for the showdown." The Emperor's Theme from "Star Wars Return of the Jedi" began playing in earnest on my internal iPod. *"Perfect."* I walked inside and immediately got to work. The creature known as Mark Galos will be here soon. I wonder what its name actually is? My insults and curses should be addressed correctly. It would be impolite for my verbal abuse to be flung at the wrong person.

I moved the recliner, so it faced the front door. Out of the gun-safe, I retrieved John's pistol. It felt right in my hand. After I loaded in the clip, like in every dream about this moment I had the feeling, *"Okay, let's get to work,"* go through my heart. I opened the front door, so the monster would have easy access to the house. No need to have him break-in. It's a fine sturdy door, and I wanted to save Mrs. Blake the trouble of replacing it.

I sat in the recliner, waiting for the time of my trial by fire. In my head, over and over, I kept hearing my mother's voice saying, "with your shield or on it." I also heard my daughter's voice telling me to "kick the mean man's ass." There are other voices too. I heard voices from a thousand different conversations giving me all kinds of advice. One voice is telling me to stay loose. Another said to keep my guard up. So many pieces of advice they churned in my head. I willed them to stop and stop they did. It is quiet in my mind now. The type of quiet you heard when you are far away from the city, people, and all things artificial. The type of quiet your ears strains to hear.

"I am ready."

As I finished the thought, a figure stood at the threshold of my door.

Chapter Twenty-Four

The creature I called a parasite stood in the shadows upon my threshold. Its silhouette showed the outline of the sledgehammer hanging at his side. "The time of reckoning is at hand. You and your family die this night," the parasite said with malice and cruelty in its voice. "Do you plan on facing your death sitting down?" He stepped into the light. My face contorted in horror at what the light revealed. A smile grew on its face as it reveled in my revulsion. The air brought a horror of its own to my nose. The odor is a foul stench. It had a sweet sickly smell of rotting flesh. It is enough to make me retch. I dismissed the urgency from my body and mind. This thing looks worse than at our last encounter. It looked worse than it had in my dreams of this moment. It looks like the monster it is. Its eyes are a dull yellow. Its teeth are speckled with black flakes. Its hair is mostly gone except for patches which reminds me of a cancer victim on chemo. Its skin is mottled grey and hung loosely on its skull. Gashes on its face are there also. In the open wounds, I can see maggots crawling in the ragged openings. The insects are gorging themselves on the dead flesh. All which is left of Mark Galos's body is the mere shell. The evil will of this parasite animates this walking corpse.

I stood and faced him. "I offer you mercy. Leave now, trouble my family and this city no further, and I will let you live. I swore revenge when the bullet hit my wife, but I will forswear the oath if you leave now. If you refuse my offer, you will face the full fury of my anger and the sting of my malice for I am a man defending his loved ones, and that gives me strength."

The creature before me croaked out a wet and garbled laugh. "You offer mercy to the merciless. Do you think me a fool? I am more than a man now. A hundred men could not kill me, but you are welcomed to try." It laughed again.

Well, the bluff didn't work. This fact reinforces my personal rule against playing poker. Without thinking, I fired three shots from John's 45. One, two, three, the rounds hit the handle of the sledgehammer. The head of the hammer fell off, and the handle splintered into a useless mass.

"You missed. How sad. You tried to save yourself and failed miserably. Your pathetic display proves you're not a man worthy of living. You don't even comprehend what you face. Do you want to know what stands before you?"

"Does it matter what you are? I think not. You're a sorrowful rabid animal that needs to be put down. You killed Mark Galos. You have killed decent police officers. You have threatened the lives of the innocent. You put a bullet into my wife's heart. It is time to pay the bill and pay you will with your life. By the way, I hit every damn thing I aimed at." I fired one shot into its ugly forehead. Maggots and bits of bone and grey matter flew out the back of his head. I fired the rest of the clip save one bullet into the center of its chest. The grouping is no larger than a fifty-cent piece. Cool. The last shot I fired into its right knee. The knee exploded into a cloud of dust and bone.

The creature fell to the ground. I tossed the gun out of reach. It is of no more use to me now. I raced to close the distance with the creature and leaped upon it. I began to wail on him with everything I had in me. After I got a couple of good licks in, he tossed me away with such strength, I flew across the room and landed against the entertainment center; I fell to the floor. My back and left side screamed in pain. The parasite's strength is unbelievable. It is even stronger than when we tussled at the corner. It doesn't seem fair. Here I live a good and decent life pay my taxes, without grumbling, I hurt no one, and if I do, I try to make it right. Helping lost ghosts travel to the next world, it is a little above and beyond. You would think I could catch a break, but no.

"This is going to end too soon. I must give my family more time to get away." Roaring a challenge, "You have plagued me and mine long enough," I shunted the pain to a part of my mind which isn't doing anything right now. I slowly stood to face him again. "I will end you."

"You surprise me, Mr. Clerk Guy. Oh yes, you said I could call you Nate. You surprise me, Nate." To my disbelief, the parasite began to rise. Gone are the various holes I had blasted into him. Somehow its knee had reformed, and the monster is beginning to rise. "Did I surprise you?" It came at me and far faster than I thought anything could move. It grabbed my shirt and lifted me off my feet. It backhanded me with such force my ear began to ring. "Your car is gone. Where did your wife and daughter go? Tell me quick, and they won't suffer long. I promise you. It will be the least I can do for the man who singlehandedly stopped me in my holy quest. Try to hide them, and when I track them down, they will experience sweet torments before their end." Its words fired me.

With a torrent of moves, I never knew I had, I launched an attack. Somehow my muscles knew what to do. My shirt tore from its hand. I gained my footing again. My blows began to land. I even fended off some of its counter attacks. It surprised me. The monster caught my right arm and twisted it almost to the point of breaking. My weight shifted, and I lost my balance. It shoved me across the room. Tumbling into the dining room table, a crack could be heard, and I felt a pang in my side. Fractured rib no doubt. As I held myself up on the table, I said, "Hate to disappoint, but I know not where they are. I sent them off with a full tank of gas and a load of cash."

It laughed, "They won't escape me."

Picking up the centerpiece off the table, I flung it at the creature. Charging as it batted the distraction away, I hit it dead center, and we went flying into the wall. It may be stronger than me several times over, but his mass is the same as a man. I reached for the lamp on the end table. I bashed it mightily in the head. My God! It is smiling again. We rolled around wrestling for leverage. The advantage is his. It pinned me down, and I couldn't move. It is over. *"Dear God, let it be I bought my family enough time."*

He smacked my head hard. So hard, I thought I saw little birdies circling my head. In my haze, he asked, "Where did you send them?"

At first, I couldn't think, then the fog began to clear. Laughing at him, I said, "Poke, prod, hit, and bash as you will. I can't tell you what I don't know. Don't think you can track her either. She is smarter than she is beautiful. Why they will melt into the surroundings when they find a backwater place. She'll never look back either. Hell, this gives her an excuse to start over." He relaxed just a bit. Searching for a memory of when I was the most pumped and when adrenalin surged through my body, I found it.

The memory of the first time Charlene and I held hands came to my mind. Her touch fired me then, and the memory of it set me ablaze now. Raging, I threw it off me. I stood before it did. No mercy no quarter I seized it and lifted it off the ground with one hand Darth Vader style. Wailing on it with one hand, while the other hand tried to squeeze the life out of it. It was honestly surprised. I stunned it into inaction for a moment, but the moment faded. It lifted a hand to the one around its throat. It pried my thumb and nearly tore it out of the socket. It fell out of my grip to his feet with me slugging him as hard and as fast as I could. It threw me against the wall. I crumpled to the floor. My breathing is ragged, and the air burned in my throat. The last of my strength is spent. My whole body screamed at me in pain. There is nothing I can do.

"You are full of surprises. You have been a better opponent than I thought. Of course, I am thousands of years out of practice. Now enough is enough. Tell me where they went to, and I will snap your neck quick and clean." It grasped me by what remained of my shirt and a great deal of my skin. It pulled me up to look it in those clouded and yellow eyes. Those eyes are dead and have no soul.

"Well, if there is a bright center to the universe they're on the planet that it's furthest from," I mocked.

"Star Trek. You're quoting Star Trek to me," It said in disbelief. It slammed my back into the wall. "Where did they go?"

"First, get your fandoms straight. The quote is from Star Wars, not Star Trek. Second, I told you I don't know where they went, but go ahead and don't believe me. Every minute I delay you here, they travel further and further away. Say I'm going to be off the clock soon, you want to take in a movie or grab a bite to eat? It will put them a hundred miles or more down the road." The look of confusion on his face is almost worth the beating.

Almost.

"Nathan, get down," I heard Charlene yell. My heart sank. Crying, I prayed, *"Oh God, no."* Why could she not listen to me this one time? "Charlene, run!"

The creature grinned a toothy grin at me. It released me, and I flopped to the floor. I looked up in time to see the effect the double-barrel Greener shotgun had on the creature's chest. The roar of the gun is deafening. His back sprayed out in chunks and mist. The pieces hung in the air for a moment and then congealed back into the wound. Charlene gasped, and John used some language which burnt my ears. It started off to deal with Char and John. They stood there, dazed. In my head I heard the words, *"With your shield or on it,"* but it is not in the voice of my mother. It is in the same voice from my attempt to murder Mark Galos. What can I do? Suddenly, a fierce barking erupted from Blossom's bed. With all the goings-on I had forgotten to send her off with the family. The creature turned to the new threat. Blossom leaped at the creature. She had gotten a hold of him and wasn't letting go. In the corner of the room, I saw the sword I helped craft. I crawled to reach it. As I reached my blade, I heard a crash and yelp from Blossom.

No time.

I stood and unsheathed the katana. My eyes pained me as light reflected off the blade. Calling for rage from my body one last time, none answered. I remembered what Karma had said, *"Your daughter's love can be a source of strength the same as your wife's love is."* In my mind, I heard my daughter say, *"Kick the mean man's ass."* Love filled my being. If felt as if I had never been in this fight. My body is renewed. I screamed a challenge to the monster fouling my home. It ignored Charlene and John and turned, once again, to me. I swung my blade down upon it and struck its right arm between wrist and elbow. His hand and wrist disintegrated as it fell to the floor. Shock covered its face when it looked upon its empty arm. I pulled my blade back up, then lunged it into the horror's chest. My blade pierced it in the same place the bullet had struck my wife. Twisting the blade, I hoped it would bring it agony. True pain did seem to reach its face. *"Outstanding!"* I removed my blade. It fell to its knees. In a great sweeping arc, I separated its evil head from its corrupted body. There was a slight tug on the blade as it sliced through what once was Mark Galos. Its entire mass fell into a pile of bits, pieces, and dust on the floor. Floating in the air is an orb of light. It wavered a little then sped toward me. It grew in my sight until it filled my vision and entered me

In my mind, I felt its presence. I quickly came up with a plan I hoped would work. My awareness turned inward. In the long corridor of my mind filled with the filing cabinets of my memories, I placed my mental minion. It has the look of being battered and bloody. A figure of a man came walking out of the gloom of my mind toward my avatar. It towered over the beaten figure of me. My avatar looked up at the monster in my mind and said, "Is this how you look or is this only another shell?" My minion started to crawl away from the intruder. "I stopped you, after all. You're not so tough," I gloated. It kept pace with me easily.

"Stopped? You have only given me a new shell to inhabit." It is smiling as it looked around my mind. Different images appeared all around. They are bits and pieces of my memory for its entertainment. Distractions until I am ready. "I think I'll like it here. Your memories are so clear and complete. I've never experienced anything like it before and believe you me I've experienced a great many things." It kicked my minion. My minion howled in pain in the confines of my mind. My minion crawled further away. "Why are you running? You can't escape your own mind. There is no place here where you can hide." After a few more steps it said, "I knew I would need a new host after this fight. I hadn't planned on it being you. But your body will do nicely. It will be a pleasure taking your wife with her believing it is you. She will be most free and pleasing with her favors for the man who saved her and her daughter's lives twice." His laughter reverberated in my mind. It pulled out a file memory of Charlene and threw it up with the other images. It is the memory of Charlene undressed and in my shower. "I believe I will enjoy your memories."

Well, I don't like this. It is gaining a bit of control in my own mind. I must be quick.

The creature continued, "I think it will be most satisfying to plunge a dagger into her heart as I bring her to the edge," he laughed again. Oh, he has so got to die. I willed my minion to jump at him. He batted the image of me easily out of the way. I willed a maze of thoughts to appear between it and the minion. "You can run for a time, but hide from me in your mind? I don't think so."

It wound its way to my minion. Step by step, it drew closer to the place I had reserved for it. One more step. It took the step unaware. I screamed, "Now," in my mind. As fast as the speed of thought, my avatar vanished and was replaced with my true self. Threads of thought began to spring up all around the entity. With each moment, it grew more and more entangled in my mind. I raged at the entity, "You have beaten my body, but this is my mind, and I reign supreme in here. Yes, I am the master of my own domain." With all my will, I drew tighter my thoughts to bind him more and more. The noose of my mental trap is closing. Tighter and tighter, I pushed it into a cell in my mind. Its screams of agony rang through my skull like Christmas bells during the holiday season. He is now nothing more than a knot of discomfort. I will take great pleasure in kicking the knot from time to time. In the end, the parasite is no more than a headache, and I have always known how to deal with those.

Waking up on the couch with Charlene fussing over me, I did my best impression of Han Solo and said, "I feel terrible."

"Jokes? Really, Nathan? You are nearly killed by… by… whatever it was, and you joke." She withdrew the damp cloth from my head, "If you can joke, you don't need this." She tried to stand and walk away. Taking hold of her hand, I pulled her back and down. I kissed her. When she was well kissed, I asked, "Where is Moiraine? I hope she didn't see any of this. Did she?"

John broke in with, "No. She is with some friends of mine down at the American Legion Hall. They would die rather than see her come to harm. Good men one and all."

"John, I asked you to take them far from here. Why did you come back? Not that I am complaining considering how it all turned out." I started to sit up. Ouch. I am sore all over.

"Well, it's like this you see," he paused to compile his words then frustration touched his expression. "You're married to her. How often have you got your way once she has set her mind on the other?"

With a half laugh, "Point taken." As I tried to stand up, the room spun, and my legs wobbled. I said, "I think I will sit here for a moment." I gave instructions to my body to send damage control parties to where they are needed. I just sat there and breathed in and out a few times. "It's a puzzle, and I don't understand. In all my visions, we died."

"My husband, in all the scenarios you played out in your incredibly thick and handsome head, did we ever come to your rescue?" She is looking at me with love in her gaze. I would bed her right now, but most of my systems will be under repair for a while.

"No. I was supposed to be a hero. No one rescues the hero."

"I was correct in saying you are thick," she shook her head and took a breath. "My husband, ever since you stood up to my father, ever since you cried in my arms over the prospect of a future alone, ever since you held our daughter in your arms for the first time and hushed her cries, ever since you took a job you hated so our future could be secure, and a multitude of others acts too numerous to mention, you have ever been a hero." I was about to say something snarky, but I think this was a moment better left unsnarked. What do you know, I guess I can learn when to keep my mouth shut.

"Nathan, what was that thing? It looked like a corpse," Char asked.

"It was a man once I think. Now? I'm not sure. I'll know more after I start interrogating it."

John asked, "What do you mean, son?"

Tapping my head, I said, "It's up here now." Both John and Charlene gasped. "Did you see the orb of light?" They both nodded. "It is its life essence I think. We had a battle of wits in here," Tapping my head again. "Don't worry, it can't escape or take control. My migraines have given me plenty of practice at keeping the monsters at bay."

Remembering what Karma said, *"Before we can start, you need to deal with Mark Galos."* Well, I guess I can cross it off my honey-do list. What are we supposed to start?

"Son, I don't know if it was a trick of the light, but your sword was shining. It was brighter than the mid-day sun on a clear day. Right, pretty it was."

"No, Dad, it wasn't a trick of the light. I saw it glowing too."

"It's news to me," Stretching out my hand, I took up the Katana. It is on the floor, forgotten. It felt warm in my hand. It wasn't glowing now. Is there a switch somewhere? I reexamined the sword I had wrought. I held it aloft and said, "Flame on." Nothing. I evoked, "By the power of Grayskull." Still nothing. "Thunder Thunder Thunder Thunder Cats Ho." If anything, the blade looked a little duller.

"Nathan, my love, stop. You look like an idiot," Char said, smiling all the while.

"Nothing new there," I sheathed my blade. What is going on in our lives? Ghosts, monsters, visions, traveling in the realm of dreams and the like, is it over or only beginning? Is my family safe? If not, can I protect them? Can I find a permanent job with benefits? The rent is due soon.

"Nathan, you look so serious. What is wrong?"

"A storm is coming." Both Char and John had quizzical looks on their faces. Pausing, then I said, "Has anyone checked on Blossom? The old girl gave that thing what for."

"Blossom is," tears started running down Char's cheeks, "dead." It is quiet in the house except for the gentle sobs of my wife. After a few moments, I looked around the house.

The furniture had been righted. There were no broken bits and pieces on the floor. Even what is left of Mark Galos' body had been swept into a pile. Ending the silence, "Cleaning Char?" John and I both burst out laughing. It broke the tension, and it even made Charlene smiled for a moment as she nodded her head yes.

It had been a long, tough day and an even tougher fight. My body ached in places I don't remember having. I took a long hot shower before going to bed. After my shower, I stepped out into my bedroom to dry off. Char had already drifted off to sleep. I finished drying and started to brush my teeth. I glanced behind me in the mirror. A tall man, taller than me, stood there smiling at me. He is dressed in a uniform similar to the one the parasite in my mind wore. I spat into the sink and looking through the mirror to the intruder behind me and said, "Give me a minute to finish up, then I will kick your ass too."

Epilogue

As I walked up to the door, my stomach is doing flip-flops. My nerves are on edge about this whole idea, but a promise is a promise. I keep my word even to the dead. After ringing the bell, the door was answered by a handsome woman in her twenties. A small child looked at me from behind the protection of his mother.

"Yes?"

"Hello, my name is Nathan Embers. I am sorry for disturbing you at home like this, but I have a letter for you from your," I swallowed hard, "husband."

"You must be mistaken my husband was killed a few years ago."

"I know. Before he died, he dictated this letter." Lying shouldn't be the answer, but the truth would confuse her. "May I come in? The explanation could take some time." She glanced back and forth for a moment and motioned for me to come into her home. She led me to their living room and offered me a seat, so I sat down on the couch. She sat down on the other end of the couch. She told her boy to play in his room while we talked. She offered me something to drink. Manners, I like that. "Thank you, no."

With the pleasantries over, she asked, "Okay, Mr. Embers? Is that correct?"

"Yes, it is. Let me start at the beginning. This is what I've pieced together. My nephew was a corpsman in the war and was treating your husband. Before he passed, he asked my nephew to write to you for him in case something happened during surgery. Before my nephew could mail the letter, he was killed. All of his belongings were shipped home. Like all well-meaning bureaucracies, the Marine Corps misplaced his effects. It was only a few weeks ago they were delivered to my sister. Going through his things, my sister found this letter. She didn't have the heart to bring it here herself. So, she asked me to find you and deliver it to you," I handed her the letter.

As she took the letter, she said, "I don't understand. The Marines who came to give me the news said he was killed instantly. They said he didn't suffer. You're telling me they lied?"

"It might be they were trying to spare your feelings. To give you some comfort in your moment of pain." She accepted the explanation. Can I be a better liar than I thought?

The letter is in her hands, but she refused to look at it. Tearing up, she sat there. She shook her head as if to snap herself out of the emotion and looked at the envelope. Her eyes widened in shock. She gasped. "I thought you said this was dictated to your nephew, but this is in my husband's hand."

"Oh crap!" Her husband and I must have similar handwriting. I can't tell her I was the one who took the dictation. Think fast. There was an awkward silence. Boom, I was struck by mental lightning. "Like I said, the story was pieced together from many sources. What I couldn't find out, I embellished. I am sorry. He must have written it himself." *"Am I sweating?"* I hope not. "He must love you very much to make sure this letter is placed in your hands."

"Mr. Embers, I want to thank you for bringing me this," she stood up and looked at me with eyes inviting me to leave. So as not to wear out my welcome, I stood up. She escorted me to the front door. Exiting the house, I stepped onto the porch then turned around.

Facing her, I extended my hand. As we shook, I said, "I am sorry for the sacrifice you and your family had to give to this country. It is my wish the words in the letter gives you comfort in the reading," pausing a moment, "The letter doesn't seem like it's enough. If I can be of service to you, please don't hesitate to call me day or night." I gave her my phone number, turned around, and walked to my car.

Sitting there behind the wheel for a long moment, I tried to recover from my shaky nerves. "It went well, sir." I nearly jumped out of my skin, which would have been messy with the blood and all. The Marine is sitting next to me in the car.

"You were there watching? I didn't see you."

"I didn't want you to see me." The Marine turned and looked out the window to his home. "I want to thank you for your kindness. You don't see a great deal of kindness once you're dead."

"It was nothing. Since you are here, do you plan to stay and watch over your family?"

The Marine took a deep breath and let it out hard. Strange. I didn't think the dead needed to breathe. Maybe it is only a habit. "No. They need to go on with their lives. If I am there, somehow I think they won't."

"For what it's worth, I think you're right. Well, can I give you a lift back to the cemetery?" He turned toward me with a slightly irritated look then faded away.

I drove home, feeling all warm and gooey about what I had done. Nathan Embers, postman to the dead. Yep, that's me. I don't think I should put it on my resume, though.

Acknowledgments

There have been many people who have helped me in this endeavor. Thank you, Linda Nagy. Your help in this project has been invaluable. I have learned a great deal. Tracy Johnston, thank you for the insight you gave me on this project. I give my thanks to Christian Bentulan who did the cover artwork. He can be reached at coversbychristian.com. I also extend my thanks to all my clients at The Men's Room Barber Shop. You gentlemen have heard all these tales and gave me encouragement.

I would also like to extend my thanks to you, the reader. If you are so inclined, I would ask you to leave a review on whichever site you purchased this copy of The Forging from. It encourages me to keep writing when I see other people enjoying Nathan's adventures. To paraphrase, "You ain't read nothing yet."

Made in the USA
Monee, IL
05 March 2021

61161304R00213